Dark Embrace

Dark Embrace

ANGIE SANDRO

New York   Boston

Copyright © 2015 by Angie Sandro
Excerpt from *Dark Paradise* copyright © 2014 by Angie Sandro
Cover design by Rebecca Lown
Cover copyright © 2015 by Hachette Book Group, Inc.

Forever Yours
Hachette Book Group
1290 Avenue of the Americas
New York, NY 10104
hachettebookgroup.com
twitter.com/foreverromance

First ebook and print on demand edition: July 2015

Forever Yours is an imprint of Grand Central Publishing.
The Forever Yours name and logo are trademarks of Hachette Book Group, Inc.

The publisher is not responsible for websites (or their content) that are not owned by the publisher.

The Hachette Speakers Bureau provides a wide range of authors for speaking events. To find out more, go to www.hachettespeakersbureau.com or call (866) 376-6591.

ISBN 978-1-4555-6273-2

For the Warrior Princess of my heart, my best friend and soul sister, Dena Taylor.

Dark Embrace

Dark Embrace

CHAPTER 1

Raggedy Man

Time slows. Colors brighten.

Scents sharpen, spreading a hunger through my body. The cheeseburger resting on the tray on the counter drips melted cheese in slow motion. I push the order toward the woman standing in front of the cash register and take her money. Her lips move, but I can't hear her. Or anyone. The voices of the patrons sitting at booths and tables in Munchies fade. The restaurant falls silent, but for the music. I draw in a breath and tilt my head, straining to hear over the rush of blood pulsing in my ears. This is not normal music. No instruments play in harmony or voices sing in tune. It's different, like a hum rising from the earth. Waves of color float through the air: dancing green, swirls of blue, arcs of red. And the black...

A chill runs down my spine as the black ribbon slithers across the floor—a serpent-like harbinger of death targeting its next victim—a raggedly dressed man hunched over his heart attack in a to-go bag, in a corner booth. He pokes a French fry into a pile of ketchup before bringing it to his mouth, totally unaware he has been marked.

As far as I can tell, I'm the only one who can see the black aura infecting the bodies of the living, heralding their impending death. Only I hear Death's song.

The newest victim's lips move as if he's muttering to himself, totally unaware his time is near. Not even I can figure out the timetable. It would be nice to have clocks counting down above everyone's head. This way you can prepare for the inevitable. Wrap up all of your unfinished business. Live life to the fullest until the timer hits zero. Then move on with no regrets. It's the randomness that drives me crazy. All I know is that once the black aura finds a victim, it's only a matter of time. A day or two at most, then *bam*. Freak car accident. Congestive heart failure. Peanut allergy. The target dies. When I first figured out what the black ribbon meant, I tried to stop it. I thought being able to foresee the future meant I could change the predestined end. How egotistical of me to believe I'm special. Death is the one thing no human can challenge or halt. It can only be put off for a time, like it was for me.

I died last year. Well, technically, I'd been pronounced brain dead. I woke from a coma three months later, only days before they were going to turn off life support. Everyone thinks it's a happy miracle. I should feel grateful to have a second chance at living out my life and doing all of the things I've dreamed of, but I don't. What nobody knows is how empty I feel, like I left a piece of my soul on the other side. I ache with loss—of what, I've got no idea. All I know is that living hurts, and sanity is a fragile precipice I navigate daily, smiling on the outside while screaming on the inside, desperate to hide the fact that I came back *damaged* from my family and friends.

So here I stand, swaying to an otherworldly music only I can hear. Wishing Death's embrace had come for me.

"Dena!" The yell in my ear and the elbow to my ribs jerks me back to reality. The transition hurts like a kick in the stomach. Air rushes from my lungs. I blink away the last of the colors floating before my eyes and focus on my coworker.

Joanna grabs my arm and pulls me toward the kitchen door. "You okay?" she whispers, throwing a look over her shoulder at the customer standing at the counter. The homeless-looking guy. When did the woman with the burger leave?

I shrug off Joanna's hand and straighten my hot pink apron. "I'm fine. Why?"

"You've been hypnotized by the candy sprinkles for the last five minutes."

"Oh, that's 'cause they'd partnered up and were doing a waltz," I say.

She stares.

"Kidding." My smile stretches my cheeks. I wonder if it's reflected in my eyes.

Apparently, she doesn't notice anything's off because she laughs. The tension in her bird-like shoulders eases, and she leans against the ice cream bar. "Girl, I thought you'd done lost your mind."

What would she say if I agreed? My mouth opens, but the

words stick in my throat. A bang from the front counter grabs our attention. The dying man, who isn't quite dead yet. He slams his dirt-crusted fist on the glass counter again. His eyes, hot and full of rage, fix on me. I'm not sure if his anger is personal. More likely it's toward the world in general. I kind of understand how he feels. I'm just better at hiding my emotions.

"May I help you, sir?" I ask, donning my mask of courtesy, while reminding myself of the rules my boss, Marcheline Dubois, drilled into me when I started working at Munchies. *Customer service is paramount. Be polite.* Even if the guy's crazy, he paid for his meal. Therefore, he's entitled to be treated with common decency. *But don't take shit from anyone.* That's my favorite rule. Courtesy has an expiration limit.

The man's stench wafts over the counter and blends with the smell of grilled beef from the kitchen. I seal my nostrils and turn into a mouth breather.

He stabs a finger in my direction. "You're an abomination."

My lips twitch, but I don't lose my smile over such a petty insult. Practice makes perfect, I guess. "Why yes, sir, I guess I am. Would you like a free refill of iced tea?"

"Someone should give you a double tap to the head and put you outta your misery."

A shiver runs down my spine.

Okay, he basically just threatened to kill me.

Joanna's gasp fills my ear. She spins on her heel and rushes toward the kitchen, leaving me alone with Mr. Charming. If I play it cool, everything will be fine. He won't break out a bolt gun to make good on his threat. I hope.

Be cool. Be calm. Be careful what you wish for. Man, the universe really has a twisted sense of humor.

I hide my trembling hands in my apron and draw in a strained breath. My eyes narrow on him, and maybe he sees the darkness hiding behind them, 'cause he steps back. *Yeah, I'm not as much a victim as you thought, asshole.*

I chew on his words, then spit them out. "Put me out of my misery…It's been tried before, sir." My fingers pick apart my hair, pulled up in a ponytail, to reveal the scar behind my ear. The bullet's still in my brain. "It didn't work." I smile again. "Now, how about that refill?"

The old man's lips press together. He doesn't need to speak; I can read his expression louder than if he shouted at me. *Great. I just confirmed his abomination theory.*

Joanna must've alerted our cook, Adam, of the rowdy customer issue. He comes through the double doors and looms over my shoulder. He's not big, more like a tiny Mr. Clean, but the carving knife in his hand and the bloodstained apron sends a loud message. Crazy guy stalks toward the front door and leaves the diner with a final glare.

Joanna wraps her arm around my shoulder. "Are you okay?"

"Are those the only three words you know?" I joke, wishing I could shrug her off. But that would only call attention to my otherness again. Before I died, I enjoyed hugging. Now being touched feels like fire ants marching across my skin—an angry, biting little horde. "I'm fine." I nod toward the kid standing at the register. "We've got a customer."

* * *

Munchies closed an hour ago. One last chore and I'm off for the night. Thank goodness. If my feet didn't ache so badly, I'd be falling asleep standing up. I wrap my purse strap across my shoulder and pick up the trash bags by the front door. I yell toward the kitchen, "Adam, you all right locking up on your own?"

"Yeah, girl. Go on."

I push open the front door, but pause when I hear "Wait."

The overhead fluorescent lights gleam on Adam's bald head as he leans through the open doorway. "Think that hobo from this afternoon's still hanging around? Won't take but a few to walk you to your truck."

"No thanks."

A frown furrows his brow. "Sure about that? No need to play it tough."

Tough's got nothing to do with it. Fatalistic is what I am, through and through. It's stupid to tempt fate, but I do it every chance I get. Still I'm not walking on the wild side tonight.

"It's okay. That guy's long gone. None of our customers saw him lurking around. And the sheriff's office said they'd patrol the area tonight in case he shows up again. Everything's fine."

"You know I'd never let anything happen to you, right?" He steps from the kitchen, but doesn't cross the room. His fingers clench the mop. "If I'd—"

Yeah, I know. "You're a good guy, Adam Pope." He really is, too. I've known him my whole life. He grew up well. Maybe he's not the brightest bulb, but he's dependable. He even came to see me at the hospital. Not many of my so-called friends did. "Night."

He nods, putting earbuds in his ears.

I step outside and let the door close behind me with a sigh.

I dodged a bullet. I can't handle any more pity declarations. My guy friends all act like they think they should've protected me. As if my well-being was and is their responsibility. Their guilt screams at me in the worry lines on their faces, and I'm sick of it. I take care of myself. Always have. Always will.

The heavy spring downpour from earlier has lightened to a warm drizzle. My grip tightens around the trash bags swinging at my sides. I squint through the haze, trying to see the trash bin at the far end of the alley. Streetlights cast shadows across the walls. Ragged bits of paper sail past in overflowing gutters.

Once I leave the shelter of the overhead awning, I'm gonna get wet. No way to avoid it. A soggy end to a crappy day. Which morphed into an even crappier night once Samantha called in sick, forcing me to work a double-damn shift on a Friday—one of the busiest nights of the week since we close at eleven. Ms. March needs to fire the girl. Given the number of illnesses Sam's supposedly contracted over the last year, the girl should've died more times than I have.

I'd find this funny if it didn't remind me I haven't gotten sick since coming back from the dead. Not once in the last six months. Even the virulent flu that took down my brothers and mother during Christmas bypassed me. One more depressing symptom pointing to the fact that all ain't right in Dena's world.

"Just keep swimming, Dottie Dee," I mutter. Some days I sing the entire song as a reminder. It may be one of those days.

A quick glance back at the glass door startles me. The reflection magnifies my eyes. They've turned into dark blue pits, threatening to overflow like the gutters. Sweat glistens on my forehead, tinting my skin with a sickly cast.

"Gawd, I look like an extra from *The Walking Dead*." And feeling more zombiefied by the minute.

With a sigh, I stare through watery eyes across Main Street to the new Chinese restaurant, Happy Dragon Eats. *What do happy dragons eat?* The randomness of the thought makes me groan. Here it is. Proof positive Dr. Estrada's diagnosis was right. *Brain damage.* What else explains this "Soylent green is people" rumble in my tummy? I can't even put my finger on exactly what makes me so nervous. Other than the obvious serial killer movie scenario playing out—girl in a dark alley, alone, on a dark and stormy night. *Duh.*

The street looks as desolate as the moon peeking from behind the departing storm clouds.

"Stop stalling," I tell myself. *Toss the trash, get into the truck, and go home.*

I step from beneath the awning. My gaze dances from shadow to shadow searching for—*nothing, just scared of my own shadow.*

With a deep breath and a roll of my shoulders, the knot in my stomach loosens. I take short, mincing steps, trying not to lose my balance on the slick asphalt. Mud churned by the heavy rain forms a sludge that squishes beneath my tennis shoes. A thump echoes eerily from the far end of the alley and I freeze, holding my breath. It's too dark to see more than a few feet away. The city really needs to put more effort into maintaining the streetlights. Sure, there's not a lot of crime in Paradise Pointe, Louisiana, but when assholes go rogue, they go on a full-out, nut-job killing spree. Like the psycho serial killer who murdered a bunch of teenage boys last year. And Redford Delahoussaye's murder spree to clean up the witnesses who could identify him as one of the men who executed Jasmine LaCroix for being a witch.

Yeah, crazy stuff happens here all the time.

My mouth opens to call out, like one of those silly girls who die first in a horror movie. I even take a breath before choking back the clichéd words, "Is anyone there?"

What if someone actually responds? *Show no fear, be brave.* I don't want to close my eyes, but I do. With my head tilted to the side, I listen to the water gushing down a storm drain, the scratching of branches scraping together in the wind, and my harsh and heavy breathing. Nothing stirs or slithers from the dark crevice of the alley. I snort, disgusted at the time I've wasted by lapsing into paranoia.

My pocket vibrates.

"Oh—" I drop a trash bag into a puddle at my feet and fumble to answer my cell. "Gabby? That you?"

"I've been waiting forever."

"Sorry, really, it's just—" I wipe raindrops from my eyes with the cuff of my sleeve. "I had to work a double shift. Sam's out sick. *Again.* I called, but you didn't answer."

"Where are you?" Gabriella slurs the words until they're almost unintelligible.

"I told you. Munchies." I bite off the name so I won't yell. If I could, I'd reach through the phone and slap the drunk-girl sober. "I turned my cell on after my shift and got your message. You didn't say why you needed a ride. Everything okay?"

"I'm fine—just buzzed."

"You sound more than buzzed." I poke the trash bag with the toe of my shoe. I wouldn't mind downing a few rum and Cokes myself right now, but no way on God's green earth am I going to the bachelorette party from hell. Not for all of the free shots and male strippers in Louisiana.

"Aren't you picking me up?" Gabriella enunciates the words with great effort. "'Sides, everyone else's drunk. Not me."

It's after midnight. I shudder to think what state the other women are in if they're still partying. Gabriella's a featherweight in comparison to most of our friends, but one person should still be sober. "Gabby, put Mala on the phone."

"I told you. She's dying." Gabriella's voice rises to be heard over the screaming that breaks out in the background. She must've covered the phone with her hand because I hear a muffled "Take it off!" before she gets back on the line, continuing where she left off. "Don't you listen?"

My jaw aches from grinding my teeth together. "I think I'd remember if you told me my cousin's dying. What happened?"

"I paid a guy. He tried to give her a lap dance. But she screamed and threw up on him." Gabriella giggles. "My God, you should've seen his face, Dee. He was so pissed. She kept saying 'so sorry' and trying to wipe him off with a napkin. And he kept trying to get away."

Oh man, Mala must be mortified. She hates getting sick. Says the smell reminds her of all the times her mama got wasted and tossed her lunch into her flower pots. To actually throw up on some random guy...a stripper. At a bachelorette party, no less. Poor thing. I should've put on my big girl panties and gone, even if it meant celebrating the pending nuptials of my most-hated-one. At least then I would've been there to help my favorite cousin.

I heave a sigh. "Where's Mala now?"

"Landry picked her up about"— she pauses— "oh, two hours ago. She said something about food poisoning and going home 'cause the shrimp's killing her."

"But you stayed, even though your designated driver went home sick?"

"I didn't want to disappoint Vanessa."

My own stomach curdles when Gabriella utters the name of the bane of my existence, my high school ex-BFF, Vanessa Purdue. "Girl, you'd better be f—"

"No, s'okay, I'm kidding. I still hate her for stabbing you in the back, but her party's fun. I met this guy. Oh Dee, you should see the way his hips move when he dances."

"Nothing good will come from a relationship based on how the man's hips swivel."

"Then you've been into the wrong kind of guy," she says, then gasps. "Geez, Dee— I'm sorry. My mouth keeps moving, but no one's home."

The brat almost sounds sober with the apology. And as pissed as I am, I can't disagree with her slurred assessment of my former relationships. I try to ignore the spurt of pain her words bring up. "Don't do anything you'll be crying in your coffee over tomorrow, Gabby." I cradle the phone between my shoulder and cheek then pick up the trash bag. Time to get this chore over with while she's on the phone with me. Drunk as she is, her voice eases my anxiety.

Except the other end of the line has gone quiet. "Hello?"

An oppressive silence answers, and I'm suddenly aware that I'm standing in the middle of the dark alley, like bait waiting to be gobbled up. My heart races as I ask, "Gabby, you still there?"

"Yeah, Dick's coming with Jell-O shots." She has a breathless quality to her voice. "Oh, yeah—I almost forgot—Vanessa."

"What about Vanessa?" My voice hardens. "Don't you dare ask me to give her a ride home!"

"I wouldn't do that. Geez, what kind of friend do you think I am?"

"The kind of friend who'd party with the girl who helped my boyfriend cheat on me, while like an idiot I..." I draw in a breath and squeeze my eyes shut.

"Uh...I thought you were okay with this?"

My head's killing me. I pull the hair tie from my ponytail and shake out my curls. "Sorry, I'm fine. I mean, I thought I was fine, but obviously I'm not."

"Look, Vanessa and Charles—I bet they divorce—six months tops. Plus, Vanessa downed six shots of tequila, with beer chasers. She's at the front of the bar puking her guts out. If I post the video on YouTube, it'll get a gazillion hits. She'll be Internet famous. Come on, please." Her voice takes on a familiar cadence, "Help me, Dena...you're my only hope."

"Stop quoting *Star Wars* at me." I sigh. "I'm coming."

As I angle inside the alley, I catch a glimpse of my shadow, outlined against the brick wall. It sprouts a second head and, in imitation of the Hindu goddess Kali, stretches multiple arms toward me. My mind rapidly sorts through the jumbled images, piecing together what I'm seeing: arms, legs, bearded face.... The picture forms, not goddess but man. *It's him.*

I throw the bags toward the guy who threatened to kill me this afternoon. He swats them from the air and rushes at me. My scream echoes against the walls, bouncing back as if mocking me. The meaty fist aimed at my face misses, but the wind of its passage lifts the hair curling around my head. I throw my arms in the air and the phone slips from my hand. Gabriella yells for me through the tiny speakers, and I scream to her for help.

CHAPTER 2

Buffy Gets Staked

The man thrusts forward, grabbing a handful of my hair and yanking my head down onto his upraised knee. Pain flares across my cheek, settling in the eye socket. My knees buckle, and I hit the ground. Jagged pieces of broken glass tear through the knees of my jeans, slicing into skin. With my eyes closed tight, I try to think through the screaming. The screaming that's only in my head because I'm too afraid to utter a sound.

My kidnapper got off on my screams. He kept me locked in a windowless room and beat me whenever I tried to fight. It charged him up. What if this guy's the same as that sick bastard?

"Get up!" He uses my hair like a puppeteer uses strings. My scalp burns as some of the strands tear out by the roots. With no choice but to follow his lead, my body slides up the front of his. He presses even closer, trapping me against the wall. I squint, straining to see him through my swelling eye.

"You ain't gonna fight?" He makes it sound like I have a choice. "I'll hurt you more if you do."

I shake my head. My face is pressed against his dirt-crusted shirt. He smells of stale cigarette smoke and body odor. I grit my teeth.

I can't believe this is happening to me again. This is what happens when you tempt fate—you get bitch-slapped.

"Say it out loud. Say it like you mean it." He jerks my hair again.

I clutch at my head. "I won't fight!"

He moves his left hand around my shoulders, holding me tighter against his body. The other hand brings the strands of hair over my shoulder, up to his nose. He inhales deeply, rubbing a curl across his cheek, then across his tongue. "Never seen hair like yours—all red and fluffy like a fox tail. When I saw you inside, I knew I'd keep some of your hair to remember you by. Whenever you look in the mirror, you'll remember Ol' Jeb's the one who saved your soul."

I concentrate on calming my mind—pushing past the fear. Despite all his talk of "looking in the mirror," I don't trust that he'll let me go after he exorcises whatever demon he thinks inhabits me.

He's crazy. Dangerously so.

"What do you want from me?" I whisper. Unable to meet his eyes, I focus on the thick beard sprouting from his face like a dandelion. A louse crawls across his lower lip, and he releases my hair to scratch his infested chin.

I don't plan it. My knee rises, aiming for his balls like Dad taught me. At the same time, I shove him in the chest. He falls back with a yell, slipping in the mud. His hands wave in the air, but he remains on his feet. I spin, half-sliding along the edge of the wall, hoping to reach the door. Adam is still in the kitchen. If I can get inside, I'll be safe.

Hands wrap around my hips, and I groan as I'm lifted in the air and yanked away from the door. I rear back, trying to slam my head into his face, but he tilts his head to the side. One arm pins mine against my chest. He slaps the other hand over my mouth. It smells disgusting, like he wiped his ass with it. I bite down on the fleshy web between his thumb and forefinger as if I've turned into a rabid pit bull. I even growl in response to the adrenaline pumping through my body. He lets out a piercing shriek and tries to jerk his hand away. No way in hell am I letting him go. I finally have the upper hand, so to speak, and I aim to survive.

Fear melts away.

He must've thought my customer service smile at his earlier taunts meant I was a helpless, pathetic weakling who'd be too frightened of the Big Bad Wolf to fight back. But that's where he messed up. Since I returned from the dead, my rage has grown stronger. At night I dream about being helpless while captured by Red. I fought him. The whole time. I couldn't stop that asshole from hurting my family, beating me, shooting me…Now this asshole wants to do the same thing. He's fucked with the wrong woman.

For the first time since I died, I *feel* alive.

I stop thinking about the danger or what he'll do in retaliation. I grind my teeth deep into his skin until blood fills my mouth.

When my teeth click together, I give a sharp twist of my head and end up with a large chunk of his flesh stuffed in my cheek. The guy screams, cursing me. Saliva splatters the back of my neck.

His uninjured hand shoves me away. My feet slip on something slimy growing on the trash lining the alley floor. Unable to get my hands up in time, my head takes the full impact of my fall. Bright lights flash across my eyes and coherent thought ceases. It takes four heartbeats to return. The spots clear in time to see the glint of metal slicing downward. My arm rises to protect my face, and the sharp bite of his knife slices deep into my skin, scraping bone.

I scream, kicking out. My foot connects with his chest, and I hear the loud crack of his rib breaking, followed by a bellow of pain. The impact sends my body sliding in the slime, and I turn the slide into a blind roll. I come to rest against the wall with my head only inches from a metal trash bin.

He grabs my left ankle with a bloody hand and drags me from the corner, waving the knife. If he thinks I'll cower in fear, he's mistaken. He should have learned by now that *he has no idea who he fucked with.*

My hand scrambles across the concrete, coming to rest on an old board lying on the mud beside me. Once it's in my grasp, I go Buffy the Vamp Slayer on his ass and shove the pointy end right at his face.

He swings his left arm, blocking the stake. It grazes his cheek instead of taking out his eye like I intended. He falls forward. The hand holding the knife drops, and I gasp, staring at the hilt sticking out of my chest. My body goes numb. I can't release the air trapped in my lungs. My eyes dart up to meet the startled gaze of my attacker. Damn. He seems as surprised about stabbing me as I feel about being stabbed. He stares at his hand then jerks on the knife. It grates on bone and I hiss. If he removes it, I'll bleed out.

He releases the knife and rocks back on his heels. He rubs at his eyes, transferring my blood to his face. "You're gonna die, ain't you?"

"Go to hell," I whisper, trying to lift arms that dangle like wooden sticks attached to my shoulders. Unable to hold myself upright, I slide down the wall. The adrenaline rush I tapped during the fight has fizzled out. I sit slumped over like a floppy rag doll.

The crusty old man drags me toward him. He's oddly gentle as he lifts my body, careful not to jostle me. My uniform shirt tore where the knife entered my upper chest, right below my collar bone. My chest burns when I draw in a shallow breath. Fluid fills my lungs. The coppery taste of blood enters my mouth. The knife must've punctured my lung. Lethargy makes it difficult to focus. Things at a distance fade, and the man's face blurs into a featureless blob.

A whisper slides up my spine, as if my soul seeps from my body with each slow exhale. My eyelids flutter, and I struggle to focus on the ribbon flowing before my eyes. It's so damn beautiful…a rainbow of interweaving colors dancing to the haunting song that death brings.

The guy doesn't notice the massive vortex opening at the mouth of the alley. It swirls, each revolution hypnotic. Tentacles of smoke whip forth, stretching toward us. My heart stutters in my chest as a spike of fear shoots through my body. It hits me. *I don't want to die!*

A burst of adrenaline sets my faltering heart racing. If the smoke tentacle touches me, I'm gone. *Sucked in, lost forever.* "No," I whimper.

The guy runs a hand over the top of my hair, like he's soothing an injured animal. "It'll be over soon. Let go."

No. I try to move my head away, but I can't.

The smoke-like tentacle weaves across the wet cement. When it reaches the guy, it expands, pulsing as if driven by a beating heart. The black column rises until it dwarfs us then hovers behind him as if deciding on its next course of action.

"Help me," I beg. Why I say it, I don't know. Hell, I don't even know who I'm speaking to, the man or the shadow. But my plea's heard.

The guy pauses at the sound of my voice. He glances over his shoulder in time to see the cloud of doom strike. It shoots a black spear through his heart. He cries out, back arching. The cloud drapes his skin, blanketing his body. He staggers toward the mouth of the alley. Like he thinks he can escape. As if the shadow isn't clinging to him. His skin smokes, and he yelps. At first, the way he dances around, shrieking and slapping himself, fills me with a sick sense of vindication. He brought this upon himself. Guess he can dish out the pain but can't take it. Except…even this lump of shit doesn't deserve to be tortured.

Not like this.

I squeeze my eyes shut, but it's too late. The image is burned into my mind. His skin has blackened—oozing on the inside—like a burnt marshmallow. The yelps become screams, drawn-out, rasping sobs pulled from deep within his chest, leaving him gasping for air. The charcoal-like stench of his cooking flesh chokes me. If I could raise my hands, I'd cover my ears. His wails rip through my body like the knife had, cutting deep to my core. As much as I want to avoid what's happening, I can't keep my eyes closed. Instinct tells me not to look away from a predator. Especially when the vortex continues to spin, searching for a soul to slurp down like a raw oyster.

My soul remains intact and safely lodged in my battered body, but for how long? Maybe only for as long as my attacker still screams.

My frazzled brain sputters and dies. My consciousness escapes into the dark, only to awaken sometime later with the scent of burned flesh clogging my nostrils. As much as I'd like to convince myself that my shaky memories are a hallucination, I know, once the moon peeks from behind the clouds again, I'll see an extra-crispy corpse lying at my feet.

This is real, and I'm screwed. My injuries are too severe. I won't survive until help arrives. I'm dying. It's the only answer. Otherwise, why would I be wondering if the tongue licking my cheek belongs to an animal or a human?

It feels like an animal tongue. But upon opening my eyes, I see a man—one who hasn't noticed I'm conscious. He runs his tongue across my face in lazy laps that trail down my neck. Then he lifts my arm to lick the oozing gash running down its length.

This whole situation has the surreal feel of a lucid dream, but I can't wake myself up. I'm straddling the line between conscious thought and unconscious delusions. And I'm not sure if I want to come back to reality. Being licked doesn't hurt. If anything, it's the opposite of pain. A sort of non-pain, not quite like numbness since I still feel his raspy, cat-like tongue sliding over the cut, which tingles as if slathered in Novocain. My head doesn't throb anymore, and while my arm aches, it's nothing compared to the mindless agony I was in earlier. He licks the cut one last time and continues downward, his tongue dipping into the bowl formed by the crease of my elbow.

Unexpected pleasure burns in the center of my chest, radiating downward with each rough slurp. It's like he has an aphrodisiac in his saliva. I grow hotter when his mouth moves to my hand. His tongue flicks across the pads of my fingers, slowly drawing each one into his mouth, like he's sucking off chocolate instead of blood.

A gasp escapes me.

I hold my breath—horrified. The guy's head jerks up. Moonlight barely penetrates the alley, but I have the impression of dark hair falling over his shadowed face. The tip of his tongue slips from between sharp teeth to lick the blood staining his lower lip. The weight of his gaze—thick with the force of his hunger—changes. He sees me, not just a tasty dish of blood for him to savor, but *me*, Dena Acker, lying beneath him, breathless.

Part of me—the strong part that fought my attacker—questions why I'm lying beneath this guy like a slab of beef. Might as well stick some carrots around me and roast me 'cause I'm cooked. I should be afraid. But I'm not. Why?

As if sensing my confusion, he rises above me. I gaze into his shadowed face. Tension vibrates between us. All my senses hum with awareness in a way they never did with my ex-boyfriend. This man's touch feels familiar. As if some forgotten piece of me recalls the weight of his body in my arms. His touch fills me with warmth and security. Part of me yearns for him, as if I've finally recovered the piece of my soul that's been missing since I woke up in the hospital.

"I know you, don't I?" I whisper. Despair wells inside, an echo of the loss, but the memory dances away each time I try to grab it. My body turns traitor and refuses to cooperate. Like it's in revolt, and wants my mind to shut-the-hell-up. It remembers him, even if I don't. I realize now that all those times I dreamed of Death didn't mean I wanted to die again. I wanted to go back to find him. To feel how I feel right now. *Cherished.*

Now he's here in my world. *Holy hell, this is real.*

Energy pours off his body. He leans forward and places large hands on my hips. I suck in a breath as his palms slide up my waist. His nose presses into the crease behind my ear, and he inhales so deeply his chest expands against me. He rubs his face against my cheek, like a giant cat scent-marking its territory. The heat of his body, burning so hot it's like he's boiling inside, pushes me over the edge.

I lose myself in savoring the softness of his smooth, silky cheek sliding across my face. I breathe in the heavy musk of his body. I want to taste him. To lick his skin like he licked mine.

He doesn't help calm the urgency growing inside me. If anything, he seems determined to explore every inch of my body with a hunger of someone starving. How can I form a coherent thought when he's licking me again? And nibbling…Oh, God, yes, there's definitely some nibbling going on.

He draws my earlobe into his mouth, rolling his tongue. I cry out as heat spreads between my legs. I squeeze my thighs together, glad of the denim barrier between us, and try to ignore the building, throbbing pressure. At the same time, I remind myself to breathe. And even with the knife in my chest, it doesn't hurt. His hand caresses my breast, squeezing the soft flesh just enough for pleasure to mingle with pain. The other hand circles the hilt of the knife and jerks it from my chest.

I sit up with a choked scream. "Son of a—"

Blood bubbles from the jagged wound, a hot trail flowing down my chest. His head dips and his tongue enters the hole until his entire mouth covers the area around the wound. He sucks hard, drawing my blood into his mouth. The numbing sensation I felt earlier spreads from my chest, up to my shoulder, and down my arm in an enervating prickle that sets my nerves jangling.

"Oh, oh God—" The euphoria spreads, and I writhe beneath him, unable to remain still. Every nerve tingles and twitches from the sensations flooding my body. I grab his hair, using the hand that refused to respond earlier, and pull. His mouth pops off my chest with a sound like a suction cup being released from a wall.

He rears back, staring into my face with green eyes that glow with an otherworldly light, before slanting his mouth across mine. His tongue slips between my lips, bringing a coppery tang, and beneath it, a sweet acidity. I drink him in, swallowing the saliva that pours down my throat until I choke for lack of air. I want him. I want to be consumed by him.

The shock of this thought brings clarity to my frazzled brain. I pull my mouth from his, drawing in smoke-tainted air, unable to clear the fuzziness from my thoughts.

A car door slams and I jerk, heart racing. I turn my head toward the entrance of the alley. Blue and red lights rotate across the wall. Footsteps…the echo of a radio and the familiar voice of Deputy Eva Winters carries on the wind. I inhale, prepared to call for help, but for some reason I hold back.

The guy lying on top of me kind of…quivers all over. His grip tightens around my hips, lifting them. He presses his face between my thighs and inhales, as if to imprint my scent in his mind. The heat of his breath brushes across my skin before he pulls away with a frustrated growl. Cold air replaces the warmth of his body, and I'm the one left shivering.

CHAPTER 3

Even Ninjas Need Hugs

I wake in the hospital, doped up on pain meds and hooked to machines. Gabriella hovers over my bed—my red-nosed, Latina, guardian angel. Tears streak her heart-shaped face. She's a crier, my best bud: hokey greeting cards, heart-wrenching commercials, and homeless puppies get her every time.

She attempts to smile through her tears as she pats the blanket over my legs. "Hey Ninja, the police filled me in. What the hell were you thinking? Taking on that guy in the alley."

I glance at my broken fingernails and sigh. "Certainly not of preserving my manicure." I struggle not to grin. Damn, these drugs are good. I'm doped up, but not foggy. The pain, both physical and emotional, is tolerable with distraction. Teasing Gabriella should do the trick. I give her a lopsided grin. "I'd ask the court to make him pay for a touch-up, except he's dead."

Gabriella's face crumbles. She falls on top of me and wails, "Oh my Gawd, stop making jokes. You're not funny. Never have been, except in your own twisted little head." She wipes her tears on my chest, and I wince. "Sorry, didn't mean to hurt you. I feel awful, and I can't pretend that everything is all right. You almost died, Dee. Dr. Estrada said that even though your injuries are pretty minor, you would've bled to death if the deputy arrived five minutes later."

Pretty minor? Guess to Dr. Estrada getting stabbed in chest is no big deal compared to getting shot in the head.

I grab the remote and raise the headboard until I'm upright. Nothing's worse than being scolded while lying flat on my back. I feel like a little kid being reprimanded by my mother, not that Pepper Acker stuck around long enough to try. I'm not in the best mood to cheer Gabriella up, but if I can't get her to change the subject soon, I'll lose it.

"Well, that's depressing." I force a wicked smile across numb lips. "Not the dying part. I always handle that with grace and dignity. I'm talking about how your face has gone all splotchy."

Gabriella balls her tiny hands into fists instead of wringing my neck. "Stop using my vanity as a distraction. What's the matter with you? This is serious."

"She's right," a deep, male voice announces from the doorway.

I jump in surprise. Pain blossoms in my chest, making my response sharp. "Haven't you heard of knocking?"

The man enters the room with the air of one used to commanding attention. He looms, appearing huge in comparison to me. I'd estimate my head would only reach his shoulders, but I'll have to stand next to him to be sure. Speaking of—his dark brown jacket nicely accents his broad shoulders and biceps. He combines the wiry strength of a long distance runner with the upper body of a swimmer, all in one nicely tailored package that makes my mouth water, until I meet his eyes.

His cold, assessing gaze cuts through the druggy haze and saves me from the seriously lustful thoughts about him wearing nothing but an itty-bitty Speedo. I shiver, feeling like he poured a bucket of ice water over my head, but refuse to break my gaze. He glides over to the bed—really, who does that? His feet don't make a sound on the tiled floor, and with each step, my heart rate increases.

"When I knock, I miss out on spontaneous confessions of guilt," he says, studying me as if I'm a dung beetle under a magnifying glass. Maybe he wants to see me squirm. The question is why? I'm the victim. When he finally smiles, it doesn't reach his dark eyes. "I admit, Dena Acker, you aren't what I expected when I learned the details of this case."

"That makes two of us," I mutter, staring at the badge pinned to his pocket. Not that I expected anyone quite like him interviewing me about my attack. I thought I'd speak to someone I knew, like George Dubois or Bessie Caine. I'm not sure if I'm happy or sad about him being assigned to my case. At least I assume he's here about the alley. He still hasn't introduced himself.

His dark-hooded eyes slide down my body, cataloguing my injuries. A frown creases his forehead when his gaze touches on the bandage wrapped around my shoulder and chest, but vanishes so quickly that, if I blinked, I would have missed it. I pull the blanket up to my neck, shielding my body. Of all the times I fantasized about a handsome man standing over my bed, I never pictured it being at a moment when my eye's half swollen shut and the rest of my face is probably black and blue from being slammed into a wall.

No, I refuse to think like this. I'm not a victim. I'm a survivor. These bruises are a badge of honor, and I won't be ashamed of them. I fought my attacker with everything I had. I faced my fear and won. No matter what, I'm proud of myself. He can't make me feel ashamed if I don't allow it.

The blanket drops. "You make it sound like I've done something wrong." The cut on my lower lip reopens when I scowl. My gaze lifts to catch his, fixed on my mouth. I slowly trace the tip of my tongue over the cut to remove the drop of blood, hiding my wince at the sting. "Am I guilty of something, Deputy?"

His shoulders tense then drop. He lifts his gaze from my lips to my eyes. They're like lasers, digging through the shield I put up. He sees more than I want to reveal.

My eyes lower to the blanket. Curse him. He won this round.

"Detective." He practically purrs. "And I don't remember saying anything of the sort. Funny you should focus on that word…*guilt*." He pronounces the word as if savoring the taste on his tongue.

I cut a grimace in Gabriella's direction. Has she noticed the same ominous vibe I'm picking up from this guy? She stares at the detective with wide, slightly glazed eyes. Guess that answers my question. She must still have a hangover from the bachelorette party. Normally she wouldn't allow drool to leak from her open mouth. If I say anything, it'll just draw attention to her, and the detective's attention is currently focused on me.

Time to move this interrogation along. Things are about to get nasty, given the direction we seem to be headed in, and I'm not in the mood. "What do you want to know, Detective…ah?"

"Anders," he says, pulling out a business card and dropping it on my lap before I can reach for it. *Asshole.* "Just tell me what happened, Ms. Acker."

I scowl at his impersonal tone. It feels like I've been judged and found lacking. I can't believe I've never met him, but I'm kind of glad I haven't. It's a small town. Gossip about a new detective should've made the rounds by now. Either he must be really new to the area or he isn't who he says he is.

My face tightens, and I wince. In the corner of my eye, Gabriella stiffens. She knows what the dark look I send Anders means—the wrath of Dena will be descending upon his pretty little head. Too bad for him. He brought it on himself with his shitty attitude. I force a strained smile. "I told the deputy who found me what happened. Don't you guys share notes?"

"As a matter of fact, I do have Deputy Winters's notes."

I shrug nonchalantly, seething, then wince as pain fills my shoulder. My fingers clench the blanket. "What more do you need to know? After ending my shift at Munchies, I took out the trash; then I was going to pick up Gabriella." I wave in her direction. "The same creep who caused a commotion at the diner earlier grabbed me from behind. I fought back. He threw me against the wall. I hit my head. He slashed my arm with a knife and then stabbed me in the chest."

Gabriella gasps, and her hand flies up to cover her mouth. She runs out of the room, sobbing.

I take a deep breath, feeling a little dizzy from spitting all that out without breathing, before continuing. "I passed out and woke when the deputy found me. I don't remember anything else."

"I find that difficult to believe, Ms. Acker," Anders says, voice lowering. It vibrates in my chest, full of unspoken reproach. And I feel bad for lying.

Startled, I meet his eyes. Seeing his misgivings reflected back, my mouth folds downward. "What? That some creep would try to take advantage of a woman?"

He places his hand on the upraised mattress beside my right shoulder. The heat of his skin warms mine. He leans forward, head cocked to the side to watch my reaction. "What I find difficult to believe is how a strong woman, one who survived a similar attack half a year ago and had the fortitude to fight off an armed assailant, came out of the experience with no memory of how the man died."

Don't panic.

He puts all his weight on his arm until he looms over the bed—so close I can see his eyes aren't brown like I thought, but jade. The light touches his sable hair, and the reddish tint catches fire. It complements a light dusting of freckles sprinkled across his nose. Bet getting teased about those as a child explains his surly attitude. 'Course, I could just be projecting my own freckle insecurities onto him.

He frowns slightly, noticing my inspection. "Explain waking up next to a burned corpse, Ms. Acker."

Hell no! I'm not explaining the part where I begged Death for help. That's locked in the do-not-go-there vault. He wouldn't believe me even if I told him the truth. He doesn't seem like the imaginative sort.

Play it cool. If he knew anything he wouldn't be grilling me. After several seconds of practicing my yoga breaths, I regain my composure and shrug. "Spontaneous combustion?"

He jerks back, hands fisted at his sides. "Is this a joke to you, Ms. Acker? Because I assure you, I take murder seriously." His voice deepens, and the tension in the room thickens.

The irritation building inside rises to a level I can no longer mask with sarcasm. A sharp pain spikes behind my swollen eye, cutting through the fuzz from the meds. *Oh, it's on now!*

"And I assure you, Detective Asshole, I take almost being murdered, for the *second fucking* time, extremely seriously myself. That the creep who attacked me died before I did is what I call poetic justice. So, do us both a favor and get out."

"This is my investigation and I dictate the terms, Ms. Acker, not you," Anders manages to reply calmly, but his expression says he's not as unaffected by the argument as he wants me to believe. "You're hiding something. I've got three unexplained deaths by your artfully described 'spontaneous combustion.' I can't even rationally explain how or why these men died. The only apparent lead is you."

"*He hurt me.* I don't care that he's dead. I hope he's burning in *hell*!" I yell. "And you can go to hell, too!"

I meet Anders's eyes and flinch at the censure reflected in his gaze. Sure, my refusal to help him solve this case is wrong, but I can't control my reaction. I flash back to the fear and overwhelming helplessness I felt during and after the attack. When I woke up from my coma, I promised to never again be so weak. Now a lunatic has made me break that promise. I thought I was going to die. No, I *knew* I was a dead woman…I'd lost too much blood.

After spending the last four months wrestling with depression, who knew almost dying again would slap the apathy right out of me.

Returning to the present, I blink up at Anders. I take a deep breath to calm my racing heart and wipe my sweaty palms across the blanket. "His death is not my problem and neither are those other murders you're talking about. Maybe if you worked on your interrogation skills and didn't make the victim feel like a suspect, you'd get the information you need to solve this case."

"Maybe if you explained why your attacker had your picture, I could bypass you as a suspect and focus on someone else." Anders pulls a wadded-up photograph from his coat pocket and thrusts it in my face.

I snatch the photo from his hand and stare at the image of me walking out of Munchies. *Was that nasty old man stalking me?*

"You said you'd never seen your attacker before, but he knew you, Ms. Acker. He'd been waiting for you."

"Impossible." I hold my hand to my chest, struggling to keep air flowing through my straining lungs. My head wags in denial. "He was just some crazy old homeless man who wandered into the diner." With a deep breath, I focus on Anders with narrowed eyes, searching his chiseled features for any sign of deceit. "You're trying to trick me!"

Anders shakes his head. Hair falls across his eyes, leaving them shadowed. "I'll tell you what I think. This man had your picture because he knew you. For some reason, you agreed to meet him, and you killed him. I just don't know why. Was he blackmailing you?"

"To blackmail, he'd need something over me. I've done nothing wrong." I stare down at my own face, then crumple the picture and throw it on the floor. "You're making this shit up as you go along, aren't you?"

"Then give me a better explanation," Anders says, voice softening. Even his green eyes lighten. He sits on the edge of the bed and leans close, laying a hand on my thigh, and I flinch, feeling my attacker's hand.

"Don't touch me." I slide my leg away. "I told you what happened."

"He had your picture, Dena. He knew who you were. He was waiting for you."

Watching and waiting. Why? A stabbing pain flares in my head, and I cry out, falling back onto the pillow. My eyes snap shut. Stars dance across my vision. It feels like someone's jabbing an icepick in my brain. Could it be the bullet? Did my head wound somehow dislodge it? *It hurts.*

Breathing deeply, I attempt to focus on anything other than the agony which has me clutching my head. Any sympathy I had for my attacker vanished upon seeing that picture, but I do feel sad for the other victims. If Anders hadn't just made me his prime suspect, I'd ask how they died. What if there are similarities between what happened to my attacker and the other murdered men?

I thought I'd been rescued. But maybe I got lucky. If my attacker hadn't been closer to the smoke shadow, I could be the one lying in the morgue, nothing but a pile o' ashes. I also don't have an explanation for why I woke up being licked like a rack of BBQ sauce-slathered baby-back ribs, or the way the guy disappeared into thin air.

Gabriella returns with Nurse Susan who, upon seeing me, rushes over to the bed and begins checking my vitals. But what's left of my attention focuses solely on my cousin, who enters after them.

The tainted shrimp didn't kill her, but Mala's still a bit green around the gills and looks ready to bite Anders's pretty little head off. She storms across the room like a hurricane. Sparks of lightning shoot from her dark brown eyes, and her voice holds an ominous rumble, "I should've known it was you acting a fool, Anders." Mala plants her hands on her hips and stares him down. "What the hell's the matter with you?"

"I should ask you the same question, Ms. LaCroix. Why exactly are you here? It's not official business since, as far as I can tell, you're not an employee of the sheriff's office," he counterattacks, voice cool. His dark gaze travels over her, giving her the same bug-under-glass treatment he gave me earlier. Hmm, I no longer feel special.

Mala's chin lifts. "Lieutenant Caine told you that I'm consulting on this case."

"Yes, but in what capacity? You're not a law enforcement officer. A simple background check shows you're unfit to testify in a court of law. You're a defense attorney's dream with your history of mental instability. Plus, your relationship with Ms. Acker is a conflict of interest."

My cousin's face clouds with every word. "You did a background check on me?"

"I'd be a fool not to."

"I see." Her shoulders stiffen. "Well, I've heard about you, too. You left New Orleans PD under suspicious circumstances. Everyone says Bertrand Parish Sheriff's Office is lucky to have someone of your caliber and experience, but—I'm not convinced. Especially since there are qualified deputies who aren't stuck-up assholes who look down on us small-town folk, who are better suited to the job."

Anders glances in my direction before answering. "Since we both have trust issues, I guess it's a good thing we won't be working together on this case."

"What do you mean?"

"As of tonight, your services are no longer needed."

"Hold on a minute…y-you're firing me?" Mala's eyes flash. "You can't…"

"Lodge a protest with Sheriff Keyes if you're so inclined. It won't change anything. Not having a partner was a condition of my hire. I've been assigned to this case, and I'll do my due diligence by interviewing Ms. Acker, the only witness to what happened last night."

Oh hell. Anders isn't afraid to play hardball. Whatever special privilege Mala operates under at the sheriff's office, Anders just stripped it away. And it's shocked my cousin to the core. What's his game? Why is he toying with her, us, like this?

Mala draws herself up. "Perhaps things are different in New Orleans, but here your jurisdiction doesn't extend to harassing the victim. Or if she's a potential suspect, interrogating her when it's obvious she's not mentally stable enough to answer your questions." She places her hand on my shoulder. I wince at the pain, but keep my mouth shut. "I'm advising my cousin not to speak with you without an attorney present."

I jump on that like a frog on a log. "Sounds cool to me."

"So, if there's nothing more, good-bye." Mala waves him to the door.

At first, I think Anders will get in the last word. His eyes flicker as if he's got another salvo on his mind, but he restrains himself. He exudes strength of will and self-control in every movement. His gestures seem designed to elicit a particular response, like how he crowded me by laying his hand on the bed. He tried to manipulate me into spilling what I knew.

But Mala's handled him like a pro. I don't know when she decided to grow up, but when I finally do, I want to be just like her. Listening to her almost makes me smile, which would ruin a perfectly good escape from Anders. But I can't resist peeking at his face, and it's at the exact moment when his eyes slide in my direction. I stare at him, waiting to see what he'll say. He simply apologizes to Susan and Gabriella, ignores me and Mala like we're invisible, and exits the room.

"What a jerk," I say, before gasping at another stab of pain. "Mala, what the hell happened? Is he telling the truth about firing you?"

"He can't fire me," she says, voice full of bravado, but the slight crinkle to her caramel-brown brow shows her worry. "Whatever happens, I'll protect you. I was serious about you getting a lawyer. I don't trust that guy farther than I can throw him."

* * *

I dream, but I can't wake up.

A man leans over my bed, his hot breath blowing in my face. I want to turn away, but I'm frozen. He pulls a knife—a huge knife, bigger than the one drilled into my chest—from the pocket of his robe. *What in the world do men with knives have against me?*

The emergency call button lies on the bed beside my hand. All I need to do is reach out a finger and push it, but my hand refuses to respond. I'm trapped inside my body, unable to scream for help. The knife falls. I pray it will be quick. I can't handle any more pain.

Out of the corner of my eye, more shadow than form, the man who licked my wounds in the alley darts toward the bed. He moves like a whirlwind, spinning the man with the knife away with a thrust that sends him flying into the opposite wall, out of my line of sight. I try to turn my head in their direction, but I still can't move. The fight's loud. Why doesn't a nurse respond? *Oh yeah. This is a dream.* A loud thud echoes throughout the room, followed by footsteps running down the outside hallway. I wait for my rescuer to return, but he doesn't.

The dream changes.

A dome of air surrounds my body, trapping me inside a bubble with no way to escape. Rage at being confined fills me. I press against the membranous edges, trying to find a weakness in the cage, but it's solid. Beneath the rage, fear curdles my thoughts. An overwhelming hunger gnaws at my insides until my only thoughts are of food—food and the hunt.

The coppery tang of blood fills the air, and I double over with pain as my stomach clenches. I stalk forward, a cloud of pure instinct. A mindless predator stalking prey. The man still holds the knife in his hand as he runs from me, but I never tire, not while on the hunt. I shadow him through empty corridors, toying with him. He must think he's escaped when he pushes through the fire exit, slamming the heavy door in my face.

My body melts into vapor. As smoke, I slip through the crack beneath the door and re-form. The man stumbles back. Tripping, he falls and hunkers down against a wall. He slashes at me with the knife, and when it passes harmlessly through my body, he screams. Both hands rise to shield his head as he cries. The terror staining his face is so different from the expression he wore when he tried to kill me. He begs for his life, but I feel no sympathy. He's not real. He's nothing but food.

I awake screaming in a puddle of my own sweat. My hands clench the blanket wrapped around my body. The pressure on my chest holds me down. My breaths come in ragged gasps. I kick to untangle myself from the blanket and slide from the bed. My legs buckle, and my knees hit the floor. Ignoring the pain from tearing out my IV, I crawl until I reach the corner of the room.

My mind feels fuzzy and doesn't cooperate when I try to separate reality from the dream. Or is it a memory? It seemed so real. Like being awake and seeing through someone else's eyes. This thought alone taps into my core, fueling my horror. 'Cause whomever I'd been connected with is spiraling into insanity. I don't want to ride the crazy train with him.

A whisper of movement in the dark brings my head up. A feather-light caress touches my cheek, and a familiar scent makes me breathe deep. Hair tickles my cheek, and lips touch mine. I lean into the kiss, chest heaving as I try to drown in my emotional response to him—this man rescued me again. Didn't he? Or is this also a dream? I don't know or care. My arms lift to circle his shoulders, but they encounter nothing but air.

CHAPTER 4

Checking Out My Assets

I spend the rest of the night trying to forget the terror from my nightmare, but it never strays far from my thoughts. When I can't stand being alone for a minute longer, I put on my robe and time my escape for an empty nurses' station. I sneak by and drift from hallway to hallway, not really paying attention to where I'm going. It's not surprising to find myself back in the Intensive Care Unit. Or that I'm standing in front of this particular door, feeling guilty for abandoning a man who still holds a very special place in my heart. I should've tried harder to find out what happened to him, but I got wrapped up in my own problems. I broke my promise.

I run my fingertips along the door, remembering the night he was brought to the hospital. I spent most of my days after awakening from my coma roaming around the hospital, getting to know the patients and staff. On this particular day, chaos broke out. Doctors and nurses ran toward the emergency room. Something major had happened.

My curiosity often gets my butt in trouble, and you'd think I'd learn from past mistakes. Nope; I hobbled after everyone else. Sirens blared from multiple ambulances as the paramedics began to unload the patients.

Susan caught me huddled in a corner. Her bloodied, plastic green smock smacked her legs, and panic filled her eyes. "Did you hear? A freak earthquake hit under the Dubois estate."

"What?" I pressed my hand against my chest. My heart raced. "Are all of these patients from Ms. March's birthday party? Mala and Landry said they were going."

"I know." She grabbed my arm when I tried to pull away. "So was just about everyone else we know. It's a disaster. And we can't handle all of the injured. Some are being transported to the hospital in Lafayette. The EMTs are triaging them on scene." Her hand squeezed my elbow, and I braced for the worst. "Dee, there were casualties. I need your help."

"But—" *Mala. I need to find my cousin.*

"George Dubois is one of the injured. Dr. Estrada is going into surgery with him as we speak. I need you to monitor his other patient." Her anguished eyes pleaded with me. "His condition is stable for the moment, and I can't do anything more for him. Can you sit with the man until Estrada's available?"

I let out the breath I'd been holding and nodded. "Of course. Just let me know if you hear anything about Mala and Landry."

Susan led me to Intensive Care. She had me wash up and put on a gown and a mask before entering the sterile room. "Don't worry," she said, "you'll be fine. Just sit with the patient, and if any of the alarms go off, get someone immediately. God, I can't believe this is happening."

I gave her a tight hug, then turned to stare at the man in the bed. Bloodstained bandages swathed his head, completely covering his face, except where a tube had been forced down his throat. The shushing of the respirator filled the room. "Was he at the party?"

"No. They found him in the middle of the road. Hit and run." She makes the sign of the cross across her chest. "We really need Estrada to pull off another miracle."

I repress my inappropriate snort. Who was I to disabuse Sue, and every other nurse in the hospital, who now called Estrada the Hand of God? After all, I was his patient. And I did come back from the dead.

"Sue, I've got this." I pushed her toward the door. "Get out there—save some lives. Do what you need to do. If anything goes wrong, I'll come get you, *immediately*. Promise."

I sat in a chair next to the bed and listened to the beeping of the machines. The room was freezing. I rocked back and forth on the chair, rubbing my arms as goose bumps rose. Icy fingers trailed down the back of my neck. My head whipped around. A sheath of darkness slithered across the far wall.

Stupid…stop jumping at shadows. I pulled the blanket over the man's chest and then took his hand, giving it a gentle squeeze. A low hum filled the room—indistinct, but growing more rhythmic. It mimicked the faltering beat of the heart monitor. My vision blurred. Colorful ribbons flashed across my vision. I'd never seen anything like it before. It was beautiful and terrifying. Unbelievable, yet not.

If anything, I thought the phenomenon a result of my brain injury. I rubbed my eyes, hoping it would go away. The ribbons faded, grayed, and then blackened as if burning over an open flame. The shadow stretched across the room and I panicked. I used my body to shield the patient from the shadow, and it stopped.

But it didn't go away. It lingered against the wall like a spider. I didn't know it waited for the man's soul to leave its battered shell and fly into the darkness' web. It took two more deaths before I understood what the black ribbon predicted. All I knew was it couldn't come any closer. I blocked its path. It listened to me. Just like it did yesterday.

The quiet, broken only by the life support machines, had frazzled my nerves. At some point, I began talking to the guy in the bed. Maybe I also talked to the shadow. I don't know. Neither answered in words, but every time my voice trailed off, the rhythm of his heartbeat dipped and the shadow crept closer.

I talked until my throat ached. I whispered for him to take another breath. I begged him to hang on until Estrada arrived. I told him not to give up because I'd stay with him as long as he needed me.

I lied. I just didn't know it at the time.

An hour later, Sue returned to the room. And I left. I thought I'd check on him if he survived the surgery, but I learned later that he'd gotten transferred to a bigger hospital. And a local got his bed. I never learned his name or found out if he survived his injuries.

* * *

I feel more relaxed when I return to my room. Rather than chancing another nightmare, I spend the day watching a *Law & Order* marathon, just like a typical Sunday at home. Mala calls to let me know she's relapsed. Turns out she has the stomach flu, not food poisoning, and won't be able to visit anything but the toilet bowl. When Gabriella bounces into the room that evening, I restrain myself from leaping from the bed to give her a bone-crushing hug. She wears her straight black hair in a bobbing ponytail and has on a frilly, blue, baby doll dress that makes her seem sweet and innocent.

I scowl at her in mock anger. "Don't you know proper hospital etiquette? Where's the horror at seeing your best friend wearing a hideous, backless gown?"

She flips her hair over her shoulder and gives her interpretation of a "grin of evil," which I know for a fact she practiced in front of the mirror to perfect during her modeling phase. "I'm busting you out of here today, sista."

"Ooh, bad girl Gabby's back in action? How are you going to do it? The nurses in this place have eyes in the backs of their heads."

"My diabolical plan involved flirting with Alonso to get him to agree to your release. Turns out he's recently divorced and has a thing for evil brunettes."

"Seriously? You really sprang me from this rat hole? A few batted eyelashes at not-so-sexy Dr. Estrada accomplished what hours of my begging couldn't?"

"Well, I tipped the conversation in my favor by bribing him with a pot of *pozole rojo*. Turns out my recipe is similar to what his *abuela* made for him as a child." She forms her fingers into a heart shape against her chest. "He says my soup is filled with passion."

Oh, she's so smug. But in this case, her ego is justified. The woman can cook. My mouth waters just thinking about her *pozole*. It's hominy goodness in a bowl.

I jump from beneath the covers. My legs waver as pain flares in my head, and I lean against the bed. "You sure I'm ready to go home? 'Cause I feel like I got my butt kicked yesterday. Oh, wait. I did."

Gabriella snorts, rushing to my side. She lays a steadying hand on my arm. "Silly Rabbit, tricks are for kids. Get back in bed until I can rustle up a wheelchair."

I shoo her off. "Really, you out-maneuvered Estrada?"

"Alonzo made me promise to stay with you. I swore that I wouldn't let you out of my sight and that you would remain in bed for at least two more days—even if I have to tie you to it."

"Kinky," I drawl, with a shake of my head that doesn't hurt too badly. "Sucks I don't have some fine specimen of hotness to spend my time with." I let out a wishful sigh, and for some reason, my mind flashes to Licking Guy. "One who knows how to use his tongue."

"Dena!" Gabriella covers her flushed cheeks.

"I know how to use my tongue," Detective Anders announces, sauntering into the room like he didn't accuse me of burning a guy to death the night before. The conceited jerk flashes a wicked grin in my direction. As our eyes meet, a ribbon of heat shoots through my body and pools in my stomach. My heart rate triples, and I get a bit breathless.

What's up with that? I should still be so pissed about our last encounter that I'd rather be licked by a dog after it licked its own ass. *Traitorous hormones.* So what if Anders epitomizes hotness and could be my muse if I had a creative bone in my body? The attraction is all physical, and physical turns ugly fast without an emotional connection.

"Ew," I say with a deliberate shudder. "I didn't need that visual, Anders. I get that you're taking my advice and working on your charm, but you've gone from creepy to extra-crispy-creepy."

His skin reddens as his brows draw down into a scowl. His mouth opens as if he has a scathing rejoinder, then thinks better of it. He visibly pulls himself together, schooling his face back into its expressionless mask. A relief to me since I know how to react to the dark side of his personality.

He glances at Gabriella. She has the same dazed eyes and slack-jawed, goofy expression she wore the night before, minus the drool.

"Ms. Gonzalez, do you mind if I speak with Dena alone?" He tilts his head toward the door in arbitrary dismissal.

"Yes, she does mind." I glare at Gabriella, willing her to agree, but instead of having my back like a proper friend, she heads toward the door like an obedient little pod person. "Gabriella, you don't have to go. If anyone is leaving this room, it's Detective Anders."

Gabriella sends a wide-eyed look over her shoulder. "Oh, no…it's fine. I'll fill out the discharge paperwork while you speak with the detective. I'm sure it's important."

I slap my palm onto the mattress and yell at her retreating back, "Where's the loyalty, Gabby?"

She ignores my outburst and flashes Anders her "winsome"

smile. The traitorous brat practiced that one, too, for all the impact it has on its intended recipient.

Anders has already focused all his attention, and it's considerable, on yours truly. "I thought we'd finish our conversation." He folds his lean body into the chair across from where I sit on the edge of the bed.

He lounges as if he has all the time in the world. His body appears relaxed until I notice the tension in his shoulders. He's come prepared for trouble, if I decide to make some. *Well, bring it on!* If he dishes out the bullshit, I'll shove it in his face this time.

I grimace, staring at my clenched hands. "You thought wrong, Anders. I said everything I intended to say to you last night. Why don't you go bug someone else?"

"*Dena,*" he says my name as if struggling to remain calm, "I'm conducting an investigation into the murder of four people. I could really use your cooperation."

"*Anders,*" I mimic his tone, "Go somewhere else to investigate. I'm not cooperating any further in your witch hunt; they never end well for the witch." I stand and turn my back to him in dismissal. "I'm being freed from this overly sanitized prison, and I need to pack. Oh, and by the way, when did I give you permission to call me by my first name?" I spin to face him, and the open flap of my gown brushes against my naked backside. "Oh crap, Anders! You peeked! I can tell by your expression. You saw my...you were looking...*aak,*" I sputter, folding the gown behind my back so I can lean against the bed.

His strong features are as still as the statue of David, but I know, just like I know he's a freak of nature, that he checked out my *assets*.

The blush rises up my chest to heat my face. I must resemble a radish right now. It'll be even more humiliating if Anders figures out why his seeing my bare butt affects me so strongly. His ego's big enough already.

"Look, Dena—" Anders pauses when I cross my arms over my not-so-substantial breasts. His eyes widen a bit before he tears them away to focus determinedly on my face. He clears his throat before continuing. "Ms. Acker, I apologize for insulting you last night." His face puckers as if he's in pain.

I don't think Detective Michael Anders—I checked the name on his business card before I threw it in the trash—has much practice giving apologies. His current attempt appears to be making him physically ill. Ironic since the effort gives him a few brownie points. He must really be desperate to get my cooperation with his investigation.

I fold the backless gown around my body and ease onto the bed, pulling up the blanket to cover my bare legs. "Okay, Anders. I think my prejudice toward you affected my objectivity." My own face puckers with the discomfort of attempting to explain my actions to him. To be clear, I am not apologizing, just un-muddying the water. "Last night I was overly emotional, and you came across as an unsympathetic jerk. If this were only about you, I'd tell you to go pound sand, but…You said other people had also been killed? Were you serious?"

He nods stiffly, jaw tight as he stares at me.

"So," I draw out the word, "maybe knowing more about the other cases will trigger my memory. I mean, I pretty much told you everything." Everything that wouldn't make me sound like a crazy person.

Anders exhales noisily, repeating, "Pretty much?"

Guilt flares and my face heats—again. "Yeah, so…umm, were there any other witnesses? Was there anything odd about how the people died?"

"Other than spontaneously combusting?"

Boy, he sure isn't making this easy. All that's needed is a spotlight shining in my eyes and a box of Kleenex sitting just out of reach, and I'd think I was in a police interrogation room.

I pull a stray thread from the blanket and twirl it around my fingers, debating how much I want to share. I meet his patient gaze, telling myself that if I see any sign of skepticism reflected in the green depths, I'll keep my big mouth shut. Unfortunately for me, he seems willing to listen.

"It looked like spontaneous combustion," I mutter, heart racing. "Of course, I was bleeding to death so I was a bit distracted. I've never seen anyone catch on fire before, and all the black smoke rolling off the body made it difficult to see clearly."

"Black smoke?" Anders raises one dark eyebrow. "From the fire."

"No, the tentacle of smoke touched him, and then he caught on fire. It burned him."

"Like…on that TV show *Lost*?"

I lean forward, gripping the blanket. What a relief. I don't have to try and explain what I saw. I'm still having difficulty wrapping my brain around the strangeness of the experience myself. At least Anders has a frame of reference to draw on.

"Kind of like that, only the smoke was actually like a tentacle. It came from a black vortex, which acts like a door. When people die, it drags their soul through to whatever's on the other side.

Heaven, hell, or purgatory in my case. No big deal, right? It's the natural order at work. Except this particular door seems to be malfunctioning. It shouldn't be able to target a living person and burn him from the inside out." My nervous grin fades in reaction to Anders's dubious expression.

I press against my pillow, wishing I could disappear. "Look, Anders, I know it sounds outlandish and it's hard to believe death's a sentient being that can target its victims, but trust me. I've thought about this all night. I'm on the right track with this theory."

Why isn't he saying anything? His silence makes me fidget, determined to hold my tongue, but I break first. "This is why I didn't want to say anything. Now you think I'm crazy. Don't you?"

"Ms. Acker, I thought you were crazy before this conversation. You just confirmed it." He leans forward in the chair. "Before coming to speak you, I was at the scene of another murder. This man burned to death right outside the hospital. He was a real person, not a character in a TV show, and he died in the most horrible way imaginable."

I blink, shocked to discover his incredulity hurts. I guess subconsciously I hoped he'd believe me and I wouldn't be in this alone. Then his words about another murder penetrate, and I reel with the memory of the dream I had the night before. Could he be talking about the same man? But it was just a dream.

I force my face into a derisive mask. It's difficult to speak without the pain and confusion coloring my voice, but I do. "And I'm responsible, 'cause, obviously, I don't know the difference between fiction and reality?"

Anders's mouth twists. "The nurse on duty last night told me you were missing from your room for several hours."

Uh-oh.

"Of course I wasn't in my room, Anders. I was busy burning an innocent man to death with my *superpowers*. I shot lasers out of my eyes and then danced around his burning body." I wave my arm in dismissal. "Give me a break! I kept having nightmares about being attacked. So I wandered around the hospital." Not that anyone saw me to provide an alibi. Darn all my sneaking around. "Cross my heart, I didn't leave the hospital. Check the surveillance cameras."

"I want to trust you, Dena. I'm just finding it difficult. Everything keeps pointing to your involvement, and you haven't told me anything that would rule you out beyond a shadow of a doubt."

I rub my burning eyes. "I don't think 'shadow of a doubt' is even applicable in this case. There is no doubt when it comes to the smoke shadow. It killed that man. It's real, Anders. Either you'll believe I'm telling the truth or you won't. Frankly, I don't care what you think."

Anders stares at the ground for a long moment, as if considering my words. Then, coming to a decision, he jerks upright. He thrusts another business card in my direction as if he knows I threw the other one away. It teeters on the edge of the bed before falling to the floor.

"I'll tell you what I think, Dena. This is all an act to hide your culpability in this crime. And I swear I won't rest until I figure out what is going on." His lip curls in a sneer. "I hesitate even to say this, but if you decide to cooperate and happen to think of anything pertinent that doesn't involve smoke and mirrors, give me a call."

"Hold your breath until you get my call, jerk!" I yell at his retreating back, feeling childish. Why do I keep regressing to toddler status in his presence?

When Gabriella returns to the room, I'm still replaying our conversation. Why did I think it would be a brilliant idea to tell the cop that Death's his murder suspect? Sometimes I despair over the state of my sanity. Anders is in good company thinking I'm two pieces short of a full meatloaf.

Gabriella sits on the edge of the bed. "So he's gone? Is he coming back?"

"I don't think so." I cross my arms, trying hard not to cry. "I think Detective Anders has all the answers he needs."

"Then why don't you look pleased? I thought you'd be happy to get rid of him."

"I am glad—sort of. I hadn't planned on divulging as much information as he managed to weasel out of me. He's sneaky."

"And pretty hot," Gabriella says with a sigh. "I'm surprised you held out as long as you did. Every time he looked at me I thought I was going to melt."

"You're one twisted sister, Gabriella. That man is obviously the spawn of some malodorous form of lichen, with the same personality."

"Malodorous?" Gabriella snorts with laughter. "So Anders formed an impression, even if it was negative. Since breaking up with Charles, he's the first man you've paid attention to long enough to even form an opinion."

I wave her away. "My experience with Charles taught me not

to waste my time with losers. If the right guy comes along, I'll know it. I'm out of my experimental phase. I'd rather be alone than stuck with some commitment-phobic jerk."

"So young and so bitter…it's such a shame." Gabriella pats my head as if I'm a stray dog. I swipe a fist in her direction.

She jumps out of reach with a laugh. "Come on, grumpy. I promise, once you're home, you can eat a carton of ice cream and whine about the evil Detective Anders to your heart's content."

"Gosh, Gabby, sometimes you're such a brat. But you are so on. Just promise not to eat all the mint chocolate chip, and I won't give you any problems until Tuesday."

I pack up my things and let down my guard enough to believe I really will be discharged without any difficulty, then Dr. Estrada tears into the room. His almond eyes widen with relief when they meet mine. He wipes a shaking hand across a forehead dotted with sweat.

"Good, good, so glad I caught you, Dena," he pants. "I thought you had already checked out."

"No such luck," I mumble, throwing an aggrieved look in Gabriella's direction. It's her fault. She spent the last ten minutes getting detailed instructions from Susan on how to take care of me. The fact that the high and mighty doctor Alonso Estrada stands there out of breath cannot bode well for my situation. He's never been much for patient care. I'm still surprised he even took me back. I have a concussion, not a bullet to the brain again, or a tumor for him to remove—unless I count Detective Anders.

He smiles at Gabriella.

I roll my eyes. Question answered, but then he turns in my direction. "Dena, I almost forgot your pain medication and antibiotics. Directions are clearly marked on the label, so even you can understand them."

Ah, the Estrada I love to hate. His nice act creeps me out. He probably feels the same about me, but he plays concerned citizen since I convinced my mother not to sue for malpractice after he pronounced me brain dead.

I grit my teeth, holding back the scathing remark dancing on the tip of my tongue. It takes a few seconds to regain control. "Thanks, Dr. Estrada. I appreciate your thoughtfulness."

Estrada's lips purse as if he's sucking on a lemon. "No problem. I hope you convey my regards to your mother in this matter."

"Ah, well, Doc, Pepper took my brothers to Disney World for Easter break. She's parenting from guilt, trying to make up for abandoning them." Wow, that sounds bitter. "I don't expect them to return until right before school starts."

The shock on Estrada's face sends a shiver down my spine, but in a matter of seconds he composes himself. "Well then, I'm sure your mother will be happy to learn how well I've cared for you once she returns." He smiles again. It looks painful. "I scheduled a follow-up appointment. The details are on your discharge paperwork." He leans in with a serious expression. "I want you to call if you have any unusual symptoms."

"Unusual," I echo, wondering what he means, then shrug. "Sure, if anything *unusual* happens, I promise yours will be the first number I call."

CHAPTER 5

Two Steps from Road Kill

Rather than heading to the family plantation, I recuperate at Pepper's house in town. She and my brothers won't be back until the end of the week, and I have a key to keep an eye on the place. It's weird living in my mother's house. We've got a strained relationship. Which shouldn't be surprising since she'd abandoned her family for five years, only returning once she found out Dad had died and I lay in a coma. Yet, she seemed shocked when I kicked her out of the family home.

The old plantation's part of the Savoie legacy, passed down through my many-greats grandmother, Tenelle Savoie, who married Herman Acker. It's my inheritance for suffering through Dad's crazy shit with a smile and a "yes sir" for years. And I couldn't stomach this woman, who I barely know, coming into my home, pretending to be a mother to me. Pretending to love me.

It's not like I don't understand why my mother—or Pepper, as she demands to be called—packed up and ran. I'm not insensitive. Or blind to Dad's faults. He was an abusive asshole. She left to survive. She thought she had no choice. He really would've killed her if she'd stayed—but why did she leave us kids? My brain knew this was how she survived, but my heart ached…still aches for those missing, silent years.

When she came strolling back, expecting to be a parent to me and the boys, I couldn't forgive her. Because of her abandonment, I lost my childhood. I'm smart. I got straight A's in high school and earned a scholarship to Texas A&M, but I turned it down to raise my brothers.

Hell, I barely had a social life. My relationship with Charles didn't stand a chance. We snuck around behind Dad's back, snatching stolen moments in the back of his pickup. I'm not stupid enough to blame myself for him cheating on me with Vanessa. That was Charles's choice. He could've broken up with me. Told me he was unhappy. He chose not to. But if I ever find someone to love again, I'll do things differently. Dying should've taught me how to live. Instead, I almost screwed up my second chance.

Almost dying a second time. Well, now I finally get it. Life's too short.

Gabriella keeps her promise to Dr. Estrada and does her best to nurse me, despite my cranky refusal to stay in bed. Bribes of ice cream and a *Supernatural* marathon can only distract me for so long. Part of my irritability comes from having the same disturbing nightmare that I had in the hospital, every freaking time I go to sleep.

Trapped in the dream, I experience an overwhelming hunger—a deep, gnawing pain in my center that obliterates rational thought from my mind. In the moment, I operate on instinct, hunting my prey—human beings. The perfect food. Part of me knows this is wrong, even if I'm only dreaming. I fight for control over the hunger to keep from killing, battling my true nature and my dream self every night.

Come morning, my muscles ache as if I've spent the night fencing with armored knights…or orcs, like in my brothers' favorite movie, *The Hobbit*. Gabriella's got no idea my mind's being splintered into a thousand pieces…eaten by the mist. And it's becoming harder and harder to pull myself together.

I'm so tired…Tired of fighting.

I sigh, rolling onto my side. The pillowcase warms beneath my cheek. I stare at the alarm clock, watching the minutes tick by, afraid to close my eyes. I can't handle another nightmare. My gaze shifts to the shadows flickering on the wall opposite the window with the light of passing cars. My breathing slows as my eyelids grow heavy. Reality bends, shifting into the world of dreams. Once again I'm trapped in a void, without physical form. Everything seems gray, hazy and indistinct, like morning mist hovering over the bayou. I can't see where safety lies. One misstep could lead to my death.

I should wake up. Even in my sleep, I know this image of beauty is false, but I'm mesmerized by the ribbons of color before my eyes—a rainbow dancing to otherworldly music. This melody calls to me, and I fall under its influence like a child lured from the safety of my home by the Pied Piper. Emotion pulses through the ribbon connecting me to the piper, to

Death, filling my body with energy. I can't fight his desire. It overwhelms...and infects.

"*Need...need...you.*" It comes as a chant in my head. Not in real words, but as a tightening in my body. A feeling which translates itself into English. This thought isn't mine.

I'm dreaming—a horrible, intoxicating dream. To believe anything else means I've gone insane.

Terror wings through me, setting my heart racing. My hands shake from the residual energy seeping from my body. Wind brushes against my cheek, and I gulp in air tinted with the lemony scent of magnolia blossoms. *The tree blooms in the front yard. How?* My eyes pop open. "Oh crap!"

I'm standing in the middle of the street. Headlights stab my eyes with a spear of light, and I slam them shut again. The car speeds toward me. *Too fast.* It's night. *The driver...does he see me? Run.* My legs won't move. I'm still asleep, at the mercy of things outside of my control. I can't break free. The hold over my mind keeps me frozen in place. *Shit! I'm gonna die.*

My muscles stiffen as I brace for the impact of the car smashing into me. Tires shriek, skidding on the pavement. The heat of the engine caresses my skin, and the headlights burn the inside lids of my eyes Popsicle orange.

The car stops inches from my body.

Still frozen, like Anna near the end of the Disney movie, I don't even twitch when the car door slams. It's only the unnerving tingle of eyes on my body that triggers my own release. My eyes open to meet Detective Anders's. Oh boy, he looks pissed, and not with his typical "you're lying, so I'm going to make you feel guilty until you confess" intensity.

The way he stares at me...whew, he's gonna blow like Old Faithful. Hopefully, he's only full of hot air. My cheeks burn with the heat of his anger, and I drop my head so my curls cover my face. The headlights set my red hair on fire, like I'm staring through flames.

Silence falls over us. He moves until his body blocks the headlights. I stare at his black boots, willing myself not to vomit all over them. My stomach's bucking and rolling like I'm sitting in my cousin's rowboat in the middle of a thunderstorm.

"What the hell are you doing, Miss Acker?" His voice vibrates with fury, and I tremble in response. He grabs my shoulders with his large hands and gives me a swift shake. "Snap out of it!"

My head falls back until I stare up at him, still unable to speak. Tears roll down my cheeks. I swallow the bile climbing the back of my throat, unable to think of anything witty to say. Witty isn't appropriate in this situation anyway. Instead of appearing tough, I'll end up babbling or burbling. Wailing also seems to be a distinct possibility.

Obviously, I haven't quite gotten my shit together yet.

He frowns, staring at my tears. "Are you trying to get yourself killed? Dispatch puts out a call about some crazy woman walking down the middle of the road, and of all people, it has to be you." Anger turns his tone harsh, but his fingers caress my shoulders.

I tremble, unable to form a coherent sentence to explain. Not that any of this makes sense. Nothing in my world seems logical since my attack—the first attack. The second one only emphasized how screwed up my life has become. This must be a new symptom to add to the others I've been collecting: rage, panic attacks, nightmares, and now—sleepwalking? Hell, Dr. Estrada was right to tell me to watch out for unusual symptoms. I'm a poster child for Post-Traumatic Stress Disorder.

Anders's mouth tightens. "You're not all right, are you?"

Bingo. I sniff, wishing my arms would move so I could wipe away the snot running from my nose. The embarrassment keeps dribbling out. Anders grimaces. He pulls a tissue from his pocket and wipes my nose like I'm an infant. The whole time he doesn't release my other arm. Maybe he's afraid I'll run if he sets me free. *Ha.*

His hands tighten once then slide down my arms, and I shiver in response. This situation stinks. I don't want to add collapsing at his feet in a boneless puddle to Anders's mega-long list of my faults. Drawing in a deep breath, I close my eyes and lean against his wide chest. His heart races beneath my ear. His arms lift, hovering behind my back, and then circle around me. He holds me tightly, but not so I can't breathe. Just enough to make me cling to him harder, soaking in his strength.

His gentle pats on my back snap me from my trance, and I stiffen. *I'm hugging Anders.* And even more shocking, he's holding me like he'll never let me go. Or is this my own messed-up longing to feel special? Maybe he hugs every deranged woman he finds wandering in the middle of the road in her nightgown. *Mm, he smells good.* I press my nose into his shoulder and inhale his spicy scent.

"Where do you live?" Anders asks.

Snap out of it. I point a shaking finger toward my house.

Anders's hand warms my upper arm. A huge contrast to how the rest of my body feels. I stare at my bare, muddy feet. The night's damp chill makes them ache. I barely feel the prick of a rock digging into my heel as I take a step, but I stumble.

Without bothering to ask my permission, Anders scoops me up into his arms. A low *mew* of surprise escapes. *God, I hope he didn't hear.* I wrap my trembling arms around his neck, determined to play it cool—like guys sweep me off my feet all the time.

Anders crosses the yard to my front door with long strides. I kind of wish he'd slow down, but he bounds up the stairs as if he can't wait to get rid of me. The front door's wide open. He enters, careful not to bump my head on the door frame, then pauses on the threshold. He scans the room before going over to the sofa and gently setting me down. I sink back against the cushions and hug myself as I shiver.

Anders lifts the cream cotton blanket folded over the back of the sofa. He wraps it around my shoulders and tucks in the sides. "Where's your bathroom?"

"Upstairs, f-first door on the left," I stammer, teeth chattering. "Oh, and no p-peeking at the lingerie hanging from the shower bar."

His head cocks to the side before he shakes his head. "I don't make promises I can't keep."

"Good enough." I snuggle deeper into the blanket and soak in the warmth spreading through my body. "Just promise to keep any comments to yourself."

"That will also be difficult."

He runs up the stairs, feet barely making a sound. His footsteps cross the bathroom floor above my head. I can even tell when he pauses in front of the shower. I picture him reaching out to lightly touch the bra hanging over the rod and grimace. At least they're Victoria's Secret, a gift from Pepper, and clean.

He returns just as quick. A slight smile flits across his lips as his eyes meet mine. I ignore it. He holds up a damp black towel. "Is it okay to use this one?"

One good wash and Pepper will never notice. I nod, reaching for it, but he pushes my hand away. He kneels and lifts my foot in his warm hands. He wipes away the mud with gentle strokes, and I wilt into the sofa, feeling like Cinderella. He comes off as such a hard ass that I never imagined his touch could be so gentle. *Hmm, magic hands...*

While he has his head bent over my foot, I study his face, tracing the curve of his brow. In the light, his brown hair glistens with lighter red and gold highlights, curling slightly at the tips to brush his ears. He glances up and catches me staring at him like a kid with a shiny toy. With a blush I can't force back down, I tear my eyes away. His fingers knead the sole of my foot. Warmth fills my toes and travels up my leg, until a burning heat settles between my thighs. My breath quickens. Each stroke builds upon the last. It feels so good. And I'm greedy, selfishly aware of my body wanting...no, needing...more.

I imagine his hands lifting the nightgown as they slide across my bare skin. He traces the curves of my calves and massages my thighs. I didn't wear panties to bed. No silken barrier stands between his fingers and me.

His thumb hits a pleasure point above my heel, and I gasp. He pauses, fingers flexing, and meets my eyes. Is that desire swirling in the murky depths?

Oh. Oh God, why care if he's turned on? Everything about this guy rubs me raw. His arrogance makes me want to scream. Only I'm not sure if it's a scream of pleasure or pain. My thighs clench, and I swallow the moan tickling my throat. I can't ignore the emotions boiling inside me, or stop myself from wondering how his long fingers would feel sliding deep inside me. *Distraction. Need one, fast.*

My voice sounds husky as I spout the first thing that comes to mind. "I thought your eyes were brown, but they're really the color of moss. Or jade, depending on your mood."

The mossy eyes narrow. "Moss? The stuff that grows on the north side of trees?"

I jerk my foot free and instantly miss the warmth of his hands. I lift my feet onto the sofa and curl into a little ball. "Moss is pretty, especially deep in the bayou where I live. This is my mom's house…" My cheeks heat even more at my babbling.

Why didn't I think of a better way to describe his eyes? Well, at least I didn't include in my less-than-poetic blurt of too much information that the gold flecks look so beautiful that I keep getting lost in them. To admit this would be a compliment to Anders, and I'm not ready to let down my guard that much. No matter how nice he's "acting" at the moment.

Fingers snapping in front of my face bring my attention back into focus. "So, what do you have to say for yourself this time?" Anders asks. "Alien abduction?"

"Oh…*ha, ha,*" I drawl, but without my usual spit and vinegar. I'm still screaming inside over the injustice of my sleepwalking situation. Anders's heroically timed rescue provided me with a convenient excuse for…ah, softening. No way would I find anything about the detective remotely intriguing otherwise.

Anders leans his elbows on his knees. "Seriously, Dena, what were you thinking? You could've been killed."

"Tell me something I don't know. Obviously, I've proved your theory that I'm completely out of my gourd. And given the circumstances, I agree with you."

"So, you're not crazy?"

Wait. What? "There you go with your selective hearing. I agreed with you. Shouldn't you be marching me to your car and driving me to the mental hospital right about now?"

The corner of his lip curls. "Crazy people usually don't realize they're crazy. If you think you are, then you must be sane."

"Again with the twisted Anders logic. I find it difficult to believe you're a detective, unless it's a *defective detective.*" I giggle at my joke. *See, Anders? Crazy.*

He doesn't laugh, just stares at me in silence. Guess he's finally revising his earlier assessment.

"So, 'Dena is *not* crazy' is your official theory," I say. "And you've conveniently discounted my story about a black shadow burning people to death...to justify this diagnosis."

"You're a little emotional."

"What do you expect? I'm losing my mind." *Damn his magic fingers and mossy eyes.* I huddle deeper in the blanket, wishing I hadn't distracted him from the massage. *Stupid, stupid, Dena.* "Aren't you going to say anything?"

Anders rises to pace around the living room. I try to see it from his viewpoint. It's a simple room with oak hardwood floors, built-in floor-to-ceiling oak bookshelves, and a coordinating computer desk lined against the north wall, separating the living room from the kitchen. Pepper painted the walls the creamy color of real butter, *not* margarine. A sage loveseat sits beside the door in front of two large windows covered with cream and sage drapes. The matching sofa I'm on is situated directly across from the doorway.

Anders stands behind the sofa. I refuse to look, but I hear him pick up the black plaster replica of an Olmec statue from the narrow table. Pepper said she bought it last year while in San Felipe, Mexico. She and her boyfriend Judd were going hot and heavy back then. She said they partied like rock stars: swimming in the gulf, quad riding along the dunes, and dancing all night. She believed they'd be together forever, but he died last year. He was also a serial killer. Pepper has atrocious taste in men.

The presence at my back sends a chill rippling up my spine. I fidget, grinding my teeth together to keep from saying anything. He bugs the hell out of me. Either ignorant or pretending ignorance of my irritability, Anders restlessly strides to the bookshelves lining the north wall. He pulls out a book, flips it open with a grunt, and snaps it closed before meandering across the room until he stands between the fireplace and coffee table.

Finally, I break. "Will you stop pacing? You're giving me a headache." I tap my head. "Remember, Concussion Girl."

He scowls, but walks around the coffee table to hover over the sofa. "I thought your friend was staying with you while you recuperated?"

"It's been the prerequisite two days since I was released from the hospital, so I sent Gabriella home tonight. I don't need a babysitter. I'm perfectly capable of taking care of myself."

He raises an eyebrow. "Obviously not, since you were auditioning for the part of road kill."

I shrug, unable to argue his point.

"From your reticence, I assume you have no intention of explaining what's going on?" He flings himself onto the sofa next to me.

I scoot my legs up, rolling into a ball in the corner, as far from him as I can get without moving from the sofa all together. I refuse to run from him despite my instincts screaming that he's too close. *Breathe, just breathe.* My nostrils flare as I inhale his spicy scent. Waves of energy race across my skin, and I rub the goose bumps on my arms. Every piece of me is hyperaware of his every move. Freaking pheromones. It's the only logical answer.

I hold my breath until my brain's about to explode, then breathe through my mouth. The fog of lust clears. I adjust the blanket until it forms a barrier between us. He notices. Everything. I'm sure of it. It shows in the way he lounges on the sofa. His fingers tap on his knees as he surveys the room, me—as if he's perpetually on guard, never truly at peace.

"Does what happened have something to do with your attack?" he asks.

I shudder. I can't help it. "*Ding, ding*, point to the cop. Your detecting skills have improved. Before being assaulted, I never sleepwalked. So, yes, it must have to do with the attack."

I search his chiseled face for cynicism, but he's doing his blank, inscrutable cop-look again. Feeling the need to explain, I say, "Before leaving the hospital after my first attack, I went through therapy. The doc said it's perfectly normal to feel depressed and disconnected from reality after going through a traumatic event. Almost dying a second time—well, oddly enough, I feel more alive now than I have in months. I thought I was okay, but…" I shrug a shoulder and give a lopsided smile. Guess only half of me is on board with spilling my innermost secrets to Anders. "On the bright side, I'm not depressed anymore."

"Are you experiencing any other symptoms aside from the obvious?"

Like being spiritually connected to the shadow of Death? "Mostly nightmares and a general feeling of doom hovering over my head. I didn't expect the sleepwalking."

Anders nods, eyes narrow. "Do you remember anything?"

I thread a straggly piece of yarn through a hole in the blanket. "I remember going to bed around nine o'clock, then waking up with your car speeding toward me. Anything that happened while sleepwalking hasn't transferred over to this waking nightmare."

"Talking to me is a nightmare?"

"What do you think? It's not like the cop that already thinks I'm *coo-cu-cachou* is the person I'd choose to find me roaming around in my nightgown."

Anders cants his body toward mine, propping his elbows on his knees. His gaze travels over my body. I can't read his expression, but I brace for the worst because, with him, there's always a worst.

"Do you know why I was in your neighborhood when the call came in about you?" he asks.

"Is this a trick question?"

"There was a murder earlier tonight a block from your house. That makes five victims and still no leads other than your *black smoke monster*."

He shocks me to the core with the news. How surprising he held on to the information long enough to chitchat. He *has* improved on his interrogation techniques, and I fell for him like a teenage girl with her first crush.

He's set me up! He knows I don't have an alibi. I told him, in the spirit of gratitude at not running me over, that I sent Gabriella home and have no memory of the last—I glance at the clock—three hours.

I cross my arms so he can't see my hands shake. "I see. So the real reason why you're being so nice to me comes out." My bark of laughter almost sounds like a sob. "You must've rubbed your hands with glee when you saw me in the road. Poor, confused Dena, so traumatized it only took a little foot rub for her to confess to the murder." My drawl mocks myself more than him. Not that he cares since he acts like he didn't even hear my words.

I bury my face in the blanket and scream, "I'm an idiot! I should've thanked you at the door and sent you packing, instead of inviting you into my house. You're like a damn mosquito…or a tick…no, a leech. You suckered me into thinking you're an actual human being."

"I assume you're feeling better now?" He studies my face as if nothing I've said bothers him in the least.

It probably doesn't. Has he lived his entire life without anyone pointing out that he has some huge—too numerous to list right now—character flaws?

"Dena, are you listening to me?"

My eyes meet his, and I flush. "No. I was counting up all the reasons why I hate you. I can share them with you, but you've got more important things to do—like sliding your perky ass off my sofa and slinking to your murder scene like a good detective. Time to hit the road, Mike." I push to my feet, wobbling a little because my legs have fallen asleep, and gesture him toward the door. "Appreciate your earlier assistance. I hope I never see you again."

Anders exhales. It's gustily full of unsaid things. Mentally, I rub my hands together in satisfaction. I really want him to squirm after all the irritating moments he's given me.

"So you think my ass is perky?" His stupid eyebrow lifts, and I want to kick him in his perky backside.

I suck in a breath and hold it until my lungs burn. *Don't scream.* When I release it, I'm back in control. "Get out."

"Dena, if there is something I should know about this case, tell me." His voice sounds like velvet as he purrs, "Why won't you trust me?"

"What more is there to say? You tricked me into spilling guts, and now I'm your number one suspect. Case closed." I march to the door and pull it open. "Good-bye, Anders. Don't come back without an arrest warrant."

CHAPTER 6

Finding a Patsy

I spend the rest of the night trolling the Internet for more information about the murders. The *Bertrand Bee* online newspaper has paid very little attention to these men's deaths, almost as if someone's deliberately keeping the news quiet. Maybe Dad's conspiracy theories about the government weren't as off-base as I thought. Given the lack of information or witnesses to the murders, I am apparently Anders's only lead.

Despite what I told Anders, I feel some responsibility for those people's deaths, since I suspect the licking guy and the black smoke are connected. I doubt it's a coincidence that both entities were in the alley at the same time. Or that I dreamed of him saving me, like some kind of guardian spirit, and a man burned to death outside of the hospital the same night.

So yeah, there's definitely something hinky going on here,

and I'm in the thick of it. What's even weirder is that, for some reason, I feel like this spirit is as much a victim of circumstances as I was. I have this…bone-deep compulsion to protect him. If I were to tell Mala about this, she'd say my behavior is "illogical" and arch her eyebrow at me in imitation of Spock. And she'd be right.

But I still don't call Anders about him. Even if it would get the detective out of my life, how am I supposed to explain some guy licking the blood off my face? And…other parts.

Another odd thing I've noticed is how quickly my wounds have healed. The chest wound, which should've kept me hospitalized for weeks, is sealed with thick scar tissue—not very attractive—but also not oozing like it should be. The cut on my arm and the head wound didn't even leave scars. The only residual difficulty from any of my injuries is a constant low-grade headache.

I enjoy reading stories involving the supernatural, but nothing I've ever read explains my situation. Dr. Estrada spoke of *unusual* symptoms before I left the hospital, and super-fast healing certainly qualifies.

When Gabriella drops by to check on me later that afternoon, I must look like death warmed over, 'cause she totally freaks out, planting her face so close to mine that I can count her eyelashes. "Oh my goodness, what happened?"

"Gabby, I'm fine…" I choke on the lie, unable to speak through the sob caught in my throat. Tears well in my eyes, turning her into a blurry brown blob.

Gabriella throws her arms around me. She doesn't say anything for several minutes, letting me cry. One of the many reasons why

I consider her a friend is she never judges or makes me feel like a loser when my emotions get the better of me.

When I finish sobbing into her new teal cashmere cardigan—so super soft that I hold back from rubbing my cheek against her shoulder and purring like a kitten—she pushes me into the kitchen and forces me to sit at the table. While she puts the kettle on the stove to make tea, I focus on something other than my own problems.

"Hey, what are you doing here?" I ask. "I thought you had to work."

Gabriella pauses in the middle of pouring hot water into a cup and doesn't notice when it overflows until some splashes on her hand. "Ouch!" She sticks her finger in her mouth. "Oh, that? Well, you know I've never really enjoyed working at the pet store. I like playing with the baby kittens and all, but really, I do have a college degree my parents spent a hell of a lot of money on. I figure it's time to grow up and find a real job with decent benefits. Especially after seeing you in the hospital. If that happened to me, I'd be up shit creek without insurance to pay the medical bills."

I nod. I'd be screwed if I hadn't received a large chunk of money from Mala. When her great aunt Magnolia passed away last year, she inherited her aunt's estate. Since she hated her aunt with a passion, she donated most of the woman's "blood money" to local charities, like the Dubois Quake victims and her immediate family. That money saved me from drowning in debt after being hospitalized for months, and why Pepper could take my brothers on a week-long Disney vacation.

I stare at my friend through narrowed eyes. Gabriella's sudden transformation into a responsible adult seems awfully suspicious.

She's avoided any type of responsibility for years. As the youngest daughter in a traditional Mexican family, she's expected to live in her mother's home until marriage. What's changed?

"So you found a new job?" I ask.

"Hmm, you know, I can't go back to the pet store knowing that as soon as I find a job I'm gonna quit. That wouldn't be fair. I put my notice in two weeks ago. Now I'm free to take anything that comes up."

I cross my arms and lean back in the chair. "Don't you think quitting might be a bit premature? Jobs aren't easy to find in this economy."

Gabriella laughs, sticking out her chest to emphasize the breasts she relies on too often to solve her problems. "Nah, I've never had difficulty finding work. The *girls* and I have good interview skills."

I muffle a sigh. Gabriella's got a lot of positive attributes. She's beautiful and intelligent, but her mother taught her to value looks over brains. She learned how to wrap guys around her little finger in high school. If the woman applied herself, she could've been a brain surgeon instead of aspiring to marry one. It would be sad, except she's happy in her own skin. How often does that happen? And who am I to judge? I've got my own issues.

Gabriella pushes the mug across the table and sits. "Enough about my problems. What's going on with you? Did I tell you earlier how awful you look?"

"If you're appealing to my vanity to distract me from the current topic of conversation, it won't work. How do you plan to pay your bills until you find a new job?"

"I told you it won't be a problem. Quit worrying about me and focus on yourself. Have you been sleeping? You look like a raccoon on meth."

I scowl at the image. "Sleeping is my problem. Frankly, I've had it with the whole process. Whoever said people need to sleep anyway?"

"Oh ho, someone's cranky pants. A full night's rest is important. It keeps you from biting your best friend's head off. Now stop deflecting and tell me what's going on."

I pour a dollop of cream into my cup of Earl Gray. "Fine, I'll share, but you'll think I'm nuts." I take a sip of tea and sigh. Warmth spreads through my chest, filling me with a false sense of peace. "Okay, so, I've had some pretty freaky nightmares ever since the night o' terror. Which I could handle. But last night…I sleepwalked." Her face blanches. "Yeah, not cool. I woke up in the middle of the street."

Gabriella grabs my hand and squeezes. "Do you remember how you got outside?"

"Nope, nada. One moment I'm snug in my bed, and the next, I'm in my nightgown about to get squished by Detective Anders's car."

"Ooh, Detective Anders." Gabriella giggles. "I bet he was surprised. Were you wearing sexy lingerie?"

"If you call a flannel nightgown sexy. Anyway, he was very polite. He helped me back inside since I was sort of in shock. Then he used my weakness to grill me about another murder. A burned corpse was found a couple blocks from here. I could practically read Anders's mind, 'Crazy girl wandering the streets, minus an alibi, with a connection to a previous murder.' I'm surprised he didn't arrest me on the spot."

"He can't think you're involved. You were in the alley talking to me. If I hadn't begged for a ride, you would've been safe at home. *This is all my fault*," she concludes in a wail.

I didn't know she felt guilty about my attack. None of what happened is her fault. "Gabby, don't—"

Gabriella slams her hand down on the table hard enough to slop my tea. "Don't 'Gabby' me! It won't change how I feel. And to think Detective Anders would harass you after all you've been through. He's so hot. But I guess he's also as big a creep as you've told me."

"Bigger," I agree with a slight growl, preferring her anger to guilt. Anger fits my mood. I can channel it into something constructive. Anders *is* hot, and the fact that his touch brings heat to places I thought would never warm again confuses the hell out of me. The man thinks I'm a murderer. And the person who probably killed those men. The guy in the alley—well, I'm drawn to him on a deeper level. Spiritual versus Physical, two keys which can unlock my heart, if I let down my guard. Time to be proactive and triple deadbolt my feelings before I end up getting hurt. "Okay, we're agreed," I say. "So what do we do to clear my name?"

A cloud covers Gabriella's eyes. "Huh?"

"I won't let Anders railroad me into taking the fall for some serial killer."

Gabriella shoves to her feet. Her dark eyes harden to obsidian. "You're right! I knew I got fired from Pet Plus for a reason. This is fate." She rises and heads to the door. "I'll be back with my things."

Fired? "Wait, did you say things?" I call after her retreating back, but I've reacted too late. Events around Gabriella move at warp speed. Once she gets an idea in her head, she runs with it. We're a lot alike in this way.

The door slams shut behind her, leaving me alone with my thoughts. But not for long. Gabriella returns an hour later with two large suitcases. I'm still sitting at the table where she left me. Sure, I moved a few times to go to the bathroom and refill the kettle, but for the most part, I'm slumped in the chair, staring out the kitchen window while trying to figure out how to fix the complications in my life.

"What's all this?" I push the chair back and stand. When I stretch, a loud crack resounds through the room as my back pops back into alignment. Muscles I didn't know existed ripple beneath my skin.

Gabriella rolls a suitcase in my direction, and I lift it over my shoulder in a smooth motion. "Been working out?" Her eyebrow quirks as she studies me like a prized bull.

"Nah, I'm hyped on the caffeine." I nod to the empty kettle. "This is my third pot."

She sighs. "Just like I thought. You need my help, *mamacita*. I'm moving in with you for a while. I can't pay my bills without a job. My car really isn't big enough to live out of, and I refuse to go home and grovel at my mother's feet for money. You've met her. Can you imagine how much pleasure she'd derive from blackmailing me into dating one of her friends' rich sons, or making me clean her house for an allowance?"

"The indignity of it all," I drawl, tapping my foot.

She nods, not catching the sarcasm. "Help me carry these bags to the spare bedroom then go shower, 'cause you smell a little ripe. After you're human again, we'll come up with a plan to clear your name."

A little ripe? I sniff the pit of my upraised arm. *Ugh.* Did I smell this bad last night? If so, Anders earned some major points in his favor by pretending he didn't notice my stench. Then again, he's trying to frame me for murder—he doesn't deserve points. He probably decided he'd get more information if he didn't piss me off by telling me I stink.

After helping Gabriella move her luggage upstairs, I retreat to the master bathroom and take a long, scorching-hot shower. I scrub my filthy body with apricot body wash. My hair's already confined in a long braid. Since I don't plan on leaving the house, I leave it alone. I don't have the energy to fight the springy curls.

Gabriella's right. The side effects of not sleeping are startling. I press a fingertip to the bruise at the corner of my eye. The purple has faded to yellow, which somehow brings out flecks of gold in the ring of emerald circling the iris. Sure, it looks kind of pretty, but keeping my eye that color means I have to punch myself in the face every morning. Maybe eye shadow will also do the trick.

Wait, duh—both eyes hold gold flecks. I lean forward, inspecting my face with a frown. What the hell? How does getting stabbed change blue eyes to green and gold? Or give the iris a catlike appearance? My brain races a mile a minute, cataloguing each feature. Nothing else appears unusual. I dodged a genetic bullet by inheriting high cheekbones set in a heart-shaped face from Pepper. She still brags about being voted prom queen four years in a row. The red hair came from Dad. It was passed down through the generations from Gerard Savoie's Irish mom. Mala's got the same red in her hair. My blue eyes were the same as my grandmother's, until they changed. The dimples set in the corner of my mouth when I smile, or scowl—well, those are my own.

While I've never been able to tan without burning, my skin looks like the sun hasn't touched it in years. Even my freckles have faded. I'm not exactly pleased about this; it took years for me to accept them as a unique part of what makes me, me. Freckles are part of my identity. Who the hell am I now?

Or rather, what am I becoming?

The stupid headache I can't get rid of flares, stabbing between my eyes and reminding me I have a concussion. Dizzy, I sit on the edge of the tub and rub my eyelids. Maybe getting knocked in the head changed my eye color.

"Whatever. Just add this to your list of unusual symptoms to tell Estrada about at your check-up," I tell my reflection.

After pulling on a navy hooded sweatshirt, black sweat pants, and a pair of black Uggs, I feel human again. I consider taking out my makeup case, but the dull throb behind my eyes makes the effort too great. Even if every whisk of the mascara brush or swipe of lipstick feels like I'm giving the finger to Dad. He never let me wear makeup, like "some kind of whore." Even though he's dead, I still enjoy my petty rebellions.

My mood lifts as I traipse downstairs. A male voice comes from the kitchen, and I miss a step. My butt hits the stair, and I bounce down the last two steps.

Gabriella runs out of the kitchen, followed by Asshole of the Year, Charles Frasier, my two-timing ex. "Dena, are you all right?" She squats down at my side, patting my cheeks like she doesn't see me staring at her in horror. "Talk to me—tell me where you're hurt."

My mouth opens, then shuts on a high squeak. No matter how hard I try, I can't form a sentence without cursing. Charles hovers over her shoulder, watching me with false concern on his scrunched, beetle-like face.

"G-gah…" I grab her hand and squeeze until she shuts up. "I'm fine. Get off me."

I roll onto my knees and use the stair railing to pull myself upright, clinging to the banister to keep from going for Charles's throat. I want to wrap my fingers around his scrawny neck and wring it like a chicken. I've been blindsided. It takes a couple of minutes to regain control over my raging emotions, but once I push aside my desire to choke him out, I look him over.

After we broke up, he wisely avoided being in the same room with me. It's been almost four months since I last saw Charles—thank God! He visited me in the hospital after I woke from the coma. I did not look my best, and given the circumstances of our breakup, I wanted to look hot the first time he saw me again, not skeletal and atrophied with part of my head shaved.

A rush of spiteful pleasure almost makes me laugh aloud. He's gained about ten pounds since we were together. His sandy brown hair also looks a little thin, probably from living with Vanessa. That shrew would make anyone's hair fall out. "Hey, Charles, what are you doing here?" It takes a huge effort to say the words in a polite tone.

"Gabriella told me about your problem and asked if I could come over and help," he says with a slight smile.

He's studying me as well. If I'd known he was coming over, I would've combed my hair and put on a little makeup to remind him of what he lost out on after he screwed his way out of my life.

Then his words penetrate. I glance at Gabriella. "Help with my problem?"

Gabriella nods.

I grab her arm and drag her up the stairs. "Excuse us. We'll be back in a moment," I tell Charles, voice strangled.

I shove Gabriella into my bedroom and slam the door.

"Hey," she protests, rubbing her arm. I've left red marks. "What's the matter with you?"

"What's the matter with me? Are you insane?" I shake with pent-up fury. "I can't believe you invited Charles over here. You told him about my problem…Charles? How could you do this to me?"

Gabriella's eyes narrow. "Get a grip. I'm trying to help you."

"By inviting Charles Frasier over? How is that going to help anything? He's my arch-nemesis."

"I thought Detective Anders was your arch-nemesis?" She puts her hands on her hips.

"He is, too," I sputter. "They're both equally arch-neme-si."

Gabriella shakes her head. Her black hair matches the darkness gathering in her eyes. "You can't have two arch-nemeses. That's against the rules. You'll have to decide on one, and frankly, I'd think the one trying to fry you for *mur…der* would be the better choice."

She's right. "But Charles? Of all the people to ask for help, why him? Why not Mala?" I pinch the bridge of my nose, breathing hard. "God, Gabby, he betrayed me. I don't want anything to do with him."

"Suck it up, Dena." Her voice has turned sharp; it cuts into me with each word. "We need an informant…a patsy."

"A *patsy*. What does that word even mean?"

"Charles is someone who can feed us information. I called Mala first, but she said she and Landry are going to New Orleans to do some digging into Anders's background. She's the one who suggested I call Charles, since he's on the inside."

"He's not a cop. He's a public safely officer. How is he going to help—tow the bad guy's car for parking in a handicapped spot?"

"Geez, Dena; you dated the guy for a year. Don't you know anything about his job? He has access to police files. He's already gathered up information on the case." She shrugs. "Lose the pride. He feels guilty about the way he treated you. We can use him to find out what Anders has on you." Determination fills her eyes. She's got my back.

"You're sure this will work?"

"Hell, yes. Now go downstairs and make nice."

"There's a limit, Gabriella." I wonder if I've reached mine.

CHAPTER 7

Arch-neme-si to the Rescue

Charles has made himself at home in the kitchen. He even figured out where Pepper hid her booze, 'cause he'd poured himself a rum and coke and was bent over a laptop on the table in front of him. When I enter the room, he smiles, and it's like a punch in the gut. This is what attracted me to him. He smiles from the center of his being, and it lights up the room with his joy. Warmth floods my body, and my own grin comes out of hiding. Thank goodness, Vanessa didn't ruin that smile.

"I guess my being here was a shock?" He tips his chin in Gabriella's direction. "I told her this wasn't a good idea, but once I found out what was going on, I had to help."

Oddly, pleasure sparks at his words. He always seemed like such a nice guy. Vanessa must've dabbled in some wicked mojo to get him to cheat. The witch!

"It was a surprise," I say, "but I'm glad you came. I need all the help I can get. Gabriella filled you in on my problem?"

Charles nods. The corners of his eyes tilt downward, and I sigh. His sad puppy eyes always send a shaft of pain through my heart. "I was on duty the night you were attacked. That's the reason...um" —he blushes—"Vanessa chose to party with the girls that night. When I heard you were being taken to the hospital, I wanted to stop by and see how you were doing. Vanessa convinced me that I was the last person you'd want to see."

Wow, Vanessa's smarter than I thought. "Thanks for the concern." I sit across the table from Charles and let Gabriella sit at the head since she appears to be the one running this show. "What have you guys come up with?"

Gabriella reaches for the Captain Morgan and pours us drinks. "Charles, you work with Detective Anders. What kind of person is he?"

Charles frowns. "Well, we don't socialize. From what I've heard, the other deputies respect him, but they're also intimidated by him. He works the graveyard shift. Keeps to himself."

Makes sense to me given his appalling social skills. No wonder there isn't any gossip about him around town. "Any talk about why he moved to our tiny parish Sheriff's Office? Must be quite a pay cut, and let's be honest: not much happens around here."

"I heard in New Orleans, he took the gruesome murder cases—the career breakers. But he's good. His record for solving heinous crimes was pretty high." Charles runs a fingertip around the rim of his glass. "I don't know why he left, but supposedly some bad shit went down on his last case. It messed him up pretty bad. This is all hearsay, so don't quote me on it."

"You sound like you admire him," I say.

"What's not to admire? He's the youngest detective on staff. He's good at his job and survived shit that would've broken lesser men."

I decide to leave the hero worship alone. "Okay, so what do you know about my case?"

Charles taps a key, opening a file, then turns the screen in our direction. "After Gabriella's call, I downloaded the case file. It isn't complete since I didn't have time to get the hard copies. If anyone finds out, I'll get in a lot of trouble. Don't make me regret helping you." He stares hard at me for a long, uncomfortable moment before continuing. "There have been five deaths. All the deceased are male. All had criminal records—mostly for crimes against persons."

"So they were bad guys?" Gabriella clarifies quickly. "Not that I think anyone deserves to die by immolation." She looks at the screen, and her nose crinkles as she studies the picture of a victim. "Ew, that's totally gross!"

Charles shifts his eyes from the laptop. His face turns a bit splotchy. "This is the dirt bag who attacked Dena, Albert Tolson." He scrolls to a mug shot, and I shiver. He has the same dead eyes in the picture as he did in person. "Tolson did a long stretch in prison for sexually assaulting a couple of college students. When he was paroled in 2008, he was supposed to register as a sex offender, but dropped off the radar for years. The warrant was still active in NCIC."

"Yikes, a really bad guy." Gabriella lets out a heavy sigh. "You got lucky, Dee."

I rub my arms, feeling like I'll never warm up. It's terrifying to think how things could've gone a lot worse for me.

Charles gives me a sympathetic smile and continues, "According to the coroner, all the victims' skins were exposed to some sort of 'unidentifiable' agent. This substance initially burned the epidermal layer of the skin. Once the victims inhaled the substance, their internal organs liquefied, fueling their internal temperatures until their bodies cooked from the inside out."

He meets my eyes. "One of the reasons why Anders is so interested in you is that the doctor found traces of this substance on your skin."

"On my skin?" I lean forward to study his face. Surely he's joking. "I didn't have any burns."

"No, you didn't. In fact, according to your medical report, upon admittance to the hospital you were almost dead from blood loss, but had no blood trace on your body except where it soaked into your shirt. Someone cleaned you off and left traces of the same substance used to kill your attacker on your skin. Only instead of burning you…it healed you."

Okay, the joke's gone too far. "How the hell do you expect me to believe that? You said I was almost dead when brought in. How did I heal?"

Gabriella grabs my arm and shoves up the sleeve. "Look, you can barely see the scratch, and it's only been four days."

I stare at the fading mark, remembering the sound of the knife as it scraped against bone. My hand touches my chest. The scar from the knife wound can be felt through my sweatshirt. "I've always been a quick healer," I argue, but only because I don't want to admit out loud that I've turned into a freak of nature.

Charles rolls his eyes. "Not this fast, Dena. According to your chart, given the amount of blood loss you suffered, your wounds were much deeper than scratches."

He laughs, but it has a hysterical quality to it. I guess learning his ex-girlfriend has turned into a mutant, like the superheroes from his X-Men comics, would be hard to process, but he works through it. "I bet the doctor is salivating at the idea of finding a way to reproduce this chemical. He could make a lot of money patenting a miracle cure."

The word "salivating" reminds me of the licking man. My wounds tingled as he licked them, and I sucked on his tongue, letting his saliva roll down my throat. My body heats with the memory. Lord have mercy, what did he do to me?

I rub the perspiration off my forehead before taking a deep, calming breath. "Why didn't Dr. Estrada tell me about my super-healing ability and the mystery element when I was in the hospital?"

Charles studies my face, scowling as if he doesn't like what he sees. "I don't think the lab reports were back yet. I'm pretty sure, yeah." He pauses, reading the report. "Dr. Estrada shared his suspicion with Anders, but until he had proof, it was just a theory to explain how quickly you healed. You were released from the hospital less than twenty-four hours after being stabbed, Dena. That should've told you something. Plus, I doubt any of this is known to anyone not working on this case, meaning only the doctor, lab technicians, Anders, and now us."

I take a deep breath. "Damn, I feel like I'm on *The X-Files*."

Gabriella grins. "I'm Mulder and you're obviously Scully—since you can't see what's staring you right in the face. So now what? Do you remember how you came in contact with the special juice?"

My cheeks heat, and I duck my head. I wondered if I'd been saved by accident—a case of being in the right place at the right time. I guess I've got my answer. The guy put a lot of effort into healing my wounds. *He licked special juice all over my body. Yum.*

"Lucky, I guess." I avoid my friends' eyes, feeling guilty for deceiving them. As much as I want to share my experience, I can't betray him without betraying myself. "At least I know more than I did before and that's because of you, Charles. I really appreciate your willingness to help me, especially after I burned all your *Battlestar Galactica* DVDs."

Charles glances away in embarrassment, or more likely, anger. He loved those DVDs more than he loved me. It had crushed him to find out they were gone, as intended. I don't know why I brought them up. Maybe subconsciously I still want to hurt him. Or I'm a bit sadistic and enjoy watching him squirm. He did cheat on me.

I lay my hand on top of his and squeeze. "Thank you." Next paycheck, I'll buy him the complete BSG series to pay him back.

His cell phone goes off. I pull my hand away and hide my snicker at the ring-tone—the chirp of a phaser. From the one-sided conversation, I gather that Vanessa's displeased about coming home to an empty house and orders him to return.

Gabriella walks him to the door while I remain seated at the table with the open file. I plan to spend the night reading through it. Maybe I'll find some clue to explain why I keep murdering people in my dreams. And I've no intention of falling asleep and having a recurrence of the previous evening's midnight stroll. Good thing I'm stocked up on my coffee supply.

Gabriella returns, takes one look at me, and slaps the laptop closed. "Oh no you don't. You're not spending all night on this. The reason I moved in is to keep an eye on you." She pulls a bell, dangling from a pink ribbon, from her pocket. "I'm a light sleeper. If you open your bedroom door, I'll hear this ring. I'll keep you from leaving the house, even if I have to sit on you."

I stare at the bell. "Uh, I don't know. Are you sure about this? 'Cause really…I have coffee. I'm sure I'll be able to stay awake."

"Sleep is what you need and what you will get. Though just in case, I suggest you wear warm clothes to bed. It's better to be safe than sorry."

* * *

I wake up crying and stuff the pillow in my mouth so I won't disturb Gabriella. Sweat soaks my entire body and bedding. My skin feels hot to the touch, as if cooking from the inside out, like the men from my dreams, and horror fills me. Not just the horror of the dreams themselves, but the horror of the spirit's existence. With each dream, we become more connected. Each night I catch a ride in his thoughts and drown in the power of his desperation. At first, our thoughts tangled with no separation. Over time, I've learned to tell the difference between the spirit's thoughts and my own.

But sometimes a third element intrudes that makes it even more confusing. Those dreams are full of rage, nothing but seething hate. When trapped in that dream, I can't think because he doesn't think or reason. In those dreams, chaos rules, and only primitive thoughts of hunting, killing, and feeding prevail. He exists on pure instinct.

Knowing his identity and how we became connected, I can't help but be terrified…for him. Little by little, he loses his battle to control his hunger. If he loses completely, no one will be safe. He'll rage without restraint, and I don't know how to stop him.

In tonight's dream, he remembered me. The memory of the alley crystallized in his mind. So he'll be searching for me. I'll have to act fast to save him. Not that I've got any idea of what I'll do once I find him. What does one do with an avenging spirit of death…worse, a slightly insane spirit of death? Invite him home for tea and cookies? Not likely. Gabriella would throw a fit.

I sigh and roll out of bed. First, I need to find him. I wore sweats to bed. No more nightgowns, especially when at risk of being discovered by a sexy but annoying detective. I throw on tennis shoes and a turquoise raincoat. My fingers freeze inches above the doorknob when I remember the blasted bell.

"Fantastic," I whisper, turning in a full circle like a bloodhound searching for an elusive trail. The streetlight outside my window casts an orange glow over the room. "This is the worst idea—ever."

Yet, I eye the window. It's not that high. If I fall, I probably won't break any bones. I slide the window up and lean out. The ground's a million miles away.

"This is an incredibly stupid idea…" With a deep breath, I climb onto the ledge. My body shakes so badly that I almost tumble out headfirst. After a couple of deep breaths, I grip the window ledge and twist around. I walk my feet down the side of the house. Too bad I can't stick to the wall like Spiderman.

I realize a bit late that I didn't plan further than me hanging from the ledge like a drunken bat. My feet dangle over empty air, and my fingertips ache from gripping the window ledge. I can't let go 'cause I really will land on my head, which upon reflection might knock some sense into me. I order my fingers to unlock, but they've got a mind of their own. It isn't until I lose all feeling in them that they release, and I fall.

I slam into something hard, but softer than the ground. Arms wrap around my back and a hand presses my face against a firm chest, protecting me as we tumble down a slight incline. We come to a halt with me stretched down the length of a muscular body I know even in the dark.

"Anders?" I touch his squared jawline with my fingertips and then trace the contours of his sharp cheekbones to brush across his sealed eyelids. "Are you hurt?"

I try to roll off him, but his arms tighten around me. *He's hugging me again.* My nose rests between the crease between his neck and shoulder. My mouth begins to water as each inhalation brings his scent, a mix of spice and chocolate. *Does he taste as good as he smells?* I want to know. *One lick.* The tip of my tongue flicks across his velvety smooth skin. It's the tiniest of tastes, barely noticeable, but he stiffens beneath me. Not just his upper body, but…Oh God, I feel him. All of him. His lengthening shaft presses against the pulsing heat between my legs. I squirm with embarrassment, but rubbing against him only drives home the fact that Anders is the perfect fit. He can unlock a part of me which I've kept sealed off for a very long time. *Holy hell, what is he doing to me?*

I ball my hands into fists, struggling not to unzip his jeans. My fingers itch to caress him. My heart races in the silence. It dawns on me that Anders has released his hold around my waist. I wiggle, inching upward until I'm straddling him. He sucks in a deep breath, and my thighs clench. *Dumb, dumb move, Dena.*

Anders's hands still cup my butt cheeks, searing the imprint of his palms through the thin cotton. "Can you get your ass off of me? I can't breathe," he mutters, with a tortured groan that's like a slap to the face. *Jerk.* I don't weigh that much. But the way he's carrying on, you'd think a Mack truck fell on him. Nobody asked him to catch said *ass.* He's the one who copped a feel first, but now he's playing the innocent victim. Well, fine. If he wants to pretend like he doesn't feel the spark between us, then I can ignore it, too.

With a curse, I roll onto the ground. "What the hell, Anders. I could've broken your back." I rise up on my knees and brush the dirt off my sweatpants. "What are you doing in my yard? Stalking me?"

"No, I thought I was saving you," he says, still lying prone. He makes no effort to get up. "Mind telling me why you were climbing out of a two-story window? Don't you have a front door?"

"It's called sneaking out. Not that it's your business. Do you plan on lying there for the rest of the night or should I call an ambulance?" I pull out my cell phone and shine the light across his face. Oh dear, he doesn't look well. Maybe I did take advantage of his incapacity. "Are you okay, Anders?"

He lies there blinking up at me with a glazed look to his eyes, and then, suddenly, he grins. "You really are insane. I never know what you're going to do."

"Glad you find me amusing. Look, do you want to come in for a bit and recover?"

Please say no! Please say no!

"I'm on duty tonight."

Relief flows through me.

Anders must not appreciate whatever expression crosses my face because he scowls, saying, "But I can come in long enough for you to explain where you were going. And how you knew I was watching your house."

I jump to my feet. "You really were watching my house?" The house in question brightens as a light comes on in the kitchen window. "Great, you woke Gabriella. You're in trouble now, buddy. She's gonna be pissed to find out you're staking out our home."

"I bet she'll be more upset when she learns you snuck out. I assume you have a good reason for that. Hmm…no? I didn't think so. Maybe we should keep this between ourselves and leave Gabriella out of it."

"Fine," I whisper. "We'll discuss this later!"

The back door opens, and the porch light comes on to illuminate the yard in its bright glow. Gabriella stands at the door, staring at us with a dumbfounded expression on her pixie-like face. "What the heck's going on?"

"Midnight tryst," Anders says with a grin. He slaps me on the bottom and laughs when I yelp in surprise. "Babe, help me up? Please?"

Babe? Gah, how cheesy.

I can't pull this off. And knowing how much I despise Anders, Gabriella will never believe such an obvious lie anyway.

Gabriella giggles. "I knew it. I knew you had the hots for each other. All those insults and smoldering glances. I thought you guys would set each other on fire…Oops," —She slaps a hand over her mouth— "well, not literally. Dena cannot set fires with the power of her lustful thoughts."

I grit my teeth. "Detective Anders dropped by to make sure I wasn't out murdering anyone in my sleep. As you can both see, I'm wide awake and in perfect control of my faculties. So I'll bid everyone good night."

"Dena?" They say in unison with the exact same tone of exasperation.

"I said *good night*!"

I sweep into the house, trying not to cry. Time is slipping through my fingers. I had a specific plan for this evening. My continuing mission, a matter of life or death. If I don't boldly go…I trail off with a sigh. *Star Trek* won't help me get past Anders and Gabriella. I can't just beam myself out of the house. If I don't find the spirit soon, someone will die, and I'll be connected to him when he kills. I can't handle seeing another man murdered.

CHAPTER 8

Charbroiled Squirrel

Since Gabriella and Anders appear content to remain in the backyard, I leave through the front. I can't take my truck without Anders hearing the engine so I run, although I'm not sure at first where to go. I move on pure instinct, but after some time I realize I know exactly where the spirit hides. He sings to me, and something buried deep and primal in my body answers. Tense expectation fills me at the prospect of being with him again and feeling that intense euphoria I associate with his touch. My skin feels so tight that it burns with anticipation.

Pockets of mist obscure the road as I head toward the outskirts of town. I'm so focused on where I'm going, I don't see the two men standing beneath muted street light until a low voice calls out to me. Fear washes away my desire, and I stumble back. The men look like gangbangers. Who else would be lurking about on a street corner in the middle of the night with bulges beneath their jackets and danger oozing from their pores?

I hold up my hand to ward them off, like that will deter them. "Look," I say, "I don't want any problems. I've been attacked once already this week, and I can't afford another trip to the hospital. So do me a favor and find someone else to mess with."

The little guy with the pencil-thin mustache has the nerve to laugh. "Why don't you do *us* a favor, come on over and show us some respect?"

"No, thanks." My shaky smile shows I'm friendly, but not that friendly. "You're probably all kinds of charming, and that knife in your hand is pretty impressive. If I wasn't meeting someone, I'd be all over that. But I've got to go."

"He gonna be as good to you as we will, beautiful?" He slinks toward me, like he stalks prey on the African Savanna.

"Well, I'm pretty sure his plan doesn't involve rape and murder." I glance around for help. The empty street has me wishing Anders would magically appear for one of his impeccably timed rescues. "Look, I'm warning you—I know karate. I learned it from *The Karate Kid*. Really, I don't feel like kicking anyone's ass today. But I will go *Kung Fu Panda* on yours if you keep heading in my direction!"

The bigger of the two guys bursts out with a laugh, leaning against the wall. "Leave her alone, Squirrel. I don't feel like getting my ass handed to me by a little girl," he says in a deep French Creole accent. He shakes his dark, bald head and motions for his friend to follow.

Squirrel doesn't seem to be as impressed by the power of my threat. The two men square up, face to face. Their eyes battle in a silent clash of wills. My heart races, and I rise onto the balls of my feet, ready to sprint if things get dicey. I'd be running already if I wasn't afraid it would trigger the little guy into giving chase. It's doubtful I can outrun him. In the end, it doesn't matter. Squirrel breaks eye contact first. The big guy wins, but when his gaze meets mine, I can tell it was a close call. I got very lucky.

Squirrel rubs a hand over his crotch like a demented mini-Michael J. "For sure, some other night."

The men almost reach the end of the street when the big guy turns back with a warning. "I know you're tough and all, but there's some strange shit going on. People dying. You should get off the street. There's a mission down on E Street that takes in girls. I bet they have a bed open."

I blink at him. *What about my outfit screams homeless chick?* "Thanks for the tip. Uh…be safe."

He waves over his shoulder, then disappears into the fog. My earlier urgency to find my shadow man fades with my adrenaline rush. I turn in a circle, trying to figure out where I am. I've never spent much time in town. And never in this part of Paradise Pointe.

Goose bumps break out on my arms from the sweat drying on my skin. The sharp, ozone scent of rain fills the air. Beneath those scents hangs the sulfuric taint of stagnant water. The bayou. *Home.*

I want to go home. Not to Pepper's house, but back to my piece of swamp. If all this craziness has to happen, I'd rather deal with it on my own turf. I'm a swamp girl, not a townie. Never will be. Yet here I am, without a real plan, trying to find a murderous spirit based on the feelings invoked by a nightmare? *I should have my head examined.*

With a sigh, I turn and trudge back the way I think I came, kicking myself for being so stupid.

Then I hear screams.

Most people, those with common sense and the instinct for self-preservation, would run in the opposite direction of blood-curdling cries. I've heard screams like this before, and I know what makes them—a man being immolated—and worse, I recognize his voice.

When I arrive, the little gangster's still smoking like a rack of baby back ribs, right beneath the arched gateway to the cemetery.

The big guy crouches next to his friend's body. "It went right past." He stares up at me with wide eyes. "As if I wasn't standing right here. It went past to get Squirrel. Like…it didn't even see me."

I walk over to him. The stench forces me to breathe through my mouth, but even that is disgusting. Charbroiled Squirrel coats my tongue. I concentrate on forcing my stomach to settle down. "What's your name?"

"Ferdinand," he says, and inexplicably holds out a large hand.

I give it a firm shake. "Ferdinand, you are a good man."

His bitter laugh cuts. "Good is not a word used to describe me, *ma petite.*"

"You're wrong." I squeeze his hand. "Whatever you may have done, inside you're still a good man or you wouldn't still be alive. That creature—it feeds on evil." I stare at Squirrel, wondering how he'd tainted his soul. "I need your help. Where did the black smoke go?"

"You mean to go after that thing?" Ferdinand rises to his full height, which is significant. "That creature is from darkness. It will kill you!"

"No, it won't. I'm not evil. I'll be fine, but I have to stop it. These killings have to end. Please help me, Ferdinand. Help me keep it from burning any more people."

Ferdinand jerks on my arm, and I stumble forward. My hand lands on his chest to catch my balance, and my palm tingles, like it's waking up after being asleep. The sensation arches through me, and the hair all over my body rises. I grit my teeth, shoving to get out of his arms.

He lets me go.

I wipe my palms on my sweatpants, breathing hard. "If you're trying to frighten me, it worked. But it doesn't change what I've got to do."

"You told me that thing killed Squirrel because he was evil. Well, you're right. He was a bad person. He's killed…not for duty, but because he liked to see blood. He served a purpose. And he was a loyal employee. As much as I felt he deserved to be taken out, his lack of conscience wasn't my responsibility."

"So he killed, and you knew and did nothing about it?"

"Still think I'm a good man?"

I shrug. "Morally ambiguous, perhaps? But it's not my responsibility to judge you either."

His head tilts, and I catch a flash of white teeth. "If I hadn't been with Squirrel tonight, he would've hurt you." He takes a deep breath and lets it out in a rush of words, "This wasn't part of the plan."

"Plan?" I ask, but…whatever. I don't really care. My foot taps. *Time's a wasting.*

He shakes his head and stares toward the cemetery. "That's no longer important. What is important is that I acknowledge the world's a better place without Squirrel in it."

"I hear you." I don't understand, but that's unimportant, too. "Just point me in the right direction, Ferdinand."

"The hell..."

For a moment, I'm afraid he'll turn caveman and toss me over his shoulder and carry me away. But he does the opposite. With a gentlemanly half-bow, he waves me forward—into the city of the dead. "Let's go. It went this way."

"You don't have to be all macho. I can take care of myself." *Lies, all lies.*

Before us stretch square, stone crypts set in white rows. Bodies are buried above ground 'cause the water table's so low. Graveyards usually don't bother me. The boys and I used to play in the family cemetery back at home. Generations of our ancestors rested beneath our feet, and none ever woke to greet us. Ghosts, the spectral kind from stories, don't exist. The dead don't linger to haunt their loved ones; they pass through the vortex into the darkness. I've seen it happen with my own eyes. Still, it's night. Fog rolls across the earth, muffling the sound of our footsteps. And I'm searching for Death. I'd be crazy if I didn't feel like vomiting.

Once Ferdinand gets going, he eats up some road. I stretch my legs to catch up. His eyes scan the rows of tombs, then he leads me forward with a wave of his hand. He moves with caution, like he's leading a platoon into an enemy city full of snipers. And it does seem like a city, with the house-like crypts laid out along quiet streets. Before long, I lose track of where I've been. We could be wandering around in circles for all I can tell.

"Seriously, Ferdinand. You should go back. Death passed you up once, but it might not be able to a second time. I think it's beginning to lose its ability to differentiate between good and bad people."

"How's that?"

"It's having a harder time telling who is good and who is bad."

He glances back with a roll of his dark eyes. "Yes, I got that part the first time. I'm not as ignorant as I probably look right now. What I want to know is how you figured out it's losing its Santa powers? You have some form of telepathy?"

"You *are* smarter than you look."

"You'd be surprised at what I know. So, about the telepathy…Are you able to read this thing's thoughts?"

"I think I am. I hadn't really thought about the form of communication we've got going, but I guess telepathy, or maybe it's an empathic connection…" I shrug. "Whatever. Your explanation is as good as any."

"I don't particularly believe in telepathy."

"You're the one who brought it up."

"Based on your description," Ferdinand says. "Doesn't mean you're right."

I scowl. The guy seems to enjoy arguing for the sake of arguing as much as I do. "Well, just 'cause you don't believe in it, doesn't mean it's not real. All I can tell you is what I've experienced. And what I was trying to say, before you got all cynical on my ass, was that I haven't completely figured out what's going on."

"Then tell me what you do know."

"Ugh, I'm trying to. Be quiet and listen?"

Ferdinand meets my eyes; his are glazed and unfocused. He

must be talking to keep from freaking out. He presses his lips together and nods.

I take a deep breath and focus on controlling the emotions that come up whenever I think about Tolson. Ferdinand's upset, enough. I don't want to make it worse. "A man attacked me about a week ago. I fought back, but he stabbed me a few times. It was about then that this smoke thing came and killed him. The shadow saved my life. Ever since the attack, I've been dreaming that the smoke is actually a man and he's dying. I have to help him."

Why did I share with Ferdinand something I haven't even told Gabriella? I glance at the man, who's basically a stranger, and sigh. *Maybe because he's seen it too?* "Do you think I'm completely insane now?"

Ferdinand gives a bitter laugh. "Hell, I'm going with you, so who's the insane one?"

A rush of desperation floods my senses, and I stumble. *The spirit. He's close.* His joy that I've arrived is as palpable as his hope for redemption. Yet, underlying all the other emotions he funnels through our connection is the knowledge of his instability, and his fear that he'll lose control over his hunger.

I stop beside a mausoleum. It's beautiful even in the darkness, with large columns bracing the slab roof. The door's open, inviting me in, and I grab Ferdinand by the arm. "Wait here. It's not safe."

"You sure about this? This isn't about you trying to prove how tough you are, is it?"

I wrap my arms around myself, shivering. "I wish, Ferdinand. I'm terrified."

"But you're going in anyway. I think that makes you one tough lady."

A rush of warmth fills me at the compliment. I face the mausoleum and straighten my shoulders. *I can do this.* Moving forward is harder than climbing out of the two-story window. When I fell, I knew I'd hit the ground. But walking through the open door to find a spirit who invades my dreams with images of death, and not knowing what to expect, eats at my courage.

Part of me hopes Ferdinand will follow. My knees knock together, and added with my chattering teeth, I sound like a one-woman percussion band. A stealthy entrance isn't even remotely possible.

I can do this. Everything will be fine, I chant over and over. I doubt whether I've the strength to continue. I talk a good game, but tend to retreat at the prospect of certain death. I'm a bit of a coward.

The only reason I haven't run back home is that I'm more terrified of remaining connected to the entity as it deteriorates. If I don't do something, nightmares and sleepwalking might be the least of my worries. Plus, he needs me.

The light from the lamp post at the entrance to this row of crypts doesn't penetrate past the mausoleum's entrance. The surname carved on a plaque on the side of the building has faded with time. Who waits inside? Do they sleep, or did Death disturb their slumber? *Oh, morbid thoughts. Go away. I don't believe in ghosts.*

Darkness waits, hungry for me to enter. My clouded breath mingles with thick fog. I see only a few feet in front of my body. My muffled footsteps on stone lend a surreal quality to the atmosphere, like I've walked into another realm. I pause, searching in the dark for some sign I'm not alone.

"Hello," I call out, voice unsteady as my breathing quickens. "Are you there?"

My voice echoes though the room, bouncing off unseen walls. A dry, musty scent, mixed with the slight ammonia of rat droppings, makes my nose twitch. How long had this door been sealed? Did the spirit open it, or someone else? It does make for a great trap, 'cause here I am about to chomp down the bait.

When nothing jumps out and grabs me, I take a deep breath and plunge forward, leaving the light behind. With my left hand stretched in front of my body, I trail the other along the wet stone wall. I whimper like a little baby, more frightened than during my attack. At least that had been a surprise. I didn't have time to think of all the horrible things that could happen to me. I hadn't already seen the destruction of a man's body as it burned.

The touch on my outstretched hand is so light that it takes me a moment to notice. By then the cold, gel-like substance coats my fingers. When I try to pull back, the sticky goop sucks in my hand, which tingles as it cuts off my circulation. It reminds me of quicksand—of how my father's body looked when they pulled his mummified remains free. His wide-open mouth filled with sand when he gasped his last breath. I never should've stayed when they retrieved him from his sandy tomb. The image is seared into my memory.

Now I'm being sucked to my death, too.

My scream bursts out and echoes against the stone walls, taunting me. I jerk my arm, but like quicksand, the more I struggle, the more I'm drawn in. My chest presses against the membranous barrier. Instinctively, I hold my breath as I fall forward.

My thoughts grow fuzzy from lack of oxygen. The need for air grows more desperate. If I don't breathe, I'll die. If I breathe, I'll die faster.

I gasp…then choke, but I don't die.

I can breathe. *How? Why?*

Who cares? I fall to my knees, drinking in air. My eyes are open, but I can't see anything. As in a dream, my emotions are magnified. I'm trapped and devoid of all hope of escape. Loneliness overwhelms me. I wrap my arms around my legs, needing the connection of touch, since my other senses are deprived. I don't know how long I sit here rocking before I hear a sob.

The broken sound cuts through my apathy. No longer alone in this hell, I crawl forward, listening for another sound. Silence falls around me like a heavy cloak, and I begin to doubt that I heard anything except my own cries. My hands continue to search in the darkness, movements becoming more and more frantic. When I touch the warmth of a body, I cry out in relief so powerful that I tremble in reaction.

I press closer. I can't believe what my senses scream out to me, but I inhale his deep, earthy scent. I run my hands up his arms, feeling his taut muscles beneath my fingers. His skin has the soft, fine smoothness of a newborn. My hands travel upward over broad shoulders to tangle in silky hair. I trace the hard angles of his cheekbones down to the indentation on his chin, and then, up to his lips. I remember this face as it hovered above mine and how his tongue felt on my body.

"I found you," I whisper, leaning forward. My mouth finds his to initiate a kiss so light it's more of a mingling of breaths.

His hands tremble as his fingers explore my skin with butterfly wing-like caresses, and I shiver. He moves hesitantly. Our chests press together. His heartbeat quickens, and my own beats in an adjoining rhythm, perfectly synchronized with his.

His head dips until it's pressed into the hollow between my shoulder and neck. He inhales, breathing in my scent. His tongue swirls over my collarbone. I press against him and cup the back of his head, my fingers twining through his hair. My other hand wraps around his waist, clenching tightly as his teeth rasp against my skin.

A distant, barely coherent part of my mind wonders *now what?* Only his lips answer my question, traversing my neck in soft nibbles with intermingled flicks from his tongue, dissolving all rational thought from my brain.

At some point, he unzips my jacket. Between one breathless moment and the next, he unsnaps my bra. His hand circles my breast, exploring every inch with kisses. The heat from his quickening breaths make my nipples tighten in anticipation of his mouth. And Lord have mercy, but he doesn't disappoint. My excitement builds with the intensity of his kisses. He's intoxicating. Addictive. *I want more.*

My hands fist in his hair, and I drag his mouth up to mine. He presses forward with a moan that vibrates deep within my body. Flashes of his emotions fill my mind. Our connection is so profound that it feels like we're one person. I've never felt so needed. His desire—an overwhelming hunger—is being satisfied by the energy flowing from my body. He inhales, mingling our spirits until his flesh hums beneath my touch.

I collapse onto my back, pulling him on top of me. His chest blankets my hot flesh. Our mouths join, the kiss deeper this time. Our tongues dance until I writhe with the need to wrap myself around him. I want to get closer. Need him to join with me.

Never have I experienced such a base need. I want to drown in the sensations and be thoroughly intimate with him in every way. I slide my hands over his shoulders, then down the muscular plane of his back. I draw in a deep breath in anticipation then stretch my reaching fingers for more, but…there is…no more.

He's cut off at the hips.

The scream rips free of my throat.

Confusion wars with shock, which mingles with disgust, at myself. These emotions barely cover how freaked out I feel upon discovering that the guy I'm making out with is a partially dis-embodied spirit. Worse, I sense his confusion at my rejection. He doesn't understand when I shove him, pushing his body off of mine enough to wiggle out of his embrace. He reaches for me, but I slap his hand away, cringing when his fingers brush my back.

The idea of him touching my body—God, I must've been crazy. I crawl blindly in the opposite direction, trying to build a mental wall to block the intensity of the hurt flowing through the link between us, but we're too connected. I feel everything, and it sends me into a blind panic. I want to—need to—escape.

Too late, I remember it's not only my sanity in jeopardy. Chaos rolls in like a dark, infectious cloud—a black hole, devouring his emotions. He gives up and allows the hunger to take over. The darkness eats him.

And it's my fault!

Desperate, I throw myself back toward him, arms out-stretched, and feel…nothing.

CHAPTER 9

Pinocchio's Broken Heart

I've lost him. Guilt smothers me, making it hard to catch my breath. The confining membrane of the goopy, whatever the hell it is, vanished with him. Even though he's gone, I can't move. I huddle against a wall, hoping he'll return.

How could I be so stupid? So what if he doesn't have anything below his torso? He'd been using the rest of his body just fine until I freaked out on him. It's not like I didn't know that, like Pinocchio, he isn't a *real boy*.

I'd searched for him with the intention of saving him from the darkness. Instead, I brought that darkness to him. My rejection caused him to give in to his despair. I only hope, in that last moment, he felt my change of heart. That he senses me begging him to come back with all of my being. *I'm sorry. I didn't mean it.*

A few rats drown in my tears before I leave the mausoleum. Ferdinand's gone. I don't blame him. Abandoning me probably saved his life. The spirit seemed to be in a killing mood when it left. *My fault.*

With a sigh, I pull up the hood of my raincoat, huddling in its warmth. I wind through the tombs, exiting onto Old Lick Road, on the opposite side of the cemetery from where I entered. Thick, oppressive, old-growth forest borders the road. The scent of rain mingles with the rotten egg stench of Bayou du Sang, or Blood River, as the non-French-speaking folk call it. Old Lick's one of the oldest parts of Paradise Pointe, and it's rumored that the ground is tainted from its blood-soaked history. Nobody comes out here on purpose. Unless they're a fool.

The large trees overhead block most of the rain, but I'm still wet, cold, and miserable. My swollen eyes strain to pierce the darkness as I navigate around the potholes in the gravel road. Lost in my own miserable world, the flashlight aimed right into my eyes comes as a shock. My arm lifts to block the glare. With my night vison shot, it takes a bit to focus on the silhouette climbing from the running vehicle, and I freeze when I recognize Anders.

Great. He's wearing his annoyed expression. The one where his chiseled jaw squares, and his eyes slant up in the corners from his frown. Yep, I know this look. I've become intimately acquainted with it over the last week.

I cross my arms to hide my shivers. "Your timing's perfect, as usual. Here to harass me?"

He flicks the light toward the ground. "Ms. Acker, I've been searching for you for hours. Where have you been?"

I ignore his question, like he ignored mine. "It's like you've got radar that lets you find me during the most vulnerable moments in my life."

Anders's blank expression hides any response to my words. Not the reaction I've got in mind. I'm spoiling for an argument—a distraction from the self-loathing burning a hole in my chest. Otherwise, I might burst into tears.

Anders studies my face for a few seconds, then softens his stance from overly annoyed to mildly piqued. "Get in the car, Dena." He opens the door.

I blink, surprised, and then give a mental shrug. I've fallen about as low as I can get. Riding in the back of a patrol car won't change anything. Or so I think, until he turns off Old Lick and drives around to the front of the cemetery. The street's filled with patrol cars, yellow tape, and a CSI van. I'm in big trouble.

"Uh, Anders? What the hell's going on?"

"You tell me, Ms. Acker."

"Ms. Acker is what you call me when you're trying to pin a murder on me." I stare out the window, defeated. "Is the false formality your way of putting distance between us, as if you didn't grab my ass earlier?" The technicians lift Squirrel into a body bag. The coroner must have already concluded her investigation. I slump against the seat. "This is the type of person you think I am? How depressing."

Anders's head tilts in my direction. If I turn, I'll catch him studying my face in the rearview mirror, so I keep my gaze firmly on the body bag being loaded into the coroner's wagon. Part of me thinks I owe Squirrel this much. Hopefully this scene isn't a prelude to the slaughter to come due to my actions tonight.

Exhaustion weighs heavy on my shoulders and I sigh. "Unless I'm being arrested, take me home. If you are arresting me, I'm invoking my right to remain silent until my attorney is present."

Only Anders's eyes are visible in the mirror, and they look flat and cold. "I've enough evidence to bring you in for questioning."

"I'm innocent, and your so-called evidence is circumstantial at best. So do what you've got to do."

"I don't want to arrest you." Anders starts the car and drives in the direction of my home. "I know you find it impossible to believe, but I'm trying to help you. If you'd just trust me—" He sighs. "I'll play good cop if you let me, Dena."

My name on his lips sends an unwanted shiver through my body. I lift my chin to prove he doesn't affect me. "I'll figure this out on my own. I'm not helpless, and I won't give up until I have some answers."

The rest of the ride continues in silence, broken only when we reach my house. Anders twists around and sticks a business card through the cage's Plexiglas window. "I know you keep throwing these away," he says with a wry twist of his lips. "Call me if you want to talk."

I stuff the card in my pocket. "Thanks for the rescue…multiple rescues. I've been a nuisance, but I don't mean to be. It's just…a lot of shit's happening." I lift my chin, searching for strength. "I'm sorry for taking it out on you. Good night."

With the last word, I fumble at the door latch. It refuses to budge, ignoring my frantic attempts to unlock it. Finally, I collapse back into the seat.

Anders seems amused, despite his current imitation of a cyborg. His dark eyes, reflected in the mirror, hold a hint of a smile in them. He exits the car and opens the rear passenger door. I stare at his outstretched hand for a long beat, wanting to ignore his help, but my legs have cramped from being stuffed in the back seat. His touch burns, sparking off a cascading reaction which floods my body with heat. *Why, oh why, does he get me all hot and bothered?*

Avoiding his gaze, I look around. Oh great. Lucky me—a police escort during that magical time in the morning when all my mother's neighbors are outside, taking their garbage to the curb, getting their newspaper, or warming their cars to go to work. I hope they're enjoying the show.

Gabriella runs out of the house. With a shriek loud enough to draw the attention of everyone who isn't already gawking at the police car, she throws herself into my arms. "Dena, where were you?" she cries. "I was scared out of my mind. I spent the night searching the neighborhood!"

Movement comes from behind, and I glance over my shoulder. Anders leans against his car, arms folded. He arches a questioning eyebrow. "I asked Dena the same question. Maybe she'll confide in you."

Gabriella disentangles herself from my arms. Her gaze travels over my mussed hair and disheveled clothing and ends on my neck. Her eyes narrow.

A blush rises, and I hastily straighten my jacket. I'm glad that Anders is behind me and can't see my face. He'd know what caused the flames to lick my cheeks. Guilt. "I'm not really in the mood to share at the moment, Gabby." I widen my eyes, glancing toward Anders. "I'd rather go take a bath and get some sleep."

Gabriella's mouth tightens in silent protest. "Fine." She faces Anders. "Detective, on behalf of my rude friend, thanks for your assistance in searching for her last night."

"For being nosy," I mutter. He didn't search out of concern for my health or safety, but because I'm his only suspect.

"Dena!" Gabriella reprimands.

I march up the driveway, listening to Gabriella apologizing—to him. How did he brainwash her into thinking he has altruistic motives for searching for me? Last night, she'd been completely on board with the idea of him trying to frame me.

I throw open the front door. An immediate sense of relief at being home fills my body, leaving my legs weak. I stumble over to the couch and fling myself across it, closing my eyes against the mother of all tension headaches. Footsteps clump across the hardwood floor, and I groan as the sound echoes in my head like a jackhammer.

Cracking open my eyes, I mentally prepare for the onslaught of questions from Gabriella, but upon seeing Charles Frasier hovering above my head with his mouth opening and closing like a lamprey preparing to feed, I shudder.

I grab the blanket off the back of the couch and wrap it over my head, burrowing as deep into the pillows as I can, praying the nightmare will end.

Charles snatches the blanket and struggles to pull it from my fingers. "Dena? Dena, let go."

"No! Go away," I yell, blinking to keep from crying. No way will I break down in front of Chucky. Not happening. Not in this lifetime.

He tugs again. This time he uses all of his strength.

I roll off the couch, landing on the floor with a bellow of pain. "What the hell's wrong with you, Chuck? Are you insane?"

"You've got some nerve asking if I'm insane," he yells back, waving the blanket in the air. "Do you have any idea how worried we were? How do you think I felt getting a phone call in the middle of the night from Gabriella, who by the way was hysterical, saying that you'd disappeared? We spent the night searching the neighborhood thinking you were sleepwalking again. Then Detective Anders calls, saying he found you near the scene of another murder!"

"I had nothing to do with that or any other murder." I shove my fingers into my hair and massage my scalp. "Anders's twisting the situation around, as usual. It's what he does best. He's a fucking cop, Chuck. Is this why Gabriella's outside sucking up to him? He got to you two, didn't he?"

"How do you expect us to react?" Charles asks in a voice thick with emotion. "This isn't normal behavior. Look at it from our point of view."

My mouth drops, and I glare at him in reproach. Wow, this is the same man who once said I was the best thing that ever happened to him.

Bitterness surges, and I contemplate the various ways I could kill him, if I were a murderer. I have him mentally impaled on a long spike when Gabriella storms into the house. She takes one look at my murderous expression and freezes.

"Uh, guys," she says slowly, as if talking down rabid dogs. "What's going on?"

Charles glowers in my direction. "I was asking Dena where she was tonight." He drops the blanket, and it falls over my head.

I snatch it off and rise, shaking.

Gabriella reaches out, but lets her hand fall before touching me. She glares at Charles. "What did you say to make her this angry?"

Out of the corner of my eye, I see movement by the kitchen and spin. *Good God, not her too?* I confront Gabriella, outraged. "You let *Vanessa* in my house?"

Vanessa's face darkens. She answers Gabriella's question to Charles, but directs her contempt at me. "Charles simply asked Dena the same questions we've all been wondering about. She's the one who became defensive and started throwing a tantrum."

I step in Vanessa's direction, but Gabriella moves between us. "Nessa, we agreed you'd stay in the kitchen until we told Dena you're here."

"I'm sorry, but I'm not coddling her just because she's mental. She's a grown woman, and she can start acting like one. Besides, I can't remain silent when *my* man is being attacked." Vanessa goes to Charles's side. She wraps her arm around his waist and gazes up at him with a sultry expression that's purely for my benefit.

Charles glances at her, and his eyes narrow. If I wasn't so pissed, I'd applaud the fact that he sees through her ruse. Instead, I watch their unspoken exchange in silence.

The sound of the door closing grabs my attention. Anders entered the house while we argued, and he's staring at Vanessa like she's some sort of toxic mold. He clears his throat, drawing everyone's attention. "Dena's had a difficult night—"

Vanessa interrupts, "Charles and I'd planned on spending the evening in bed. We came to help because we thought Dena was in trouble, and I'm not going anywhere until I get some answers."

"I didn't realize where I went tonight would be the object of everyone's scrutiny," I say. "And did I ask any of you to butt into my private life?"

"Oh. My. God!" Gabriella shrieks. "I know you're embarrassed, Dena, but I don't think a little courtesy is too much to ask, given the circumstances. I was worried. I promised to watch out for you. To wake you if you started sleepwalking again. I totally lost it when I couldn't find you. That's why I called Detective Anders and Charles." She throws a glare in Vanessa's direction. "Not her, though. She invited herself."

"I see," I reply.

Overheated, I unzip my jacket and toss it onto the sofa. "I guess I owe all of you an apology. I'm sorry I worried you." Silence greets my semi-heartfelt apology, and I throw my hands in the air. "Now what?"

"Is that a hickey?" Vanessa squeals, jumping forward and thrusting the neck of my sweatshirt down.

I slap her hand away. "Personal space, Vanessa."

She falls onto the sofa, giggling so hard that black tears stream from her mascara-enhanced lashes. Unfortunately, she seems to be the only one in the room who finds the condition of my neck amusing.

Charles glares at my neck. His face turns the shade of an overripe cherry tomato. "Who were you with?"

"I'm not your girlfriend, *Chucky*," I say. "You cheated on me with Vanessa, so don't be so sanctimonious when it comes to my love life. It's none of your business."

Anders clears his throat and leans forward. "That explains a lot."

Glad to be distracted before I say something I'd regret, I turn to him. "What do you mean by that?"

Anders flashes a grin. How have I never noticed his dimples? They soften the hard angles of his face, reminding me of how attractive he is, and I blush.

He saunters over and brushes a finger across my burning cheek. "Nice."

"What?" I blink, confused by his non-cop-like behavior, and then remember I asked him a question. "Explains what?"

"Usually it doesn't take this much work for me to charm a woman."

My voice comes out as a breathless whisper. "Is that what you're trying to do?"

"If you have to ask, then I need to work harder."

His finger trails down my neck, and I swear I almost do an old-fashioned swoon right into his oh-so-very muscular arms. *What the hell?*

Gabriella's eyes widen at my expression. "Um, right…Okay, so this is awkward."

The doorbell rings. Anders shoves his hands in his pockets and steps back with a chuckle. Once he no longer invades my space, and I can't smell the spice of his aftershave or gaze like an idiot into his green eyes, my brain starts to function again.

I run to the door, throwing it open only to freeze as I take in the tall form lounging in the doorway.

"*Konmen ça va*?" Ferdinand asks, searching my face. "I saw the cop pick you up so I followed you home."

"Gee, thanks," I say, opening the door wider. "Please come in, Ferdinand."

Ferdinand grins, stepping forward, then pauses when he takes in the group of people standing in my living room. His gaze darts to meet mine. A spurt of raw panic blanches his midnight skin, and I know he recalls his earlier comment.

Vanessa jumps to the offensive...literally. "So, Ferdinand, you're the guy Dena was out with tonight?"

Ferdinand's mouth tightens, and his fists clench at this sides. He seems on the verge of hitting someone. "Yeah, what about it?"

"So...you were *with* Dena tonight?" Vanessa's eyes fill with a wicked light.

"Yes, I was with Dena," Ferdinand repeats slowly, as if speaking to a toddler. "Obviously, she already told you about it."

"No, I didn't," I interject before he can say more.

Gabriella's mouth drops. "She was about to spill the whole story."

"You're not Dena's type," Charles says. "She usually goes for men who wear their pants with belts."

"It's not how a man wears the pants, but what's in them," I say with a grin, enjoying watching Charles's face redden. Hmm, the conversation has taken an interesting turn.

"You seriously expect me to believe you let this guy get in your pants? He's a thug."

"Wow, way to stereotype, Charles."

"He's a gangster!" Charles shrieks, putting his nose right in my face. His appears splotchy. For a scary moment, I think he might have a heart attack. "It's not a stereotype if it's fact!"

Ferdinand smoothly inserts his body between Charles and myself. "I'm a big guy. I feel more comfortable in baggy clothes. It's a fashion thing." He stares down into the other man's eyes with a menacing glare, but he continues in a calm tone. "I'm not a gangster. I own a private security company in New Orleans."

"So, you're like, what? A bodyguard?" Gabriella's eyes brighten as they run up Ferdinand's massive frame. "Oh my, I'm impressed. This is perfect! Dena's in need of a little personal protection lately."

"Not funny, Gabriella," I complain, but in truth, I need to have a private conversation with Ferdinand about the earlier events of the evening.

Anders has remained quiet during the exchange, but even without looking, I can sense exactly where he is in the room. The crackling tension between us increases with each step as he walks up from behind. When he reaches my side, facing Ferdinand, the back of his hand brushes my arm, and I shiver.

"It's interesting that you were out with Dena tonight." Anders again wears the gruff cop-look I'm beginning to hate. "I picked her up in the vicinity of a homicide. What do you know about a man named Anton Terrie?" He crosses his arms, which he then flexes—every woman in the room notices. Is he trying to intimidate the Ferdinand? Or is the mouthwatering display for me?

Ferdinand seems more bored than impressed. "I'm sorry," he says, giving the apology in a tone that's anything but apologetic. "I know you, right? Anders? Yes, we've had this conversation before. As you know, any information I have on my employees and clients is confidential, unless you have a court order."

"That can be arranged since Terrie is dead."

"When I see one, we'll chat. In the meantime, I'd like to speak with Dena alone. If you'd excuse us." Ferdinand touches my arm. "Is there someplace where we can speak in private?"

"Sure. I'll take you to my bedroom." I lead him toward the stairs, only to pause and look around. "When I come down, the only person I want to still be here is Gabriella."

CHAPTER 10

BFFs Forever

Ferdinand follows me to the master bedroom. It's strange to have a man in here, and the more I think about it, the more uncomfortable I feel. Hurrying inside, I kick a lone pair of panties under the bed. I really need to clean or Pepper's gonna kill me when she gets back.

Ferdinand glances dispassionately around the room, then sits on the edge of my bed. "So what happened after I left?"

On the way upstairs, I decided to trust Ferdinand with the whole story. He saw what happened to Squirrel. Plus the way he handled Anders impressed me. The detective doesn't intimidate him, which gives him mega-points in my book. I need help, and nobody else has seen what we've seen. They wouldn't understand.

I crawl on the bed and cross my legs. "I'll tell you what I know if you promise to keep it between us. I need help, and I don't know who to trust. My friends think I'm having a nervous breakdown, or worse—a psychotic episode."

"Look," Ferdinand says, "I saw Anton get killed. It wasn't normal, even among the things I've witnessed in my life. I don't think you're crazy. Tell me about your earlier experience; maybe we'll be able to figure this out together."

"I already told you about my initial encounter with the spirit and my theory that he's trapped in that form. I know it's hard to believe. I didn't believe it at first, and I witnessed it."

I try to gauge Ferdinand's reaction but his features remain composed. He must get a lot of practice keeping his face expressionless during his security work. Especially if the majority of his clients are a bunch of criminals like Squirrel.

"After my first contact, I began having vivid dreams. In them, I channeled this guy's—this spirit's—whatever he is— his emotions. His pain. His horror at being trapped. His despair at the hunger that drives him to feed on humans."

"Did he feed on Anton? Is that how he died?"

"Yeah, I think so. But…you have to understand, it's not by choice. I think he tries to fight the urges, but it's…instinctual. I mean, I would love to lose weight. Starving would solve my problem, except I have to eat. If I didn't, I'd die. So my survival instinct kicks in and I pig out on snack cakes."

"So Anton's a Little Debbie."

"More like a Boston Crème. See, the spirit denies himself by fighting the hunger. He waits for a more palatable food, for a man like Anton, who is rotten inside from hurting the innocent."

Ferdinand nods. "I get it. How exactly did you become telepathically linked to him?"

Heat burns in my chest and rushes to my face. "The doctor who patched me up after the attack found this mysterious substance on my skin. Don't ask what it is—I've no idea. But it came from the entity, and it healed my wounds quickly."

I hold out my arm to show him where the knife had slashed it. "I got this five days ago. The knife cut down to the bone."

Ferdinand traces a finger lightly across the scar. "Impressive."

"My, you are the master of the understatement." I take my arm back.

"You told me you could stop him from killing. It's the only reason I let you go into that crypt alone." Ferdinand draws in a deep breath. "You disappeared."

"That must have been disconcerting." The memory of passing through the barrier brings a shudder. "What did you think happened?"

"Hell, I didn't stick around long enough to put much thought into it. I'd already reached my car before I talked myself into going back for you. I saw the patrol car pass by with you in it."

"I have the worst timing ever when it comes to that man," I mutter. "Detective Anders is investigating Squirrel's death, and he's convinced I know more than I'm sharing."

"You *do* know more than you're sharing," Ferdinand says. "Anders is trained to tell when he's being lied to. I bet he's furious at being unable to get you to trust him. He has good instincts."

"Too good," I agree. "But there's nothing I can tell him that he'll believe. I mean, I told him about the black smoke. He called me crazy."

"What do you think the thing is?"

"It's not a thing," I snap, feeling protective. "He's a person—maybe not a normal person, but he has feelings and emotions. He needs my help."

"And what do you think you can do for him, Dena? You said earlier that you had to save him. When you disappeared into the crypt, did you find him? Did you save him?"

I slap my palms over burning eyes, pressing them until white spots dance behind my eyelids. "No, I messed up. I was so stupid! He was so happy to see me. I mean really *happy*." I squirm. "The way a normal man would be happy to see a woman. At first I was glad to be with him, too. I forgot the fact that he's different and got lost in the moment. His emotions swept me up." I shiver. "Jeez, this conversation would be easier if you were a woman."

Ferdinand sighs. "Misunderstandings happen. The woman I'm interested in thinks I deceived her, and she'll probably never forgive me." His dark eyes soften. "See, woman or not, I understand the pain of hurting someone I care about."

Poor guy. "I'm sorry."

He runs a hand across his bald scalp and smiles. My breath catches. *Wow, Ferdinand's hot.* I couldn't see him well in the dark, but now, he totally reminds me of the actor from *Murder in the First*, Taye Diggs. Only taller. Mala had the biggest teen-crush on the actor. She dragged me along to all of his movies. I bet if she met Ferdinand in person, she'd pass out. Starstruck.

Stifling my inappropriate giggle, I say, "It's strange. We haven't known each other very long, but for some reason, I trust you. Thank you for opening up to me."

He raises his hands, palms up. "I've made mistakes in my past. The spirit searched my soul and allowed me to live. Perhaps I still have a shot at redemption."

Maybe we both do.

"I hope so. It's strange how he makes me feel. I've never been so intense, so soon, with anyone else." Except Anders, but I'll deny my attraction to that jerk until the day I die. I stare at my fingers, remembering the spirit's soft kisses. My reaction to him scares the hell out of me. "What if my feelings for the spirit aren't real? Do you think the chemical creates false emotions?"

"What?"

"I think he secretes an aphrodisiac. I find myself craving his taste when we're together, but it fades when we're separated."

"Like a drug addiction?"

I shrug. "I guess it doesn't matter if the emotions are real or false. What matters is that it *felt* real. I responded to him as if it was real. That's what makes what I did even worse. I could feel how much he needed me, and I panicked." My stomach knots up in shame at the revulsion I felt. "I rejected him."

Ferdinand cups my hands in his large ones. "Dena, I know you feel horrible, but given the circumstances, your reaction was justifiable."

"Yeah, maybe. Still doesn't change the fact that I blew my chance to help him. If anyone else gets hurt, it'll be my fault."

"Blaming yourself won't change the situation."

I sit back, considering all I know about the entity. "You're right. I need to fix this. He needs something from me, Ferdinand. I have to believe that. Otherwise, why choose me in the first place?"

"To know the answers to that question, you'll need to figure out how he came to be in this state and what he is."

"How exactly do I do that?"

"You have a couple of clues, the first being your connection to him."

"The dreams?"

"If you are more connected to him during the dreams, perhaps you can use this altered state to discover what happened to him."

"Shit! I barely remember the details of the dreams once I wake up."

"I have a client who is a hypnotherapist. I can call her and schedule an appointment." He grins. "She'll get a kick out of it. She's really interested in things like alien abductions and past lives."

"Is she pro or con?"

"I'll let you discover that for yourself. Second, you should find out more about that chemical on your skin. Talk to your doctor."

"I have an appointment for a follow-up this afternoon."

He nods. "Last, you need to find out whether there were any unusual occurrences around the time when the murders began."

"Like a freak meteor shower or a particle accelerator explosion that makes a giant thunderstorm?"

Ferdinand slaps a hand on his thigh and rises. "Stranger things have happened. At least it's a start. Unless you plan on sitting around beating yourself up over what happened or what might happen in the future."

He's got a point. I practically float as I walk him to the front door. After spilling my proverbial guts, a huge weight has lifted from my shoulders. I have a plan and a co-conspirator, always nice things to have in a crisis.

Ferdinand pauses at the door. "I'll call after I speak with my client about the appointment. I also suggest putting a notebook beside your bed to record the details of any dreams you have immediately upon waking. Call me if anything new pops up." He pulls out a card and hands it to me.

Gabriella waits in the kitchen, dispelling the notion of vanishing back into my room without getting caught. She slumps in her seat at the table, a steaming, untouched mug of tea sitting in front of her. When I enter the room, she lifts her head, but refuses to make eye contact. That, coupled with the redness of her nose against her butterscotch skin, indicates she's been crying. I need to talk fast to make things right with her.

Guilt swamps me. As her alleged best friend, I should've confided everything to her in the beginning. Now the situation has become so confusing that I don't know how to begin, or whether she's willing to hear my explanation.

"Dena, sit down. We need to talk."

"Look Gabby, I'm so sorry…"

"Please, this will be easier if I don't have to stare up at you." She waves me into a chair.

I sit, lip poked out in a pout. Unfair—I know—but I don't care. I'm terrified of what she plans to say. What if she tells me she doesn't want to be my friend anymore?

I hadn't realized how much I depended on her unwavering support until this moment. How much I'd leaned on her after the breakup with Charles, getting released from the hospital…hell, for more things than I can count on one hand. I need her friendship a hell of a lot more than she needs mine.

"Look," she says, "I know you've had a rough go of it lately. I've tried to be supportive, and up until today, I thought we were tight. I mean you're like a little sister to me…"

She pauses to take a breath, and I jump in. "You're like a sister to me, too, Gabriella."

"Let me finish. You hurt me today. Do you get that?" She scrubs away her tears. "I was so worried. I almost lost you the night of the party, and tonight, not knowing if you were alive or dead, brought back all the terror of seeing you in the hospital."

"I know. Please forgive me. I'd never deliberately do anything to hurt you. I wasn't thinking straight."

Gabriella sniffs. "I know you weren't. That's why I think you need to see a shrink."

"I agree."

Her jaw drops. "Seriously? Are you some pod person that's taken over the body of my friend?"

"Nope, no body snatching here" —*although it would explain how fast I'm healing*— "at least I don't think. Would I know if I were?" *Oh my God, what if I'm an alien?* I take a deep breath and brush the thought aside with my exhale. Now isn't the time to freak out. "Don't worry. I know I can't deal with this situation alone. I need help."

"I'll always be here for you."

"I hope you will be, but I won't take your friendship for granted, Gabby. If I lost you…well, in that direction lies madness and despair." I grin to show I'm joking. "Seriously, I don't know what I would do if you weren't around. Probably take up knitting again."

"You made some pretty cool blankets in your post breakup days. Thank goodness I convinced you to stop moping over Charles and go partying with me." Gabriella laughs then sobers. "About that shrink?"

"Actually, I took care of that tonight. I told Ferdinand about my problem, and he's scheduling an appointment for me to meet with a therapist friend of his."

"Isn't that a conflict or something, seeing as how you're in a relationship?"

"Relationship?" I choke on the word. *With Ferdinand?* Then I remember the debacle over the hickey. "We're just friends."

"Why? He's handsome, employed, and handsome."

"Don't forget, old enough to be my father."

"He's the best kind of guy. He can be your sugar daddy."

"Are you eating Nutella, Gabriella? I don't need any man barging into my life, telling me what to do. Dad's dead, and I'm free to do whatever I want. I'm not falling into a relationship trap until I'm good and ready."

She laughs. "I knew he wasn't your type, yah big faker. It was funny watching Charles turn all red and splotchy at the thought of you with another man, though."

"He was totally jealous," I agree with a wicked grin of my own.

"I thought Vanessa's head would explode with envy. After you went upstairs with Ferdinand, she physically held Charles back to keep him from following."

"He's a self-righteous jerk. I don't know what I ever saw in him."

"I always wondered the same thing. If Ferdinand wasn't the guy you were spending time with, then who was it? Detective Anders?"

"Are you kidding?"

"No. Haven't you noticed the way he watches you? How he's always showing up unexpectedly?"

"Where do you get these crazy notions? You read too many romance novels. I have absolutely no interest in Anders."

"Right…"

"Seriously, I don't. I mean, he is attractive, but he's got a giant stick up his ass. I've never seen him relax. Everything he says is calculated for effect, like a robot."

Gabriella giggles. "Anders reminds me of Sam Worthington in *Terminator Salvation*, where he plays a hot cyborg."

"Looks only go so far. Eventually, you need to hold an honest conversation with your significant other. Anders puts up a shield and only shows what he wants me to see. "

"Just because he's shy doesn't mean he doesn't have a personality."

"Shy my left butt cheek. He's a manipulative bastard who's investigating me for multiple homicides."

"He's not, Dena. I asked him myself. He doesn't think you're the murderer." She pauses, staring at me with wide doe eyes. "He thinks the murderer's stalking you."

CHAPTER 11

Hypnotize Me

I'm exhausted when I roll out of bed at noon. A feeling of dread lingers. As much as I once despaired of having nightmares, it's the only way to connect again with the spirit. The problem is I tossed and turned for most of the morning, unable to fall asleep. The idea that the dead men were targeting me freaked me out more than my nightmares. It's time for me to get some answers, starting with Dr. Estrada.

I shower and dress in comfortable clothing: a navy T-shirt and jeans with a black corduroy jacket that will be easy to remove during the appointment with Dr. Estrada. Next, I tackle my hair, always an arduous undertaking. After a liberal dose of conditioner to tame my unruly copper curls, I feel presentable.

Gabriella drives me to the hospital and waits in her car while

I go in, 'cause I don't think the appointment will take long. Boy, wrong. I expect a routine examination, where Estrada checks my wounds, says how great I'm healing, and explains how the mysterious substance affected my body. Afterward, we go our separate ways in mutual satisfaction. Instead, twenty minutes after I come in, I'm sitting across from Estrada while he threatens to call in an orderly to hold me down while he draws my blood.

I hate needles! Estrada has a really big one sitting on the table next to him, which makes me nauseous. "Repeat the part about needing three vials of my blood, please?"

Estrada's face flushes. "We've been over this twice already. Nothing in my answer is going to change. Roll up your sleeve so we can get this over with."

"Well, my answer hasn't changed either. As I said earlier, I don't do needles unless it's for a very good reason. You haven't given me one. So I'll ask again. What you are hoping to find?"

"I want to run some tests."

"I get that. Tests for what?"

"It's routine," he repeats, slowly, as if I'm stupid.

"Is my blood special, Alonso?"

"No!"

I lean forward. Beads of sweat pop up on his forehead. "I heard you found an interesting chemical on my skin…"

Estrada's whole body stiffens, starting with his face and moving downward until his fist clenches on his lap. "Where did you hear that? No, it doesn't matter. I assure you this is a routine test. I need to be sure you weren't exposed to any pathogens when you were assaulted."

"Why didn't you just say that in the beginning? I've already been tested, and Tolson's body was tested during the autopsy. He was clean."

I hop off the table and pick up my jacket and purse. About to exit the room, I pause, deciding to give him one last chance to tell me the truth. "Alonso, I know something strange was found on my skin. I know that I healed amazingly fast. I also have some other *unusual* symptoms. If you had been honest with me up-front, instead of skirting the issue, I would've been willing to help you."

"Dena, I assure you there's nothing..."

I hold up my hand. "Never mind. I hate being lied to, especially when it has to do with my body. Maybe you think you have a good reason—that you're hiding this information for my benefit. But I'm done with being taken advantage of by men. You're loosely included in this category, but the results are the same. I'll be transferring to a new doctor. I expect my records to make it to *her* without any problems."

Estrada's amber skin flushes. "I'm sorry, but I won't be able to do that, Dena. This is my case. I refuse to give anyone access to the compound I found on your skin."

"Are you kidding? Just because you interpreted the lab results doesn't mean you own it or me."

"It's my discovery, Dena. It's a miracle substance. Imagine how many lives will be saved if I discover how to reproduce this compound. The regenerative properties alone make what's in your body worth a fortune."

"It's my skin, my miracle, Alonso."

"I think Pepper would agree with my proposal..."

"What does my mother have to do with anything? Are you planning on tattletaling to my mommy about my lack of cooperation?" I pour the sarcasm on thick. "Go ahead. Maybe she'll try to ground me until I comply."

"Don't be ridiculous. I'm simply begging you to reconsider. Your mother trusts my judgment. She would agree with me about the benefits of cooperating. If money's not an incentive, consider that you would be helping to save lives."

I lean forward, nostrils flaring. "Maybe my mother *would* put money over my welfare; she has before. But I don't trust you. I won't become your lab rat, no matter how much money you wave before my face. And I know for a fact that you aren't doing research out of the goodness of your heart, with high moral principles like saving mankind. As far as I can tell, you don't even have a heart, Alonso."

I storm out of his office feeling like shit. During my hospital stay, I'd heard rumors about Estrada's ruthless self-promotion, compromising his ethics when dealing with patients. It infuriates me that he'd try to use Pepper to coerce my cooperation, let alone ignore the illegality of discussing my case with my mother. *I'm not a child.*

I check my text messages on the way to the car. Ferdinand scheduled an appointment for me to meet with his hypnotherapist friend, Downey Flood. I grin at the name. I text Ferdinand back, letting him know that I'll be there.

Gabriella sits with the seat pushed back. Her foot's propped on the steering wheel as she paints her toenails. "Oh," she hisses when I slide in beside her, slamming the door so hard she paints half of her big toe. "You have the worst timing."

I pull nail polish remover from her manicure kit and hand it to her. "I can drive if you want."

"No way, Concussion Girl. I want to make it home with my pretty toes attached to my feet. Passion pink." She dabs a cotton ball on the mess I created.

"Sorry about that." I lean closer to inspect her artistry. "Pretty."

"Do you want me to paint your fingernails?"

My nose scrunches. "I thought redheads weren't supposed to wear pink."

"I dare you to defy stereotypes."

Why not? "Defiance is my middle name today."

She catches my sigh and frowns. "That bad, huh? Did Alonso tell you more about the mystery goo?"

"No, it was a total waste of time. He spent five minutes checking my wounds. The next twenty he tried to get me to give up my blood."

"Bet that was a lost cause."

Gabriella and I sing in unison, "I don't do needles," then laugh.

"You should've seen his face. He was so angry, I thought he was going to throttle me."

"I would've enjoyed seeing that." She snorts, jostling her hand. This time she paints the wheel. "I've been looking for an excuse to *throttle* you since we met."

"Very funny, but really, he was a complete jerk. First, he denied finding the mystery substance on my body. Then he tried to trick me into giving him my blood. Said he wanted to test it to see if I'd contracted a blood-borne illness from Tolson. What if I had believed him? I would've been a nervous wreck waiting for the results, with him knowing the whole time that I'd already been given a clean bill of health."

"Why would he do that? You'd think he'd want you to cooperate. It's not like he hasn't known you long enough to know how stubborn you can be." Gabriella clears her throat. "He's a strange man. Remember the condition of your early release from the hospital? I promised to go on a date with him. Well, we were supposed to go out Tuesday, and he was really upset when I postponed because I was taking care of you. He sent a text before you walked out, asking if we could reschedule for tonight. I said yes, but maybe I should back out?"

"No," I say, considering his motives. "He's probably desperate."

"Dena," Gabriella squeals, slapping my shoulder.

"Oh, sorry; that didn't come out right. I meant, he probably can't see through your façade of a flighty, naïve ingénue. He thinks you can be manipulated into helping him."

"That retraction doesn't make me sound any more attractive, Dee. You don't think he's interested in me?"

"A normal man would be," I say, wincing at her hurt tone. "But Alonso's egotistical. The only thing he's attracted to is his reflection in a shiny surface. Be grateful he doesn't find you appealing. It would be an insult if he did."

Gabriella remains silent as she seals the polish up and drops it in her purse. I can't tell what she thinks of the matter. Maybe she really does enjoy flirting with the man. And isn't sharing out of sisterhood-solidarity. If that's the case then she needs to be filled in on the rest of the conversation with Estrada or she won't be of any help.

"Do you know what Estrada had the nerve to tell me after I confronted him about his lies? He said my mother would approve of his experimenting on me. That we'd make a lot of money selling a compound that could save millions of lives."

Gabriella snorts. "What? So you're supposed to agree to let him stick holes in you—for money?"

"And because the compound can heal people with life-threatening illnesses." I bite my lip, feeling guilty, but also knowing it's a slippery slope. After I awoke from the coma, Estrada conducted test after invasive test to find out why. He used the same argument about saving lives to get me to comply. It wasn't until after the bone marrow biopsy that I realized he didn't see me as a patient, but as a test subject to be exploited. "I'm not sure if I can handle being turned into a human pin cushion again, but if this mystery goop could save lives then wouldn't it be selfish not to help him?"

Gabriella pats my hand. "You're so strong, I sometimes forget how much you've suffered. It's okay to be selfish."

"I need to figure out what he's really thinking before making a decision, 'cause right now, I trust him about as far as I can throw him."

"So I need to practice my feminine wiles before going on my date?" She bats her eyelashes and pokes out her bottom lip.

I laugh, my mood lightening at her sultry pout. "Don't go overboard, Gabby. He's older than he looks. If you come on too strong, he might have a heart attack, and I'll never figure out what he knows. See if you can get him to lower his guard long enough to let something slip. He'll be trying to do the same with you."

"It's still weird that Alonso's being so secretive. Have you spoken with Anders?"

"No, not yet. I just got through one agonizing experience and already you're pushing me to have another."

"Dena, you're being melodramatic. Anders is not that bad."

"Yes he is! Can you imagine how much satisfaction he'll get once I finally use one of the stupid business cards he keeps throwing at me? He'll be insufferable."

"Drama queen, just get it over with and make the call." Toenails finally dry, Gabriella slips on her shoes and starts the car. "Where now? Popeye's for their famous fried chicken? Maybe the mall so I can find a dress for tonight?"

"Sounds good. I could use a little retail therapy before my actual therapy. I've got an appointment with my shrink at four."

"Ferdinand works fast."

"He wants me to meet with a hypnotherapist who is going to try to interpret my dreams." I wiggle my fingers in the air. "Maybe read my aura or something"

CHAPTER 12

Astral Hijinks

Downey Flood works out of her home, a modest one-bedroom cottage painted my favorite color—a pale yellow, with blue-trimmed shutters—too cute, like her name. A variety of plants dot the small yard. The atmosphere she's created seems designed to lull a person into a more relaxed frame of mind, but I can't relax.

Ferdinand and Downey meet me at the car. The house is the polar opposite in aspect from Downey. If I'd seen the home first, I would've thought a flower child resided here. Instead, Downey seems perfectly modern. She wears her chocolate hair in a short bob that brushes her jaw line. Tailored brown slacks match her hair and compliment a teal, turtleneck blouse. Rings glitter on her manicured fingers. Since I'm dressed for comfort, I feel shabby in comparison.

Despite her upscale appearance, Downey comes across as amazingly laid back. She gives me a welcoming smile, and the hand grasping mine holds on long enough to show her pleasure at our introduction. Ferdinand promises Gabriella that he'll drive me home after the session concludes, while Downey places my hand on the crook of her elbow and leads me toward the house.

I nod to Gabriella, who gives a little wave.

When I turn, I catch Downey studying me. "Ferdinand shared that you began having nightmares after being attacked and that recently you sleepwalked?" Her voice swoops upward on the question.

"Ferdinand told you all that, huh?" From his expression, I can tell he hasn't divulged the whole reason for the meeting, which is fine by me. The whole entity angle's a little difficult to swallow unless witnessed firsthand.

"I hope you're not upset?" Downey frowns slightly. "I typically schedule sessions a month in advance. He had to provide a good enough reason for bumping up your appointment. He felt the sleepwalking posed a risk to your safety."

"I wondered about the quick service. If you think you can keep me from wandering into traffic again, I'm willing to try anything you ask."

Downey leads me into her home, and again, everything seems perfectly normal. It's a bit of a letdown. I guess she leans toward "con" when it comes to believing in the supernatural aspects of hypnosis. The sofa's a boring brown, but it's plush. I sink into it with a sigh, exhausted from my nights with so little sleep.

Downey sits in the chair across from me. "Are you thirsty? I made tea."

"Yes, please. I love tea."

"Good, it's a special blend. It'll help you relax." She waves her hand toward what I assume is the kitchen. "Ferdinand, the kettle's on the stove. Could you bring Dena a cup while I get to know her?"

Ferdinand nods and leaves the room. How the big guy moves so soundlessly is beyond my comprehension. He's got catlike reflexes.

"I hope you're not too nervous about this?" Downey asks.

Again with the swoop to her voice. Since Downey's the professional, shouldn't she be trying to ease my worry, not the other way around? I catch myself about to roll my eyes and vow to use this opportunity to work on my patience and tact. "Not yet, but give me few minutes and my answer might change."

Downey laughs. "I appreciate your honesty. I'm a bit nervous myself. I usually get to know my clients for several sessions before attempting hypnosis. You don't know me. The tea will help loosen you up a bit. Ah, speaking of…" She angles her body toward the kitchen door.

Ferdinand returns with single cup on a tray and places it on the table. I give it the evil eye. "Are you saying the tea's drugged?"

"No, it's made from a special blend of herbs designed to relax you. I grow them in my garden. I've found that a person's receptivity to hypnosis is greater if there is trust between the client and therapist."

I need this hypnosis thing to work to find the spirit before he kills anyone else. My hands shake as I reach for the cup, and I down the tea in one gulp. The flavor lingering on my tongue tastes strange—a blend of licorice and cinnamon.

Downey takes the cup from my hand and sets it on the table. "Okay, lie back and get comfortable. Even with the tea, some people have difficulty going into a hypnotic state the first time, so this will be a trial run."

Great, if this doesn't work I have to come back again. Nerves hold my body tight with tension, but as I listen to the soothing sound of Downey's voice, I relax. Damn, she's good.

I stretch out my senses, attempting to locate the connection stretching between the entity and myself—I really need his name. Surely he has one. My spirit elongates then separates from my body. From above, I look down. My body lies boneless on the sofa. A silver cord connects my body to my spirit self like in a book I read about out-of-body experiences. The book also warned that if the cord gets severed then my body will die—not a comforting thought when the cord looks so flimsy.

I drift upward, passing through the roof of the house and into the sky. I search the city for anything that might pinpoint the spirit's location and catch a swirling darkness forming downtown. Thinking about the darkness draws my spirit toward the churning energy of the shadow. He senses my presence. The cloud coalesces, spiraling in agitation, and I feel his hesitance in approaching.

Mentally, I reach out, drawing him closer. *"I'm sorry,"* I send, infusing my apology with the intensity of my emotions. *"Please, come back. Trust me. I won't hurt you again,"* I beg—pleading for him to return from that dark place he has been lost in since our last encounter. It hurts to know he fears my rejection. My actions make him vulnerable. If I don't earn back his trust, he won't let me get close enough to read his thoughts.

On this plane, he manifests as humanoid in form. Featureless but for wounded, dark eyes staring at me with a hunger that reaches deep into my core. His energy flows outward, inching closer, then envelops my own. I drop my defenses and let him in, but I'm not consumed.

Our spirits join. We become one.

Tranquility fills my body, spilling out in a cooling wave of utter peace that flows into him. His rage drains, rinsed away by the clarity of my thoughts, like new rain washing the dust staining a rose petal. He drinks it in. The darkness in his aura lightens. If asked to describe how the change affects us both, I don't think I could find the words. His embrace fills with warmth and light. He draws our energies closer. We dance, whirling. I imagine, if anyone can see us, we look like twin tornados, twining together higher and higher into the clouds.

The tug from my body shocks me. I grab onto him, unwilling to go without learning why he's trapped. What he wants from me.

"What's your name?" I ask, fighting to hold on to him. "Tell me."

The tug on my body's harder this time. It hurts.

"Please, tell me."

Ashmael... The name floats through my mind, lavender letters against the darkness filling my thoughts. I release my hold. "Follow me," I beg. "Please..."

I fall toward the earth, so fast I become dizzy.

My eyes open on a spinning room. I roll sideways and my stomach heaves, splattering vomit across a pair of shiny brown pumps.

Downey's worried face fills my vision. Sweat dots her forehead.

"She's awake," she cries, patting my back as I gag again. "Ferdinand…"

Ferdinand runs out of the kitchen with a telephone clutched to his ear. "I'm sorry, false alarm. She's awake," he says to the person on the line.

I frown up at him, uneasy at his panic-stricken expression. "Who's on the phone?"

"Ferdinand called 9-1-1," Downey says in a shaky voice. "I lost my hold over you. I couldn't get you to come out of the trance. You stopped breathing…"

I draw in a deep breath in response. "Oh; that's not normal?"

"Definitely not! To get that deep is dangerous."

"I wasn't deep. I left my body behind. I remember looking down and seeing myself on the couch. I saw both of you, and then, I was out there…in the world. It was the most amazing experience—ever."

"You're talking about astral projection?" Downey's lips purse. She grimaces at Ferdinand, who shrugs. She shakes her head. "Are you sure what you remember is accurate? Sometimes the mind invents a scenario in which we confuse ourselves into thinking we've left our bodies. It's really just another form of a dream."

"It felt real." My face flushes.

I glance at Ferdinand to see whether he shares her skepticism, but he still appears shaken. "I think I should take Dena home," he tells Downey. "We'll talk about this tomorrow."

"But we need to analyze this now, while the memory's fresh."

I reach for the hand Ferdinand holds out to me. He helps me to my feet, and I lean on him for support. "I'm a little woozy. I don't mind putting off the deep psycho-babble for another time."

Whew, astral projection really takes a lot of energy out of the body…*literally*. Despite the nausea, I'm delirious with happiness. More than a little giddy. I found him…my deadly shadow, Ashmael.

Ferdinand refrains from making a scene until we're in the car and heading home. He stares at the street with an intensity that leaves me afraid for anyone who dares to cut him off. "Okay, promise you'll never do that again," he says in a clipped tone that accentuates his accent.

"Are you referring to astral projection or hypnosis in general?"

Ferdinand shoots a glare in my direction. "I haven't known you long, but I've noticed you revert to sarcasm when confronted by extreme emotion. You know you're not funny, right?"

"And I've noticed you get all analytical on my ass when confronted by the same." I cross my arms. "And I am funny. I'm an acquired taste—I'm considered too spicy for most people."

His jawline tenses, highlighting the sharp angles of his cheekbones. "Dena, you stopped breathing. Some people aren't meant to slip their skin."

Slip their skin? What an unusual, but accurate description of what happened.

"You could've died." He glances over at me to hammer in his point. "Again."

"For some reason, I'm not too worried. From what I can tell from my many near-death experiences, Death's on my side." I'm joking. Except it also feels like the truth.

"Immortality goes against the natural order of the universe. It comes with unforeseen consequences. I also speak from experience here."

The laugh bubbles up from deep in my stomach, releasing all of my pent-up tension. "Right; very funny."

Ferdinand's lips pinch shut. He closes himself off, as if he builds an invisible brick wall between us. *Shit!* I swallow my laugh and lean back in the seat. *I screwed up.* Was he serious about "immortality" and "unforeseen consequences"? If so, what the hell?

My closest ally and I totally threw his concern in his face. How stupid can I get? "I'm sorry, Ferdinand. I didn't expect to stop breathing. I also shouldn't have joked about dying. I know I'm not immortal."

His hands clench on the steering wheel.

"Come on, I didn't know I'd be in danger when I agreed to hypnosis. Downey should've warned us that something like this could happen." Remembering the shock on Downey's face, my own anger rises. "It's not like I planned to almost die again. I just wanted to fool around in my dream a little bit."

"And did you?" Ferdinand's foot eases off the gas. "Fool around, I mean? Did you find the spirit?" Seeing my expression, Ferdinand's lips quirk. "From the shiny glow on your face, I assume the contact went well."

"It was good for me." I grin.

"So, did you figure out why he's linked to you?"

I reflect on the main points of my experience. "My initial intent was to gather information about what caused him to be a vengeful spirit."

"He's more powerful than a vengeful spirit," Ferdinand says.

"Yeah, he's not like ghosts you see on TV." *I can't believe I'm even talking about ghosts like they're real. When did my life get so surreal? Yeah, right after I came back from the dead.* I cough to cover the hysterical laugh bubbling up from deep in my gut and continue, "Once I found him—Ashmael, that's his name—I realized how betrayed he felt by our last encounter. I had to do some serious apologizing to get him to come close and, well, the apologizing was nice. It was different being on an equal plane of existence. Two spirits floating in the clouds…" I rub at the goose bumps on my arms. "Okay, I know this is an alternative relationship that doesn't have a shot in hell of working out since he's not…human or…alive, but I'm not creeped out like I should be, or as much as you probably are looking in from the outside."

"It's extremely creepy, Dena, but for your sake I'm trying to keep an open mind. That's why you pay me the big bucks—for my objectivity."

I frown. "Pay?"

"After what I had to put up with today, I'm definitely charging for the stress and anxiety you've put me through. Don't worry. I'll give you a discount."

"Great, my own personal bodyguard…" I mutter, looking out the window. We've parked in front of my house before I notice Ferdinand's isn't the only car in the driveway. I slide lower in the seat. "Oh no, is it too late to turn around? Ugh, he saw us."

Anders steps out of his car.

"Maybe…maybe you could come in for a while," I stutter, unable to take my eyes from Anders's clenched fists. He notices me watching and stuffs his hands in his pockets.

Ferdinand has the nerve to laugh. "Not a chance. You're on your own."

CHAPTER 13

Sabotage the Control Stick

I stomp to the door and let Anders in with a wave of my arm. "What are you doing here? No murderers to catch?"

Anders takes off his jacket and lays it across the back of my armchair, as if he plans to stay awhile. I do the same, suddenly overheated in the corduroy jacket. Tension stiffens the muscles in my shoulders, and I roll them a bit to loosen the strain. Being alone in the same room with Anders scares the hell out of me. He's so unpredictable. I never know which Anders I'm going to meet: Suspicious Anders or Flirty Anders. Either one plays my body like a well-tuned violin. I'm afraid…no, terrified—not so much of him, as of what I might be tempted to do to him.

He faces me with his arms crossed. "Charles called—"

"You and Charles got a thing going? Great, it'll give Vanessa a taste of how it feels to be cheated on." His scowl at the interruption deepens to the point where I fear his face might freeze in that expression. I clasp my hands together so I won't give in to the irrational desire to smooth the lines marring his face. "Sorry; continue."

"Charles was in dispatch when Dixie received a 9-1-1 call requesting an ambulance for a Dena—who wasn't breathing. He was understandably concerned that the call was about you."

"If I didn't know better, I'd think you were also concerned." I imitate Gabriella's flirty expression by fluttering my eyelashes in his direction. He stares back stone-faced, and I sigh. "But we both know that sentimentality doesn't affect the mighty Anders."

His own thickly lashed eyelids lower. "I don't let my emotions interfere with how I conduct my job. Being emotional leads to mistakes. Mistakes get you killed."

"Sounds like you speak from experience." I step closer, studying his face. *Damn, he really is handsome.* "Have you almost gotten killed?"

His mouth opens as if he's on the verge of sharing something profound, and then he shuts it. His expression remains closed, but a distant look enters his eyes.

I cave to temptation and touch his cheek with the tips of my fingers. "Anders? What happened?"

He blinks, focusing back on me. The moment's gone. "I see that reports of your demise were premature."

My hand drops into a fist at my side. "Yes, I'm breathing just fine. It must've been a prank call." I hope the lie doesn't show on my face. "So you've done your duty. I'm still alive. Anything else you'd care to talk about? Like the case? Found out anything interesting?"

"Dr. Estrada called. He said you knew about the chemical he found on your skin. Why were you so resistant to helping him?"

"Why wouldn't I be? He blindsided me with needles. *Needles*," I emphasize with a shudder. "And he lied to me. I hate liars." I pause in my tirade, slapped in the face by my own hypocrisy. Hell, I've done almost nothing but lie to this man. "Unless there's a very good reason for the lie. As far as I can tell, Estrada doesn't have one."

"I asked him not to tell anyone about the substance."

My eyebrows jump up my forehead. "I don't understand. Why tell him to keep this information from me? It's my body. I'm the one being affected by this stuff!"

Anders raises his hands to halt my advance on him. I hadn't even realized I've moved toward him. Or that my hands are clenching and unclenching.

His hands circle my wrists, keeping me at arm's length. "Dena, I've been trying to convince you that I'm concerned for your safety for days, but you've repeatedly said you don't trust me."

"I don't trust you for this very reason." I struggle to pull away. "You knew I was sleepwalking, and not once did you say, 'Hey Dena, the mystery goop might be causing your problems.' Nope, didn't care enough to let me know I'm not going crazy."

He tugs on my wrists, and I fall against his chest. His heart races beneath my palm. "Dena, it's my job to withhold information about an ongoing investigation. I did it to protect you." He stares into my eyes, no longer concealing his sincerity. "And to protect myself."

My own heart speeds to match the flutters in my stomach.

I step closer, breathing in his familiar scent. He smells of fall—fresh mown grass with a slight musk like crushed leaves. With each inhale, my chest brushes his. My sensitive nipples harden, and I become hyperaware that only my bra shields my arousal. Warmth spreads from my core to fill my body. My cheeks must glow like lampposts.

I avert my face, hiding behind my hair.

Anders releases my wrists and steps back. He blows out a breath. "I don't know why you rattle me so badly."

Rattle? Is he kidding? Unlike me, he's barely sweating. I can almost see the hamster wheel in his head spinning as he considers how to turn my arousal to his advantage. No matter how often I deny what I'm feeling, my body screams the truth: *I want to fuck Anders.*

Right here. My eyes drop to land on the bulge straining the zipper of his trousers. *Right now.*

What the hell's wrong with me? First Ashmael, now Anders. Ever since the alley, my libido has been turbo-charged, like the aphrodisiac effect of the mystery substance still courses through my body. I close my eyes and silently count to ten, trying to regulate my breathing. If I can't get myself under control, I don't know what I might say—or do.

He's still staring at me. We're alone.

Desire surges, and I clutch the back of the sofa, digging my nails into the cloth. *Play it off, Dee. Don't let him see how he affects you.* "Okay, fine, Detective. Convince me why I should accept your apology," I say, pleased my voice doesn't reflect the strain I'm under. "Gabriella said you think the murderer is stalking me. Why? And shouldn't you have told me all this yourself?" I grimace, then wave away the accusation. "Ignore that last part. Just explain your reasoning."

"Will you sit down and promise to stay calm and hear me out?"

"Like you, I don't make promises I can't keep." I force a conciliatory smile. "Let's just agree that if my voice rises to uncomfortable decibels, you'll make a quick getaway."

He studies my face for a long, uncomfortable moment then nods. "How about if I explain what led me to think you're a target?"

I motion to the sofa and watch him sit down before I curl up next to him. I wrap the blanket across my shoulders, scrunching down in preparation for what he'll reveal. He crosses and uncrosses his legs, then leans forward with his elbows propped on his knees.

I swear if he doesn't stop fidgeting I'm going to scream.

As if reading my mind, he meets my eyes. "Okay," he says, "the fact that you've remained silent this long is unnerving."

"While normally my main purpose in life is finding ways to sabotage the control stick shoved up your backside, I'm working on my patience today." I grin, and this time, it's genuine. "Don't worry. I swear to be on my best behavior, but you'd best get on with this story before I break."

He clears his throat, staring down at his hands, then squeezes them together. "I'm pretty sure Charles revealed the contents of the medical report from Dr. Estrada." He waves away my murmured protests. "He told you about the incident I was involved in last year…"

My eyebrows rise in surprise. "You're giving Charles too much credit for duplicity. The only thing he talked about was how much he admired you. He was all…*blah, blah, blah*, Anders is Great. The *blah, blah* part is where I tuned him out. Charles has a serious case of hero worship. I tried to talk him out of it, but he was determined to only mention how respected you are."

Anders frowns down at his folded hands. "For once I agree with you, Dena. I'm the last person anyone should admire." His hands tremble on his lap.

I lean forward and lay my hand on top of his. "Hey, no fair. Talking smack about you is my job."

Anders's eyes darken, and I shift, uncomfortable with the emotion reflected in their jade and gold depths.

He lets out a deep breath. "I have…*had* a partner. We were investigating a string of cold case murders spanning several decades, which were reopened after we linked them to a particular suspect, the so-called Hoodoo Queen of New Orleans. Her web of influence stretched from the lowest street peddler to the mayor's office. Drugs, guns, money laundering, murder for hire—she controlled the French Quarter. Hell, probably most of Louisiana."

"So a mob boss."

A hint of a dimple flashes in his cheek. "The Hoodoo Queen wasn't a typical gangster. She allegedly trafficked in black curses."

Is he serious? I nod, as if I understand what he's talking about. "She sounds scary."

"Scary," he echoes. "Yes. Fear is a huge motivator. With fear of the supernatural—well, for those who believe, she held absolute power over them. People whispered that she controlled an indestructible army of undead. Men whose souls were trapped in their rotting corpses, damned to an eternity of servitude to the Queen.

Nobody dared speak her real name, let alone testify against her for fear she'd fix a curse on them. The one informant who did spill, Étienne Thibodaux, disappeared before he could give an official statement. Rumor has it the Queen turned him into her personal zombie slave."

My nose scrunches. "*Tssh*, I don't believe in zombies. Dead's dead."

He sighs. "Neither did I, but my chief ordered us off the case. Said it was too dangerous. We didn't listen. My partner got a tip about some big deal going down in Paradise Pointe, involving the Queen. It was outside of our jurisdiction, but we thought we'd finally caught a break. We went in without backup. My partner got killed," he says in a monotone, almost like he's reading from a book. Except his cold fingers close around mine. I doubt he realizes he's holding my hand. "After Jimmy died, I couldn't let her get away with murdering him. I left New Orleans and got hired by Bertrand Parish Sheriff's Office so I could keep investigating the link between Paradise Pointe and the Queen. And I finally found out her real name."

He glances down. Seeing our fingers intertwined, he removes his hand. "You know what's ironic? I'd been investigating a dead woman. She died the same night my partner did. Maybe you remember the night of the big earthquake?" At my nod, he continues. "Magnolia LaCroix died in the quake. All of her assets, including the title of Hoodoo Queen, went to her niece..."

It takes a moment for his words to sink in. *Well, hot damn!* "You're talking about Mala."

His hostility toward my cousin, and to a lesser degree to me, makes sense now. Of course he'd believe I was capable of casting a spell to burn a man to death if I'm related to the Hoodoo Queen.

"Malaise LaCroix is the next link in the chain. I need to find out if she's continuing her aunt's criminal activities."

"Swear to God, she's not." I raise my hand in the air. *No way. Oh my God, Mala…Does she know her aunt was a criminal? Is this why I'm being stalked? Calm down. Focus. Breathe. First things first. Clear Mala with Anders.* "She sold off most of her aunt's estate. Donated the rest to charity. She's the most honest person I know." *Unlike me.*

Anders remains silent, studying my face. *What does he see?*

"Please believe me. I'm telling the truth."

His penetrating gaze drops. "Maybe you're right, but if not her, then someone else is in charge of Magnolia's empire. The first three men burned were low-level street thugs, drug addicts. At first I thought they'd gotten caught up in some turf war between rival gangs, fighting over the vacancy left open with Magnolia's death. Or they were targeted by Magnolia's people. Then I found your picture on Tolson."

"He'd been stalking me, waiting for a chance to catch me alone." I shudder. The idea of him following me around, taking pictures. It's unnerving. "At least he's dead."

"He wasn't the only one following you, Dena. We found the second body outside of a beauty salon, Luscious Locks. It's on—"

I lean forward. "Wall Street, it's where I get my hair done. I go every other month for a trim."

Anders nods. "I know. I spoke to your beautician, Bai Sung. She gave me a detailed schedule of when you come to see her. She said she spoke to another man who wanted the same information. He told her he wanted to ask you out. She thought this was fantastic since you'd been celibate for so long."

Great, Bai! Thanks for hooking me up with an assassin. My face burns as I meet Anders's gaze. *Can I bury my head under the blanket now?* "So basically this guy was lying in wait for my exit from the salon, but the shadow got him first."

Anders rolls his eyes at the word "shadow." "Someone found him. The fourth body was found in an alley beside the hospital with a knife in his hand the morning after your attack. Records show he'd been admitted for observation after he complained of chest pain."

My breathing quickens. I flash back to the dream I had in the hospital of a man standing over my bed. Of watching the knife descend toward my chest. The terror returns, surging through my body, and my stomach clenches with nausea. I close my eyes and try not to vomit. "Where was the next body found?"

"We found him last night, a block over from your house. He died around the same time I found you sleepwalking. This guy was different from the others, a contract killer. He broke into the house behind yours, murdered the couple, but left their baby alive. A neighbor reported the child crying this afternoon."

My hands shake. "Why did he break into the house?"

"We found a sniper rifle in the master bedroom. The window is directly across from your kitchen and bedroom window."

"S-So he planned to execute me?" I meet Ander's eyes in disbelief. "That's what you think, right? He killed that couple and planned to watch my house until he had the chance to kill me."

Anders's voice is cool. "That's what the evidence suggests. Only someone stopped him."

Another nightmare that's turned out to be real. The thought of the dead assassin doesn't bring up a shred of sympathy. He killed my neighbors. Might've gone after their baby, only Ashmael stopped him. Saved the baby. Saved me.

"Dena—" Anders's voice jerks me back.

My heart warms as his face fills with sympathy. It's a new expression for him, but he wears it well enough that it may be genuine. "So my sleepwalking was more of a gift than a curse. It's lucky I wasn't inside, right?" I laugh shakily, unsure which of us I'm trying my hardest to convince. I must sound deranged. Nothing he's said is the least bit amusing. Somebody wants me dead. And they're willing to go to great lengths to make it happen. "Why keep this from me?"

"Like I said, I thought Mala was involved. I didn't trust you, and your association with Magnolia LaCroix's ex-employees pointed to your complicity."

My head's spinning. Everything he says confuses the hell out of me. This is what comes from wanting to know the truth? Ignorance is bliss. There's a reason this idiom is still relevant. Same with "knowledge is power", which is more in line with what I believe. No matter how much I want to, I won't bury my head under the blanket and pretend this is all a crazy dream.

I let out a heavy breath and ask, "What employees?"

"Ferdinand Laffite and Anton Terrie."

Oh, my God! Squirrel. "Wait…Ferdinand? My Ferdinand?"

"He owns a private security company in New Orleans. Anton was one of his employees. Magnolia LaCroix was Ferdinand's client. He was in Paradise Pointe with her when she died." He runs his fingers over a seam in the couch. "He visited you in the hospital right before you woke from the coma, along with Mala, Landry, Magnolia, and Magnolia's secretary, Sophia. If rumors about Magnolia are true, she brought you back from the dead."

"What a load of crap!" I shriek, then dial back the shrill before I lose my voice.

"Dr. Estrada said you were brain dead. Yet you woke up right after their visit."

"Estrada? The idiot misdiagnosed my condition. He was going to kill me. Now he's covering his ass by lying."

"He knows your waking up should've been impossible. A miracle." Anders stares at the ceiling with a frown, and I hold my breath, waiting for what comes next. 'Cause there's got to be more. I don't think I can handle anymore.

"Estrada showed me the CCTV video. Magnolia, Mala, and Sophia went into your room. Landry and Ferdinand stayed in the hall. Then something happened. Landry broke open the door and rushed in."

I'm shaking my head *no*.

Anders's lips purse. "If you don't believe me, ask them. Ask your mother. Pepper was there, too."

Pepper never... I rub my burning eyes. *Brain dead*. She was taking me off life support. Then, holy miracle of all miracles, I woke up. Right after being visited by the Hoodoo Queen of New Orleans.

My throat feels tight. Like the time I ate squash and almost suffocated from anaphylactic shock. "Dead's dead. I'm not dead. Or a zombie. Or whatever..." This time it's Anders holding my hand and me jerking away. "I'm not dead. I'm not."

"You're a thousand times more beautiful than the zombies from *The Walking Dead.*"

The unexpected compliment pierces the bubble of shock I'm stuck in. "Good." I let out a heavy sigh. "'Cause Gabriella's mom once made me brain tacos, and I wasn't a fan. Swear."

I sniff. *Damn, how long have I been crying?*

I wipe my face with the blanket. The pounding in my head echoes the words flashing through my brain: *STUPID, STUPID, STUPID.* Too trusting. Too stupid. Everyone but me knew the truth. Mala, Landry, Mama. Ferdinand…he worked me over like a master liar. I spilled my innermost secrets to him, like he was my long-lost BFF. He acted like he didn't know me. He kept the fact that he was the Hoodoo Queen's muscle to himself. *Why?*

I close my eyes and pinch the bridge of my nose. My mind's cluttered. Full of…of crap. Loads and loads of crap. *Focus. One thing at a time. First Ferdinand.* Why keep his identity a secret? So Mala won't find out? He seemed sincere about wanting to help me. But maybe his motivation is more selfish. If someone is targeting Magnolia's staff then Ferdinand's at risk, too. Which means he's on my side, if only to keep himself alive.

"Are you okay?" Anders asks.

"Yeah, I guess you had good reason not to trust me."

He blinks, and the right side of his mouth lifts enough to flash his dimple before he sobers. "Don't feel too bad. My partner's the only person I ever truly trusted. You're growing on me. It'd be easier if I wasn't still confused as hell."

Confused…This makes me giggle. My poor brain's twirling like a pinwheel. "You and me both. So let's break it down and consider the players involved. You've got a dead mob boss. My cousin, who refused the 'Hoodoo Queen' mantle of power, leaving Evil.org without a leader. A whole lot of incompetent—I call them this since I'm still alive—dead assassins. And me. We need to figure out who took over in the vacuum left by Magnolia's passing."

Anders's eyes sparkle as he shifts on the couch. "Right. Maybe this person's picking off those loyal to the old Queen. Like Ferdinand and Anton."

I shake my head. "The black shadow killed Anton. He died because he was in the wrong place at the right time." Except he'd also threatened me. Could this be the common denominator? Anything that threatens me, Ashmael crispy creams. "The shadow killed the assassins who came after me. It's protecting me."

"Not that I believe this shadow exists, any more than I believe you're a zombie. But if it did, why?"

I shrug. "It…he…likes me."

"I like you, too, but not enough to burn people to death for you."

"Well, I hope not, Anders. We barely know each other." I rub the blanket across the tip of my nose, soothing myself with the repetitive motion. The whole time, I firmly steer my mind from dwelling on the mini-confessions of interest Anders keeps slipping into the conversation. It's getting harder and harder to act like I haven't noticed he thinks I'm more beautiful than a zombie. He likes me but not enough to kill for me. And he needs to protect himself from whatever seductive wiles I may throw at him. Okay, the seductive wiles part is my own interpretation.

I sigh and wrap the blanket over my head. "The more important question is why am I being targeted?"

"That's what doesn't make a lick of sense, Dena." Anders stabs his fingers through his sable hair again. For some absurd reason, it strikes me as endearing. Maybe because he seems genuinely flustered. I don't think this is one of his calculated emotional responses. This time, I'm reading the truth in the emotion stamped on his face.

He scratches the rough stubble on his jaw, staring at the coffee table, then meets my gaze. "If one of Magnolia's business rivals is taking out the competition, then why not target Mala? What's so important about you? I'll do my best to protect you, but I can't stop them until I figure out why you're such a threat."

Without saying it outright, he thinks I'm doomed. I've got a giant bull's-eye plastered on my back. The only reason I'm not still crying: I'm not alone. Anders has my back. And so does my guardian angel of death. Ashmael kept me safe before I knew of the danger. Everything will be okay. *I'll be fine.*

"Sorry for calling you a stalker for staking out my house." I force myself to smile. "I get it now. All this time I thought you were a perv. Instead you're my knight in shining armor, carrying a Glock 9-mil in your shoulder holster instead of a sword. At least I don't have to worry about you lopping off my zombie head."

Anders frowns. "This isn't a joking matter, Dena."

"Yeah, I know…but I have to laugh to keep from crying." I get up and motion him toward the kitchen. "Come on, hero, I'll get us a drink, and you can brag about how many times you've saved my life this week."

"I haven't saved your life this week," he mutters, following me into the kitchen.

"Yet…I feel so undead, Anders." I pull a six-pack from the

fridge and place it on the table. "Want a beer? Or are you on duty?"

His gaze travels across my face. "It's my day off," he says with a frown.

"Really? Then I admire your dedication to your work. Come on. You have no excuse. Let's get drunk and forget about all the problems plaguing us like pesky mosquitoes out for blood. At least for a little while." I gesture toward the extra chair.

It's at this point that I break Anders.

CHAPTER 14

Lover Boy and Anchovies

Anders throws his hands in the air. He turns in a half circle, as if to storm out of the kitchen, then lunges forward to grab a beer from the table. He downs it in four long gulps, before snatching my can from my frozen hand. I stare, mouth open, in complete shock. My laugh bursts from my chest, catching both of us off guard. The man completely disarms me by chugging a beer, like any other normal guy.

"Why don't you order us a pizza?" Anders loosens his tie and unbuttons the top of his dress shirt.

My eyes are drawn to the sliver of bare skin revealed. "Pizza, huh?" I lick my lips, mouth dry. I take another can from the table. "Plan to be here awhile?"

"Can't have beer without pizza. It's un-American."

Pizza, too. Damn, score another one to Anders. He's just leveled up in hotness points. My heart races and each breath comes with effort. I tear my gaze from his chest, pulling my cellphone from my pocket as an opportunity to clear my head. I hit the pre-set number to my favorite hole-in-the-wall pizza joint, Santiago's, and hold the phone to my ear.

Back in control, I face Anders with a raised eyebrow. "What do you want on it?"

"Pepperoni, olives, and extra anchovies."

I give a delicate shudder. "Whatever turns you on, Lover Boy."

His eyes do that thing—where they darken— and my stomach clenches. "A lot of things turn me on," he says, his voice like silk sliding across my skin.

Whew, it's warm in here. Fanning my face, I stare out the kitchen window. I won't let him see how his words affect me. Nope, no blushing. Not this time. I keep my voice steady when I place my order. "Yeah, give me a large pizza: half pepperoni and olives, and half veggie delight hold the olives— anchovies topping both sides. For delivery, please; you have my address."

Anders grins when I look at him. "I see we have a love of eight-ies movies in common. Tell me, do you tip well?"

Oh God! Of all the movies to references, why did I pick *Lover Boy*? "Better than most women." *Ugh, I suck at flirting.* "Who doesn't like little salty fish and Patrick Dempsey as a gigolo pizza delivery boy? I actually have the DVD. We can watch it while we eat." I grab another beer and sit down at the table.

Anders follows, sitting next to me. Maybe he senses my dis-comfort at the topic of conversation, because he tips the beer toward me in a salute. "Thanks, I needed this."

I salute back then take several large swallows. "I could tell. You were wound a little tight."

"Murder usually affects me that way."

"I can't even imagine all you've gone through." I set the beer on the table and fold my hands. "If I forgot to say this earlier, I'm sorry about your partner. I'd gotten lost in a pit of self-pity over my own drama and forgotten my manners."

Anders smiles, shaking his head. "I'll leave that last part alone since you're being civil for once and enjoy it for as long as it lasts. And thanks for the condolences. He was a good friend and a better partner. He saved my life that night."

"What do you mean?"

"I told you about Étienne Thibodaux—"

"Magnolia's zombie servant."

"Chauffeur…. And for a dead guy, he had excellent reflexes. Jimmy and I had followed Magnolia to the Dubois estate. Thibodaux tried to run me over with her big ass Cadillac. Jimmy shoved me aside. The impact killed him. I cracked my head on the pavement, but I got lucky. Dr. Estrada put the shattered pieces of my skull back together like a jigsaw puzzle."

"Oh, I'm so sorry. That's awful. Wait. Estrada—" My words cut off with my gasp. I put together the pieces of information he shared earlier—the Dubois Estate, Magnolia—to solve my very own puzzle. "You said this happened the night of the earthquake."

"Yeah, why?"

"Because I think you're my mystery patient. The night of the earthquake an injured man was brought to the hospital. I watched over him."

His lip curls, and he shakes his head, disbelief stamped on his face. Not that I blame him. I hardly believe it myself.

"Why would you be there, Dena?"

"I'd woken from my coma a few days before. That night…" *Was the first time I heard Death's song.* "I've never seen anything so horrifying. So many of my friends didn't make it." I blink back the memory. "The hospital had too many patients coming in and not enough staff. The nurses were overwhelmed so I helped to monitor your status until Estrada could operate. You joked about Estrada putting you back together like a jigsaw puzzle, but I saw…Anders, you almost died. It scared the hell out of me." *I held your hand and blocked Death from stealing your soul. What kind of crazy fate do we share for this to happen?*

He stares at me through thick lashes, and I shiver. The intense bond I formed with the unnamed patient that crazy night stretches between us—a fragile, unbroken cord. I never got over him. I've been wondering why I feel such an intense attraction to him. Now, maybe, my conscious self knows what my subconscious has been shouting since the first moment Anders scowled at me. I only wish I'd recognized him sooner.

Guilt forces my head down. "I'm sorry. I promised to find you after the operation, but I didn't. They moved you to another hospital, and I never got your name."

"Jimmy and I went in undercover. I didn't have my identification on me. I ended up at the hospital in Lafayette, then after I woke up they moved me to New Orleans."

"Yeah, well, I still should've tried. This is so crazy."

"What? That I found you instead?" He takes my hand and lays it on top of his. With the other hand he opens my fingers, one by one. "I wondered why this hand felt familiar." His soft lips press a kiss to the center of my palm. Right on my love line. Coincidence? Knowing Anders, I think not.

His green gaze traces the curves of my face, pausing for a long, breathless moment on my mouth. I don't breathe. My heart's about to fly out of my chest. I wet my bottom lip with the tip of my tongue, and Anders's pupils dilate. I can't conceal the blush warming my cheeks, but I can redirect this situation before it gets out of control.

Clearing my throat, I ask, "Do you know how Magnolia found out about your investigation?"

"No, Jimmy spoke to the informant. He told me that Magnolia would be at the Dubois estate, and the informant would meet us there with enough proof to indict Magnolia for her crimes. Only I can't remember if we met this person before Thibodaux tried to kill us. My memory's spotty."

"Did anyone else in your department know about the meeting?"

"It wasn't sanctioned. We kept quiet in case the informant didn't show. The captain had already ordered us off the investigation."

I lean forward, elbows propped on the table. "What do you remember about that night?"

Anders raises the beer to his lips and takes a deep drink. "Not much. That's the problem. I read statements given by the victims who survived the quake. Nobody remembers Magnolia being at the Dubois party, but her remains were found in the debris. Along with Étienne Thibodaux."

I lift my own beer and shake the empty can. I don't remember drinking it, but I won't guzzle the next one. I grab the last can from the table before Anders nabs it.

Anders stretches back in the chair, kicking his legs out. He rakes his fingers through his hair again. "I was put on administrative leave after the incident. My captain wanted me to see a shrink and convince him I was fit for duty. I left instead. Sheriff Keyes knew my history, and he still hired me. Even now, I worry he's waiting for me to screw up. I've heard that some of the guys think I'm responsible for my partner getting killed. That I ran away rather than facing sanctions for what happened."

I slide my chair next to his, so close that I can smell his clean, spicy scent. "There's no way. I've only known you for a week, but there is no doubt in my mind. You're not capable of betraying your own partner," I state firmly. "It must be difficult not knowing if somewhere in your mind is the answer to all of the questions you've been asking yourself. That maybe you know more than you remember."

Anders's eyes flicker, reflecting a vulnerability that tugs at my heart. He breaks our gaze, staring down at the table as if to shield himself before I peel off the protective layers he uses to conceal his pain. He reminds me of myself.

Neither of us trust worth a damn.

But I want to. Does he?

The question must be stamped on my face. I don't mean for it to show. Or expect an answer. The corners of his eyes soften as he slowly puts down his beer. "You're such a contradiction. I feel…" He releases a heavy sigh, but remains silent.

"Huh?" *Feel what? Enraged? Annoyed?* Maybe it's better if he doesn't answer. Do I want him to admit to feeling this connection between us? That he feels something deeper than the frustration and distrust he shows so often? It would only complicate our already complicated relationship. Maybe some things are safer if left unsaid.

I shift my focus to the word before the hiccup of a confession. "What do you mean by 'contradiction'?"

Anders angles his chair until I'm sandwiched between his legs. His muscular thighs press against mine, holding me hostage. "Shut up, Dena! Just for a moment, please."

I seal my lips, acutely aware of the heat of his legs. It would be so easy to reach out and slide my palms up his thighs. Even easier to rip the buttons from his shirt so I can explore the contours of the chest peeking out, teasing me. I clasp my trembling hands together and stick them between my knees, fighting the temptation to touch him.

Anders frowns. Does he read the desire in my eyes? At this point, I can't hide it. Two—maybe, three—beers equal inhibitions shot to pieces. I'm screwed, or rather, hoping to get screwed, six ways to Sunday.

Anders lifts my hands from my lap. His fingers wrap around mine, holding on tight as if afraid I'll pull away. "Dena, the men are targeting you for a reason. I don't think they'll stop until they've accomplished their objective, which appears to be killing you." He punctuates that last statement with a light squeeze. "The only way to stop them is to figure out what they want, why they picked you. I know you don't fully trust me, but I'm begging you—be straight with me. What secret are you holding back?"

I try to reclaim my hands. I guess I am a contradiction. One second, I want him to touch me. The next, I want to escape, and he refuses to let go.

"Dena, how did you get downtown last night?"

I struggle against the illusion of intimacy. He's using it as a weapon to coerce me into trusting him. Manipulating my desperation. And I'm such a sap, it's almost worked. How pathetic. The last time I softened toward him, I spilled the secret about the black shadow. He called me crazy. What will he say if I tell him about my semi-corporeal makeout buddy?

Deliberately obtuse, I shrug. "I don't understand."

"When I found you last night you were five miles from home. You didn't take a car. Who picked you up?"

Now my confusion isn't faked. I shake my head. What does he mean by five miles from home? Had I really been that far away? It didn't feel so far. I ran it in about five minutes. I wasn't even out of breath.

I stop trying to pull away and clutch Anders hands, my own sticky with sweat. Our eyes meet. Concern fills his jade and gold depths. It feels real. Maybe I'm subconsciously deluding myself, but as I stare into his eyes, my fear and uncertainty drifts away. *Darn that beer.*

"Dena," he whispers, a little befuddled himself, judging by the shifting darkness in his eyes. His head tilts toward mine. He runs his tongue across his full lips. "Who is he? Gabriella didn't know. She was as shocked about you being with another man as..."—his head dips, gaze dropping—"...I was." Pain pinches the corners of his eyes when he looks at me through his thick lashes.

Am I responsible?

He clears his throat. "What's his name?"

Is this jealousy? Or something else? I pull my hand free and rub my neck. Are the love bites Ashmael gave me still visible? Or did they heal as fast as my other bruises? "How do you know it was a man?" My voice sounds strained.

Anders grunts. He lays his fingertips against the racing pulse in my throat. My eyes close as I lean into the warmth of his cupped hand. Heat radiates through my body. "I know," he whispers, a tinge of amusement lightening his husky tone.

His fingers tangle in my hair, tracing across the bullet scar behind my ear. My first instinct is to grab his hand, but I don't. This scar reflects the one inside me. The pain of it has healed, but it's a reminder not to take life for granted. No matter how much living hurts. It took a long time to accept this. I'm not ashamed of him seeing it.

His fingers move from the scar to sweep my hair over the opposite shoulder. Gently, he massages my neck and then trails his hand down to my shoulder. My muscles relax, and a small moan escapes my lips.

Anders scoots to the edge of his chair. "Did he make you feel like this when he touched you?"

Did Ashmael? What does it matter now? I shut off the part of my brain trying to overthink my complicated relationships. *This is real. A dream will only ever be a dream.*

I focus on enjoying the warmth of Anders's hand against my thigh. My legs part, and I lean closer. I slide my hands across his chest, wishing for bare skin instead of a cotton shirt. His heart pounds beneath my palms. *Is he as nervous as I am? As turned on?*

His hands settle on my hips, and with a tug, I fall into his arms. He pulls me so I'm straddling his lap. He unbuttons my jeans and slips his hands past the waistband, cupping my bottom in both hands.

He laughs at my startled expression. "I've been obsessed with your ass ever since you flashed me in the hospital."

Warmth fills my cheeks, and I press my face against the side of his neck. His body shakes as he laughs…at me. *God, I'm so embarrassed.* The doorbell rings, saving me from coming up with some lame excuse to cover how silly I feel about my sudden attack of shyness.

I glance at the clock and frown. "It's only eight." Too early for Gabriella to be returning home from her date. Unless Estrada bored her into an early escape with his egotistical droning.

Anders must think the same. "Does Gabriella have a key?"

"Yes." I shift, self-conscious. If Gabriella catches me sitting smack dab on Anders's lap, she'll die laughing. I'll never hear the end of it. Especially after all my denials about being attracted to the sexy man in my arms.

Anders's lips nuzzle the juncture between my neck and my shoulder. "Don't answer it."

I want to ignore the doorbell out of spite alone. Who'd be rude enough to keep ringing someone's doorbell, over and over, without waiting for an answer? A real jerk. And the only jerk I'm acquainted with is kissing my neck. This thought cuts the haze of alcohol-induced bliss clouding my thoughts.

Anders groans as my thighs tighten around him and I prepare to stand. "Shit. Really, Dena?"

No…yes, ugh. I don't want to move. His arms form a protective circle around me, and his muscular chest is perfect for cuddling against. His tongue does some flick/lick thing to my earlobe, and the resulting shiver runs from my head all the way down to curl my toes. My eyes close, and I take a deep breath. *I'm losing control.*

No, he's stealing my control, one kiss…lick…nibble at a time. And I want to let go. So bad. But I can't with Anders. No matter how delicious his mouth tastes as he kisses me. Or how my body reacts as his tongue duels with mine. If I go too far, too fast, I'll get hurt again.

With Ashmael, it's different. He's not real.

A relationship with a spirit won't complicate my life. I won't be tempted to think I can have anything long term with him, only to find out he doesn't feel the same. *I need to stop.*

My hands clench Anders's shoulders, and I push up, breaking the seal of his arms around my waist. Instantly, I miss the heat of his body. "Maybe Gabriella forgot her keys. Besides, we've both been drinking. If we stop, there'll be no regrets tomorrow…" *But more than a few right now.*

I adjust my disheveled clothing and stride to the door. Anders follows. A quick look over my shoulder and down to the bulge in his jeans gives clear evidence to his frustration. I give him a sympathetic grin. His frown returns in response.

Oh well. His reset button has been pressed, and he's back to being annoyed with me. I'm kind of glad for things to return to normal. This sudden twist in our relationship has me a little too confused. I need time to process my emotions and anger's a fine distraction.

Another loud pound hits the door, and a gruff voice yells, "Pizza."

I twitch, throwing a guilty glare over my shoulder at Anders.

I'd forgotten we ordered pizza. "I'm coming—hold your horses." I open the door. "Sorry it took so long—"

The barrel of the sawed-off shotgun pointed at my face cuts short my apology.

Anders grabs the back of my shirt and jerks me from the doorway. I fly backward, airborne for a long second, then hit the ground, sliding across the hardwood floor. Anders jams his shoulder against the door, slamming it on the gun as it discharges.

The sound reverberates through the room.

Screaming, I crawl toward the end of the sofa farthest from the door. Jagged shards from Pepper's blasted Olmec statue rain down upon my body.

Anders struggles to hold the door closed, but another hole explodes in the wood, only missing his head by inches. He throws himself to the side, landing on the loveseat and bouncing off the cushion to fall onto the floor. "Stay down!" he yells, pulling his gun. He scrambles across the floor, using the coffee table and sofa to shield himself from the spray of bullets that fill the room, until he reaches my side.

I peek around the end of the sofa. A large body blocks the doorway. A man wearing a ski mask fires the shotgun in our direction. Anders presses my head down. Heat from a shotgun pellet grazes the side of my face. I cry out, clapping my hand to my bleeding cheek.

"Keep your head down before it gets blown off!" Anders's voice sounds muffled through the ringing in my ears.

The man with the shotgun steps into the room, as if unafraid of retaliation. A second assassin crowds behind, also trying to enter the room. Whoever sent them must've said I'd be helpless, but what they hadn't counted on was Anders being at my house. And Anders is armed. He rises to one knee, shooting. Three bullets hit the man in the upper chest, throwing him back into the second man. Tangled together, they fall to the ground.

Anders follows. "Sheriff's Office, put the gun down!" he orders the second man, who is pinned beneath his partner but still trying to shoot us.

"Anders!" I scream as the man lifts his gun and pulls the trigger.

Anders staggers to the side, but doesn't hesitate. He shoots the man twice in the only place visible. Blood and chunks of skull splatter my front step. Pieces of the man's brain sit in my azaleas. My stomach heaves, and I scramble to my feet.

Anders's head jerks up at the sound of my movement. The shock in his eyes turns them completely black. I catch my balance then break for the kitchen. "Are you okay?" he calls after me. "Did you get hit?"

"Fine...sick." I choke and wave him back to the bodies. My stomach twists again. I stumble over to the kitchen sink in time for the beer to explode from my stomach with a force that leaves me gasping for air.

Anders calls 9-1-1 requesting medical assistance, but the only thing those two men need are body bags. The image of the gruesome artwork on Pepper's front porch flashes through my head, and my stomach heaves again. I stick my head back in the sink. I hadn't realized I drank so much. On an empty stomach, too.

A cool hand touches the back of my neck and brushes the hair away from my face. "Anders—" A cloth covers my mouth, cutting off my scream. The sharp edge of a giant knife presses against my throat. I don't resist as I'm pulled against a wide chest. My brain races to put the pieces together. This third man must've come in through the back door while his friends hit the front. *So blind…* I didn't see him when I stumbled into the kitchen.

"You fight, I kill you," he whispers. His modulated tone is deadly calm and obviously meant to intimidate me with how ruthless and badass he is. I have no doubt in my mind that he means the threat.

He's the difference between a professional assassin and a homeless creep who assaults me in an alley. The only reason I still breathe is because he wants me alive. I have absolutely no doubt about that either.

I nod, and his arm loosens. He pulls me toward the back door. The whole time I think that Anders will notice I'm missing and check on me, but apparently he's lost interest in my well-being after he heard me puking my guts out.

The man forces me into the backyard. Sirens wail in the distance, heading in our direction, but they're still far enough away that he doesn't seem nervous. He holds onto my arm and drags me through the neighbor's yard, keeping us in the shadows. With each step, we get farther from Anders.

When the man judges it's safe, he begins to run and pulls me after him. I stumble, feet tangling together. I try to keep my balance, but he yanks on my arm, almost wrenching it from its socket. I choke on a scream.

"Keep up," he orders.

"I can't," I gasp, trying to pull away. "Too fast!"

"Not fast enough." He jerks on my arm again. This time I do

scream. I focus on my legs, willing them to steady. I imagine them moving...

"Faster, faster, must run faster," I chant. *Before he gets pissed and kills me* is how it ends in my head. I concentrate so hard on running that I'm not aware of our speed until I glance up. Trees whip past my eyes—charcoal-dark smudges staining the night. In the blink of an eye, we're past them. *Flying...it's like I'm flying.*

CHAPTER 15

Bionic Upgrade

What the hell am I thinking?

Shock has screwed with my mind. There's no other reason to explain leaving the house with a man holding a knife. I'll be an even bigger fool to keep running farther from Anders and safety.

Rather than fighting the hold on my arm, I stop running and let my legs go slack. The pain in my shoulder as it's wrenched in the socket is instantaneous. I cry out, jerking my arm toward my chest, and pretend to faint. Not much of stretch of my acting skills, given I'm out of breath and exhausted from running at speeds a horse would have trouble maintaining.

As I crumple to the ground, the man curses. He drags me by the arm for a few feet before he realizes I'm not budging. Too afraid to keep my eyes closed, I watch him from behind half-closed eyelids. He looms over me, barely breathing hard. He toes me in the side, and I moan.

A stronger kick in the side. "Get up!"

I grit my teeth and hold my breath so I won't scream. The bastard still holds the knife. I can't fight until it's out of the way. I won't get stabbed by accident, like the last time.

He curses again.

Now I'll know his true motivation. If he wants me dead, he'll use the knife. If I'm needed alive, he'll put the knife away and pick me up. My chest hurts from holding my breath for so long. My muscles keep tensing up, but I force myself to appear unconscious.

Bastard shoves the knife in his belt sheath and bends over. *Finally!*

I mule-kick him in the chest.

He flies through the air and slams into the passenger door of a car parked on the side of the street. The impact of his body against the metal rings out like a gunshot, and the door crumples. He collapses in a boneless heap.

My breath hiccups as it rushes from my lungs. I sit up and run a trembling hand down my leg. It feels normal, but it can't be. It's got to be bionic.

Clearly, I've gotten an upgrade.

The man's concaved torso jerks upright. He inhales, and his head lifts. A flap of skin brushes his cheek. Black blood oozes down his neck from where his ear used to be attached. He lifts a hand and pushes the ear back into place. It sticks as if hot-glued back on. He pushes up from the ground, sliding his body up the car until he's on his feet.

"What the fuck?" I slap a hand over my mouth. *Shit on toast. I'm so screwed.* I wasted my opportunity to escape without a fight.

He stands, ignoring the fact that my kick shattered most of his ribs. Hell, they're already moving back into place. The pop of reknitting cartilage makes my skin crawl. He points the knife in my direction.

Oh crap. My hands fly up over my head in surrender. "Sorry."

The bastard spits a wad of blood at his feet then smiles with black-stained teeth. His gloating rubs me raw.

I drop my hands and ball them into fists. "No, screw being sorry. That was badass."

The man wipes his bloody hand across his chest. "Yeah, good kick. They said you'd been Xena Warrior Princess'ed. I thought this was too easy."

"Well, I didn't know." Confidence floods my body as my endorphins kick in. I may not be bionic, but I'm not a normal human anymore either. "Now that I do, I'm not going without a fight. Do you think you can take me on?"

"That was a cheap shot. I wasn't expecting it." He flashes another black smile. "It's one thing to be super-powered and another to be able to fight. Can you fight, little girl?" He pivots his body and lowers into a boxer's crouch. The hand fisted around the knife stays pointed in my direction. "'Cause I'm willing to bet you're all talk. Get up. Now!"

I roll to my knees, but getting up is a lot harder than falling down. When I put weight on my ankle, pain shoots up my leg. "Ow, ouch!"

"Think I'm falling for that again?" The man shakes his head. "If you've been given the juice then you can heal. Boss said to bring you alive, but I think that's too much trouble."

"Well, if your boss wants me alive…alive it should be," I say, considering his words. The pain in my ankle has begun to fade, but he doesn't need to know. "Besides, maybe I didn't get super healing with the *juice*…whatever that's supposed to be? I don't suppose you know?"

"I'm only told what's needed to complete my job." He steps forward. The flap of skin that peeled off has fused back to his head. He's been *juiced*, too. If it comes down to a fight, I've got no real advantage over him.

He stares with narrowed eyes at the hand I hold out to him.

I flutter my fingers in the air. "A little help up, please? You win. You're better and stronger, and I'm a helpless woman who's fallen into your evil clutches."

God, I hate pretending to be weak. Or stupid. But it works. He grabs my hand and yanks me forward so hard that I almost face plant onto the hood of the car. I catch my balance and turn toward him. I've procrastinated for as long as possible, but time has run out. I need to make a decision.

He opens the undented back passenger door. "Get in."

"Do I look like I'm outta my damned mind? There's no way I'm stealing a car. Stealing is against the law."

"So is kidnapping."

"Yeah, another reason why I'm not going anywhere with you." I run around the front of the car, moving so fast my surroundings blur. I blink to refocus my vision, trying to get over the dizziness. I need to get my head together or I don't stand a chance. "What the hell's going on with my body? Who told you to kidnap me? Is it the person who took over Magnolia's criminal empire? Tell me before you kill me, 'cause I'm not going anywhere with you, asshole."

He leaps forward, sliding across the hood of the car like a stunt man in a movie. I jump back, expecting to land on the trunk of the car. Instead, I fly through the air and land in a crouch twenty yards away.

I slant a stunned grimace over my shoulder. "Cool," I whisper and sprint toward home.

This time I keep my wits and push my legs to the point where the muscles ache. The man follows. He runs faster than I do, but I have a head start. I maintain my lead until we're a couple of houses from Pepper's. He grabs a hunk of hair, and my head snaps back.

"Jerk!" I scream, whirling around. "You almost broke my neck."

I grab my hair, tugging it from his hand. At the same time, I spin into a roundhouse kick. His nose breaks with a loud crack, and he grunts. "Nobody ever believes me when I say I know martial arts—two years of Tae Kwon Do at the youth center." I bounce back on the pads of my feet then jump into a front kick that doubles him over. "Plus, I'm on expert level in kickboxing—Billy Blanks, baby!"

Panting, since his nose hasn't healed enough to allow him to breathe through it, the man raises the knife. "Enough. You got questions. Well, my boss's got answers. She'll tell you all about how you got juiced. Think you're fast now, just wait. Healing, quick reflexes—those things are just baby steps."

I freeze, hands rising in the air. "Why am I wanted alive now? What changed?"

"Someone else put a bounty on your head—fifty grand—dead or alive. Think you can fight off every bounty hunter in North America? Think you can protect your friends or that detective sniffing around if they get in the way? Come with me. You're one of us, Xena, and we protect our own."

Damn, if he's telling the truth, then those assassins won't stop coming after me until I'm dead or captured. My friends are in danger. Anders could've been killed tonight. Is my life more important than theirs? A life I shouldn't even be living. I got a second chance, and I don't even know why. But maybe this guy's boss does. And getting answers is worth the risk.

I let my fists drop. "My name's Dena, not Xena," I drawl, infusing my tone with false bravado. "And since I'm a survivor, I'd be a fool to refuse your protection."

He gives a smug smile and sheathes his knife. "Good choice."

"Yeah? Well, if you'd explained the situation instead of kidnapping me, I wouldn't have broken your spine." I walk over to the man.

He pulls a cell out of his pocket and makes a call. "I've got her," he says, then hangs up. He gives me a sharklike grin. So pleased with himself. But I guess he's got a right to gloat. He just earned fifty thousand dollars with my capture.

His fingers wrap around my wrist, like a shackle. "Time to go."

Black rage fills my mind, and I snatch my arm from his grasp with a snarl. His cell phone falls to the ground, and I pick it up with a warning. "Touch me again without permission and I'll break your fingers."

The guy holds out his hand, laughing. "Sorry, Xena."

"Dena!" Heat boils inside. *He dares to touch me? Sure, I turned myself over to him, but I'm not his property. He can't control me. He thinks we're the same, but he's nothing. Less than nothing.*

I grit my teeth against the invading rage. It infects me. This isn't my anger. It has the feel of my nightmares. I sense rather than see the black smoke coalesce around the guy's body 'cause of the shadows we stand in. But then one of the shadows strikes.

"No…no, stop!" I shout at the shadow, willing it to obey like it did in the alley. Only it's too filled with rage to hear. I need this bastard to get answers. I won't have any way of figuring out the truth without him. But it's too late.

The man screams—a wordless cry of agony. He beats at his skin as it chars, flaking to ash. Fat runs from his frame to form a spreading puddle at my feet. He burns, and I scream in incoherent fury at the shadow.

A hand grabs my arm and whips me around. I'm still screaming, only this time at Anders. Too late, he's finally come to my rescue. I slap at his hands, not sure what I'm yelling. I think I'm ordering him to stop or telling the shadow to stop. It doesn't matter in the end.

Anders stands over the man's burning remains. He steps back and clutches his stomach as if he's about to vomit. "What did you do?"

It takes a minute for the accusation to sink in. I stare at him with my mouth hanging open. My brain shuts down, overloaded. I don't know what to say.

Anders's hands grip my shoulders. "Answer me, Dena." He punctuates each word with a shake. Spit flies from his lips, sprinkling my face. A pulsing vein stands out on his forehead. "You killed him. How?"

"I didn't!" Shaking my head, I twist my shoulders and pull free, careful not to use my new strength. That would be disastrous. "I didn't kill him. I tried to stop it."

Anders thrusts his face in mine. "Don't lie. You touched him, and he caught on fire. I'm not sure how, but I'll figure it out."

"You're delusional…" I back away, shaking out my clothing. "How would I set him on fire? Do you see an accelerant? I know, I puked gasoline all over him. Did you taste the gasoline I drank with my beer when you kissed me?" My words jumble, coming faster and faster. Not making a lick of sense. But neither does his accusation.

I pull my pockets inside out. "No matches." I choke on a sob. "Come on…You know the shadow killed him. You were right here, Anders. You saw it. I know you saw it!"

"There's no such thing as a murderous shadow. The only thing I saw was you!" He snatches for me. I lunge backward, ducking his outstretched arm, then pivot on my heel and sprint toward the flashing lights of the patrol car pulling in front of my house. I'm verging on the edge of hysterics by the time I reach my yard.

Deputy Winters, the same deputy who found me in the alley, grabs me as I try to run past. "Dena? Stop, stop you're safe." She pulls me to the side of the driveway. "What happened?"

"She's being detained for suspicion of murder!" Anders yells, coming up from behind. He spins me around and snaps a handcuff on my right wrist. Surprised, I jerk my arm to the side a little too hard and the metal cuff strikes Anders on the head. He falls to his knee, and I stumble away from him.

Another deputy who outweighs me by a hundred

pounds—he's a big boy—blindsides me. One minute I'm on my feet, and the next, I'm eating dirt. He presses a knee into my spine, wrenches my arms behind my back, and slaps on the dangling cuff.

More concerned with dragging air into my lungs, I don't think about fighting. I'll only be in worse trouble. Winters and the other deputy each grab an elbow and haul me upright. I feel woozy. Rather than two deputies, I see four…or six. My stomach rolls, and I heave. Winters sidesteps the vomit, but doesn't release her hold on the handcuffs.

"Put her in your car, Kyle," Anders orders the deputy holding me upright. "After the scene's secure, I'll take her to the station. Eva and I will prep for the crime scene techs."

Kyle grunts his assent. He half drags me to the car as I stumble, off balance. My head's spinning. It's all I can do not to vomit again. Part of me wants to shout. To protest how unfair this is, but what's the point? Anders sees and hears what he wants. All his talk of trust…lies. His kiss, manipulation. He lulled me into a false sense of security. None of what happened earlier reflects the truth.

I'm done appealing to him. But self-pity is a luxury I can't indulge in. My only lead's a burned carcass in the middle of the road, and I'm going to jail for his murder. How crazy is that?

The area in the back of the patrol car is tight, and my legs begin to cramp. I eye the giant leaning against the side of the car, making sure he's not paying attention to me, then lift my legs and scrunch my butt up over my hands until I'm cuffed in the front.

I wrap my arms over my raised knees, wiping my face on my

jeans. These are the last tears I plan to cry. I'm strong. I'll figure out what the hell's going on. The first problem is dealing with my arrest.

I stare out the fogged window. I flash back to the second gunman's head exploding upon impact from the bullet. From my position in the car, I can see the dead men piled one on top of the other like cords of wood, bodies nothing but lifeless husks. One moment they were trying their best to kill Anders and me, and the next, they were dead.

As I focus on the bodies, sweat breaks out across my skin, and I shiver. I'm missing something…I replay the scene in my mind. The first gunman burst in through the door. He blocked the entrance. Anders shot him. He fell back onto the second man, pinning him to the ground.

I blink and rub my eyes. The position of their bodies has changed. The first man, the one who fell on top of his partner, lies on the ground. Did the officers move the bodies? I doubt that's procedure. From everything I've seen on TV, they're supposed to wait for the medical examiner. I scrub the condensation from the window, trying to see.

The movement—a twitch of his outstretched arm—jars the body of the man lying beneath him and spills a little more gray matter onto my porch. The man's head rotates. The whites of his eyes blaze as they roll in my direction.

The scream seems yanked from my chest. Full and deep, using every bit of the air I hoarded from the moment I realized the man still lives. When the sound trails off, I scream again, trying to get someone's attention, but Anders and Winters are inside the house.

The other deputy, Kyle, stands on the opposite side of the car from the bodies, oblivious to the supposed dead man who rolls into a crouch and moves toward us in a laborious, lumbering shamble that quickly gains speed. I pound on the window. The sound of the cuffs striking glass rings out.

Kyle glares, throwing open the driver's-side door. He leans in to slide open the Plexiglas window dividing the front half of the car. "Shut up," he orders, pulling out a can of pepper spray. He aims it at my eyes.

I freeze, not from the threat of being sprayed, which is what Kyle obviously thinks, but because the man reaches him. Before I can warn him, he grabs Kyle by the waist and pulls him from the car. One arm wraps around his neck. Kyle wraps his hands around the arm, but he can't break the dead man's grip. His face reddens then darkens to purple from lack of oxygen. His fingers scratch bloody furrows in the dead man's arm as he suffocates. The wounds stop bleeding almost immediately.

It doesn't take long for Kyle to lose consciousness, but the man doesn't release him. Even as I scream at him to let Kyle go, he keeps on the pressure. His cold eyes, devoid of emotion, remain locked on mine. After several minutes, he smiles and releases Kyle, who slides to the ground.

He reaches for the door handle to open the rear door. I grab the arm rest, using all my considerable new strength to keep it closed. He jerks the door. The sound of ripping metal fills the air as he tears the door from the car.

"Oh shit!" *Dude's crazy.* I roll onto my stomach. The safety lock on the opposite door refuses to budge. I scream, repeatedly, for Anders or Winters. Either one would be better than nothing.

The man's hands clamp onto my ankles. I kick my feet, trying to break his grip. He grunts and drags my body across the seat.

My fingers scrabble for something to hold onto. Every time I get a good grip, he yanks on my feet and tears my fingers loose. Blood runs down my palms from my torn nails. With a final pull, I'm jerked from the car. My head hits the sidewalk.

* * *

The pain of my skin being scraped off wakes me. I'm being dragged down the street by my heels. Blood soaks my shirt. I twist, rolling sideways and kicking my feet to break the man's grip. From behind, Anders shouts for him to stop.

The man moves unnaturally fast. He releases one of my ankles, turns, and fires his gun in one graceful movement, like a ballerina doing a pirouette.

Anders flies backward. His body smacks the ground so hard that he bounces. I pray for him to get up, but I can tell by the contorted position of his body that he's been hurt bad. He's not getting up any time soon—maybe never—and my chest tightens. The only thing giving me hope is that I don't see the vortex. It hasn't come for his soul.

Come to think of it, if I'd thought to look for it when the assassins got shot, I would've known they'd come back as zombie terminators.

Winters runs from the side of the house where she'd been concealed in the shadows. She slides across the grass like she's heading for home plate, rolls into a protective crouch over Anders, raises her gun and fires. The impact of her bullets thrust the man holding my leg backward. Blood flowers on the front of his shirt. He releases my ankle to point his gun at Winters.

"Watch out!" I yell.

Winters glances in my direction, and then her body bucks as the bullets strike her chest. She falls onto her back, arms splayed.

"No!" I crawl toward them.

The assassin mutters something. His hands brush across my legs, but I kick them away. He darts to the side and runs forward. His foot lashes out. The toe of his boot rams into my side. Air explodes from my lungs along with the sound of cracking bones. I tumble through the air as if punted, then hit the ground with a heavy thud. I push up onto my elbows, but my eyes cross and I collapse onto my stomach.

The thick grass cushions the man's heavy steps so I'm surprised when nails dig into my scalp. He pulls me upright until I dangle by my hair, with only the tips of my toes touching the ground. With my head pulled back at an unnatural angle, I stare into the man's bloodless face. Madness fills the bloodshot whites of his eyes as his other hand closes around my throat and squeezes.

A bang fills the air, and his hold on my throat releases. I drop to the ground, gasping for air as the man stumbles. My eyes shift in the direction of the gunshot. Anders has rolled onto his stomach. He has his elbows planted on the ground, supporting the weight of his gun as he fires. The bullets strike the ground inches from my body. Chunks of gravel fly up to cut my face, and I do an old-fashioned duck-and-cover.

"Damn it, Dena. Get out of there!" Anders shouts, climbing to his knees.

His gun remains pointed at my assailant. How the hell does

he expect me to go anywhere? I'm injured, unarmed, and smack dab in the middle of a gunfight. But, really, anywhere else is better than here. I cover my face with my hands and throw myself sideways, rolling toward the curb.

The man lunges for me, but slips on the blood pooling at his feet from his numerous gunshot wounds. He collapses to his knees, and I think for sure he'll stay down, but he doesn't. He gets on his feet and points his gun at my head. *My God, it will never end. Why the hell won't he fucking die? Die already!*

He pulls the trigger.

CHAPTER 16

Common Ground

The trigger clicks. The chamber is empty, and I live to see another day.

Anders fires again. The bullet blows a chunk out of the assassin's hand, and the gun drops. The man screams with rage, but he doesn't come after me again. This time he runs.

Thank Jesus. Thank the Blessed Virgin. It's over.

And I'm finally going to listen to Reverend Prince and take my heathen ass back to church. If they let me back in after this.

Anders runs a few steps after the man, then collapses. The look on his face appears so shocked that I almost feel sorry for him. Then I recall the man wouldn't have been able to get to me if Anders hadn't handcuffed me in the back of a patrol car like a *fucking criminal*.

"Dena, are you hit?" he asks, crawling over and wrapping his arms around me. I press my body against his warmth. *I'm so cold.* My teeth chatter, and I'm trembling with shock.

Anders runs his hands across my body, inspecting every inch of exposed skin. "Where's the blood coming from? Is it all the other guy's? Are you okay?"

My injuries are healing, but my mind's stuck on stupid. I can't even form words. Nodding, I draw my knees into my chest and wrap my arms around them.

"Okay. Stay here while I check on Eva and Kyle," Anders says, pushing up from the ground, and I panic. I clutch his arms, afraid to let go. If he doesn't hold me together, I'll fly apart.

He presses a kiss to my forehead, then rises without a backward glance.

Sirens ring in the background. Now that the gunshots have stopped, neighbors flock from their homes. Dr. Eugene, the podiatrist from next door who's sweet on Pepper, runs over to give first aid to Winters. My legs hold my weight so I go over to assist him. Despite being shot several times, the deputy was wearing a Kevlar vest. No vital organs appear damaged, but the vest didn't cover her stomach.

"Hang in there, Eva. You'll be okay," I say, pressing a gauze pad against her wound. She kept me calm after she found me in the alley. Now I return the favor.

I thought Kyle was dead, but he's as tough as he looks. He still has a faint heartbeat, and Anders gives him CPR until the paramedics arrive to attend to the injured officers. Anders waves them off when they want to check him for injuries, claiming he's fine. Which doesn't sit right. I saw him get shot.

Then they check my injuries.

Given my rapid healing factor, the fact that my ribs are still cracked and I have a mild concussion means my initial injuries had been pretty serious. The paramedic checking me out asks if I want to go the hospital. I gaze around the yard filled with sheriff deputies, crime scene technicians processing my house, nosy neighbors bringing out their lawn chairs to watch the show, and the body with chunks of his brain drying out on my front porch. Plus I recall the pesky fact that while Anders acted like he cared after the shootout, he could remember he planned on arresting me at any moment.

Suddenly, a trip to the hospital seems like a vacation.

* * *

Susan sets me up with a bed in my own private corner of the emergency room. Not in the mood to be disturbed, I pull the drapes shut and think on what happened. How I'm able to move so fast. Became so strong that I can jump over a car. If I want answers, it's time to agree to Estrada's terms and give up the blood.

Susan bustles around the drapes. She has a wobbly grin on her face as she inspects my wounds. "Don't have time for a visit, but I wanted to give you an update. Deputy Winters's in surgery. One of the bullets punctured her intestine which complicates the procedure, but her prognosis is positive. Deputy Kyle is breathing on his own and will make a full recovery. You, on the other hand, look like shit."

I snort laugh. "They said I managed to get through this with no major injuries."

"Lucky you, second concussion this week, and of course,

Estrada isn't answering his cell phone. He's probably on a date and hopes to get lucky."

"He went out with Gabriella tonight. See if you can reach her cell."

"I'll let you know if I hear from either of them." Susan pours water into a glass from a pink plastic pitcher. "Does the sheriff's office know who those men were?"

"Not a clue. I'm barely on speaking terms with the detective in charge of my case." I shrug and wince at the pinch in my ribs.

It's difficult to feign detachment. Whenever I remember Anders's accusing tone, filled with rage and horror, demanding to know how I'd burned a man, I want to cry.

Speaking of burned, the drape slides open and Charles steps around the corner. A frown puckers his brow, and worry tightens the corners of his eyes. Upon seeing me, his expression relaxes, and he smiles. Warmth surges in my chest. Forgetting how much I hate him, I jump out of bed and throw myself in his arms. He hugs me tight against his chest, patting my back. "Shh, you're okay. Everything's okay."

I shake my head against his chest in denial. Everything most definitely is not okay. I am far from okay. Snot drips from my nose, and I've stained his shirt with my tears, but he lets me cry. Susan slips around the curtain, giving us the illusion of privacy. Charles shifts aside with my body still pressed against his, and pulls the drape closed. As it slides shut, my gaze meets Anders's across the room. A flash of emotion narrows his eyes, vanishing so quickly I can't be sure what he feels...relief, a touch of regret, longing. All of this flows through me as the shutters fall across his eyes. He turns away, leaving a lump of pain in my chest.

My face burns. I step away from Charles and grab a couple of tissues from the box on a stand next to the bed. I pass some to Charles and use the rest to mop up my face. "Sorry. It would be a shame if Vanessa got the wrong idea about this." I wave my hand between us. "It's just..."

"You need a friend."

I nod, biting my lip. "God Charles, I'm so glad you're here. I couldn't hold it together much longer. I'm sure the staff will be glad I won't run screaming through the ER."

Charles chuckles. "Why don't you get back in bed? I'll be here as long as you need someone. Speaking of, where's Gabriella? I didn't hear anything about her being involved."

I clutch at my chest.

Charles lurches forward at my reaction. "What the hell, Dee? Are you all right? Should I get Susan?"

I draw in a couple of deep breaths, massaging my chest to open the air passages that constricted when he mentioned her name. "Oh God, I don't know what to do," I whisper. "Gabriella, she's..."

"She's what? Dena, you're scaring me. Was she in the house? Is she...*dead*?"

"No, she's fine. Sorry." I take his hand, biting my lip. "Luckily, she went on a date. If she'd been home when those men attacked, they would've killed her." God, I feel so helpless. I need Mala. She'd know what to do, but she's not here. Plus she's been through enough trauma because of my family. I shouldn't drag her or anyone else into this, but I can't figure this out on my own.

I stare into Charles's open face. Once, I trusted him completely. His betrayal hardened my heart. I cut off my emotions and turned bitter. Sad. Lonely. For better or worse, I'll put my trust in him again.

"Charles, swear to keep what I tell you to yourself. Don't talk to anyone—not Vanessa, and especially not Detective Anders."

He takes a deep breath and nods. "Spill it."

"The men who attacked my house tried to kidnap me. If Anders hadn't been over, they would've succeeded. One of the men said I've got a bounty on my head. And before you ask, I've no idea why." Though I've got a pretty good guess it has to do with being juiced.

Charles's mouth opens, but I press my fingers to his lips.

"This guy said the only way my friends would be safe is if I went with him." I squeeze his hand, making sure he understands. "He said his boss would give me answers, and I'd be protected. I was going with him, but then he died."

Tears trickle from my eyes again. I hate crying. What purpose does it serve? But I can't stop. I feel so helpless. Useless.

Charles sits on the bed and pulls me down next to him. He wraps his arm around my shoulders, and I lean against his chest, remembering the feel of him. But I also compare it to Anders's solid chest. His skin had been so smooth. He radiated heat when he pulled me into his arms. Even mad at him, I felt a crushing sense of loss when the bullets struck his chest. He said he hadn't been injured, but I *saw* him get shot. If he'd been wearing a bullet-proof vest, he would've been undamaged, but I felt his bare chest against my palms before the doorbell rang. He hadn't been wearing a vest.

"Charles, can you track down an address for the last number called on this phone?" I hold out the bounty hunter's cell phone.

"If it's possible. But this is outside my jurisdiction. You should speak to Anders, get authorization…"

"No, leave him out of it. He never even bothered to ask what happened to me. I was kidnapped, and he didn't care. If I did burn the assassin, it would've been in self-defense. But maybe it's for the best. We've got time to find proof of my kidnapping. Anders won't be able to ignore me then."

"Then report it…Anders's accusations, all of it, to Lieutenant Caine or Sheriff Keyes. They'll believe you."

"That's what I'm most afraid of. What if they start a huge investigation? They'll only get hurt trying to protect me. Just like Winters and Kyle."

"Shit, Dee. You're asking me to put my job at risk."

"I know."

"You'll be in danger." He shakes his head.

"I'm already in danger. They won't stop coming after me. This is the only way I can think of to get answers. It's probably the stupidest plan ever. I'd never ask you to get involved, but I'm desperate."

Charles's arm tightens around my waist. I can tell he's working through the situation in his mind. My feelings toward him have softened. In the last week, he's repeatedly put himself out to help. So maybe he's not my One and Only, but we can be friends.

"Okay, we'll do it your way until we get more information." He lifts a hand up, halting my words. "I think you need to involve Anders, but I understand your objections. There's a way to trace the cell, but it's not legal. And it'll take time. I'll let you know when I find anything."

I give him a hard squeeze of relief. Of course, this is when Vanessa walks in. She shakes her head, as if unable to believe what she's seeing. I know the feeling. I did the same when I walked into Charles's apartment and found them going at it doggie style in the middle of the living room.

Funny how the memory doesn't make me sick to my stomach anymore.

I lean away from Charles, flushing. "V-Vanessa," I stutter, then give in to the urge to explain the situation. I don't know why. It would serve her right to stew in her own jealous juices. I guess I don't feel up to a fight and Charles deserves happiness in his life. "It's not what it looks like. I just…"

Vanessa walks to the bed in silence, face inscrutable, but her chocolate eyes are full of emotion. I have time to suck in a deep breath before her arms wrap around my neck, squeezing.

Vanessa's trying to kill me. I struggle to pull free, but her skinny little arms tighten around my neck. I'm debating whether I should use my newfound super-strength to rip her arms out of their sockets and club her in the head with them, when it sinks in that she's sobbing. Charles also has tears in his eyes. He watches us embrace with what looks like paternal satisfaction. What a fucking reunion.

It's good I took a deep breath before the hug 'cause several minutes pass until Vanessa pulls it together and releases her hold. Charles pulls her onto his lap, and she curls up like a cat, mewling as if her best friend passed away.

"You almost died," she chokes out, echoing my thoughts. "Again…"

I almost say something scathing, like, "Why would you care if I died?" But I guess what Uncle Ben said is true, with "great power comes great responsibility." Time to stop wallowing in self-pity. Charles won't be so willing to help if I keep insulting his fiancée, especially when she seems to be undergoing a metamorphosis of her own.

I'd tuned out and missed part of her seemingly heartfelt apology, but now I cobble it together enough to be gracious. "I'm fine, Vanessa. I accept your apology."

"I miss you, Dena. You were my closest friend. I wish I'd done things differently with Charles, but…I love him. I didn't know how to tell you."

Of course, love excuses betrayal. I shake my head, brushing the thought aside. Being magnanimous is difficult. "Look, Vanessa. It's all water under the bridge. I can say with absolute certainty that I'm no longer physically attracted to Charles." I suppress a slight shudder, revolted at the idea of seeing Charles naked again.

Hurt flares in his eyes, and I quickly continue, "My feelings for him are platonic. I've grown up a lot in the last week, and the ability to forgive is a skill that grows over time." *But I'll never forget. I learn from my mistakes.*

"Are you sure, Dee? I know I've been a bitch, but I've been insecure. Your attack, plus the fact that you're seeing another man put things in perspective. I'd like for us to be friends again."

Ugh, self-centered…It's always about her feelings. She feels bad. She wants to be friends. Never mind how I feel. Exhaustion makes my voice thick. "Vanessa, please. I've had a hard day. I'll talk to you both later, okay?"

Charles meets my gaze with a covert nod. He'll let me know if he finds anything. He pushes open the curtain and leads Vanessa away. With each step she takes, my tension releases. I curl up in the bed, staring at the ceiling.

I've been in schoolyard fights. Kids used to tease me and my brothers all the time. Pepper left right after I hit puberty so I didn't have a woman in the house to talk to. Mala's mama—well, Ms. Jasmine wasn't the best role model. She tended to use booze or sex to cope with her problems. I'm not the sort to let people run all over me or my family, but I've got a gift for gab that could talk myself out of most sticky situations. The martial arts training I took in case words failed. I've never thought of myself as a particularly strong person, especially when I compare myself to my cousin. But the one thing I've discovered about myself this week is that, when push comes to shove, I shove. I fought Tolson, almost to death. I fought those men tonight with every ounce of my strength and, like that man rising from the dead, I'm a survivor.

Susan sweeps in to check on my recovery. "Not seeing double? What about nausea?"

"Fine and fine. What about Anders? He came in earlier. Was he injured?"

"No, he said the blood's Winters's. He's checking on the guys then will probably go down to the morgue."

I sit up, surprised. "Are you saying the man whose brain spilled all over my porch is at the hospital? Not the coroner's office?"

"He still showed signs of life, so they brought him here. He passed in the operating room."

Signs of life? With that injury. Good God Almighty. This isn't good.

Susan frowns. "Are you sure you're all right? You're looking awfully pale."

I force a smile. It probably looks ghastly. "Sue, tell me I'm being ridiculous to worry. People don't come back from the dead. Right?"

"Not unless they're Jesus," Susan says, then pokes my arm. "Or you."

I chuckle, but hate where my thoughts are going. God, *please let this be over.* The guy in the morgue lost half of his brain. Even on *The Walking Dead* there's no healing from a head shot. The problem is, a man came back to life tonight, without medical intervention. The laws governing life and death have already been broken.

CHAPTER 17

Don't Be a Hero

The fact that I've snuck into the morgue to verify that a dead man has stayed dead says a lot about the state of my sanity. That I'm running down a faintly lit hallway toward the screaming rather than away, once again verifies I'm certifiable. The last time I found myself in this position, Squirrel ended up a casualty of the shadow. This time, it might be me. Still, I don't hesitate. I'm the only person who stands a chance of neutralizing the man who shambles in my direction like a damn zombie straight from a horror movie.

The missing part of his brain must've controlled rational thought. All that remains is a capacity for mindless violence, and judging from the blood trail he's left, someone has already fallen victim to his rage.

Bones grow back together over the ragged hole in his skull.

The pieces reform, coming together in a transparent, fragile matrix that seems to have the consistency of gelatin and the color of freshwater pearls. He screams when he catches sight of me, an inhuman roar. He lurches in my direction and then turns on his heel, quick…quicker than the eye can follow, even if it's slower than he'd be if uninjured. He looks over his shoulder and screams again.

A security guard exits a side room. He stares at the undead man, stunned, before he shouts, finger reflexively pulling the trigger of his gun. Each bullet thrusts the man back, then he staggers forward a few steps and back again, each time getting closer to the guard. With a final leap forward, he grabs the guard's outstretched arm, using it as a lever to throw him—toward me.

I shout, lifting my arms. The guard slams into my chest, and we fly back. I hold onto him as we slide across the linoleum, feeling a sense of déjà vu.

I release the guard and roll toward my attacker rather than away. My legs wrap around the man's calves and I twist, summersaulting backward. The force of the roll throws him over my head. He smashes headfirst into the wall. He slides down in a motionless heap.

I crawl back to the security guard. The nametag says his name is Pete. He can't be more than twenty-five. He stares into my eyes, his own filling with pain and pleading for help. I've never felt so useless in my life.

His fingers fumble at his belt. "Radio…call for backup."

I remove the radio. "Please, someone…anyone, I need help in the morgue."

Pete's eyes begin to glaze. He hears the music…Death's song, an ethereal flute playing its seductive melody. It soothes his pain, mesmerizes and cajoles. He's falling under its spell. Soon he'll let go. My vision shifts as the veil to the other side thins in preparation. The aquamarine of his aura fades, then grays. But it's not black. There's still a chance for him to pull through, if he gets help soon.

I slap his cheek. "Don't you dare," I snarl the order. "Stay awake. They're coming for you."

He blinks, nodding. His gaze moves over my shoulder, and his eyes widen.

"You've got to be kidding!" I hunch into a protective crouch over Pete and then leap to my feet.

The assassin slides up the wall. Rage fills me. The jerk just won't stay dead. He charges, and I throw myself toward him, arms outstretched. Our bodies impact in the air, driving the breath from my lungs. Darkness rolls across my vision as we hit the ground, but I push it back. I hold onto him, kicking and gouging at his body as we roll across the floor. The returning blows are as mindless, but damn it, they hurt. With a solid jab of his knee, he thrusts me off of him and I slide across the floor like a turtle on its shell.

He rises, unstoppable. And unlike me, he doesn't seem to feel pain. The elevator dings. Someone has answered my radio for help. I have to lure the assassin away because I can't allow anyone else to get hurt.

So I do the most practical thing for everyone involved. I run away.

His bellow of rage echoes through the corridor, bouncing off the walls. I glance over my shoulder. Once I'm sure he's following me, I head down a hallway leading away from the voices exiting the elevator.

Never having been on the lower level of the hospital, it doesn't take long before I'm lost. The shambling steps follow. I slow enough for him to keep up, almost feeling the heat of his rancid breath on my neck, but not enough to be caught. There has to be a staircase leading upstairs. Or a weapon to help me kill this creature from *Night of the Living Dead* who refuses to die.

When we're far enough from the elevator for the responders to be safe, I pick up my speed 'cause I really don't want to fight him again without a weapon. I skid around a corner, losing my balance and ricocheting off the opposite wall. He still follows, but he's far enough behind that I can't see him. The long, empty corridor ends at a blank wall. Given my high degree of panic, it's no wonder that I've cornered myself in a dead end.

I huddle against the wall, gasping for breath. My head feels stuffed full of cotton, and I sway with dizziness. I'd ignored the pain from my injuries with the spurt of adrenaline filling my body during the fight, but that's fading. My body's one giant throbbing bruise, but miracle of miracles, I don't think anything is broken.

The halting steps get louder. Soon he'll come around the corner and will have a clear view of me. I imagine his satisfaction at seeing me trapped—if he's capable of any feelings. I've given up hope he'll collapse from his injuries. Those will be healing like mine.

The overhead lights flicker like crazed lightning bugs. One by one they pop, exploding with a flash of light. The corridor darkens until only the light directly overhead remains, then it too ignites. I shriek, raising my hands over my head as sparks drift down, burning my skin, and an answering bellow fills the corridor.

Shit! He's here… His shuffling footfalls move toward where I crouch in the corner. I can't see him—my monster in the dark.

A hand grabs my wrist. My mouth opens, prepared to scream again, but another hand closes over my mouth. My feet leave the ground as I'm lifted into the air. My body slides up the wall. It's dragging my sorry ass across the ceiling. I kick my legs wildly, unable to break free. A body climbs under mine, holding me up, and I'm now a fly stuck to the ceiling in a sticky paper. Gravity defied, except for my hair, which trails down in a ragged waterfall around my face.

My brain screams that what's happening is impossible. It's illogical. My perception's twisted upside down. It feels like I'm lying on top of a warm chest, but my back presses against the ceiling. My arms are pinned between our chests, and I can't move. A cool nose touches my neck and inhales. All the trapped air in my lungs rushes out in a sigh of relief.

"Ashmael," I whisper, as my shadow man breathes in my scent.

He responds by licking a tear from my cheek.

Footsteps drag closer until they're beneath us. My mouth opens with an inhale, and Ashmael's mouth slants across mine. His tongue slips between my parted lips, and the sweetness of his saliva fills my mouth. I drink him in, savoring his taste. Fear fades. His tongue caresses my tongue, coaxing it to dance in time to his kiss. My chilled skin warms, then tingles. The aphrodisiac I swear is in his saliva loosens my tense muscles. My aches disappear. The kiss deepens. His hands slide down my hips and grip my thighs. Wrapping my legs around his waist, he draws our bodies closer. We melt into each other, which given his incorporeal nature might not be strictly metaphorical.

A groan from below acts like a slap to the face. The lust boiling inside vanishes. *God, this is so surreal.* I'm suspended from a ceiling in a spirit's embrace, while a murderous, zombie-like creep thrashes around directly beneath us.

Kissing no longer seems like the best idea.

Gravity hangs heavy on my body—an irresistible force drawing me toward the ground. I don't know how Ashmael suspends us in the air. I'm not a scientist, and whether this is a manipulation of electrons or something equally mystifying, I don't know. I do know if his mojo gives out and he becomes incorporeal again, I'll fall.

In the distance, a voice I recognize calls my name, and I shudder. The man below hears him, too. He bellows in response, and his footsteps pound down the hall. "Anders!" I shout, thrashing against the body restraining mine, "Anders, run!"

Anders yells my name again. This time he's closer.

"Put me down." I wiggle against the spirit. "Please, I have to help him. It's Anders…that thing is going after Anders."

Rather than releasing me, Ashmael pulls my body closer. His lips move to my neck, nibbling the underside of my jaw. His hand caresses my thigh, heedless of my pleading for release. I refuse to fall into his lust trap again. Frustration grows until it's a palpable wave flowing through me. I heave against him with all my strength. A pop rings in my ears, and I fall headfirst. I throw my hands up to protect my face. Arms circle my waist, and I'm jerked back against Ashmael's chest.

I reach out with trembling fingers and touch the ground, only inches from my face. "Oh, Ash," I breathe, "thank you. Thank you."

A hand brushes my fingers then tightens. I'm lifted to my feet. The spirit leads me through the dark corridor until the blinding light of a man burning in the distance allows me to see again. I step forward, but invisible arms wrap around my shoulders like steel cords.

"Anders is up there." I push at the arms until he releases his hold. I search the empty hall for the presence I feel just out of sight. "I'm sorry, Ash. I promise, I'll find you later. Thank you for saving my life... again."

I inch closer to the burning man, who minutes before had been trying to kill me. He thrashes around, still on his feet. I cough, choking on the smoke. The acrid smell makes my stomach clench, and I swallow the vomit inching over my tongue. The man collapses to the ground, still smoking. I'm scared to step around him. He's stopped flailing about, but what if he regenerates? His ability to heal has surprised me too many times to count tonight.

On the plus side, now I know the only surefire way to kill the undead, and it's not a bullet to the head. I have to burn them.

Anders moans, and I meet his glazed eyes through the flickering flames. Blood coats his face, but I don't see an injury. He blinks. His eyes clear and drop to the body then flash back up.

Crap, I know that look. It's blame-game time, starring Dena Acker, the wicked evildoer, as contestant number one.

* * *

Anders drives me to the sheriff's office. I've maintained a steady silence since we left the hospital, not bothering to argue the injustice of being arrested. From experience, I know trying to defend myself won't do any good. I was found at a crime scene—again—and my guilt was a foregone conclusion once the security guard gave Anders my description.

Anders dumps me off with a bored-looking deputy who escorts me to an interview room. A hidden camera has been fixed behind a light in the corner. Mirrored glass shields the observers on the other side of a large window. The deputy handcuffs me to a chair. Both the chair and the dirty table across from it are bolted to the floor. The requisite box of Kleenex sits in the middle of the table, just out of reach.

I stare at my hands as the door shuts behind the deputy. Then I wait and wait…long enough that I really need to pee, though I will never beg Anders for a bathroom break. I'd rather pee my pants.

When Anders finally comes into the room, he moves until he hovers over me like a dark, malignant shadow. No, worse than a shadow. Ashmael has never arrested me and made me hold my urine for hours. I hate Anders, and I wish with all my heart that he hadn't pushed me out of the path of that bullet. I'd be better off dead. My life sucks.

"Why am I here?" Silence greets my question. I meet Anders's cynical gaze and cross my arms. "I want a lawyer."

He leans over the table. "Dena, you're only making the situation worse."

"Despite the fact that you never Mirandized me when I was arrested, I know that I'm entitled to have a lawyer present before being questioned." I refuse to look at him. It hurts too much. "Give me my phone call."

"Dena..." he growls. " I didn't read you your rights because you're not under arrest. I need you to answer my questions."

"If I'm not under arrest then I'm being illegally detained. Undo these cuffs, I'm leaving. Now!"

A knock on the mirrored window startles me, but not as much as when Anders's hands slap the table loud enough that I jump. The cuffs bite into my wrists. I grimace, clamping down on the huge part of me itching to give a hard tug on the cuffs and snap free. He storms from the room. His raised voice comes from the other side of the door, and when whomever he was yelling at responds, he doesn't sound pleased.

Sheriff Keyes storms into the room a few minutes later. "Dena, I had no idea you were the one brought in. I'm sorry." He takes off the handcuffs. I shake my hands to get the circulation flowing again. He pauses, staring at me in silent expectation.

"Thanks, sir," I say with a slight nod. He's always been good to my family. I follow him from the room to the outer office, where my cousin paces like a caged lion.

I run to her, but not at supersonic speed 'cause she doesn't pass out from shock. I pick her up and spin her around. "Hot damn, Malaise Jean Marie LaCroix. It's about time you showed up."

"Waydene Madonna Acker, if you drop me—" Mala can't finish the threat for laughing.

I set her on her feet, so relieved she's back that my legs feel spongy, like I've got jellyfish tentacles attached to my torso. "You've no idea how happy I am to see you."

Her arms tighten around my waist, holding me upright.

"Saints, cuz, how do you manage to get yourself in trouble every time I go to New Orleans?"

"I'd like to know the answer to that myself." I let out a huge sigh and step back with a shrug. "Guess you need to stick around town."

"Babysitting you isn't how I planned on spending my spring break, but I guess I owe you." She smiles, but guilt flashes in her dark eyes. Damn, I didn't mean to upset her.

With a sigh, I tilt my head toward the door. "Let's get out of here."

As we leave the station, Anders stands in the parking lot. His face is washed of expression, but I know him well enough to tell when he's pissed. Tension holds his shoulders stiff, and as his hand goes into his pocket to pull out a set of keys, I notice his badge and his gun are missing from his waistband.

Mala follows my gaze. "I can't believe Anders is still harassing you."

"He's also saved my life."

"That's his job. Well, it was his job. Cocky jerk took advantage of his position. He's suspended."

I glance over my shoulder, but Anders is gone. My chest tightens. "Why?"

"Why do you think?"

"Because of my arrest? Couldn't Sheriff Keyes cut him some slack? He saved my life after those three men attacked!"

"Calm down, Dee. No point getting upset over Anders. He created his own problems, and they've nothing to do with you. Sheriff Keyes and Bessie filled me in on what's been going on, but I can't help without more information."

"What can I tell you?" My voice has a slightly hysterical quality to it. I focus on steadying myself. "It's all so crazy—guys stalking me, breaking into my home, burning bodies." I bite my lip. "Whatever's going on is Twilight Zone weird. I hate to drag you into my mess after what you went through last year, but I don't have a choice."

"Wait. Slow down and tell me what's happened since I left."

I follow her to her truck and climb in beside her. Her dark eyes shine in the dark. Now that I've had a chance to think, I don't know what to say without sounding insane. Guess it's best to just spill it on the table and let the chips fall where they may.

"Gabriella said you went to New Orleans to dig up info on Anders." At her nod, I continue. "Well, I did some digging on my own. Anders told me the murdered men were after me." I take a deep breath. "He thinks they used to belong to a gang run by your aunt Magnolia. After Magnolia died, someone else took over the organization. That's why he didn't want you on the case."

Mala lets out a strangled gasp. "What?"

"Don't worry. I told him you didn't know your aunt was a mob boss. And you certainly didn't take over her business once she passed away."

"Of course I didn't take over her business. It was pretty obvious that Magnolia had some shady ties to the underworld. She employed a bunch of thugs she called "private security guards," for goodness' sakes. And she used their leader to try to kill me. I'd be a fool to let myself get trapped in whatever web she spun to control me."

A bitter taste fills my mouth. "So Anders was right. You knew?"

"I suspected but hearing it confirmed by Anders only verifies it was the right choice to dump my so-called inheritance." A frown forms between her brows. "So Anders thinks the person who put the bounty on your head took over her business?"

"Yeah, he…" *Oh wow.* "Mala, it's too easy."

"I still have to talk my lawyer into giving me the name of the buyer, but this is a concrete lead. Which is more than what Anders has." She lets out a cackle that leaves me rolling my eyes. *Drama Queen.*

"Let's get out of here."

Mala starts the ignition. "I can't wait to see his face when I solve this case. He'll regret the day he fired me."

"I'm sure he's already considered this angle. Just like how he thinks that Magnolia was responsible for bringing me out of my coma." I hold my breath, waiting a few seconds for denial, then continue, "He saw the video feed at the hospital. You were there, too." I choke out a pained laugh, remembering the conversation. "I told him I wasn't a zombie, but I'm not sure that's the truth."

"Oh well." Mala's dark eyelashes dip to conceal her eyes. "It's complicated. Your body didn't die, but your soul…"

"Magnolia raised me from the dead?" My heart squeezes. It's hard to catch my breath.

"No, I did."

Crazy. I've finally gone crazy. "Oh." A shiver rattles my teeth. *So cold.* I flip the heater on. Warm air blasts from the vent. "So you really are a Hoodoo Queen?" I ask in a teasing tone, still waiting for her to bust herself out. She's got a terrible sense of humor. And she laughs at her own jokes. I don't know how Landry stands it.

This joke isn't funny. She's taking it too far. *Play it off, Dee.*

"Hoodoo Queen." Mala slaps the vent closed on her side. "Stupid title. No, I'm the last LaCroix. All the power from generations of women in my family spilled into me after Mama and Magnolia died. The ability to see the spirits of the dead is only one of my abilities. Another is pulling souls from the other side and stuffing them back into their bodies."

"Like me." *My hands are so cold.* I cross my arms and stick them under my armpits. *Why isn't she laughing?*

She gives a slow nod. "Dark magic goes against the natural order. It came with a high price tag—a life for a life. I killed Redford Delahoussaye so you could live. He had you trapped in purgatory. I couldn't let him keep torturing you." Her liquid brown eyes melt. "I played God. I don't regret getting you back, but…everything that happened the night of the earthquake is my fault. It's a price I'll never repay."

Oh God, she's serious. I hunch into the seat. Her explanation's too elaborate. She's a good actress, but not this good. *Why can't I warm up?*

"Dee," Mala whispers, "say something."

She looks so sad. I should hug her, but I don't. Now I know why I hear Death's song. Why it's drawn to me. *I'm dead.* I stare at my hands. The cuts from my fight are healed. A zombie can't be killed. It's already dead. *I'm dead.*

"Dee, I'm sorry. I should've told you everything. I will now."

"No! Later." I swallow hard. My head's gonna explode, and probably reform like the morgue zombie's if I hear any more. The tears I should cry 'cause I'm dead start to fall. "I'm so scared, Mala. So scared…"

Mala pulls me into a hug, and I sob into her T-shirt. Inhaling her strawberry shampoo, I'm transported back to when we were little girls. Back then, it was Mala and me against the world. Together, we weren't afraid of monsters; we slayed them. Her life wasn't all sunshine and daisies, but somehow she managed to see magic in the world. I had the rose-colored glasses ripped from my eyes when Pepper abandoned us and Dad lost his ever-loving mind. After that, I saw life as it is. And until I died, I found nothing magical about it.

Everything is different now.

I'm the monster in the dark.

And I have something to fight for and protect to the bitter end. Mala saved me from Redford Delahoussaye. It's my turn to protect Mala and Gabriella. Time to stop feeling sorry for myself and pull it together.

'Cause the cool thing about being dead is, I've got no life to lose.

I sniff and regain control. "I need you to take me over to a friend's house. Can you do that for me?"

"I'd rather take you home. Landry and the Rev will help...." Her eyes are puffy, but her expression is calm, thoughtful even, as she leans back in the seat. "But you don't want them involved, right? And if I force you, you'll just climb out a window like you did in high school for that Carrie Underwood concert."

I laugh, wondering what she'd say if I told her my last attempt at climbing out a window landed me on top of Anders. I sober at that image. "I'm done climbing out windows. I'm old enough to use a door."

I text Ferdinand about needing a safe place to hide. No questions asked, he sends the address of some "friends." They live off the grid, in the one place nobody goes: Bayou du Sang. I thought we lived rough until we turn off Old Lick onto a narrow, muddy road. Despite Ferdinand's directions, we get lost several times. The road winds through the high areas of the swamp, not following a straight path.

Mala clutches the steering wheel, muttering, "I hate this place."

I blink into the darkness of the old-growth trees overhead. "They say the ghosts of the dead walk here."

My cousin's head whips in my direction. Black pits where her eyes should be bore into me.

Shivering, I rub my arms. "What? You said you see ghosts."

"Yes," she whispers. "They're all around us. Can't you feel them?"

"God, I shouldn't have encouraged you. Stop being so dramatic; you're freaking me out. And watch the road."

Her foot eases up on the gas. "Now who's being dramatic? I'm barely going five miles an hour." The road ahead branches out at a crossroad. Mala stops the truck. "Your friend's directions suck. Do they say which way to go?"

"Left."

Mala slams on the brakes, and I yelp. My hand slaps the dashboard. "What the hell?"

"We've hit a dead end." She twists in her seat. "I can't turn around. The road drops off on either side. You'll have to get out and navigate."

I've never liked how the swamp sounds once the sun sets. I'm not afraid of the dark. Or the mosquitos buzzing around my ears. It's the chittering and creaking in the air. The cry of a bobcat in the distance, like a woman shrieking for help. It's the way the bushes rustle, and the wind moans through the branches overhead. My mind plays tricks on me as I walk backward down the dark road with only the flashlight from my cellphone. The hair rises on the back of my neck, and I swear eyes watch from the darkness. I'd pass this off to paranoia if I hadn't felt the same way right before Tolson attacked me. If I'd listened to my instincts that night, I would've gone back into Munchies and asked Adam to walk me out.

I catch myself staring over my shoulder every few steps, my body tense and ready to fight. My feet squelch in the mud. A light drizzle blurs the red glow of the taillights, leaving me blinking as if my vision will suddenly clear. I can't stop shivering.

It's a relief when we reach the crossroads.

Mala pulls a U-turn and points the truck in the opposite direction. Her fingers drum on the steering wheel when I climb in. "Landry's gonna kill me. He expected me home hours ago. And if I get this truck stuck in a ditch, holy hell, I'll never hear the end of it." She points at a downed tree in the road. "How exactly are we supposed to get past that?"

I sigh. "Guess I'll walk in."

"Hell no. Not by yourself," she says in her law woman voice. Whenever we played cops and robbers as kids, she pretended to be her hero, Deputy Bessie Caine. Calm and deadly. I know there's no point in arguing, but I try. "What about your truck?"

"It can take care of itself. You can't."

Maybe not before I died, but I doubt much can take me out anymore. Mala, on the other hand, is still human. I remind myself of this as I slide protectively in front her—'cause wouldn't you know it, her words are put to the test the moment we exit the truck.

CHAPTER 18

Allies and Puppies

Two figures melt from the shadows, one big-boned and the other thin to the point of looking emaciated. The metallic glint of the thin guy's machete flashes in the high beams of the truck parked on the other side of the fallen tree. He steps forward, and I'm able to see him clearly. He's Latino, mid-twenties, with buzzed black hair. He's dressed in an oversized, black button-up shirt, baggie jeans, and black boots.

"Who sent you?" he asks.

"Ferdinand," I say, ignoring a sharp hiss from Mala. She grabs my elbow, and I pat her hand. Throwing bravado into my voice, I tip my chin. "He said to ask for Angelo?"

"He didn't say nothing about two girls," the same guy says. I assume he's Angelo.

"She's my cousin. She's dropping me off."

"She doesn't look nothing like you."

"Most people think we look a lot alike." When he remains silent, I snap back. "We come from different branches of the family tree. Why? You got a problem with black people?"

Mala squeezes my elbow in warning, and I back down. I hate when people judge. Like I can't call her family 'cause our skin's different shades.

"Didn't say that." He sounds indignant. Maybe I shouldn't be so judgmental myself. "I'm saying you can come in free, but your cousin has to pay. This ain't no free shelter."

Mala steps forward with her jaw jutted like a bulldog about to chomp on a skinny little bone. "Like I'd trust her going off alone into the backwoods with the two of you."

Angelo steps back, and the hand holding the knife jerks up. "Step off! I owe Ferdinand a favor, but not big enough to deal with two PMSing females."

"I'll show you PMSing," my cousin hisses. This time I grab her elbow and jerk her back. Things have gotten off on the wrong track. As annoyed as I am with the little man, I need him.

"Both of you, relax. Mala won't be staying, Angelo. Once I'm safe, she'll go home—"

"But—" Mala begins, but I override her.

"Or Landry will come looking for you. Do you really want to explain this?" I wave my hands to encompass the whole stupid situation. "Ferdinand wouldn't send me out here if he didn't think I'd be safe."

"About Ferdinand. Are you talking about Ferdinand Lafitte? Guy who used to work for my aunt?"

"Yeah. Why?"

"'Cause I'll lay down money that the bastard knows what's going on. Ferdie and I are long overdue for a chat." Mala steps forward. "Angelo, I'm going in or we're both leaving. What do you think Ferdinand would do if he found out you screwed this up?"

Angelo drops the knife down to his side. "Shit; fine."

He and the big guy get back in the truck. It doesn't take long for them to wrench the tree to the side. Mala and I follow them down the road in her truck. When I question her about Ferdinand, she says it's a long story and she needs to concentrate on navigating.

I lean back in the seat and rub the goose bumps on my arms. A quiet Mala is a scary Mala. She only clams up when she's strategizing. Whether the plan she devises will be any good or a load of crap remains to be seen. But it won't be the first time I've waded into some nasty business without my rubber boots.

Another five minutes of bumping down a narrower path ends at a gate. Barbed wire lines the top, as well as the fence encircling the property. Motion sensor-activated spotlights light up the driveway and yard we enter after passing through the keypad-operated gate. For being set off in the middle of nowhere, I expected it to be more rundown. Instead, it's set up with high-tech surveillance equipment, which I assume is powered by a generator somewhere on the property.

"I think these guys are drug dealers," Mala whispers, as if they can hear us. She pulls the truck in behind theirs and shuts it off. Neither of us move. Shadows streak from all corners of the yard, barking and growling. Dogs scare me. I once got bit by a stray and had to get rabies shots. It sucked, big time.

Angelo stands in front of our truck and waves at us. Yeah...
hell no.

I roll down the window. "Can you put the dogs up?"

"You'll be fine. They know you're with me." He scratches a
pit bull behind the ears then slaps his leg and whistles. The dogs
scatter. He heads toward the house, not bothering to see if we'll
follow. He probably doesn't care.

The renovated farmhouse has been set up on stilts to protect
the base from flooding during the rainy season. Angelo waits on
the porch. No dogs remain in sight, but I keep an eye out for a
reappearance. I might end up using my bionic legs to jump on the
roof of the truck if they reappear. And no, I'm not proud of this
thought.

Angelo waves us into his house. Mala and I follow, keeping one
eye on our backs. Despite his sudden welcome, there is no way in
hell that I'll fully trust Angelo.

The interior looks like a typical frat house. Beer cans and card-
board pizza boxes are stacked in piles on the table in the corner.
How nice. They didn't bother to clean up for company.

The heavyset man walks to the sofa facing a big screen TV,
where *Call of Duty* has been paused. Soon the sound of rifle shots
fills the living room.

Angelo frowns at his friend then glances around with impa-
tience, drawing down the corners of his lips. "Flaco, get your fat
ass up. We got company."

Flaco tears his eyes from the game in obvious surprise. Screams
come from the television, and he looks at the screen and curses
when he sees his soldier has been eaten by a wolf. He tosses the
controller onto the couch and stomps from the room.

Angelo gathers up the stray clothes covering the other side of the couch. He motions for us to sit down. "Ferdinand said he'll be here in five. He also said I'm to be respectful." He gives Mala a slight nod and a sappy smile. Obviously now that he's seen her in the light, he's overtaken by her beauty and charm. Well, charm's a bit of a stretch.

My cousin gives a disdainful sniff. She picks a plastic knife off the table and brushes a grimy, supersized pair of boxers onto the floor, then settles next to me on the couch. She rubs her arms as if chilled and stares off into a corner of the room. Prickles run across my own skin. It always freaks me out when she gets that distant glaze to her eyes. It's like she sees into another world. Now I know she actually does.

Angelo blushes and kicks the underwear underneath the coffee table. "Sorry for being such a hard ass earlier. We don't get many visitors out here. You're right about Ferdinand. He'd kill me if he found out I disrespected his friends."

"Literally," Mala mutters.

Angelo acts like he doesn't hear, but his next words seem directed toward her. "I owe him big. I got caught up with a negative element as a kid, and he kept me out of juvie."

"Really?" I raise an eyebrow. "Were you innocent?"

"Innocent that time." Angelo snorts with laughter. "All the times before that I'd been guilty, just hadn't gotten caught. The one time I had nothing to do with the crime, I get picked up. Ferdinand hired a lawyer for me and convinced the guilty party to step forward. He's pretty persuasive."

Mala plunks her elbows on her knees and leans forward. "Was that the last time?"

Angelo's eyes go glassy as he focuses on my cousin's chest. I kick the table, toppling his beer can pyramid, and he jumps. The tips of his ears turn as red as his shirt. "Huh?"

Poor Angelo. I hide my giggle behind a well-timed cough. "Your boobs are distracting him," I say. "He missed the question."

Mala scowls. With her obsidian eyes and hawklike nose, she can be pretty intimidating. "I'm just curious whether Ferdinand wasted his time. Or did you learn your lesson?" she asks.

Angelo looks sheepish. "I learned, but it took me being on probation to get straight. I joined the Marines after high school for the GI Bill, and after my tour, got a job with Ferdinand's security firm."

"Wow," I say, nodding. "Ferdinand seems to be a good influence. I'm kind of impressed."

"Yeah, like I said, I owe Ferdinand. He grew up poor in Haiti, but he turned his life around. Started his own business. He does right by his people. My family came from Puerto Rico before I was born. They struggled to keep us kids fed and clothed, but I thought what they did wasn't enough. Turned to crime. Ferdinand taught me to want more for my life. I won't be sitting in this shack when I'm thirty, smokin' weed and playing video games like Flaco."

"I heard that, man," Flaco's plaintive voice trails out of a back room.

"You were meant to hear, you lazy *hijo e puta*," Angelo yells.

A knock on the door ends Angelo's tirade against the hapless Flaco. Angelo holds up his hand and motions for us to be silent. Mala grabs my arm and pulls me to the far side of the room where we'll be concealed behind the door. Angelo waits until we're out of sight then pulls a gun from beneath his shirt, not hard for us to miss given his baggy clothing, and looks through the peephole.

"It's Ferdinand," he tells us, opening the door. "Hey, Boss."

Ferdinand enters the room, stealing a glance over his shoulder. I step into sight and the tension releases from his shoulders. I grin in response, running over to give him a self-conscious hug. "Thanks for the help. I don't know what I'd do without you."

"I'm tacking rescue services onto my bill."

I roll my eyes. "If I survive, I'll cash out my non-existent retirement fund."

Mala steps around the door and the mood shifts. Tension arcs between her and Ferdinand, as if the air's become electrified. Curls on my head straighten—the copper strands standing upright around my face. But the scariest part is the way my cousin's eyes shift—the brown taking on a yellowish cast.

I step back from them, sensing I don't want to be in the middle of whatever wicked mojo's being tossed around right now.

Which is stupid. Why would they be on the verge of fighting? They worked together to raise me from the dead, so I assume they were on friendly terms at least, if not BFFs.

I swallow hard. "What's going on?"

"Ferdinand…it's been a while," Mala says. Not like she's pleased to see him. "Bessie will be interested to know you're in town."

"Since our last meeting ended with her hitting me in the face with a lamp, I thought it would be best to avoid her."

Mala steps forward. "You should've avoided me, too, you son of a bitch." Her hand whips out, fingers bending into claws. She twists her hand to the left.

Ferdinand cries out, clutching his head. "Stop."

"Aren't you proud, Teacher? I've been practicing." Her hand clenches into a fist. The prickly feeling intensifies. My gums tingle. The air crackles with energy, and the smell of ozone fills the room. Any minute I can imagine lightning shooting across the ceiling to strike Ferdinand. And maybe it does, only I can't see it.

Ferdinand screams again, staggering in her direction, then he topples.

Angelo and I share shocked glances and leap toward them.

"Whoa, hold up!" I grab for Ferdinand, catching him before he hits the ground. Angelo goes for Mala. I doubt he understands what's happening any more than I do, but it's not hard to figure out Mala's the cause. My cousin doesn't even look at Angelo. She sweeps out her other hand, and Angelo flies into the air. He slams into the wall and slides to the floor.

Ferdinand twists in my arms, screaming. Blood trickles from his ears and nose. If I hadn't been juiced, I'd never have the strength to hold onto him.

"Stop!" I scream. "Mala, you're killing him."

"Serves him right." Her voice vibrates with rage, but she's not out of control. This attack is not at all like her. She bluffs like a card shark, but never straight-out attacks first. Her attention never wavers from Ferdinand. Hate rolls off her—as dark as anything I've felt in the shadow dreams.

"Do you know how many people he helped Magnolia kill?" She spits out the words. "They almost killed Landry, my father, and Aunt March. Georgie." Her voice drops to a whisper. "Mama."

"Ms. Jasmine?"

"When Magnolia tried to possess me, I saw her whole evil plan. Start to finish, years in the making. She twisted the minds of the men who killed Mama. Took their free will and set them loose on her like rabid dogs."

Daddy…did she corrupt him too? I don't have the stomach to ask. What if Mala says no, and he really was evil?

"Oh God. Mala, I'm so sorry." I lay Ferdinand on the ground. He doubles up in a fetal positon. His eyes have rolled up in his head, and he convulses. "But Ferdinand's not Magnolia. Killing him won't bring back the dead. Let him go; you're better than this. Please."

Mala's panting. Sweat dots her forehead. A splotch of crimson stains her right nostril, then spills down across her lip. Her body trembles, and she collapses to a knee. Whatever she's doing is killing her, too.

"Malaise, please."

She lets out a sob, and her hand drops. "I can't…I can't do it."

Thank God! I glance over at Ferdinand. He lays on his back, breathing hard. But he's still alive. I run over to my cousin and wrap my arms around her. "Fuck! What the hell?"

"Cussing sounds weird coming from you." She presses her face into my shoulder, and I pat her back.

"Yeah, you're a bad influence."

"I know."

Angelo glances over at me with wide eyes. He seems more shocked than hurt. I nod in Ferdinand's direction, and he crawls over to him. Ferdinand's bloodshot eyes are open. When they fall on Mala, guilt fills them instead of anger. What the hell happened between them? And why did neither of them bother to tell me?

It takes a good thirty minutes and four Tylenol for Ferdinand to recover enough to hold a conversation. Mala's not much better. Angelo and I take care of our patients, avoiding each other. When both are mobile again, we meet back in the living room.

Mala sits in a recliner while I perch on the armrest. Ferdinand stretches out on the couch. Angelo flanks him, standing guard with crossed arms. And I swear he cradles his gun beneath his shirt like a security blanket.

When the silence in the room becomes oppressive, I break the ice. "Okay, I don't need to hear your story from the beginning. It feels like it'll be overly complicated, and I'm a bit"—I wave my hands in a circle—"distracted."

"Don't you mean slow?" Ferdinand quirks a pained grin. "Don't worry, it's understandable. You've been through a lot in the last twenty-four hours. The attack on your home is all over the news."

"I'm famous or infamous, depending on the perspective," I joke, trying to keep the atmosphere light. "I know Anders... Never mind, who cares what he thinks anymore."

Ferdinand shares a frown with Mala. "He still believes you're involved in the murders? I thought he had more sense."

So did I, but he's in deep denial when it comes to the shadow. Unless...what if he just can't see it?

I open my mouth to explain, then shut it. It'd be better to explain the situation to Ferdinand in private since everyone's hanging on our words, including Mala, who hasn't been completely briefed on my supernatural predicament. Of course, after witnessing Mala almost kill Ferdinand with the *power of her mind*, my cousin, aka Hoodoo Queen extraordinaire, probably won't be shocked when I spill the whole sordid truth. Angelo, on the other hand, is on a need-to-know basis.

Recognizing the conversation has been abruptly concluded, Mala addresses Ferdinand. "I'd like to know why you've ingratiated yourself with my cousin. Why did you bring her out here?"

Ferdinand nods. "It was a security measure…"

Mala interrupts with a raised eyebrow. "Meeting in Bayou du Sang? The same place where Magnolia had Gaston murder all those kids for her soul-swapping spell." She waves a hand to indicate Angelo's house. "It's not a coincidence. Tell me why you chose this house?"

"This farmhouse was built in 1918. I converted it."

"An entire family was massacred in their beds in this house. Both parents and four children. The veil between our world and the other side's so thin, anyone who dies here is cursed to walk the land."

Ferdinand sits up on the couch with a groan. "You keeping your shield up?"

Who? What shield? I scratch my head, looking between them. Spirits. Death. Yeah, I get this on some level since I've got Ashmael protecting me. Zombies, ditto. What's killing brain cells is the fact that Mala and Ferdinand are holding a cryptic conversation about it. It's like they speak an alien language. Any minute I expect one of them to break into Klingon.

"Yeah, shield's activated." Mala crosses her arms and shivers. "The spirits are beating on it like a drum. Okay? Now explain why we're here."

Ferdinand rubs a hand across his bald scalp. "If you'll stop interrupting, I'll explain. As you're aware, Dena has been the victim of several attempts on her life. This is but the most recent."

Mala lets out a gusty sigh. "Don't talk to me like I'm stupid—"

Ferdinand ignores the outburst. "However, the attempts have escalated. They won't stop until they've accomplished their objective, which appears to be Dena's death."

I raise my hand, clearing my throat. "Actually their objective changed. Tonight they tried to force me to go with them. They started trying to kill me after I resisted."

"And how did you do that, exactly?" Mala asks. "And why does Anders think you're the one who burned the assassin?"

I shrug modestly. "Well, that Tae Kwon Do class helped. Plus Anders wasn't thrilled that one of those men thrust a gun in my face then tried to kill him. About burning the assassin, it's complicated, and he doesn't believe me."

"Anders has a limited imagination," Ferdinand says.

Mala nods. "And a history of involving himself in dangerous situations. I talked to a gossipy records clerk at New Orleans PD. He got put on admin leave while they investigated the murder of his partner. Most think he had something to do with it."

"I told you; it wasn't Anders," I snap.

Mala's eyebrows lift.

I stifle my groan, embarrassed I've opened my big mouth. But I couldn't stay silent when they were attacking his honor. He isn't here to defend himself, which makes him seem vulnerable to me. For some crazy reason.

Mala's eyes narrow on my face. *What is she thinking? Hell, what am I thinking?*

I shake my head and continue, "Anders believes whoever took over Magnolia's organization after she died is coming after me, and I agree. I also think I know why." I go silent for a long moment, ideas churning through my mind as pieces come together. "Hey, Angelo. Mind if I speak with Ferdinand and Mala alone?"

Angelo looks to Ferdinand for permission. At the big guy's nod, he goes to the door. I wait until he goes outside before turning to face Ferdinand. A sudden chill runs down my spine. "You know, don't you."

Ferdinand's head tilts to the side, and his lips quirks in a tiny grimace. "What?"

"Don't play me for an idiot. You brought me to a place where Mala says the veil between life and death is thin for a reason. Tell the truth." I studied his face. "You know about Ashmael."

CHAPTER 19

Aren't Avatars Blue?

Ferdinand stills. "I do."

I suck in a deep breath and hold it. You'd think by now I'd be used to the pain of betrayal by people I care about, but it stings every time.

Mala looks between us. "Who is Ashmael, Dee?"

My lungs deflate in a heavy sigh. "That's what I need to know, too." I shift my attention back to Ferdinand. "So the night we first met wasn't an accident like I thought?"

"Squirrel and I were tracking the spirit. I'd only seen you briefly in the hospital, and I didn't recognize you at first. That's why I tried to warn you off." My chest tightens again when his lips lift in a teasing and totally inappropriate smile, given his confession.

The smile vanishes as if it never existed. "Of course, you're stubborn like your cousin. You never listen."

"That's because you're a liar," Mala snaps, shifting in her seat. "And a murderer."

"I've killed, but never murdered anyone."

"Bullshit!"

"I'm telling the truth. Magnolia betrayed me as well. I was as surprised as you when everything went down at the party."

Mala's face remains tight. "Your lack of action spoke louder than words. You did nothing to stop her, so save your excuses for someone like Dena who still cares."

Hurt flares in Ferdinand's eyes, and I wince, unable to maintain eye contact. Everyone lies, even if it's by omission. We lie because it's easier than telling the truth. The worst lies are the ones we tell ourselves to rationalize our guilt. Those scar deeper than any physical injury. Ferdinand's scars are reflected in his eyes when he looks at my cousin.

"Stop arguing!" I squeeze my eyelids together. "Sorry if this seems selfish, but my problem supersedes whatever happened between you in the past. Ferdinand, why did you hide the fact that you knew about Ashmael?"

"I thought I was protecting you." Ferdinand turns to my cousin. "Sophia gave you her grimoire. Her book of spells," he explains to me. "Can you explain to Dena what you learned about Magnolia's plan?"

Mala gives him the stink-eye, but she moves to stand in front of the coffee table, as if giving a lecture. "The Loa of Death used Magnolia's body to live in our world. If I hadn't destroyed the Loa before it could complete the body swap, I would've been its next victim."

"This is the simplified version," Ferdinand says.

"Fine. How about if you explain the more intricate details of her plan, Professor X?" she snaps, and I hide my smile behind my hand. Girl's obsessed over Patrick Stewart. I'm surprised she hasn't asked Landry to shave his head.

Ferdinand drums his fingers on the edge of the couch. "Magnolia's spell needed a tremendous amount of power, more than what she could cast on her own, so she combined her magic with Mala's. When your cousin retrieved your spirit from the other side, the door between realms remained open because it's linked to you."

I lean forward. "By door, do you mean the vortex that opens when people die?"

"Yes," Ferdinand says. "It's a manifestation of the conduit which transports souls to their final rest."

Mala gasps. "You've seen the black hole thingy?" Her scowl creases her eyes. "You didn't mention seeing spirits too when I confessed."

"I'm not a ghostbuster. I see death as a ribbon of fate." I sniff, kind of liking how poetic this sounds. I can speak in an alien language, too. I catch their confused glances and sigh. Okay, I guess I should stick with English. "What about Ashmael?"

"He's the avatar of Death. When Magnolia died without closing the door, he was trapped in our world."

"So to free him, we close the door. How?" I ask.

Ferdinand gives me a look so full of pity that I scrunch in my seat.

Mala's about to hyperventilate. I reach for a Popeye's bag for her to breathe into, but my hand fists when I see the green cast to the chicken bones in the bottom. Silence stretches in the room. Finally, I whisper, "Ferdinand?"

He swallows. "The door opened for your resurrection."

"So…" *Don't draw it out…Just say it…*

"It only closes with your death."

"No!" Mala hisses.

I ignore her. "Killing me isn't as easy as it used to be."

Ferdinand nods in agreement. "Only the conduit can reclaim Dena's soul. Magnolia used her people even after they died. She'd bring them back. Year after year, they worked for her. Undying. Indestructible. The conduit has been reclaiming those souls, restoring balance. Which is in direct opposition to the goals of the two contenders for Magnolia's throne. They are opposing powers, shoring up their resources and cleaning house by disposing of everyone who was loyal to the old queen. What they didn't expect was that Ashmael would protect you, even though your death would break the spell holding him."

I shake my head. "Why?"

"For some reason, he likes you."

For some reason…ha! "'Cause I'm awesome! Awesome, redhead, dead-girl walking." I throw my hands in the air. If the spell breaks, he'd be free. *He likes me.* This thought gives me warm tingles, but guilt and the image of gold-flecked green eyes quickly shoves it aside. "Holy crap. So basically, because I came back from the dead, Ashmael's trapped."

"Well, not exactly *trapped*, Dena. Somehow you freed him the day you were hypnotized. He's no longer tied to the other side, but to you. He draws strength from you. And you…you've gained so much from him. Your fates are entwined. To send him back to the other side and close the door means you have to die."

I listen to him, mouth hanging low enough to fit my fist inside. I almost eat a knuckle sandwich to keep from screaming. I hear what he's saying, and I understand what he's saying, and frankly: *What the fuck!*

"You...you're the one who sent those men to kill her!" Mala yells, going for Ferdinand by jumping over the coffee table like she's Wonder Woman. Her foot lands on a slimy piece of...well, not sure. Maybe avocado. I throw my hands in the air, catching her fall, but rather than learning her lesson and chilling the fuck out, she tries to go after Ferdinand again.

"Let me go!" Mala struggles to break free. Ferdinand could break her into bite-sized pieces and spit her out if inclined, but he doesn't move from the couch.

"Cut it out."

"Who else would want you dead? He's the one, Dee." She wiggles like a trout, almost slipping through my fingers. "I won't let him hurt you."

The rage I've been holding back all day surges, and in that instant rational thought doesn't cross my mind, and I react. I grab my cousin by the shoulders and lift her into the air, shaking her the way Anders always tries to shake sense into me when I've done something stupid. Now I know why.

"Hurt me?" I growl, punctuating each word with a shake. I stare into Mala's horrified face. She gapes at the ground under her dangling feet. "You mean fix what you broke by bringing me back."

Hurt, followed by anger, turns her eyes into obsidian daggers. "Thou shalt not kill. You know what that means?" She jabs a finger into my chest. "I sacrificed my soul to bring you back. I killed Red. For. You. There's no fixing that, Dee."

"I never asked you to."

"Doesn't matter. I made my choice the moment I found out the two of you were trapped on the other side. He tortured you. Drove you insane. I had to get you out."

My laugh bursts out. "It matters to me. Not knowing what you did, living while knowing I came back wrong, but not understanding what happened to me or why…" I throw her away from me. She lands in the recliner. A loud crack fills the air when it collapses. She scrambles to her feet, breathing hard.

"Look at me, Mala! I'm stronger, faster, can leap cars in a single bound." I'm laughing through the tears falling from my eyes. I grab a knife sitting beside the Xbox and hold it to my chest. *Dramatic much?* But I want to make my point. "Do you know what else, cuz? If I stabbed myself in the heart, it would hurt less than the way I feel right now. I've been fighting to stay alive. For what? I shouldn't even be here."

"Stop! Just stop, please, Dena," she begs as I raise the knife, not knowing that it won't do anything but give me a bad case of heartburn.

"Then stop fighting with Ferdinand. He's the only one who knows what's going on. My only chance of getting out of this without sacrificing myself. But I will, if I have to," I warn, staring at her expectantly.

Mala staggers over until she stands in front of me. She reaches out and turns the knife until it presses against her own chest. "You're right. This *is* my fault. I weighed the consequences and made a choice. I never thought—" She scrubs a hand across her face, and I realize she's crying, my cousin who hardly ever cries. "I didn't know anything bad would happen to you. If I had—well, I'd be lying if I said I wouldn't make the same choice. But I'd never keep it a secret." At my frustrated growl, she steps closer. The tip of the knife digs into her skin, leaving a crimson dot on her shirt. "I won't lose you again. I'll fight death and the beyond for you. If you don't believe that, then kill me now. I don't deserve to live."

I frown, backing away. Crap, we both inherited a flare for the dramatic. We stare at each other for several minutes, unwavering in our intent not to be the first to blink.

This is ridiculous. "Fine, I believe you." With a roll of my shoulder, I flip the knife in the air, spinning it until it blurs, then throw it at the wall. The blade impales a poster of a half-naked woman.

"Guess I'm also more dexterous." I frown down at my hands, clenching them into fists.

"Yeah, my cousin the superhero." She shakes her head. "I'm so sorry this is happening to you."

"Yeah, well, stop. I didn't mean it when I blamed you." I shrug. "You know how my temper gets…"

"Dena the slow-burning smokestack." Mala laughs. She goes to sit in the chair and stumbles back up when she remembers it's broken.

"How about a group hug?" Ferdinand says, holding out his arms.

Yeah, right.

Mala's eyebrows shoot down into another scowl, and I want to punch him. She'd gotten so angry at me that she'd forgotten about him. Then he goes and makes a lame joke and ruins it.

He rubs his bald head. "I guess that's a no."

"Hugs are for sissies," I say, shoving at his chest. He stumbles backward, and I mumble, "Sorry, super-strength."

"Don't push it, Ferdinand," Mala says, looking like Grumpy Cat. "If you aren't trying to kill Dena, who is?

"I don't know. What I do know is the Loa who possessed Magnolia didn't escape from the other side alone. It was only the first. You're not fighting normal humans, but entities who played at being gods. They are more cunning and evil than you can imagine. And as long as the door to the other side remains open and Ashmael hunts for them, their time on earth is at risk."

All the bravado in my cousin deflates with his words. She hunches in on herself, wrapping her arms across her stomach. "It's not over. Magnolia's dead, but it's still not..." She chokes on the word, breathing heavy. Spots pink her cheeks.

I grab the Popeye's paper bag off the table and dump out rancid bones. "Breathe into this before you pass out."

"Thanks." One big inhale, and her skin pales. "Don't follow me!" she yells as she sprints for the bathroom. She slams the door shut behind her, but I can still hear her retching through the walls.

"Gross. She's gonna make me sick."

Ferdinand gives a slight smile. "You'll heal."

True. I go knock on the bathroom door. "Are you okay?"

Mala grunts and flushes the toilet. Guess that means yes.

"Ferdinand, what I don't understand is, if my death closes the door, why kidnap me?" I ask.

"It changed the moment you freed Ashmael. In order to close the door, they need you and the avatar."

"Ashmael."

"No. Death is a function of the natural world. Ancient. Unthinking, unfeeling, uncaring of human life. Until it connected to you. It tasted life. It wanted more"—he points—"it wanted you. But to manifest, it needed a mortal to give it human form. Teach it human emotions. An avatar through which Death became Ashmael."

Mala comes from the bathroom, wiping her mouth on a paper towel. She still looks pale and a bit wobbly, but determination hardens her eyes. "So, out there, some poor human is possessed by the spirit?"

"He is the spirit. They are now one. And we must find him before our enemies do."

Wow, Ferdinand's like a bald, Haitian Gandalf. "What exactly are we supposed to look for in the host avatar?" I ask. "He's not blue, right?"

Before Ferdinand can speak, the door flies open. Angelo hustles into the room with a worried frown. "Time to move out. They're coming," Angelo says. His face, flushed with excitement, darkens when he sees his broken chair.

"It's her fault," I say, pointing at Mala.

My cousin huffs. "Stop blaming me for everything."

Angelo takes a deep breath. He turns to Ferdinand, "Sir, I say this with respect. You owe me."

Ferdinand sighs and reaches into his wallet. He pulls out a stack of hundreds, counts out ten, which he gives to Angelo, and the rest he places in my hands. "In case we get separated."

"I'm taking off, Dee," Mala says.

"Wait, what? Angelo says those guys are on the way."

"We need more information than what Ferdinand can provide, and I think Sophia's book of spells can help. Don't try to talk me out of this. I'm going."

"They're dangerous—"

Mala wiggles her fingers. "So am I. Keep in touch." She turns to Ferdinand and Angelo. "Get my cousin someplace safe," she orders.

"Wait…" I cry, stepping forward, but the door shuts in my face. I spin to Angelo. "Should she leave like that?"

"Flaco will point Mala onto a safe route. I rigged this whole area with false trails. What good would it do to be trapped if the shit hits the wall?" He stares at Ferdinand. "Mind sharing who you think is coming after this girl and why she's so important?"

"If I told you, I'd have to kill you," Ferdinand says, and I'm not sure if he's joking.

CHAPTER 20

Zombie in the Dark

Angelo's cell rings. He answers in monosyllables that even I can understand with my limited knowledge of Spanish, and then slaps his phone closed. Whatever he heard bleached the color from his face. He turns to us. "Flaco says one of the cars followed Mala. The other belongs to the Russian, Zakhar Ivanov's man, Victor. " His hand trembles as he stuffs his phone in the back pocket of his baggy jeans. "You know what this means, sir? For them to send the best assassin…"

Ferdinand nods. "Victor's coming with guns blazing. No prisoners."

Angelo's bleak gaze fixes on me. "We'd better jet."

Their words solidify the *we're-in-some-deep-shit* niggling in my bones. Part of me knows I should play martyr. A real superhero would fight the bad guys until everyone got to safety. But I've been a normal human for most of my life. It's been less than a week since I've known I'm more. Habits of a lifetime are difficult to break.

I'm scared…I'd be a fool to deny or ignore the terror choking me into silence. It's greater than my shame and guilt over bringing these men into my mess.

Angelo ushers us from the living room and down a narrow hallway that ends at his kitchen. He goes to an electrical panel on the wall and flips a button. "The floodlights are disabled," he says, then opens a sliding glass door. His head swivels as he scans the area, then waves us forward.

I grab his arm. "Wait. What about your dogs? Aren't they in danger?"

Angelo smiles and pats my hand. "You're sweet. My pups aren't guard dogs. Their bark is all show, no bite. I kenneled them while you all had your *private* conversation."

Relief releases the air in my lungs. Even though I'm terrified of dogs, I'd never want one hurt or killed because of me.

Ferdinand and I follow him outside. The back porch also acts as a fishing dock. It stretches out across black water. It's too dark to see the far bank. Water laps against the logs, and the croak of frogs fill the night. The only light comes from the quarter moon. Shadows line the shoreline. Most are trees, but I swear one of them is man-sized and moving steadily in our direction. It's still a distance away. Even squinting, I can't be sure it's not a figment of my overactive imagination. Still, the rising hairs on the back of my neck give fair warning: *The Russian's here.*

I hunch my shoulders, wishing one of my powers included invisibility. Angelo heads to the end of the dock and unties a rope attached to a rowboat. I expect him to climb into it, but he shoves it off.

I watch the boat float away. "Wh—"

Ferdinand covers my mouth with a hand, and I nod, feeling stupid for forgetting. *Covert escape mission. Duh, Dee.*

Angelo climbs down a ladder attached to the side of the dock. I listen for the splash as he enters the water, but only hear a slight slap, like feet stepping into a puddle. Ferdinand follows him down, and I stare over the side. They're standing on top of the water like they've had a Come-to-Jesus moment. Ferdinand beckons for me.

Shaking my head, I climb down the ladder. I hold my breath as my feet touch the water, but instead of sinking, I stand on a solid concrete beam. Angelo unhooks the ladder and pushes it beneath the dock.

"The path's only twelve inches wide," Angelo whispers. "Follow my steps exactly or you'll swim with my pet gators."

Gators… I shiver, searching for the telltale red glowing eyes in the water.

I hold onto the back of Ferdinand's shirt as he follows Angelo. I slide each foot across the narrow underwater bridge. Our steps barely make a sound, blending in with the slap of waves against the shoreline. It would be different if we tried to row the boat across the pond. The noise from the oars would be amplified by the water. Victor would have no trouble following us.

A slight buzz fills the air. Angelo pulls out his cell, hiding the light behind his hand. "Hurry! Flaco says Victor's pounding on the front door."

I gasp. "Flaco's still in the house?"

"Yeah, he's gonna play the Xbox and pretend ignorance, not that it's a stretch for him. Maybe it'll buy us some time."

Panicked, I try to spin around, but my foot slips on algae. Ferdinand grabs my hand and steadies me before I topple into the water. My heart races as I whisper, "Angelo, text him to get out. This guy's dangerous."

Angelo shoves his phone in his pocket and continues to walk toward shore. "He knows the risks. If the Russian wants you, he won't waste time on Flaco."

That's what I'm afraid of.

I slide closer to Ferdinand and whisper, "Tell me about Ivanov."

Both men have picked up the pace, but the water lapping at our feet and the lack of light limits how fast we can travel. The fact that Ferdinand clears his throat and begins to speak makes me believe he thinks we're safe from Victor for now.

"The Russian and his mercenaries worked for Magnolia, and her Second, as enforcers. They handled the dirty side of the business while I strictly supervised her private security. The deal was Ivanov stayed out of Louisiana unless on a mission from the queen."

"When the Second and Third went to war, Ivanov became a free agent." He sways on the narrow plank, and I steady him this time. This must be ten times more difficult for him with his large feet.

He pauses, catching his breath, and then inches forward. "Ivanov works for whichever side pays the most. And I have no idea which side is paying him to go after you."

"Does it matter?" I whisper.

His grip on my hand tightens, and I wince. "Information is power. If we knew who to fight, we could take the battle to them. I hate playing defense."

"Yeah…I'll worry about that after we get out of the swamp." *The faster I get out of here, the safer everyone else will be.*

Angelo speaks with awe in his voice. "Ivanov's guys are serious heavyweights, ex-soldiers, mercenaries with major firepower. Victor's his right-hand man, a fucking legend. I ain't gonna pretend like I'm not shitting-my-pants scared. If I'd known Ivanov's people were the ones after you—let's just say I'd have found a way to say no when Ferdinand called tonight."

* * *

It's a relief when we step off the bridge onto the bank. I scramble after the men up a steep hill, afraid they'll leave me behind. Twigs and brush scrape across my bare skin. The muddy ground tugs at my shoes with each step. I'm breathing hard, more from fear than exertion. My legs tingle with the need to run, but I won't abandon my rescuers. Any of them.

I gulp in a huge breath and hold it for a few seconds. Release it, then take another, trying to calm my racing heart. My eyes dart from side to side, studying each shadow for movement. Each creak and bump makes my skin itch.

Ferdinand follows Angelo into the woods. He hasn't let go of my hand. I'm strangely comforted by the warmth of his long fingers. Part of me is afraid that, if I let go, I'll lose him to the darkness.

Angelo cups his cellphone between his hands, limiting its

flashlight's glow to only a few feet. Clusters of thick vines snake across the narrow path, snagging at my ankles with sharp thorns. I keep my eyes focused away from the light so I don't ruin my night vision. It doesn't help to alleviate my fear. *I really hate the dark.*

When we reach a wooden fence, Angelo shoves aside two loose boards. Ferdinand twists his wide shoulders, barely squeezing his oversized frame through the narrow opening, then holds out his hand to help me through. I pause, looking over my shoulder toward the house. *Did Victor get inside? Is Flaco okay?*

Angelo pushes me, and I stumble forward. "Go on, it'll be okay. A short run through the woods and we'll be at Ferdinand's truck."

I let them take the lead, lagging behind to give the illusion I'm unable to match their speed, until there's a significant distance between us.

Angelo and Ferdinand continue down the path, not noticing I've turned around. I know they're more concerned with getting away from Victor than keeping an eye on me. Not that I blame them. I don't want to put Ferdinand and Angelo in danger and, from their description of him, Victor isn't the type to leave them alive. I need to distract him long enough for the others to escape. I just hope they're right about Flaco being able to take care of himself.

A scream echoes across the water.

I freeze, stunned by the tortured wail that follows—a sound no human throat should produce.

"Flaco!" Angelo yells. He turns, running back toward me.

I meet him in mid-run. The impact of his body against mine knocks him backward. I grab him around the waist, halting his fall. "It's too dangerous!" I holler. "Go with Ferdinand. I'll get Flaco."

"No!" Angelo cries, yanking on my arms, but he can't break free of my grip. The look in his eyes when he realizes I'm holding him—the terror filling his face—it's like a punch in the gut from Zombie Assassin Number One.

"You're wasting time," I say, trying to make my voice sound deep and dark. I'm totally shocked when it doesn't squeak. "Go with Ferdinand. Get the truck and come back for us."

I shove him in Ferdinand's direction and run back down the path. The guys shout in surprise. From their viewpoint, did I move so fast it appeared like I vanished?

Flaco's screams stop long before I reach the fence. I don't want to be pessimistic and think the worst, but the slap of approaching footsteps moving at great speed reveals the truth. An explosion of boards fly through the air. I throw up my arms to protect my face and leap back. Wooden slats rain down around where I stood moments before. A shadowed hulk stands in the wreckage.

Holy hell! I'm out of here. I race back the way I came. Shadows fly past. The path opens into a clearing. Where the hell did Ferdinand and Angelo go? They said the truck was just ahead. Did they abandon me? I choke on a sob, slowing down. *Which direction do I go in? Where's safety?*

Anders...Ashmael. Help me!

Fingernails dig into my shoulder, and I'm thrown into the air. My back slams into the trunk of a tree. Air shoots from my lungs in a choked scream. My brain goes dark. I clutch my chest with both arms and roll onto my side. The toe of Asshole's boot slams into my spine, knocking me into a mud puddle. Everything from the neck down goes heavy. I can't feel my arms and legs, my skin, or lift my head from the water. I'd be drowning if my lungs worked. The cold and wet don't bother me, and neither does the pain. I almost cry in relief. Then every muscle in my body clenches. My back arches, and I grit my teeth against the agony from my regenerating nerves. I flop in the puddle like a fish escaped from a bucket.

Footsteps come toward me at a run. I roll onto my back, done with this fool using me as a soccer ball. Now that my legs work again, I can kick, too.

I wait until he gets close, then jam my heel into his knee. It dislocates with a pop, and he screams. He should've been labeled with a BEWARE FALLING DEBRIS sign, 'cause he topples like a demolished skyscraper. I lift my hands to protect myself from being pancaked, but I also lash out at him again, a double kick, like I'm stomping on cockroaches. Why? 'Cause payback's an evil bitch named Waydene Acker.

The heel of my right foot jams his testicles so far up inside him that he can probably feel them in his throat. When he doubles over, the second kick slams into his jaw. Blood flies from his mouth, and his neck cracks, twisting his head to the side at an unnatural angle.

The moon shines through an opening in the foliage above, casting its light on his ugly face, and I want to puke. Angelo had been right to be scared. I know the man lying on the ground. Victor is the assassin who took several bullets to the chest and still escaped from Anders. He was badass even before he got juiced. Now he's terrifying. A broken neck won't stop him for long.

My breath comes out as a ragged sob. I scramble to get to my feet, but keep slipping in the mud. Every time I fall, my panic doubles, making it harder to think. My mind traps me in a loop, replaying the memory of Victor's hands wrapping around my neck and squeezing. My chest aches as I relive how I struggled for a single precious breath.

I suck in air, but my lungs resist, expelling it in huge puffs just as fast. My vision blurs. I'm lost to myself, but not gone. When Victor's outstretched fingers twitch, I instinctively kick at the hand like it's a tarantula skittering across the ground. His hand wraps around my ankle, but I twist free.

I hear the car engine before the lights speeding toward us penetrate my brain. Victor disappears beneath the undercarriage of the car with a loud squelching sound. My stomach heaves. I end up on my knees, with my head hanging over my hands as I spew vomit against a bloody tire. My insides feel shredded, leaving me gasping for air.

I guess I'm also crying, 'cause I can't see—or maybe it's Victor's blood on my face. Hands wrap around my waist, holding me out of my own filth, until I finish emptying my stomach. I'm exhausted. The process of healing the injuries Victor gave me is sapping my energy.

A hand presses my face against a familiar, warm chest. I inhale his clean scent. "Anders," I whisper and snuggle closer. "You smooshed Victor."

"Dena," he sighs my name. He caresses my back with long, slow strokes.

I like how he makes me feel. Tingly and giddy. My arms slide around his waist. For the first time in what feels like forever, I feel safe. "Thank you for saving me."

His body jerks, like he's been stung by a jellyfish. Or he realizes he's embracing me like he never wants to let go. Either way, it's enough to give a girl a sliver of hope. And in his arms, I can't deny the fluttering of my heart.

Anders loosens his grip enough that my head tilts backward. Our eyes meet. The vulnerability reflected in the jade and gold depths sweeps me up in an emotional tsunami that threatens to drown me.

His gaze shifts to my lips. *He going to kiss me.* I hold onto him, fists clenching in his shirt. The pulse in my throat races as his eyes dilate. I try to focus on the curl of his plump bottom lip, but it blurs. *No…don't pass out. Not now.*

CHAPTER 21

Body Dumping 101

I'm cocooned in warm, fluffy clouds. I want to sink deeper, until no worries bother me, no fear. Memories edge around the drowsing corners of my awareness. If I open my eyes they'll return, and I don't want them to. *I want to float. Is that too damn much to ask?*

Of course it is. My eyelids flutter, sticky from sleep, then open. And like the light flooding in, so come my memories. Panic wings through my body. I roll over the side of the bed. The blanket goes, too, falling over my head. Everything I suppressed returns in a jumble of horrifying impressions. Flaco's screams. Victor getting squished. And to top it off as one of the worst days of my life, I fainted right as Anders's soft lips pressed against mine. *Oh my God.*

Fabric muffles my scream. *I can't breathe.* The blanket has become smothering, rather than comforting. It won't let me go, like it's alive and determined to eat me. *Fluffy clouds my left butt cheek. More like a cotton cannibal stuffed with downy fluff.* I twist and kick, trying to find the edge. I'm all tangled up, which increases my panic.

What if Anders didn't get me free? Victor's out there, and I'm trapped.

Hands grab my arms. "No!" I yell, lashing out. *I'm suffocating.* "Get off!"

A heavy weight lands on top of me. No matter how much strength I use, he won't budge.

"Stop punching me," Anders says, pulling the blanket from my face. My nose gets flattened against his wide chest, and I inhale his familiar scent and return to my senses. I peek up at his face. *Uh-oh, he looks all kinds of pissed off.*

"Did you hear me, Dena? I said calm down."

No, I didn't hear you the first time. My mouth draws down in a pout. "I can't breathe," I mumble, scrubbing my face against his chest.

"This was my last clean shirt." He rolls off and sits with his back against the side of the bed. Annoyance is stamped on his chiseled face. So much for the dreamy concern I remember from when he saved me. I could kick myself for fainting and missing that opportunity. It may never come again.

"How long was I unconscious?" I sniff and rub the back of my hand across my eyes. "Where are we?"

"Only a few hours. And my house."

"Oh. Why?"

Anders gives his patented long-suffering sigh. "Because we're hiding from the bad guys trying to kill you, Dena."

I laugh. The sound comes from out of nowhere. There's nothing amusing about what he said, but the exasperated way he said it tickled my funny bone.

I pull the blanket out and peek down. "So—uh—where are my clothes?"

"I thought it'd be easier to keep track of you if you were naked."

"Wanted an excuse to see me in the buff, huh? I *knew* you liked me from the moment you checked out my ass in the hospital." I wrap myself up like a burrito. The effort leaves me shaky and sweaty, and not at all sexy, in my opinion. Maybe Anders doesn't feel the same. He watches me with a strange light in his eyes. I take a deep breath, trying to calm my racing heart before I stroke out.

I'm also on the verge of tears. I should be outraged that I'm naked, but I'm not. I've wanted to get naked with Anders for a while now. It just sucks that I'm too messed up to enjoy his very obvious interest. Rather than test driving his bed during a round of hot sex, I'd rather snuggle in his arms and go back to the drifty place where nothing can hurt me again.

I sigh. Both ideas are selfish. I can't hide from my responsibilities. "Where are Ferdinand and Angelo?"

Anders glares in my direction. "Why do you care?"

This snaps me out of my lusty haze. "Because they're my friends, Anders. They were trying to help me!"

"If they're your friends, then where are they?" He climbs to his feet and begins to pace in front of me. "I'm the one who's here, not them."

"That's what I'm asking." I force my voice to sound calm,

soothing. I refuse to engage in unbecoming behavior, despite how many buttons Anders pushes. "Where are they? What happened after I passed out?"

"What do you think happened? I rescued you—again. I killed a man for you. Don't you get that? I'm a cop, and I murdered a man to save you."

What's up with everyone blaming me for murdering people? "I appreciate the fact that you rescued me, but I never asked you to murder anyone!" I pinch the bridge of my nose. "And if you're talking about Victor, don't worry. You didn't kill him. Not any more than you killed him the last time you shot him. He didn't stay dead then, and I seriously doubt that running him over killed him this time."

Anders stops pacing. "What are you saying? That this is the same guy that broke into your house?"

"Yeah, the one you kept shooting, but he kept on kicking like the Energizer bunny on steroids. It takes a whole lot of damage to kill him."

"Shit! You're serious." Anders's eyes widen, and he runs from the room.

"Wait—" I jump up and tuck the blanket securely around my body and then chase him down the hallway, through the kitchen, and into the garage. He's reaching for the trunk of his car when I grab his arm. "Is Victor" —I close my eyes—"in your trunk? Please, please tell me you didn't—"

"I thought I killed him."

"But your car? What the hell were you thinking?"

In a swift move, his hands lock around my wrists. He jerks me forward, and I fall into his arms with a sharp gasp. He wraps his arms over mine, pinning them to my sides, like he's afraid I'll pull away. *Not a chance.*

I lay my head against his chest. My heart races, but it's nothing compared to the rapid beats beneath my cheek. My hands lift to his hips, settling on the v-juncture between his waist and pelvis. I tilt my head back and meet his haunted eyes. "Anders—"

He brushes a finger across my cheek. "What was I thinking?" He slides his fingers into the curls at the nape of my neck. "Nothing."

His head dips down, and he brushes the tip of his nose down mine, and I forget to breathe. "I saw you lying in the field, bleeding, crying…I don't know what came over me. Or how I could…" His arms tighten around me. "The next thing I know, I've run him over with my fucking car."

"You saved my life."

"I almost died myself when you passed out. I thought I'd gotten to you too late. I wasn't thinking about the consequences at the time. I panicked and stuffed Victor in my trunk. I figured I could throw the corpse in the swamp later."

My body warms. I want to believe what he's saying and run with it. But he's gone cold on me so often that I can't let my guard down all the way. I give his waist a tickle. "Wow, Anders likes me enough to dispose of a body for me. I'm flattered."

His jaw clenches. "Stop teasing."

I give him a lopsided grin and pull him away from the trunk. "Look, you won't win Detective of the Year for this save, but thanks to your quick reflexes, I'm alive. I owe you. And I pay my debts. We'll take care of Victor together." Damn, that speech was badass. He's impressed, I can tell. An ax hangs on the wall, and I go over and grab it.

"What's that for?"

"In case he's not dead." I secure the ends of the blanket before giving the ax a test swish. It whistles through the air. One good chop and, like a vampire, Victor will be dead without a head. I take a deep breath and move to the trunk. "Open it and move out of my way—fast."

Anders twists the key, throws open the trunk, and jumps back. I leap forward, swinging the ax. The sharp blade slices into Anders's spare tire.

"He's gone," I state the obvious. My legs waver, and I catch my fall on the edge of the trunk. My hand feels wet. *Blood.* I scream, holding my palm out to Anders. So much for my tough girl act.

Anders uses the edge of the blanket to wipe off my shaking hand. "It's okay."

"No, no it's not." How long before I stop seeing the red stain on my hand? Months? Years? *Ugh.* I double my fingers into a fist. "You're an amateur, Anders. I bet Victor remembers to disable the emergency release whenever he transports corpses in his trunk."

"I've learned my lesson in Body Dumping 101. I won't forget next time."

We study the ground. Bloody shoeprints lead to the side door that exits the garage. They're so obvious that I'm surprised we didn't notice before. We got lucky. "Go check to be sure he's not lurking outside," I say.

"You're the one with the ax," Anders snaps back, but he pulls the ax from my hand and goes to the door. I hold my breath while he peeks outside and then locks the deadbolt.

"He'll be back," I say.

"How could he survive? It doesn't make any sense."

I should tell him about what I learned from Ferdinand and Mala, but he can't even wrap his brain around the shadow. How would he feel about zombie assassins, and the avatar of death? Still, I owe him the truth, even if he doesn't believe me. "The only thing I've seen kill them is fire, like the guy in the morgue by the shadow—"

"That was you, Dena." Anders rubs his face, shaking his head. "I saw—"

"Nothing!" I yell. "The truth is staring you in the face, Anders. You're deliberately being thickheaded. Everyone, including Sheriff Keyes, knows blaming me for those men's deaths is absurd. What is the accelerant? Damn it, your theory makes less sense than the fact that Victor and his partners are almost indestructible. I won't continue this argument with you. I need your help—so suck it up."

I swear a smile flickers around Anders's lips, and I narrow my eyes at him.

He shrugs. "Fine, but saying we're not going to argue is like me saying the sky is green."

"Anders, a green sky would be ridiculous."

He rolls his eyes. "We need to get out of here."

"I agree. Victor will be back with reinforcements."

"How about if we hole up in a motel and come up with a plan?" He opens the car door then pauses when he sees I haven't followed.

"We need clothes and supplies." I wave a hand down my body. "I'm not scandalizing the town by running around in a blanket."

His hot gaze sweeps from my toes to my barely covered

breasts. "I've grown fond of the blanket." He grins slightly before sighing. "Otherwise, we go back inside."

Fear sweeps over me at the thought of reentering the house. What if Victor didn't leave?

Anders places a steadying hand on my arm. "I grabbed some clothes from your house. Everything's in the kitchen. It won't take but a few minutes to get what we need."

I wrap my fingers around his and squeeze. "I don't want to go back in there. Maybe…maybe we should get in the car and go while we have the chance. I mean Victor…"

"Victor's long gone, or he would've come for us by now. We were both so out of it, he could've killed us a thousand times."

I grip his hand tighter. "I do need clothes." I take a deep breath and nod. "You're right. He's gone. We're being paranoid."

Anders leads the way back in to the house, and I tiptoe behind him. The light of dawn peeps through his windows, giving the room that first shimmer of sun. My duffle bag sits on the counter of the center island, separating the kitchen from the dining area. The room is cozy, and definitely not the kind of kitchen where I would've imagined Anders cooking breakfast in the morning. He doesn't come across as a granite countertop kind of guy. Let alone a wrought-iron pot rack with cast iron pots and pans. In fact, the entire house seems more upscale than what I imagined a cop could afford. Not that I know much about what upscale looks like.

I walk over and grab the duffle bag from the counter, but Anders heads toward the door leading to the rest of the house.

"Where are you going?" I ask in a shaky whisper that carries too loudly.

Anders whips around, bringing his finger to his lips. "Shh."

I shrug, arms flying up as I silently mouth, "Let's go!"

He holds up one finger. *Seriously?* "My gun's in the bedroom. I'll be right back."

He glides from the room. I rock from foot to foot, listening as his footsteps cross the house. It doesn't sound like Victor's attacking him. The tension I've been holding onto drains. I take a deep breath, and the stupid blanket slips again. I open the duffle bag and find a bra, panties, a navy blue sweatshirt, jeans, and tennis shoes. Not high fashion couture, but then, I don't own any.

I pull the panties on under the blanket, keeping an eye on the door, then drop the blanket to pull on the bra. I'm bent over, adjusting the cups when feet move in front of me. I suck in a breath to scream, one hand rising to cover my breasts and the other fanning across my privates.

Victor attacks just as it dawns on me that I'm an idiot.

I dart around the island, putting it between us. The first thing my hands touch is the toaster. I yank the cord from the wall and throw it at Victor's head.

He ducks, and it crashes against the wall. "Enough!" he yells, batting away a waffle iron.

"Not on your life."

"What about your friend's life? You want to see her again? Stop causing problems."

I freeze, hands gripping frying pan. "What friend?" I'm afraid I already know who he's talking about before he smiles, but I ask again because I need to hear him say her name. "Who are you talking about?"

His voice twists with malicious glee. "Your little roommate wasn't as much trouble."

His words hit as if he's punched me in the stomach. "Bastard, where is she?"

I run toward him, not caring about anything except that he has Gabriella. Forget the fact that he's bigger than I am, or that he might be lying. All I know is that I'm going to dig my fingers into his throat and choke the information out of him. His hands grab my shoulders, and we both fall to the floor. My head slams into the tile, and everything goes shimmery for a moment. Long enough for Victor to toss me over his shoulder like a sack of potatoes.

Footsteps tear down the hallway, then Anders bursts into the room. He aims his gun at us, or rather at me, since I'm dangling over Victor's shoulder, blocking his shot. "Put her down."

Victor whips around, and I'm airborne. Anders tries to catch me, but the force of our bodies colliding sends us flying back to the floor. I land on top of him, unable to catch my breath. Victor grabs my waist and flings me aside. I roll across the slick, granite tiles until I crash against the wall.

I hear Victor and Anders fighting, but my body hurts. I can't move. My eyes won't open until the gunshot echoes through the room. I grab the edge of the counter and pull myself up from the ground.

Dizzy, I'm not sure at first what I'm seeing. It takes several head shakes and eye squeezes to clear my doubled vision, and I choke on my scream when I see Anders and Victor tangled together in front of the refrigerator in a spreading pool of blood.

Neither moves.

CHAPTER 22

Reversal of Fate

Anders!" I cry, staggering forward. Pain shoots from my right ankle, and I catch myself on the counter. *Why doesn't he move?* I try to take another step, but my ankle won't hold my weight. I drop to my knees and crawl across the room.

Victor lies on top of Anders. He looks dead, but he looked the same way on the porch. Doesn't mean a damn thing. He could be faking. Waiting to grab me. I'm afraid of falling into his trap, but I can't...I stifle a sob. *Oh God, Anders, be okay.*

My hand darts out, shoving Victor's shoulder. He rocks and I flinch, scrambling back. A low groan comes from the pile, and I shift forward again. *Please be Anders.* "I'm here, Anders," I say. "Hang on, I'll get you out."

With a deep breath, I slide my hands beneath Victor's chest and roll him to the floor. His glazed eyes stare at the ceiling. *Faker.*

Shaking my head, I study Anders. Blood stains his shirt, but I don't see an injury. Maybe the blood came from Victor, but if so, why doesn't Anders open his eyes? I shuffle forward on my knees and press trembling fingers to his neck. At the same time, I lean my cheek over his nose, feeling for a breath and watching for the rise and fall of his chest.

He's alive. "Anders?" I pat his cheek. "Come back to me."

His eyes open, squinting from the shaft of sunlight over his face. Relief stops my heart for a split second. I don't think I've ever been this scared in my entire life. Which tells me a whole lot.

Anders's arm wraps around my waist. "I'm okay."

"Thank God, you scared the hell outta me," I say.

He shakes his head, as if clearing the cobwebs. I wrap my arm behind his shoulders and help him sit up. His gaze falls on Victor. "Asshole's heavy." He touches the base of his skull and pulls back bloody fingers. At my gasp, he gives a faint smile. "Don't worry, I'm hardheaded."

"Yeah, I know. Stubborn as a mule, too," I joke, but I don't like the squiggly feeling in my stomach when I glance at the trail of blood running down his neck. "Hurry, you need to get up. My ankle…" It must be broken if it hasn't healed yet. Another fifteen minutes and it'll be fine, but we don't have that kind of time. "I can't put any weight on it yet."

Victor twitches and I flinch. He's healing. Faster than I am. Anders isn't in any condition to fight him again, and if I'm honest my ears are still ringing from the knock on my head. Even if I could find something to tie him up with before he regained conscious, I can't guarantee he couldn't break anything short of chains. But if we run, it means letting go of any chance of getting information from him about Gabriella. Hell, I don't even know if he was telling the truth.

"Anders," I brush my fingers across his cheek, "about Victor. He said he—"

"I shot him," Anders whispers, hand tightening around my bare waist. His face dips into my hair, and he breathes in deeply.

"I know. I'm so proud of you." I pat him on the back. Victor lies at our feet, looking as dead as he did the last time Anders shot him. His chest rises. Once. *Shit.* We've run out of time. "Hurry, we've got to go. He's almost healed."

"I shot him in the heart. He's dead!"

God, I'm tired. "We are *not* having this conversation again. Remember? No arguments."

I half drag, half carry him toward the garage. Every two steps, I glance over my shoulder, expecting Victor to be up and running after us. I grab my duffle bag as we exit into the garage. Why didn't we bring the ax in the house? A beheading would've solved all of our problems, except I don't think I could pull a Ned Stark on the assassin. Self-defense is one thing. But…execution, I don't know. Plus I'll need him alive if he really has Gabriella. Once I'm sure, I'll be ready the next time he comes for me. And I know he will.

Anders's hands tremble when he pulls his car keys from his pocket. I try to take the keys from him, but he snatches them away. "It's my car; I'm driving."

Victor's coming. Hurry. I bite my lip, studying his eyes. He gaze remains steady; the fog dulling the green has lifted. "Fine."

He slides behind the wheel while I limp-run around to get in on the passenger's side. His hand shakes. I reach over and shift gears. The garage door creeps upward. I grip the armrest, holding in my scream. It tickles the back of my throat, ready to burst free.

In the corner of my eye, I see something move by the kitchen doorway. Panic floods through me. My uninjured foot lifts and jams on top of Anders's, hitting the gas. "Go!" I scream. The car leaps forward and slams into the washing machine. The crunch of metal hurts my ears, and I cover them with my hands.

Anders curses as he hits the brake. "We have to go back, Dena."

"I am not going back!" I grab for the wheel.

Anders shoves my hands and leg onto my own side. He shifts the car in gear. "No. Reverse. The car needs to be in reverse."

"Oh…" I mutter, staring at the empty doorway. "Yeah, sorry. I thought…I'm sorry I broke your washer."

"It's okay. I've been eying a front loader at Home Depot," Anders says, backing the car out of the garage and merging into traffic with one of those lighting swift turns that only police officers on TV make look simple.

I twist in the seat, staring out the back window as we drive down the street. Nothing leaps out at us or stops us. Sirens scream in the distance, heading in our direction, but Anders avoids the first responders and turns onto a one-lane road. The housing development he lives in was built smack dab in the middle of acres of farmland. The developer touted the community as secluded and safe from unsavory elements. Guess we ruined its image.

We're a quarter of a mile from the highway onramp leading to town before I finally stop staring out the window and settle in my seat. I'm still not thinking straight. It takes getting ogled by a snaggle-toothed man driving a John Deere tractor along the shoulder of the road before it occurs to me that I'm in my bra and panties, and those are covered in drying blood.

I lean forward and riffle through the duffle bag pressed between my knees. "I assume you grabbed the clean bra and panties hanging in the bathroom."

"No, the ones stuffed under your bed." Is he joking? I can't tell. He wears his distant expression again.

"Anders—" Oh my God, he looked under the bed when he searched the house. Pepper keeps a bunch of kinky sex toys in a trunk under there. The idea of my mom strapping on...*ew*. No, I refuse to picture it. He'd better not be fantasizing about me wearing it either. Sharing toys in this case is not okay.

I shudder, gagging a bit. *Too gross.* "That trunk is my mom's."

"I didn't promise to keep my comments to myself, but I will." He cuts a sideways glance in my direction. His eyes dance. "I didn't know how long it would be before you'd be allowed to reenter your home since it's a crime scene."

I brace myself for more teasing and let out an inaudible sigh. "That was nice. Thanks."

Surprise lights up his face. "I think that is the first sincere thanks I've gotten. You're welcome, Dena."

A snappy comeback pops into my head, but I don't want to ruin his smile. It brings a return of the warm tingly feeling, and I'm too chilled from everything that has happened to send it away. Maybe my lack of clothing is what's causing me to feel so exposed. Vulnerability doesn't sit well; it makes me itchier than the dried blood on my skin.

I pull on a blue sweatshirt, and then a pair of jeans, wiggling in the seat. "Where are we going?"

Anders nods to a motel just off the highway. "Super Delight? I figure it'll be safe enough."

Yeah, I doubt anyone will think to check for us here. Everyone knows better than to stay at the Super Delight unless they want bedbugs, dope, or a prostitute. Mala's mother used to turn tricks out of one of the rooms. I always avoided looking at the place when I drove past, afraid I'd catch her with some man. Or, if our eyes happened to meet across the parking lot, she'd read the pity in my eyes. I shudder, rubbing my arms as we turn into the driveway.

Anders parks in front of the main office. Nothing can sneak up on us without being seen. He turns off the engine and faces me. "Do you trust me now?" he asks, in a voice hoarse with exhaustion.

I glance at him from the corner of my eye. He almost appears to glow in the dim morning light. "With my life. Obviously." The corners of my lips lift. "You've earned it."

The muscles in his shoulders relax, and he lays his cheek against the headrest. "Then tell me what's going on. Starting with what Victor said before he grabbed you."

I swallow the emotion tightening my throat and tell him what I know about the bounty, the assassins, and about Gabriella. I leave out most of the metaphysical crap, figuring he'd just get annoyed. I can picture him saying, "Just the facts, ma'am. Just the facts."

I manage to get through the whole story without crying, until Anders presses a soft kiss against my forehead and says, "Okay then, we'll find her. No matter what."

* * *

Anders and I go into the main office together. Neither of us argue for separate rooms, almost as if we're afraid to be alone. Gosh, I don't know why we'd be paranoid after the night we just endured. We end up with the honeymoon suite, not for any other reason than it faces the parking lot. Nobody can sneak up on us. Hopefully no one will try, because I'm exhausted from the all-nighter. Passing out does not equal a full night's sleep.

I go into the bathroom and turn on the shower. While waiting for the water to heat, I shake out my hair, which is covered in dried blood and other things I don't want to think too hard about. Anders also packed my shampoo and conditioner, and despite how long it will take to get the curls untangled, I can't go a minute more without getting clean.

The hot water beats down on my bruised skin. I scrub at the blood, which doesn't seem to want to come off. Clumps of my hair blend in with the red wash of blood sloughing from my skin, swirling around in the water at my feet. At some point, I begin to cry. I know don't when, since the tears mingle with the water flowing over my head—as my cousin says, denial's not just a river in Egypt. Once I'm aware of the tears, all the emotions I've struggled to control erupt. I cry out, sinking down to huddle beneath the warm spray, rocking back and forth, unable to put myself back together again. Like Humpty Dumpty, I've taken a great fall.

Between my sobs and the pulsing water, I don't notice Anders until his hand settles on my shoulder. He perches on the side of the tub and gazes at me with eyes so full of concern that it makes my tears fall even harder.

With a deep sigh, he opens his arms. "Come here, Dena."

I squint at his blurry face.

"Please." He lifts me up, and I let him. He turns off the shower while I stand in the tub, naked in more ways than one. His hands are gentle as they slide across my shoulders, gathering my curls on top of my head and securing them with a towel. My mouth dries as he takes another scratchy towel from the rack and leisurely rubs it across my shoulders, over my arms, down my back. He captures each bead of moisture from my skin, running the cloth across my breasts, then my belly.

His eyes smolder with unleashed passion as he kneels in front of me, holding the towel in his hands. "Do you want me to stop?"

Do I want this? Him? My lips part, and a plea slips out. "Yes." His eyes lower to his hands, and I realize what I've said. "I mean, don't stop."

His dimple flashes. "If you're sure."

I lay my hands on his solid shoulders. *This is real.* "I'm sure."

Nudging my legs open, he slides the towel between my thighs; all the while he rubs in gentle circles that make my muscles tighten around his hand. Heat blossoms inside me, spreading fingers of fire along my limbs. My breathing matches the speed of his hand.

Anders groans, pressing his face against my stomach. His hot breath warms the sensitive skin between my legs, sending ripples of sensation through my body. I lean against him, my legs quivering with the intensity building inside, readying to explode. My breath escapes in escalating pants.

"Yes," he says. "Let go."

Flames rise within me. I arch my back, pressing into his hand.

The orgasm starts in my center then radiates outward. I bite my lip, holding in my cry of release. My knees buckle and, like always, Anders catches me before I touch the ground. He always seems to know when I need him. He kisses the curve of my stomach and then flicks his tongue into the saucer of my navel.

My fingers dig deep into his hair, holding on for dear life, as he rakes his teeth across the shallow juncture above my hip. "Why?" I whisper. *Not that I'm complaining.*

Anders's head tips until he can look into my eyes. "I can't stand seeing you cry." His voice vibrates deep within his chest. An echoing vibration runs through my body. His green eyes have a softness I've never seen before, a vulnerability he quickly conceals. "Tell me to stop and I will, Dena, but do it quick."

I shiver at the intensity of the desire reflected in his gaze. "I'm a big girl. If I didn't want this, you'd know."

"I thought so. But a gentleman cares enough to find out what his woman wants." He slides his hands around my hips and stands, lifting me out of the tub and sitting me on the countertop. I shiver from the cold tiles and press against the hard length of his warm body.

"Tell me what you need." He leans forward and flicks his tongue over the tip of my nipple, and I gasp as it hardens. He takes the nipple in his mouth and rolls his tongue around it. I arch against him. He pulls his mouth away. "What do you want? Tell me."

He wants me to think. How can I when desire burns my thoughts to ash? Sanity be damned. Protect my heart? It's too late. No matter how much I fight the truth, I want him.

"Touch me," I beg, arching my back. "Help me forget."

"Where?" His fingers clench around my thighs as he steps away from the tub.

My hands fist in his hair as I pull his mouth down to meet mine. "Here," I whisper against his mouth. I run the tip of my tongue across his lower lip, then slip it between his teeth. His arms wrap around me, holding me tight. The kiss sears any residual thoughts from my brain, burns through all my protective layers, and flays me open. I shove everything I am into him and he takes it, then returns it twofold. All barriers drop between us.

Anders pulls away first, gasping for air. He kneels over me, propped on his hands, and I realize I'm lying down. When the hell did we reach the bed? He still wears clothing while I'm naked. Somehow this doesn't seem fair. Before I have a chance to make things more equal, he captures my mouth, and I lose myself again.

When we pull apart this time, we're both struggling for air. Anders tugs the towel from my hair and lets it fall to the floor. He tenderly brushes aside the wet curls sticking to my cheeks. "You're beautiful, like a phoenix rising from the ashes," he murmurs. "The first time I saw you in that hospital bed, looking so vulnerable but fierce, your face was burned into my thoughts. I can't get you out of my head."

"I'm sorry." I trace my fingers over his cheeks.

He pulls my hand from my face and kisses my palm. "That's not a complaint."

"Oh—"

His mouth captures my words, and I'm drowning. I can't

breathe. I can't think. I sink beneath the wave of sensations crashing over my body. Each caress of his hands on my sensitive skin makes me feel like I'm about to explode. The pulse between my legs calls for more than his fingers, dipping and sliding between the folds of my sex. I want the length of him, pounding deep within me, touching a place long neglected.

I wrap my legs around his waist and fumble to unbutton his jeans. His hard-on makes it difficult to get a good grip on the button. My angle's all wrong. "Take it off." I groan, tugging on his waistband. "I want to feel you."

Anders leans back, putting his hand over mine. "God, I want you so much." He pants and his eyes cloud. "But we can't…do this."

I tighten my legs around his waist and pull him back down onto his hands and knees where I can reach him. "Can too…almost got the damn button."

Success comes in the form of an unzipping fly and Anders's cock in my hand. I grin as I caress the hard, velvety shaft all the way to the base, then back up. I rub my thumb over the wet tip. Anders's hips jerk, but I don't let him go.

He falls forward with a groan. "God, Dena. Wait."

Hmm, Dena, Goddess of Hand Jobs. I kinda like the sound of that. I embrace my new role, adding a slight squeeze at the base of his shaft. Anders breath quickens.

I arch my hips, rubbing his tip through the folds of my sex. "I want you inside me, Anders."

"And I want to be inside you, but this isn't right." Anders pulls himself from my hand and rolls to the side. Since my legs are still wrapped around his waist, I end up straddling him.

I stare into his face. "Oh?" I breathe, pressing my hands on his shoulders. I slide my breasts up his chest until my mouth reaches his neck, and I nibble along his jawline. "I've only done missionary style. You'll have to show me what to do." I sit up, positioning myself over him. "Do I just slide on?"

"God, Dena," Anders moans.

"Goddess. I'm all woman." I give him a smug smile. "As you're about to find out."

"You're killing me."

"Maybe afterward." We'll both pass out from exhaustion by the end, if I have my say. I've fantasized about what I'd do if given this opportunity. I won't waste a second of it.

Anders grabs my shoulders and pushes until I'm upright again. "Listen, Dee…"

I sit on his stomach, nothing between us. All the passion we'd built up slowly drains from us—*him*, judging by his softening manhood against my bottom. "What's happening?" I ask. "Did I do something wrong?" My eyebrows shoot up my forehead. "Oh, we forgot a condom."

He scrubs his face with a hand. "I have a condom in my wallet."

I giggle, leaning forward to peck his cheek. "That's my Anders. Planning ahead."

His hand caresses my back then presses against my shoulder again. "I'm sorry; I didn't plan to go so far. I swear."

I shake my head. "What?"

"This is my fault. You were naked, and I lost control when I saw you in the shower. I thought you'd be the strong one. I thought you'd get mad and tell me to leave you alone."

"Well, that's just stupid."

"Tell me about it." He rubs his forehead. "I messed up. Got selfish."

"Hold up now," I say slowly to be sure I'm interpreting the situation correctly. "Are you saying you kissed me 'cause you *wanted* to piss me off?" I scoot off him. "Was this an attempt to make me angry?"

He sits up, face lightening in relief. "It's just that you were in shock. I mean you were hysterical. I wanted to help, and I thought a distraction—"

"A distraction," I echo. I want to kick him.

"I hated seeing you cry, and I thought being angry would be better, especially since we still need to figure out how to find Gabriella."

"Gabriella," I sound like a parrot, begging for a cracker. Shit! He's right. My friend's out there, God knows where. My priorities are skewed.

I slide off the bed. My face burns, and my head pounds. I can't form a coherent response. My frustration's too raw...too thickly tainted with anger at being so *fucking* emotional. His distraction worked too well. And it takes every shred of dignity I have left not to beat him upside the head with a pillow.

He sits on the bed looking so calm, so pleased that he...what? Seduced me out of being upset over almost getting killed? Sexy, hot Anders—such a stud muffin—worked his mojo. One moment of weakness and I forget everything.

"Dena?" Anders leans forward. "Say something."

"Idiot!" I grab the towel off the floor, march into the bathroom, and slam the door with all my strength. Which, of course, breaks the damn door.

I stand in the light, my graceful exit ruined, holding the door in my hands. The surprise on Anders's face would be comical if I wasn't pissed off. I sniff, refusing to cry. It might cause Anders to feel so *bad* he'll try to fuck me better. *Idiot.*

I prop the door against the wall. "You'd better have enough credit to pay for this, 'cause it's your fault."

Anders crawls off the bed. "You tore it off the hinges…"

"I'm well aware of what happened to the door." I stomp my foot. "Can you please give me some privacy while I get dressed? I'm sure flaunting my naked body is distressing to you since the only reason you touched me in the first place was to piss me off so you wouldn't have to listen to me having hysterics."

"Do you not have to take a breath when you talk now either? Because that was the longest run-on sentence I've ever heard." He stands in the doorway. *Too close.*

"Get out of the bathroom, Anders!" I yell, hugging my breasts. His eyes drop to my chest. I reach out and lift his stubbly chin with the tips of my fingers. "Look me in the eyes when I'm talking to you. These breasts"—I motion to the items in question—"are officially off limits. You had the opportunity to have them all to yourself and you got buyer's remorse. You sent them back without fully inspecting them."

Anders scowls, staring steadily into my eyes. "I had a taste."

"I offered more than a taste. Remember it was your choice to stop, not mine. You wanted me angry and focused on the problem of finding Gabriella. It worked. Now leave me alone so I can get dressed. And if you hear me crying again, stay out!" He steps out of the bathroom, and I pick up the door and prop it over the entrance.

I glare at my reflection in the mirror. I look terrible. My blood-shot eyes have dark circles under them, and my skin has a yellowish cast to it, like I'm jaundiced. Maybe from losing so much blood. Whatever the cause, it's not attractive, and definitely not sexy. No wonder Anders has had second thoughts. He probably thought I'd barf on him in the middle of sex.

Forget it! I don't have time for self-reflection. Although I'm pissed at Anders's method, it worked. I need a plan to save Gabriella. Hopefully it's not too late.

Anders's knock rattles the bathroom door. He'd better not want another heartfelt talk because, until I can control myself, I plan to steer as far away from his sphere of influence as possible. He isn't the only one to blame for losing control.

"Dena, I've left you alone as long as I could, but I'm covered in Victor's blood. I need to take a shower. And we need to talk."

"Fine," I grunt, figuring he makes a good argument. I'd forgotten he isn't as fresh as a daisy, any more than I had been. I slide the door along the wall.

Anders blocks the exit, and when I step forward, I stare straight ahead. At his bare chest. I swallow hard, but otherwise refuse to acknowledge his existence, and wait for him to move. His chest rises in a heavy sigh. "Dena, we need to talk about what's going on, the door…everything you're still hiding from me."

"You're right." My eyes slide down his tight abs, and I clench my fist. *I will not count each muscle to see if he has a six pack. Won't do it.* I inch around him, careful not to touch him, which isn't easy given his size. Up close, he sort of looms. "We'll talk later."

The back of my neck tingles. *Is he staring?* I chance a quick glance over my shoulder and catch a frown marring his beautiful face, shoot—*homely face*. He reaches out, fingers brushing my arm. I twist away and watch his hand fall.

"Promise you'll be here when I come out," he says. "Don't go off on your own just because you're pissed. You attract danger like there's a homing beacon attached to your backside."

My lips twitch as I try not to smile at his lame attempt at a joke. "Since you find me every time I need help, I'm glad the beacon works." I shrug. "'Sides, I'm not silly enough to think I can handle Victor on my own. Especially half-dead from exhaustion." I glance at the king-size bed. "I'm going to nap while you shower. I just hope I don't have nightmares…" I stumble on the words, realizing I've overshared. I don't want to force intimacy on Anders. I keep forgetting he's a cop and protecting me is his job. All I can do is respect his wishes and back off until he's ready.

Funny thing is, when did I become ready? And why the hell aren't I terrified?

Anders leans against the door frame. "I promise I'll wake you if you do. I'll also hear if you try to leave so don't worry about the sleepwalking."

The concern in his voice fills me with warmth, and I sag in relief, knowing he'll keep me safe. "Thanks. Wouldn't do to wander out in traffic with the highway so close."

The huge bed calls to me. I slide beneath the covers on the side farthest from the bathroom and stack the extra pillows in the middle of the bed, separating the sides. As long as Anders stays on his side and I stay on mine, everything will be fine. No more fighting off unwanted attraction, right?

It's already eight a.m. A couple hours of sleep will help more than hurt my chance of coming up with a plan to save Gabriella. The first step is to find her. Estrada seems to be my only link, unless he's still missing. Maybe Charles has traced his cell phone. I also need to contact Mala and Ferdinand. The problem is that I've lost my cell phone and I never memorized any of their numbers. *I'm too tired to think straight.*

I roll onto my side, hands cupped under my cheek. I stare at the bathroom door, listening to the soothing sound of the shower. My eyes drift shut, and I give myself permission to fantasize about Anders while I fall asleep. I picture him standing under the warm spray of water with his eyes closed. He tilts his head. Water plasters his hair to his scalp and separates his thick lashes. It runs down his strong, lickable jaw, over his wide shoulders, and across his chest to pool at his feet. He picks up the soap and rubs it in slow circles over his muscular chest. His hand glides lower, sliding back and forth…

Umm…

…nice.

The warmth of a solid chest presses against my back. A hand caresses my right hip then slides past the waistband of my sweatpants, finding the place between my legs that craves more attention. Fingers slip inside with no hesitation, and I moan, back arching. My head dips into the hollow below his chin. A tongue traces along the edge of my ear, definitely an erogenous zone, and I shiver in response.

His fingers move faster, until I moan in tune with the intensity of the orgasm creeping up in a crescendo of sensation. I cry out, throwing my hips forward, then fall back into his arms.

I roll onto my back, trying to catch my breath enough to ask Anders why he changed his mind. And I realize I've made a huge mistake.

He's not Anders.

CHAPTER 23

Death Becomes Him

I should have noticed.

It's not like I haven't been licked or kissed by the spirit before, but I didn't expect Ashmael, or to find Anders beneath the covers on the other side of bed, seemingly dead to the world. The spirit doesn't seem overly concerned with the whole situation. Not normal behavior, true; but he isn't exactly a normal guy.

But I'm not exactly operating under normal parameters either. Here I am, lying next to one man while making out with another. And rather than running, I'm majorly turned on. This has to be a dream. The ultimate sexual fantasy. Real life can't be this bizarre.

I suddenly snap out of my head, realizing Ashmael's hands are doing a thorough job of exploring the contours of my body. Like a sculptor smoothing clay, he kneads my skin with gentle, reverent strokes. His touch warms my skin, turning my muscles pliant and relaxed. Even if I should tell him to stop, I don't want to.

Of all the times Ashmael and I were together, we never had the opportunity to *enjoy* each other. I was either bleeding to death or running for my life. Oh, and the whole astral projection incident when I stopped breathing. So if this is also a dream, or astral projection, or whatever, why shouldn't I enjoy being desired for a change? Would it be so wrong to give in to the pleasure building with each stroke of his hands? All too soon, I'll wake up and face the real world. We both deserve some happiness, even if it's not real.

Ashmael caresses my face, oh so gently, like a blind man seeing his partner in the darkness. His fingertips trace across the fragile skin over my eyelids and then brush down the length of my nose. He slides his thumb across my lips, and I kiss it. He stiffens, then shifts over me. He touches my lip again. This time I nip his thumb.

He begins to shake. I freeze, afraid I've hurt him. His arms wrap around me, and I'm pulled against his chest. He's silently laughing.

The conduit of Death is happy. Maybe for the first time in its existence. All the pain and rage he projected in the earlier dreams has vanished. *Because of me. I did this.*

Raw, unfiltered joy warms my chest, and I hug him back. His lips find mine in a soft kiss. He takes his time, savoring each brush of our mouths. Each tiny flick of his tongue teases. I shut off my mind—it never gives good advice anyway—and soak up the heat filling my body. I float, perfectly content to go on kissing him forever, but then the kiss deepens. His tongue delves into my mouth, stealing my breath and my sanity.

Gasping, I pull away. *I want to see him.* How can I feel so strongly for a man I've never known except by touch, never held a conversation with?

"This is a dream," I tell him, breathless. "When I wake up, you'll be gone. I'll be alone again." But I won't, not completely, since I can reach out and touch Anders, who forms a large, dark lump under the covers.

I force my eyes away, straining to see the man who feathers kisses down the length of my neck. I bite my lip to keep from whimpering.

I cup his face with one hand, lifting it until we'd be able to see eye to eye, if not for the darkness. "It's like you have an aphrodisiac in your saliva. You're addicting. I want to be near you, taste you." I run a finger gently down his spine, stopping at the curve of his back. Lesson learned in the cemetery. I'm not pushing my luck by going farther.

"Why do I react to you this way?" I press my palm against his chest. "You don't even have a heartbeat. I don't think you're real. Yet, somehow, you always manage to be there when I need you." *Just like Anders.* "Why is that?"

He must be tired of all the talking, because his mouth covers mine again. He pulls my sweatshirt over my head, then slides his hand down the top of my sweat pants again. I lift my butt so the pants and my panties slide down my hips. He kisses his way down my chest, spending a lot of time on my most sensitive spots. He dabs his tongue in my navel and nips the sides of my hips until I squirm and giggle. Seemingly satisfied by my response, he heads further south.

When his tongue slips inside me, I almost come up off the bed screaming, but I suck in a deep breath instead, allowing the sensations coursing through my body to build until I gasp again as I come. My fingers clench in his hair, and I yank his head up to mine for a bruising kiss that leaves him shuddering in reaction.

I'm writhing beneath him, literally rubbing against him in anticipation. I want Ashmael deep inside me, until we become one being, connected for eternity. It's this thought that brings me crashing back to reality.

My eyes close as he parts my legs, and I try not to get my hopes up. *Whatever happens next, don't scream.*

He lifts my legs and wraps them around his waist. *He has a waist.*

I press up with my hips.

Yes, hallelujah—Pinocchio has man-parts.

And he's learned how to use them.

My muscles clench around his length as he slides into me. *Oh shit, I should've thought this through.* But it's too late now, because my body takes over. My hips lift to accommodate his thrusts, moving in unison. He draws himself in and out in smooth strokes, and I squeeze around him. The internal pressure builds, spiraling outward in concentric waves. My back arches, drawing him in deep, and I cry out, unable to hold myself silent.

My screams energize him. He pumps faster, sliding me up the silk sheet. The top of my head slams into the wooden headboard, and I'm snapped out of my euphoria with a painful jolt. White light flashes behind my eyelids. I squeeze them shut with a whimper. The pain fades, along with any residual desire. I'm fully inside my body. I doubt I'll find release now, but I will make damn sure Ashmael never knows.

Heavy breathing comes from above. I grab Ashmael's shoulders, holding on to keep from getting knocked unconscious. His skin feels different, rougher. Sweat runs down his chest, and his arms tremble from holding himself over me.

"Now, Ash. Now." I clench myself around him.

With a final thrust, he yells with his release then collapses on top me.

I thought I'd lost my ability to ride the wave with him, but I was wrong. It takes a few minutes before I return to myself.

Ashmael's cheek lays against my shoulder. Sweat plasters his short hair to his scalp. His skin's burning to the touch, feverish. "Ash?" I brush his face. His eyelids are closed. I shake him, but his head rolls against my shoulder. *Oh God, I've killed him.* "Ashmael, wake up," I scream, panicking. It's not like he had a heartbeat before. *Is he breathing?* Air flows across his lips. I feel a rapid pulse in his neck. It's beating too fast. He's still buried inside me when I roll him onto his back and lean over to flip on the lamp.

I squint down at the man lying beneath me. "Anders…" His name clogs my throat. *This isn't happening. How?* I rub my eyes then pinch my cheeks. *I'm still asleep.* "Why can't I wake up?" *I should be waking up.*

Unless Ashmael's the dream.

This is reality.

My heart races. I draw my legs up until they're pressed against my chest. The throb between my legs tells the truth. *I had sex with Anders, not Ashmael.*

I lean forward to study his face. His cheeks are flushed. I press the back of my hand to his forehead. Heat radiates from his skin. So hot. He groans, rolling toward me. I throw myself backward and slip right off the mattress. I'm lying on my back, trying to catch my breath when Anders leans over the edge of the bed. He stares at me with wide, bloodshot eyes. A blush rises in response. I grab the blanket and cover my naked lower half.

Where did Ash throw my sweats?

"Dena?" Anders squints down at me. His eyes have a weird green glow from the lamp. Or maybe it's the fever making them glitter. He sits up. "Did you have a nightmare?"

"Uh…no. Not a nightmare, but I guess I was dreaming."

He nods, scrubbing his hand through his hair.

Does he not remember? I keep my eyes averted as I pull the blanket up to my neck. "Sorry, I didn't mean to wake you."

"It must have been pretty intense." He reaches out a hand. "You woke up screaming."

Yeah, you don't know the half of it. "Uh huh, intense."

I blush again, hesitating before letting him pull me up. I stand beside the bed, rocking from foot to foot, trying to decide whether I should tell him about what we did. Only, how? Do I apologize for taking advantage of him when it's now obvious he's sick?

His eyes drift shut, but his fingers tighten around my hand. "Do you want to talk about it?"

"I'm fine, Anders," I say before taking a deep breath. "I'm more concerned about you. How do you feel? You look like crap." Well, not totally, since he's wearing nothing but a pair of boxers, blue and very tight. My eyes widen on the large bulge framed like a pretty blue picture. Was he wearing those while he was inside me?

Why don't I remember feeling them? It takes all my strength to force my eyes away and say, "I think you're running a fever."

Anders lays back against a pillow. "I run hot sometimes."

You sure do. I find I'm nodding my head.

He scowls, his normal expression when confronted by Dena-logic. "Why does it feel like you're hiding something from me?" He pulls the sheet over his lower body and pats the bed. "Talk to me?"

I perch on the edge. I refuse to let him know he's rattled me with his insightfulness.

"I'm not going to bite, Dena."

"Oh, I don't know," I drawl, mouth turning down.

"Why are you acting like I'm about to jump you?"

I try to appear relaxed, but I'm ready to run for the bathroom if this confession goes sideways. Hiding is not beneath me, especially since I don't know how he'll react once he finds out what we did. "I'm not afraid of you, Anders. I respect you. You've made your position on this subject very clear. That's the problem."

"And you're still angry about that? I should have known." He sighs, running a hand through his hair. "Look, it's my job to protect you. I don't want to compromise our situation by making it more intimate. It's getting harder and harder for me to remain objective when it comes to you."

"Don't you get it, Anders? It's hard for me, too." The look I send him would've burned his chest hairs off, if he had any, and he doesn't from what I can see. Just smooth, muscular chest. I exhale, willing myself not to get distracted. "I was perfectly fine keeping this"—I wave my arm to indicate the whole situation we found ourselves in—"platonic. But you keep sending me mixed signals. You're the one who pulled me on your lap and groped my behind. You're also the one who took the towel to uncharted territory after my shower. I've shown amazing restraint. What's happened isn't all my fault," I finish in a huff and the tied ends of the blanket unravel.

Crap, I'm naked. I grab for the blanket, but it slips between my fingers.

Anders hisses and shoots from the bed. He grabs my arms and pushes me onto the mattress and throws a sheet over me. I almost slug him.

"Where are your clothes?" He leans over me, scowling as his hand goes to my neck, and tilts my head to the light. "This hickey…I don't remember…"

"I don't know what you're talking about." My voice shakes. I don't think he believes me, because of course I know what he's talking about. And now, I'm sure I shouldn't tell him the truth.

"Did I—" Anders frowns as a faraway look enters in his eyes. "I did this, didn't I?" He rolls off the bed and walks across the room. "When you woke up, you screamed. You were yelling at me, weren't you? I took advantage of you in your sleep."

"Of course not!" I snort. "That's utterly ridiculous." I put my hand up to my neck, rubbing it carefully. It's a little sore but not too bad. "Wouldn't you remember? Or am I so forgettable that you'd have to ask?"

"Stop angling for a compliment. You're the least forgettable woman I've ever met—under normal circumstances. Look, don't protect my feelings. You're a terrible liar. You get this squinty look in your eyes, like you're about to throw up."

Indignant, I cross my arms. "Do not! I'm a wonderful liar." *Damn, I've gotten sidetracked.* "Besides you know me well enough to know I wouldn't spare your feelings. Half the time, I don't think you have any."

The look Anders gives me is full of anguish. "Please, Dena. Tell the truth."

"I am. For some reason, you don't believe me. You've never believed." I throw up my hands. "Why should I even bother? I've opened up to you on more than one occasion. You've barely reciprocated. I know next to nothing about you, Michael Anders."

Anders steps forward then pauses. He stares at my neck a moment then turns his back. "I told you about the ambush and what happened to me."

"Yeah, you did." I pick up the blanket and lay it on the bed. "What do you want me to say? So I know one thing about you instead of nothing. My mistake; sorry. I guess I'm being melodramatic."

"God, Dena. You really don't make sharing personal secrets easy. Just can't stop attacking me, can you?"

"If you're trying to tell me something—spit it out."

Anders stalks to the bed. I scoot back until I'm pressed against the headboard. My mouth dries. I can't speak, even if I had anything to say. I refuse to apologize after all the aggravation he's repeatedly heaped on my head. My mouth draws down in pout, but I keep my lips zipped.

When he doesn't get a response, he sits down. "I've frightened you. Good, you should be frightened. You should have run from this room screaming when I put that hickey on your neck. No, don't deny it." He raises a hand to halt my protests.

"After I got out of the hospital, I began having blackouts. Whole chunks of my time are gone. Sometimes I'll find myself sitting in my car, and I'll realize hours have passed. I have no idea what happened during those missing hours. People tell me they've seen me. That I've spoken to them. But I don't remember it, or them. Do you know how terrifying that is?"

I shake my head, unable to say anything reassuring.

Whatever Anders sees reflected in my eyes makes him turn away. He runs a hand over his hair. "Don't feel sorry for me. I didn't tell you this for sympathy. I wanted you to know that I didn't mean to hurt you."

I gasp. "You think getting the hickey hurt?"

"I mean a lot of things."

"Are you saying you don't remember the bathroom? The fact that we almost made…love?" My voice cracks on the word, 'cause now I understand what I feel for him goes beyond physical attraction, although I definitely desire him. As much as I'd never in a million years be the first to admit this, at some point in the chaos of killing crazed zombie super-soldiers, I fell hard for him. It just sucks, because I doubt he feels the same. *Sucks, sucks…sucks.*

With Ashmael, my emotions are equally complicated. The spirit filled the emptiness in my soul. I'd been so cold before him. Like my heart remained dead inside me, waiting for the spark that would restart it. Ashmael's fire woke me up, but it's Anders who makes my heart race. Every damn time. The two of them complete me. Complete each other. And it's this revelation that sends a chill racing down my spine, 'cause it will shatter Anders's world. Our world.

Oh hell… I want to squeeze my eyelids shut, but force myself to meet Anders's beautiful green gaze. Familiar eyes that mesmerized me the first time I saw them, glowing in the darkness of the alley. And I have to ask myself, *Is Ashmael looking through them now, too?*

I crawl off the bed and walk to him. He allows me to take his hand. "You don't remember touching me?" I place his hand on my breast. "I mean I'm not vain enough to think they're the most impressive breasts in the world, but certainly they're memorable."

Anders snorts then draws his hand away. "I didn't think I'd ever forget touching you, but apparently I have since I don't re-member what happened after I got into bed."

My heart's breaking. After all the lies told to me, I now under-stand why sometimes a white lie is necessary. People tell them to protect someone they love from being in more pain. I heard the fear in Anders's voice as he shared his story. How can I tell him my suspicions about Ashmael? I doubt he'll believe me anyway. I barely believe it myself, even though the truth resonates deep in my soul.

I force out a careless chuckle. "Oh, you remember everything you are supposed to remember. I'll tell you again. You did not give me the hickey. I'm embarrassed to admit that I had an ex-tremely erotic fantasy last night while you were in the shower. I may have gotten a bit carried away in pleasuring myself, since you didn't seem to be in the mood."

Anders blushes, eyes wide. I'm not sure if he believes the most ridiculous lie ever told or not, but I'm pretty sure the only thing revealed on my face is the memory of the shower fantasy, and if lying gets rid of the guilt stamped across his face, then I'm cool with keeping our first experience a secret.

The dulcet tones of Shakira singing, "Hips don't

Lie,"—strangely appropriate if "hips" was changed to "lips"—fills the air.

"Hey," I cry. "That's my cell phone. I didn't know it was in the bag." I dive for the duffle bag, digging through the clothing like a mad woman before holding it up in triumph. Unfortunately, it goes to voicemail before I can answer it.

I twist on my knees to find Anders crouching next to me. He reaches for the phone. I push aside his hand. "Hey, Mister Grabby, it's mine."

"Dena, now's not the time to play games. Who's calling?"

"Maybe it's my mysterious boyfriend. Not everyone can resist my charms for the greater good."

"Now you're being childish." He snatches the phone from my hand and looks at the caller ID. "It's Susan Jones? Isn't she the nurse that works at the hospital?"

"Yes, better let me call her back. You're not one of her favorite people."

"We have to be careful about who we contact. We don't want to put other people at risk. The men who are after you are ruthless. They don't mind taking hostages to insure your cooperation."

"Duh, Anders." I grab the phone out of his hand and listen to the voicemail. The news Susan relays is surprising in a really fantastic way. My face must light up like a child's on Christmas morning.

"What? What did she say?" Anders asks. He's gotten dressed while I listened to the message. The flexing of his taut buttocks as he pulled on his jeans distracted me from fully paying attention to the message, but the gist was that Dr. Estrada finally showed up at the hospital. He also asked for me. I don't tell Anders the last part. As soon as he hears that Estrada's back, he runs for the door.

I jump up. "Hey, hold on. I'm coming with you."

"No. You're staying here where it's safe. I'll come back for you."

"Like hell I am." I push him from the door. It's harder than it should be given my extra strength. "The call was for me. If I hadn't said anything, you wouldn't have known. I've as much of a right to be there as you do."

"If Victor kidnapped Gabriella, this is most likely a trap. You being there is a liability. I can't protect you and interview Estrada at the same time."

"I never asked to be protected, Anders."

"It's my job."

"No, we're partners." I grab onto his arms.

He shakes me off. "My last partner died. I won't lose someone I care about again."

My heart warms at his words. *He cares*... I shake my head. I won't be distracted. He's only saying what he thinks he should to get me to obey like a little automaton. "You're not responsible for what happens to me. I make my own choices. So did Jimmy. What happened to him isn't your fault. So stop blaming yourself."

He's not listening. "I'll come back."

Fine, I'll flip it around and play the protection card since it means so much to him. "Don't leave me here alone. What if Victor finds me? Can't I stay with you? Please."

He stares at me, eyes squinting in suspicion over my sudden reversal. I shove the very real terror Victor inspires into my eyes. No joke. Thinking about him finding me again sends a chill down my spine.

Anders sighs and steps away from the door. "If you start crying, I'm out of here."

"Let me get dressed." I grab the duffle bag and dart into the bathroom. I don't bother with brushing my hair. It curls in a wild halo around my head. My breath doesn't smell much better since Anders forgot my toothbrush. I'm out of the bathroom in less than five minutes, but Anders is gone.

Running into the empty parking lot, I yell, "Sneaky jerk!"

CHAPTER 24

The Dark Side of the Force

I kick the curb, then stalk back inside. Muttering curses…such a waste of time. And I don't have a lot left. Anders charging into the unknown by himself is bad enough. Anders, who may or may not be the avatar for Death, running right into a trap, *grr*.

I hate maybes. They leave too much room for interpretation. I never should've let him out of my sight. He's suffering from a hero complex that will get him killed, and it'll be my fault for not telling him my suspicions. This is what happens when I'm nice.

I call Ferdinand, after discovering he's left several messages. When he answers, I jump into the conversation with a quick, "I'm sorry and help!"

"Where have you been?" His yelling forces me to hold the phone away from my ringing ear. "We thought you were dead."

Okay, not expected. "Why? You knew I was with Anders."

"How would I know that? You disappeared. Angelo said you went back for Flaco, and he saw Anders run you over and stuff you in the trunk of his car before taking off!"

"What?" My voice warbles from the high pitch. "Is Angelo nearsighted? Why in the world would Anders do such a thing? He's a cop, for goodness' sakes."

"That's what Angelo thought he saw happen. Since you were missing, I didn't have any other answer for why you would disappear with Victor on your tail."

"Did you report me as a missing person? Are they after Anders?" Because that's the last thing we need. *Ugh*.

"I told Mala. I didn't know who else to call. She was the only other person who knew what was happening. With her connections, I thought she would be able to figure out what to do. I don't know what she did with the information."

"Mala." I groan, dropping onto the bed. "She must be sick with worry."

"To say she's upset would be a vast understatement. I suggested she wait a bit before taking action. She's not the easiest person to calm down when her loved ones are in danger. At least she has pull with the sheriff's office. Angelo and I are lucky we weren't arrested, especially after they found Flaco. Victor really messed him up. He's at the hospital in critical condition, and I'm heading over to check on him. They don't know if he'll survive."

Guilt makes my voice hoarse as I say, "God, Ferdinand. I'm sorry." I lean against the dresser, trembling with shock…and remorse. Flaco may be dying because he tried to protect me. My life isn't more important than his. Yet I'm so grateful for their protection. Ferdinand has more than earned his security fee. "I'm at the

Super Delight. If you could pick me up, I'd like to ride to the hospital with you. Victor told me he kidnapped my roommate. He was probably lying to get me to go with him, but I need to know for sure. The doctor who saw Gabriella last night wants to talk to me."

"Good. Maybe you'll finally get some answers. I'll be there in five, and you can finish filling me in on what happened after your disappearance. Don't forget to let your cousin know you're safe."

While I wait for Ferdinand, I call Mala. When she picks up the phone, her voice brings fresh tears to my eyes. "Dena, I was so worried."

"I'm sorry. Ferdinand told me that you thought I was dead. Stupid Angelo. I don't know what he was thinking to make up a story like that. Uh, you didn't tell the deputies about Anders, right?"

"What was I supposed to say? Detective Anders killed my cousin, but my only proof is the word of a suspected drug dealer?"

"Given the fact that I'm still alive, I'm grateful you considered the situation in that light. Everything else Angelo told you is the truth. Only Anders ran over Victor and stuffed him in the trunk."

"He what?" she shrieks.

"Yeah, Victor wasn't happy." I chuckle darkly, remembering our mad search of the trunk. In hindsight, it's kind of funny. Probably only 'cause we survived the encounter with Victor. I fill her in on Gabriella's possible kidnapping. Ferdinand's gray truck pulls into the parking lot. I wave in greeting and slide into the front seat. He raises an eyebrow, and I cover the mouthpiece to whisper, "Mala."

He nods, pulling out of the lot.

"What about Anders?" Mala asks. "Are you still with him?"

"No, he went to the hospital. Dr. Estrada turned up. Since he was the last person to see Gabriella, maybe he has a clue to who took her. Anders thinks it's a trap. He left me behind 'cause he didn't think I'd be safe." I sigh. "I'm afraid he's in even more danger than I am."

"Hey, don't worry about him. Victor's after you."

"No, I'm pretty sure Victor only needs me to lead him to the avatar…" I sigh again as my voice trails off. "What if Victor finds him, and I'm not there to protect him?"

"Finds who? The avatar?"

"Yeah."

"We don't even know who it is. Besides, I thought you were worrying about Anders, not some unknown…" Mala goes silent, then whispers, "Wait, unless you're saying…Is Anders the avatar?"

"Yeah, remember me telling you about the guy I sat with at the hospital the night of the earthquake? How I felt connected to him? I think that's when it happened." When death came for Anders, I thought I blocked it. But what if Death found him through me—the spirit of Ashmael was born from Anders the night he should've died. All of the bad things that have happened to him since are my fault."

The next thought hits like a hammer to the heart. *What if Anders only likes me because of this mystical connection between us?*

Ferdinand glances at me with a raised eyebrow. "What about the avatar?"

I shake my head and squeeze my eyes shut. No wonder Anders

fights the attraction. *His feelings for me are as fake as the life he leads during his blackouts.*

Mala must've heard Ferdinand's question because she pipes in, "Is that Ferdinand?"

"Yeah."

"Don't tell him about Anders," she says quickly. "I know you trust him, but I still think he has more to do with this than he's saying. If he sent those assassins after you, then he's working both sides. He may only be pretending to help us. Like he said, they need you and the avatar to close the door to the other side. And I'm not sure I want the door closed. Not if keeping it open means we can drag the other escaped Loa back to hell."

I glance at Ferdinand again and give him a reassuring smile. "Okay, but—"

"Landry and I will meet you at the hospital."

She leaves me with more questions than answers. And underlying all the turmoil and anxiety stirred up by the conversation is the contradiction of my feelings for Anders. Deep inside, I hope he's not the avatar. I want to believe his feelings for me aren't due to a mystical confluence of events. He said he ran over Victor because I got hurt. Then he freaked out and stuffed him in the trunk because he worried about losing his job. Anders is a real person. *Not some ghost.*

Ferdinand has been silent, but he's been listening to my responses to what amounts to a one-sided conversation. The look he turns in my direction is heavy with unasked questions and sympathy.

"I'm guessing you understood what that was all about," I say, fighting to control myself, because I'm verging on freaking the hell out.

"Anders is Ashmael, and Mala doesn't want me to know."

I point my finger at him. "Bingo." I brief Ferdinand on *everything*, including the humiliating aborted seduction by Anders, the eventual consummation by Ashmael, who turned out to be Anders, who doesn't remember a damn thing. *How did my life become so complicated?*

Ferdinand listens without cracking one joke, a novel experience. He appears thoughtful as he says, "If I whip out what I remember from my college Abnormal Psychology class, it sounds like Dissociative Identity Disorder."

"Is that like multiple personalities? I watched a series on Showtime about this before my dad disconnected the cable…*United States of Tara*. I loved seeing the different personalities, but I also felt so sad at how the illness affected the character's relationships with her family." I glance back at Ferdinand. "So you think this is similar to what's happened to Anders?"

"It's only a theory. Except the alternate personality isn't one Anders created to protect himself from a forgotten trauma. In this case, it's more that Ashmael assumes aspects of his personality. He is both separate and a part of Anders."

"But does being an avatar change the person?" I whisper. "Is Anders still Anders? How much influence does Ashmael have on him? His underlying personality doesn't change, does it?"

Silence stretches for several minutes before Ferdinand breaks it with a groan. He rolls his eyes in my direction. My jaw tightens as I raise my hands in exasperation, "Now what did I do?"

"It's your expression. You had the same stubborn look on your face the night you talked me into helping you track the shadow after it killed Squirrel. Even if I warn you to stay away from Anders, you won't listen. Just like you didn't listen to Mala." He laughs. "Anyone else would have stayed far away from that mausoleum, but not you. You walked right in hoping for the best."

"It worked out, didn't it? There haven't been any more murders."

"Not unless you count the men who broke into your house and tried to murder you, no."

"It's all related. At least we know why Death was killing Victor's men. What I'd like to know is what the one guy meant when he said I was juiced. Even though Mala brought me back from the other side, I didn't heal this fast. It all began in the alley."

"That was the moment Ashmael exposed you to the mystery substance."

I nod. "But how did those assassins get juiced? I can't see Ashmael licking their bodies." *Ick.* I shudder, gagging a bit at the image. "This is what we need to find out. It may be the answer to why all of this is happening."

We pull into the hospital parking lot, and Ferdinand shuts off the car. He scrubs a hand over his eyes. "Let's go find our friends."

Ferdinand and I enter the hospital, heading toward the ICU. Angelo sits on a plastic chair with his head held in his hands. Four other beefy guys, dressed in black-on-black security uniforms, also pace the corridors. One of them stands with his hand on Angelo's shoulder, and he squeezes it when we draw closer. Angelo looks up.

I back up a step in response to the anger tightening his eyes. "Uh, Ferdinand, maybe it's better for Angelo if we split up. Tell him I'm sorry. For everything."

He stares at me for a long moment, then nods. "See if you can find Anders, but wait for backup before confronting Estrada."

"Sure," I lie, straight-faced. I'm not eager to walk into a trap, but seeing Angelo, I know I won't put my friends at risk. I can't handle the guilt. I'm already mostly dead. Putting this body to rest if it keeps my friends safe isn't a hard choice. But I won't sacrifice myself without putting up a fight.

I turn and run for the elevator.

Angelo shouts from behind, "Hey, get back here!" His feet pound on the floor as he runs after me. A quick glance over my shoulder shows Ferdinand now has him in a bear hug. Their loud voices follow me into the elevator, and I collapse against the metal wall once I'm inside. By the time I reach the fourth floor Neuro Unit, I'm calm.

Susan Jones sits behind a computer at the nurses' station. She barely lifts her eyes from the screen when I walk up. "I see you got my message about Dr. Estrada?"

My fingernails drum out a rhythm on the countertop. "Yeah, where is he?"

"Everybody's been asking about you. Mala and Charles call every few hours asking if you've been admitted. You look healthy enough to pick up a phone so your friends won't worry."

Scalded by the heat in her scolding, my face flushes. "I didn't have cell reception in the backwoods. I'm sorry for worrying you and everyone. Mala knows I'm safe. I called her before coming here." I let out a deep breath. "About Estrada—"

"His office." Her fingers pause on the keyboard as she shakes her head. "He's acting really strange."

"Define strange. Estrada isn't exactly normal."

She barks out a laugh. "I'm constantly amazed at the stuff he gets away with. It's frustrating how the higher-ups cater to his every request. They've given him more money for his research projects than most…Oh, who am I to poor mouth the man? I've seen the miracles he's worked. You being one of them."

We both roll our eyes and say in unison, "Hand of God," then crack up. I adore her. I would've gone insane from boredom without her during the month before my release from the hospital.

I cross my arms on the countertop and lean forward. Ever the professional, she turns the computer screen from my view. "What about Detective Anders?" I ask. "You remember him? Long, lean, hotness in a suit with a shitty attitude. He interrogated me after I was brought in the last time. Have you seen him?"

"I haven't seen anyone else go into Estrada's office," Susan says with a shrug. "Not that I was paying much attention to people coming and going. I do have patients to care for. Okay, I'll stop lecturing you. I know you're anxious to see Estrada. Go on in." She waves me off with a quick smile, then starts typing again.

I stand another minute outside the door, gathering my courage. All the doubts and fears dragging at my heels weigh me down. I should wait for Ferdinand or Mala. But what if Victor's behind those doors? I don't want them to get hurt because of me. Alone, I can choose whether to fight or let him take me to Gabriella. If Victor's not there, then I don't need them to interrogate Estrada. I can handle that all on my own. *With pleasure.*

The question is: What am I willing to do to get the truth?

Anything.

My hands ache. I crack each knuckle—the popping soothing my anxiety—then shove the door. It slams against the wall, and I stride inside the large corner office, ready to browbeat some answers out of Estrada if necessary.

Estrada sits behind the desk. "Ms. Acker?" Sweat dots his forehead, and his eyes shift over my shoulder. "Now is not an ideal time for an unscheduled appointment."

"Wow," I mutter, squeezing my hands. "That was anticlimactic."

"I thought the same thing," Anders says from behind me.

I jump, twisting to face him. He stands in the doorway to the bathroom. The look he gives Estrada is ferocious, and anxiety rears again in my chest. I've never seen so much emotion on his face. Even while being attacked he retreated into a studied calm. The only time he ever seemed to be anywhere close to being in danger of losing control was after he thought he'd murdered Victor.

"I came expecting to get some answers." He walks toward the desk with stiff, jerky steps. His fists clench and unclench, bunching the muscles in his arms. "I thought I'd finally learn what happened that night."

Keeping my body between him and the desk, I move closer, trying to turn his focus from Estrada. Tension radiates off him in a wave that washes over my skin in a zinging rush.

"So he doesn't know what happened to Gabriella?" I whisper, a little breathless from disappointment at the dead end, but also because of the anger building in Anders. I don't want to set him off. "I hoped he'd have answers, but I'm not surprised—"

"I meant the night I almost died," Anders says, continuing to stare at Estrada. "You experimented on me, didn't you? Put me back together wrong."

His words echo the thoughts I've had since waking from my coma. Only I now know the answer to the question for both of us. Wrong? Hell yes, we came back from the beyond wrong. We're Frankenstein's monstrous couple.

Again that prickle of unease washes across my skin. All the hairs on my arms stand on end, like static electricity has built around my body. A dusky shimmer hovers over Anders's skin as the energy coalesces into a malignant, smoky cloud.

I glance back at Estrada, who remains frozen at his desk. He appears aware of the danger brewing in front of him. The terror in his eyes must mirror my own. Anders isn't himself—not even close. This must be one of the blackout episodes he warned me about. The moment when I should run like hell and get as far away from him as possible. But he is Anders. And he is Ashmael. All swirled together. And I love them both.

"Anders," I beg, desperate to find some connection to the man I thought I knew, but terrified at the same time that he never existed. I step toward him. "Michael, please..."

His eyes fix on my face, and I flinch. The eyes are no longer Anders's eyes. I've gotten lost in the jade green depths on multiple occasions. These eyes, set in his familiar face, belong to something inhuman, closer to being feline, with elongated pupils the color of green bottle glass and so bright they appear to glow.

I know these eyes, too. I've seen them in my dreams. Not the kinky ones, but ones where we hunt men. These are the eyes Death wears when he eats souls.

"Michael...come back to me." All my latent emotions go into that plea. I don't know how I speak so calmly, except if I lose control, he will, too. "Babe, I know you're in there."

My trembling hand moves toward him but doesn't touch the oil slick darkness forming an inch above his skin. The shadow. Ferdinand said it kills abominations like me. That's its sole purpose: To fix the damage caused by Magnolia LaCroix's spell.

Anders's eyes travel from my face to my reaching hand, and he stretches his own toward mine. A ribbon of darkness lifts from his skin and strikes my fingertips like a cobra.

"Anders!" I yelp, hiding my stinging fingers behind my back. *He's lost control.* Stricken with terror, I forget to breathe. *Why is this happening? He's never attacked me before.*

CHAPTER 25

Pontificating Villains are Annoying

Out of the corner of my eye, I see Estrada stand. I edge sideways, and Anders turns with me, putting his back to the desk. My mouth opens, shuts, and opens again. I want to warn Estrada to run, but I can't say anything without reminding Anders of his presence. Estrada's eyes widen as he darts from the room.

So much for being rescued. With a deep breath, I return my attention to Anders, afraid but also glad he didn't notice Estrada leave. He no longer seems fully of this world. With each passing second, he fades, growing more wraithlike. His body is barely visible. Only the green glow of his eyes, still locked on my outstretched hand, prove he'd once been...or rather looked...human. The problem is he's not Ashmael either. I don't know how to communicate with this...this...

Ferdinand said Death didn't think or feel, but I sense its rage.

That's the only reason why I know Anders is still in there. Fighting. He hasn't lost the battle for control of his body. Yet.

I choke on a helpless sob.

Unnoticed by Anders, Estrada reenters the room. I almost cry out in relief. His eyes narrow in warning, and he raises a finger to his lips. He creeps behind Anders, and in a lightning quick move, sticks a needle in his neck.

Anders's back arches, and his mouth gapes wordlessly as he convulses. He claws at his neck, pulling the syringe free and throwing it against the wall where it shatters. Blood-tinged flecks of foam dot his lips as he half turns. The vibrant green in his eyes and the rolling cloak of darkness bleed away as he glares at Estrada. He sighs, and his legs fold as he collapses. I catch him before he hits the ground, sitting so his head rests on my lap.

Anders's eyes focus on my face. "What happened?" he murmurs, but he's unconscious before I can answer him.

I glare at Estrada. I want to be angry, but all I feel is relief. "What did you give him?"

Estrada purses his lips. He crouches beside us and checks Anders's pulse. "Just a sedative. A very strong one." He sits back on his heels, and his lab coat brushes the ground. "How long have you known he's the one responsible for the murders?"

"He didn't murder anyone." I can't help the tremor in my voice.

"Ha. My dear, I am a genius and an expert in my field, something you keep forgetting in your personal distaste for my quirks. Put aside your bias long enough to study this problem logically. Look at Anders." He waves a hand at the prone man. "Did he seem normal to you? Unthreatening? Or did he seem like he was seconds away from burning you alive?"

I brush Anders's hair from his face. He looks so young sleeping.

Estrada pushes to his feet. "Don't worry. There is a scientific explanation behind what we witnessed. And just like I found a way to neutralize him, I'm also close to discovering a cure to reverse the effects of the pathogen infecting your bodies."

My eyes widen. "Bodies?"

"I found the substance on Anders first. He accused me of putting him together wrong. My dear, he'd already healed by the time I was able to perform the operation."

Estrada chuckles at my stunned expression. No modesty there, the egotistical prick, but if he's actually discovered a cure—a way for us to go back to living a normal life—then he has the right to be arrogant.

"Detective Anders needs to be moved to a more secure location," he says. "I don't know how long the sedative will work on him."

My arms tighten around Anders. "Alonso, I appreciate the help, but I won't let you squirrel him away somewhere or let you dissect him like a lab rat."

Estrada's head twists in a birdlike manner that's unnerving. "He's too dangerous to be set free."

"He doesn't remember what he's been doing," I whisper, but only because I can't think of anything else to say, or do. The idea of agreeing with Estrada about anything sets my teeth on edge, and I prolong the moment as long as possible.

Estrada leans forward, obviously sensing he's wearing down

my resistance. "Which makes him even more dangerous. If I hadn't stopped him, you would be a burnt smudge on the floor. You can't save him from himself. And the Anders we both know wouldn't want you to."

He stares at me a moment longer, and I'm forced to nod. He's right. I don't want to admit it, but I know it. Right before Estrada entered the room, Anders didn't recognize me. It would devastate him to find out he was responsible for murdering Ivanov's men, but to be set free to kill again would be unacceptable.

Estrada leaves the room and returns with a wheelchair. I lift Anders into the chair, earning a grin from Estrada. "Is super strength one of the unusual side effects that you neglected to inform me about? What other powers have you mastered?"

I grimace in response. "It would've been easier if you'd explained what the mystery substance was doing to my body, Estrada. Why did you keep it a secret the day I came in?"

"Silly girl," he laughs. "Would you have believed me if I told you?"

"Point made." I follow Estrada as he wheels Anders into the hallway. "So what have you learned in your research, other than figuring out a way to cure me?"

He gives a quick look at the patients and nurses walking the hallway. "I'll tell you everything once we reach my secret lair."

"God, you're creepy." I let out a huff. "You're acting like this on purpose. Just to annoy me, aren't you?"

Estrada pushes the wheelchair to the elevator while I follow in silence. I won't leave Anders alone. I'll protect him as much as I can.

Estrada brings us down to the basement. Stepping out of the elevator, I'm assaulted by bad memories. I hate this place. The walls close in. The ceiling presses down. Underneath the dank, dark paint, mold grows. And under that, the scent of blood lingers. The twisty turns soon have me completely lost, but we end up in an older section of the basement that must've been built in the early half of the twentieth century. This is where Estrada has built his secret lair...lab.

He smiles and points to a door with a blacked-out window. "This is mine. The hospital promised me a place where I could conduct research in private. No one comes down here any-more."

"So no one will hear if I scream," I joke, but the look I receive in response is not amused. "Okay, tell me what you've learned about the substance you found on our bodies. And how do you intend to fix us?"

Estrada smiles. "Of course." He unlocks the door to his lab. The light is already on, and I follow him inside.

A cry jerks me to a halt.

Gabriella throws herself into my arms, a boneless weight that I hold effortlessly, despite my shock. Victor steps from a shadowed doorway, and I stumble back. My heart races as he stalks forward, takes control of the wheelchair from Estrada, and rolls Anders out of the room.

"What the hell?" I gasp. "She's been here? The whole time? You sold me out to Ivanov."

"I'd hoped you were smarter than you looked," Estrada says with a chuckle. "I thought you would've figured it out sooner. Gabriella *was* with me when she disappeared."

"I warned her you'd be a horrible date. Sucks to be right."

"Wrong. I treated Gabriella like a queen. She had no complaints about the first half of our date. Not even when I tied her up. It was only afterward, when I wouldn't let her leave, that I had to drug her. Tell me the truth: you really didn't suspect me?"

"I thought Ivanov's men had you both."

"And then I came to your rescue? Saved you from big bad Anders and you forgot everything in your gratitude?" Estrada chuckles again, a sound I'm thoroughly beginning to loathe. Why do bad guys always feel the need to gloat?

I hug Gabriella protectively against my body. "Fine, you're the super-genius. I'm your dimwitted protagonist. I never seriously thought you were involved."

"After everything that happened, I would have thought you'd be questioning everything and everyone associated with you. Obviously, Detective Anders is not the person you imagined him to be. Why would you trust me?"

"'Cause you're my doctor, Estrada. Sure, you're an arrogant jerk, but I thought you lived by certain ethical standards. Even I know doctors follow the Hippocratic Oath: First do no harm."

"That's a common misconception. First, that's not part of the actual oath. Second, an oath is optional and unenforceable. Totally nonbinding. I chose to opt out, since my morality is a bit ambiguous."

"Good to know. A little late, but I won't forget."

Gabriella's head rolls back. She smiles, as if she trusts me to get us out of this mess. Anger makes me quiver. "Will she be okay?"

Estrada gives a negligent shrug. "Of course. I wouldn't do anything to harm her. That would ruin my plan to get you to sacrifice yourself for your friend. I didn't think you'd be so...*difficult* to procure. But now I have another hostage to use against you."

Victor returns to the room. He stands to the side of the door, blocking my escape. I can't outrun him carrying Gabriella. Plus Estrada is right. I won't leave Anders to his tender mercies. And I'd rather not wait for the cavalry to ride in. If anyone's going to get hurt, it'll be me. I heal fast.

"Just hang on, Gabby," I whisper. "I'll get you out of here."

Estrada holds a syringe in his hand and motions me toward the operating table in the corner of the room. "If I'd wanted you dead, you would be. I need those samples you refused to give earlier. Cooperate and I'll let you and your friends go."

"Please, like I'm gonna trust you now. Let them go. Put a stop to this before anyone else gets hurt."

"You're wrong, Dena. It's inevitable that someone will get hurt." Estrada mops the sweat on his forehead with a tissue. Seeing it gives me a bit of hope. He isn't as calm as he portrays. "I made promises to Ivanov. In return, he paid me a lot of money—I mean a *lot*—to come up with a serum from the substance I discovered on Anders's skin. Ivanov calls it the super-soldier serum. Kind of a cliché, I know, but it's accurate. What country wouldn't pay to have soldiers who are stronger, faster, and able to regenerate from damage that would kill a normal person?" He laughs, but it isn't happy. "Ivanov tried the first batch I came up with on his own men, but it caused some pretty negative side effects in the test subjects."

"Like mental instability?"

"That was one. Look at Victor, for example." He circles his ear with a finger. "Cuckoo."

Victor's expression remains detached. I have to wonder whether Estrada's been sampling his own product, 'cause he's not right in the head either.

Estrada motions me toward the table again. I step back, and his lips tighten. "Procrastinate all you want, Dena. It won't change the outcome. You're going to do as I ask."

"You still haven't explained why you need samples from me."

"I have a responsibility to my employer. I promised Ivanov a viable serum without all the glitches."

"But Ivanov's going to use it to kill people. Please, Estrada… Alonso."

"He'll kill us." Estrada nods toward Victor, finally letting go of his lackadaisical attitude. His body practically vibrates with fear and determination. "Do you understand now? Ivanov is not the sort of person who accepts failure. I don't know how you and Anders got infected. Hell, I'm not sure I even know what Anders is. None of the men who have been given the serum have the ability Anders displayed."

I glance across the room to Victor, but super hearing doesn't appear to be in his bag of tricks. The only thing Anders and I have going for us is that Ivanov doesn't seem to want me because I'm the key to capturing the avatar. He's just greedy for his own materialist brand of power. "We both saw that Anders didn't exactly pass his sanity check," I whisper. "He almost killed us."

Estrada holds up the syringe. "That's why you're my test subject. However you were infected, you're the only human to undergo the transformation without any negative side effects. The key to reproducing a working serum is inside your body. Please, stop fighting this. If you cooperate, it will be much easier, but I'll force you to comply if necessary." His voice rises with conviction as he motions to Victor. "Take her to the table and strap her in. If she resists, hurt her friend."

Victor smiles and starts forward. I try to throw Gabriella over my shoulder, but she slips down, arms flopping. Victor grabs Gabriella by the waist, pulls her from my arms, and tosses her to the side. I cry out, lunging forward, only to be caught from behind by Victor.

"I said hurt her friend, not kill her!" Estrada rushes to Gabriella and checks for a pulse. "If she dies, we have no leverage to induce Dena's cooperation." He turns a glare my way.

I stop struggling and lean against Victor. "I'll do whatever you ask. Just don't hurt her anymore, please."

Victor lays me on the operating table. I stare at the ceiling, praying Estrada will keep his promise and let Gabriella go. Estrada lifts Gabriella and carries her from the room.

"What's he going to do to me?" I ask Victor. "Will it hurt?"

Victor grunts, pulling the strap securely on my left arm. "You give your body to science. What is nobler than to die so others may live?"

"That is not reassuring." Tears fill my eyes. "Especially when the others you speak of are murderers."

"This is about money," Estrada says, returning to the room. "Governments will pay a high price for this kind of power, and we will profit from their greed."

"What are you going to do to me?"

Estrada puts a mask over my face. "Breathe in deeply. You'll sleep, and when you wake up, it will be over." He sticks an IV needle into my hand, and it takes every bit of my willpower not to thrash around. I've never liked needles, especially those wielded by money-hungry maniacs.

CHAPTER 26

Binding of the Three

I fight the sedative he injects into my IV line, but it's a losing battle. I fade away. My soul slips from my body, and I drift upward. This time I control where I want to go. I float in the corner of the room. When Estrada pulls out a scalpel and cuts into my chest, I can't stomach anymore.

I float through the closed door to the room where Estrada carried Gabriella. She's laying on a cot with a blanket pulled over her. Another presence tugs my essence toward it. I follow the path to Anders. Victor has him tied to another operating table. An IV is attached to his arm, and he's sedated. Around his body, the dark cloud rolls thick and angry, snapping with sparks, but it's bound to his unconscious body by a thick tether. This is Anders's rage, and it's magnificent. His fury and fear manifested in darkness.

I remember when the spirit and I joined while I was hypnotized. How hungry he had been when he fed off my energy. He teetered on the edge of insanity, but I brought him back. I can do it again. Ferdinand said we're linked. I call it symbiosis. We need each other to survive, 'cause in my world there can be no light without darkness.

I feed Anders my strength, my love, and my hopes. It pushes back his rage, leaving him bathed in a shimmering golden glow.

Anders stirs on the table. His eyelids open to reveal orbs of otherworldly green—Ashmael's eyes—full of love. He focuses on me hovering above him and blinks. The glow dampens, but doesn't disappear as he brushes his hand though my spirit. "Dena?"

I silently send a message to him. *"Welcome back, Sleeping Beauty. Time to get up and save us from the evil madman."*

Anders frowns and rolls his legs over the edge of the table. He jerks the IV from his arm with a wince. When his feet touch the ground, he staggers, almost falling, but regains his balance. He rubs his eyes, shaking his head. "Dena," he whispers, "is that really you?"

I kick an incorporeal foot at his perky ass. *"Yes. Now get a move on before Estrada carves me up like a Christmas turkey."*

"This can't be happening," he mutters. "You've finally driven me insane."

"You're not insane. Anymore." I float closer, focusing on pushing my thoughts into his head. *"But you're right about this being my fault. You're as much a victim as the people who died in Magnolia LaCroix's spell the night of the earthquake. None of this would've happened if not for her...and me."*

"What are you saying?"

"*I'm saying you've got some powerful mojo inside you. You can either let this break you or you can use it to get us out of here.*" I concentrate and form the image of him in Estrada's office. I focus first on his eyes, the glowing green shining from his face like lanterns in the darkness. I show him the ribbon of electricity rising from his body to strike my fingers.

His breathing quickens. "No!"

My heart bleeds for him, but he needs to know. It's the only way for him to control what has been happening. He's repressed this part of himself deep in his subconscious. But buried emotions always resurface. They wiggle up like night crawlers in a rainstorm—a veritable feast to be eaten by that which preys on the weak. Only by facing his rage will he find the strength to overcome Death.

The memories hit Anders hard. He jerks in reaction and sinks to his knees, holding his head in his hands. Blackness thickens across his skin, coating every inch of him. I wish more than anything to be able to touch him. To be able to drape myself over his trembling body and protect him, but I can't.

I'm scared. So very, very scared.

"*Control it, Anders,*" I beg, not knowing if he can even hear me anymore. "*Don't let the rage continue to feed off you. It'll take over, and you'll disappear. Please. I need you.*"

Wholeheartedly. I need his strength, 'cause I'm growing weaker. Thinning out. Death's song plays in my head, growing louder with each passing second. Like a plucked harp string, the vibrations resonate along the silver cord connecting me to my body.

If it snaps, I'll drift away.

"I'm not ready to die, Anders." We have to stop Estrada's experiments. He can't get away with what he's done. With what he's doing to me right now. *"Help me."*

Anders blows out a deep breath. The darkness over him fades to gray, but doesn't vanish completely. For now, he's in control of his anger. How long he can contain it, I don't know. Hopefully long enough to get us through this mess. He pushes to his feet and walks over to his clothing piled on the floor. He picks up the gun, then pulls on his jeans. In my opinion, dressing is a waste of time. Who knows what Estrada's doing to my body in the other room?

My eyes caress the contours of his muscular backside until it vanishes in denim. *Such a shame.*

Fingers snap in front of my face, and I twitch. *"What did you say?"*

"Where are you? Your body, I mean?" He shakes his head. "Are you here?"

"Follow me." I glide back into the hall then freeze. Victor leans over the cot holding Gabriella. She's still unconscious, but Victor has her skirt pulled up. He's unzipping his jeans with his free hand, so caught up in his sick fantasy he fails to notice Anders. He doesn't even turn as Anders comes up from behind and smashes him in the head with the stock of his gun.

"Hit him again!" I cry out, furious. My own aura darkens. Sparks fly from my fingertips as energy shoots from my fingers. There's a loud sizzle, and Victor convulses. His pants catch fire and begin to burn.

"What the hell?" Anders gasps. He grabs the blanket from the floor, throws it over Victor's burning crotch, and stomps on it to put out the fire. The man groans, but doesn't wake up. "How many times do I have to tell you not to burn people?"

"I don't," I protest, then bite on my lip. Obviously, I have the ability. Oh crap, what if those dreams of me hunting really were of me hunting? Only like Anders, I don't remember. What if I'm as responsible for sending those men to the other side as Anders? *"He deserves to burn! Maybe not to death, but he doesn't need to pee standing up."*

"You can't take the law into your own hands." Anders pulls his handcuffs from his back pocket and locks one end around Victor's wrist. He drags him over to an exposed pipe across the room and cuffs the other hand. I don't bother to tell him Victor can easily break free. If we can take care of Estrada, we'll get back before he wakes up.

I glare over at Victor, fingertips burning. *"Piece of shit trying to take advantage of an unconscious woman. It's his fault she's here."* I finish my rant with a hiss.

"Get back in your body if you're going to behave like this," Anders orders, then pinches his nose with two fingers. "I can't believe I said that."

What I can't believe is that I'm still capable of getting angry. My emotions are but wisps of what I'd normally feel. With each minute that passes without me being in my body, the less of a connection I have to it. Tendrils of spirit drift from my form in misty contrails. Whatever surgery Estrada performs is playing havoc with my system.

I take Anders's advice and float back to the operating room. My stomach heaves when I see my ribs have been cracked open, leaving my internal organs on display, including my beating heart. Not a sight one ever wants to see.

Anders staggers into the room then freezes. "Oh God, Dena…" He points his gun at Estrada, but obviously he doesn't know what to do.

Estrada glances at him then continues with his work. "She's beautiful, isn't she?"

Anders swallows thickly. "Whatever you're doing to her, stop."

"You are not in a position to give orders." Estrada raises the scalpel then lowers it into my chest. "One flick of my wrist and she dies. All it takes is for me to nick an artery or plunge this into her beating heart."

"What are you doing?" Anders asks.

"I'm studying your work. I assume you did this to her. Surely you understand why I needed to see what makes her different from the others. Look at this heart, how strong it is, and her lungs. Simply amazing." Estrada's eyes crinkle at the corners. "She has none of the degradation of organs and none of the mental instability found in the test subjects provided by Ivanov. If only I had been able to study Dena before I practiced on them."

Estrada nods toward the gun. "Put that on the ground and kick it over to me. I don't want any accidents in my surgery. The fact that you're in here without a gown and mask compromises my sterile field. It's lucky Dena's body has evolved. She appears to be invulnerable to disease or injury."

Anders's gun hand trembles. His finger flexes, caressing the trigger, like he debates whether to take the shot. I hope he goes for it. That he denies Estrada what he has gone to such extreme lengths to obtain. My life or death shouldn't factor in when the stakes are so high.

Estrada points his scalpel at my chest cavity. "I don't think you want to test that, do you? Of course, I *am* curious whether the test subjects are able to heal from catastrophic blood loss as quickly as other wounds."

"Don't!" Anders yells, voice thick. He drops the gun and kicks it to Estrada. "No more. Sew her back up."

Estrada picks up the gun and points it at Anders. "There's no need to sew." He motions toward my body and laughs. "Look at that..." he breathes. "Isn't she amazing? Her body is already re-generating. Just like yours did."

Hovering over the table, I watch the muscles and bones begin to knit back together again.

Anders's face takes on a greenish tint. He wavers, leaning against the wall. His breath comes in ragged gasps, and his red-rimmed eyes meet my own. The darkness representing the door-way to the other side—the vortex of death which used to be a separate entity—has now fully integrated with him. He stands on the threshold. If he falls into it, he'll be consumed. I can't let that happen.

"Fight it, Anders," I say, flexing my bicep. *"I'm tougher than I currently look. I'll be okay."*

A single tear runs down Anders's cheek. Seeing the pain he can no longer hide from me almost breaks my non-corporeal heart into tendrils of misty vapor. He straightens from the wall, and the darkness fades. "You got what you needed, so go," he says. "Don't forget I don't need a gun to kill you."

"Oh," Estrada says with a sigh of wistful awe. "I'd kill for more time to play with her. I assume you incapacitated Victor on your way in. Did you kill him?"

"I hit him in the head."

Estrada nods. "But he hasn't come back in the room. I imagine his healing factor is much less rapid than Dena's, but what about *yours*, Anders? I never did find that out." He raises the gun and fires. The impact of the bullet twists Anders to the side, and he slumps to the ground.

Estrada's face is devoid of sympathy, even as he apologizes, 'cause he's a *big, fat, lying psychopath.* "Sorry about that, Anders, but given that you're suffering from amnesia and don't remember you asked me for help means I've become the villain in your little tragedy. I'm making a hasty exit before you recover."

Anders presses on his wound. "Estrada, wait. What don't I remember?"

Estrada kneels beside him. "I'm sorry, my friend. You know what this is about. You've always known, but you weren't able to deal with the truth. I can't help you now." He rises and flashes the vials of my blood and tissue. "Don't worry, I haven't forgotten about my promise to your partner, even if you have. I'm doing this for Jimmy."

Estrada leaves the room.

And I can't do anything to stop him. I float in the corner, growing stronger as my body heals. My vision blurs, then darkens. When my eyes open, I'm back inside my body. I stare at the ceiling, concentrating on not throwing up from the excruciating agony filling my chest. As long as I don't breathe, I can think. Moving? Not an option.

Until I remember that Estrada shot Anders.

I tilt my head to the side. He's lying on the ground in the same pose I am, as if too afraid to move because of the pain.

"Give me a minute or four," he whispers.

"Not really ready to move yet myself. Take your time," I say, then reconsider. "Except the bad guy is getting away while we're lying around. It's not like we're not invulnerable or anything. A little pain won't kill us."

"Speak for yourself," Anders says. "This feels worse than when you fell on top of me. I can't breathe. He shot me in the lung."

"Cry me a river," I mutter, tugging at the restraints on my arms. They won't budge. "Super strength doesn't work on these. Too bad I can't shoot lasers out of my eyeballs."

"Have you tried?"

I scowl at him. "If I could, you'd be on fire right now."

Coughing, Anders sits up. Blood dots his lips. "I'm having a hard time believing all of this. If I'm supposed to be this powerful thing, why don't I remember anything?"

"It's pretty complicated." I decide to give him the scaled-down version. "The night you were injured, Magnolia LaCroix worked a spell to open a doorway to the afterlife. When Death came to claim your soul, I was in the hospital with you. I fought it, thinking I was protecting you, but I actually caused it to merge with you."

"Merge."

"Maybe 'blend' is a better word. Your body became the avatar for Death. Rather than fully embracing your dual nature, it split you into pieces. Your loving side comes out as…a, uh, sexy, protective spirit named Ashmael. Your rage manifests as the black mist, and its strength is so great that it acts out on its own. But you're the glue that holds everything together." *Including my heart, if you want it.*

Anders holds his arm against his side as he limps over and unbuckles the restraints tying my arms to the bed. "So I'm the black smoke monster you kept telling me about."

"The one you kept telling me didn't exist, even when you were staring right at it? Yeah, pretty much." I rub my freed wrists while he tackles the ankle restraints. "Your mind blocked out your traumatic memories. It makes sense you'd be in denial of a smoke creature."

"What else don't I remember?"

"Oh. Well…" I clear my throat, damning myself for the decision to embrace honesty. "We made love this morning…in the motel."

"Dena—"

My mouth draws down. "Sorry, I should've told you."

He rises and leans over me. I focus on the lips hovering inches over my own. "So I gave you the hickey."

"And I enjoyed every minute. So did you, even if you can't remember."

"Maybe I do," he breathes. He runs the tip of his nose against the side of my neck and inhales. "You smell so good."

"I smell like blood and guts."

Anders smiles and shrugs. He helps me sit up. My whole body aches. I clench my teeth against the pain. My eyes lose focus for a few seconds, but I push aside the dizziness. My chest hasn't completely closed. It seals, one layer at a time. I also realize—only because of the expression that crosses Anders's face—that my ripped shirt leaves me exposed from the waist up. "Crap, I need clothing. I'm not running around the hospital half-naked."

"But it would've been okay if I'd only worn my boxers."

Heat rises up my chest and into my cheeks, and I gasp. "How?"

"Remember, I could hear your thoughts." He nods toward the back room. "My shirt's in there."

"Fine, I admit to being a hypocrite. But no peeking. I'm embarrassed enough that you saw my internal organs. Talk about an invasion of privacy," I mutter, crossing my arms over my chest.

"It's not like I haven't seen your breasts before, Dena." His lips quirk in the smuggest of all smirks. "They're pretty much branded behind my eyelids. I picture them every time I blink."

Is this a bad or good thing? I shake my head, refusing to ask. "I doubt seeing them covered in my blood makes them more attractive."

"Dena, you're damned hot, blood and all." The heat in his voice almost melts me into the table. His hand practically burns my skin as it wraps around my waist. He pulls me into his arms and slides me down the front of his body. *Oh yes, I really do light a brushfire in his britches.*

The sudden surge of lust shoves down my residual horror from being eviscerated. But now I need a distraction from my distraction before I lose control and use my super strength to rip his jeans right off.

I slide from between him and the table. "So I have a theory. Do you want to hear it?"

"Do I have a choice?" His fingertips trail across my thigh.

I lean into his hand, still too weak to stand on my own. Touching him gives me strength. "I don't know. Personally, you're the only thing holding me together. If you suddenly go bat-shit crazy, I won't be far behind."

"I've handled being told I'm the insane incarnation of Death pretty well." He frowns. "From what I remember from my Comparative Religion class, avatars are used by Hindu gods to come to earth to restore balance in the midst of chaos."

"Oh, I don't know. All I had to go by were the blue aliens in the movie. Once we find Ferdinand, he can explain it in a way that doesn't sound completely Looney Tunes."

"It makes sense to me. Maybe you've already gone bat-shit crazy," Anders drawls, hand tightening as I stagger.

"Are you messing with me?" I pause, turning in his arms to stare at him. His eyes meet mine. Turmoil darkens them until only a slight edge of jade shines through.

"Dee, I'm responsible for the murders I've been investigating. I don't remember killing those men, or know how to keep from killing anyone else. So forgive me if the only thing holding me together is fucking with you, since I can't actually fuck you."

I stare at him for a long moment then wrap my arms around his neck. "I prefer to use the term 'make love.' It more accurately describes how I feel right now." My fingers tangle in his hair as I pull his head down. I kiss him the way I've always wanted to kiss him, without reservations, and for once he kisses me back the same way.

The sound of someone clearing their throat breaks us apart.

Gabriella stands in the doorway, pressing her hand to her swollen cheek. "Uh, guys…what's going on?"

My arms cross to cover my breasts. "Gabriella…we were coming to rescue you."

"*Really*?" she asks, voice strained with incredulity. "'Cause it looked an awful lot like the two of you forgot about me while making out in the *super villain's* secret lair!" She thrusts Anders's shirt into my hands then stomps toward the door. "I rescued myself."

Anders and I share a guilty look and run after her. My chest no longer hurts, and Anders appears to have recovered as well. Which is a good thing since Victor's missing. The handcuffs lie in pieces on the ground.

Gabriella picks up the broken pipe and gives it a test swing. "Just wait until I find those jerks. I'm gonna get medieval on Estrada's ass after what he did to me. And Victor's gonna be pooping through a metal straw."

I meet Anders's eyes, and he shakes his head. Even though I can't hear his thoughts, I know what he's thinking, 'cause I'm thinking the same thing. The only thing that kills these guys is the black mist. Anders's rage when released completely destroys them. While the idea of Anders running around burning people to death is not my favorite, if he's ever able to harness the darkness, we may have a weapon to use against Ivanov's men.

We have no idea how many of his men have taken the serum, and now that Estrada has my blood, he'll be able to make his serum stronger. We need to find him and get my samples back before that happens.

CHAPTER 27

Team Death for the Win

Anders holds my hand as we race through the maze of corridors. With every dead end, every U-turn, I want to tear out my hair. We run at human speed to match Gabriella. I won't leave her behind. But I also can't drag her deeper into my secret.

We reach the elevators at the far end of the hallway. The down arrow above the elevator A is red, but I jab the up button a few times anyway. Then we wait, impatient. I even side-eye the stairs. I'm fast. I step in that direction, but Anders pulls me back. The door opens and Gabriella yelps as a man bursts out. Before I have a chance to react, she bashes him with pipe, then hits him two more times before I realize she's beating Estrada to a pulp.

I grab her arm and snatch the pipe from her fingers. "Enough, he's down."

"Let me go!" she yells. "He deserves this after what he did."

No doubt. He deserves this and so much more, but I shake my head.

The doctor lies on the ground with his hands wrapped around his head. When he realizes he's not being hit anymore, he stops screaming long enough to beg, "Help me. He's coming."

Who's he? I look at Anders, but he's down on one knee, searching Estrada. "The vials are gone," he says, then lets out a string of curses. He grabs Estrada by the lapels of his lab coat and hauls him upright. "Where are they?" The doctor dangles from his hands as he shakes him. "Did Victor take them?"

"Yes, yes. He's gathering the rest of my supplies." He grips Anders's hands, but he pleads with me. "We can catch him if we leave now. I know where he's going. I'll get them back."

"Why? Breaking your deal with Ivanov doesn't make any sense. He'll kill you."

"Not if you protect me. I'll do whatever you ask. Just save me now." A bell dings. "No...oh no, he's here. It's too late."

Both of the elevators' doors open. Ferdinand, surrounded by his security guys, emerges from one and steps into the hallway. Seeing their black vests, shirts, and cargo pants, and the guns on their hips has me slumping in relief. The cavalry has just arrived to save the day. Two guards rush forward from the second elevator, and Anders thrusts Estrada in their direction. In less than thirty seconds, the doctor's handcuffed and led onto elevator B. He's still crying for me to save him when the doors shut.

Ferdinand scowls at me. "Didn't I tell you to wait for backup?"

"I didn't need no stinking backup," I say, grinning at him. "But I'm glad you were here to take Estrada. My roomie has already committed great bodily injury to the man. It's best they go their separate ways."

I motion Gabriella forward, but she edges closer to me with a squeak. "Who are these guys, Dena?"

"Friends. Don't worry; you're safe now."

Angelo pushes the button to open the elevator door. He gives Gabriella a saucy wink and grin and waves her forward. My bestie giggles, fanning herself as she follows him inside. As the doors closes, I catch her practicing her seductive lip pout and eyelash flutter on him. Poor Angelo. Trapped in a metal box with no way to escape her feminine wiles. Of course, he started the game first.

"What about Victor?" Ferdinand asks. "Is he still down here?"

I bite my lip. *Something's not right.* "He got away with some vials of my blood and tissue samples. Ivanov plans to use them to perfect a serum of the mystery substance. It'll make his men invulnerable."

"Ivanov will find that task difficult without his pet doctor," Ferdinand says.

Anders's fingers interlock with mine. "We still need to try to recover them. My guess is Victor's still around waiting for Estrada. Let's get out of here." He steps forward, but then stops when the guards spread out to flank us. He shifts to the side, blocking me with his body. My heart races at the unease he tries to conceal. I know him too well not to be nervous.

"What's going on, Ferdinand?" I keep my eyes directed on the man I thought was my friend, but I watch his men through my peripheral vision.

"Step away from the avatar and come over here, Dena."

Hot damn, he's a traitor after all. Mala called it. She'll never let me live this one down. I'll have to listen to her tell me *I told you so* until the day one of us dies. Which may be today, 'cause nobody's taking Anders away from me without a fight.

I move in front of Anders, raising my fists. "No."

Anders grabs my arm and pulls me beside him. "Don't block my line of fire."

Right. He has a gun. He keeps it pointed at the ground. Which is smart. The situation's tense enough without everyone bringing guns into it.

Ferdinand crosses his arms, looking totally badass and scary. "This is not up for debate, Dena. He's dangerous. So are you…" My wise Gandalf is gone. As is the joking confidant who lowered my defenses, allowing me to feel comfortable enough to divulge my innermost secrets. I was lonely and isolated until he entered my life. He took advantage of my weakness.

Fucking Ferdinand picked the wrong time to be two-faced. "Glad you understand the situation. Rather than putting your guys at risk by messing with us, you should be going after Victor. Unless you work for him, too. Are you one of Ivanov's men?"

"No, I've simply decided you're safer under my protection. Hell, Paradise Pointe's safer if the avatar is detained. Too many people have died protecting you. Your freedom comes with a price I'm not willing to pay anymore."

"I should've let Mala fry your brain, traitor." I hold up my fists. "Fine. If you really want to make this a fight, I guarantee you won't win. I'll take them all down."

"Enough," Anders says, stepping around me. He raises his arms above his head. "I give up."

"Are you crazy?" I yell. The soldiers come at us in a rush. Anders doesn't even try to fight the man who grabs his arm. I pull him off Anders, blocking the punch aimed at my face. I grab his arm and fling him into a second man who staggers back. The third moves in while I'm distracted, which doesn't seem very fair.

Anders lunges for me, but I dodge. My quick reflexes usually don't work on him, but I'm in the groove now. I keep my body between Anders and the soldiers. There are too many of them. And I'm afraid to use my full strength 'cause I don't want to hurt them. They won't heal like Victor.

"I've got this!" I tell him. "Really. Trust me, I do." A kick from behind knocks me into the wall. *Okay, maybe I don't...ow.* A sharp pain explodes in my head. The hallway blurs, then goes grainy. My chest burns, and I struggle to catch my breath. *I'm running.* A sharp prick hits my shoulder, and I yank out a feathered dart and throw it to the ground. I try to rub the sting away, knowing the arm and pain aren't mine.

"What's happening?"

This isn't my thought either. *Mala?*

"H-Help. Help me."

"Mala...she's screaming." I'm no longer in my own head. I see from my cousin's eyes and feel her pain. Her terror threatens to overwhelm me. She broadcasts her panic directly into my brain, no filter, just a straight infusion of fear.

The drug in her system confuses her. Her thoughts come in ragged impressions—visions I struggle to interpret. She's still in the hospital, running down a long hallway. Red doors flash past. All of them closed. The one doorknob she jerks on won't turn.

Where are all the people? Her legs turn watery. Each step gets harder.

A hand grabs her arm, jerking her around. She looks up, and I see a familiar ugly face. *Victor.*

Damn, I should've killed him when I had the chance. He pulls his arm back and slams his fist into her chin.

Pain rolls my eyes back. "Mala!" I scream, falling with her.

Anders wraps his arms around me. "What's wrong?"

I press my face into his shoulder. Sobs leave me breathless. I shake my head, trying to dispel the fuzzy aftereffects of the vision—the taint of the sedative. It felt too real. "Victor grabbed Mala. I saw it." *She's so frightened.*

Ferdinand's voice comes from above us. "Mala and Landry were searching the fourth floor. She's fine."

"She's not. I'm not sure how, but I'm seeing through her eyes. He shot her with a dart gun." In my mind's eye, I see Victor's face from below. He carries her to an ambulance and climbs inside. Two men also load a stretcher onto the same ambulance. I can't see the person lying under the blanket. Is it Landry? He wouldn't let anyone hurt her without a fight. Oh God, what if Victor killed him?

Pain eats the vision, and I blink. "They're in an ambulance in front of the ER. If we hurry, we can stop him. Please."

Anders releases me and stands. "Promise you'll find Mala, and I'll go without a fight."

Ferdinand taps on his earpiece. "Beta Team, target's been sighted in the ambulance bay. He has hostages so proceed with caution." He motions for Anders. "Let's go."

"Stop…" I push to my feet. Three guys move to block me. I

have to go through them to get to Anders, but he's already in front of Ferdinand. He holds out his arms and handcuffs are locked around his wrists.

"It's better this way, Dena." Anders says, not meeting my eyes. "I'm dangerous. I can't control this alone. I need help."

"You've got me. We're a team." I raise my hands in the air as I approach Ferdinand. "I call a truce. Here's the deal. I'm going with Anders. We won't be separated. He needs my help to control the shadow, and guys, if the shadow breaks free, you're all a bunch of toasty marshmallows on a spit." I turn to Ferdinand. "In return, promise you won't hurt him?"

Ferdinand elbows his way between the soldiers and pauses an arm's length away from me—where's the trust? "You have my word."

With those four words, I give up.

I follow the men onto the elevator, planning my escape once we reach the first floor. If Ferdinand thinks he can trust me then he doesn't know me very well. Anders refuses to meet my eyes. Is he also biding his time? Or does he really believe he's too dangerous to be free?

The elevator doors open. We shuffle out, and the doors close behind us.

The silence catches my attention first. The entire lobby is empty of people.

Everything happens next in a blur.

Sheriff deputies run from all corners of the room, forming a wall of black and tan uniforms barring our exit. Guns point in our direction.

"BPSO, drop your weapons!" Lieutenant Bessie Caine orders. "Put your hands up!"

I reach for the ceiling. *Oh my God, I've never been so happy to see this many cops in my entire life.* I've known Bessie my whole life, and she's never looked cooler or more in control than at this moment. Her eyes are hard chips of ice. There's not a sign of weakness or compromise in them. If Ferdinand's men don't comply, she'll shoot them. I believe that.

Ferdinand's men believe, too. They hesitate, looking to him for direction, and I hold my breath. What is he going to do? Fight?

Ferdinand raises his hand over his head. "Lieutenant Caine, there's been some sort of misunderstanding."

"Only if you resist. Guns on the ground."

He pulls his gun out of the holster and tosses it in Bessie's direction, then interlocks his fingers over his head and drops to his knees. His men do the same.

Deputies rush forward, but I don't watch as Ferdinand's men are taken into custody. I rush over to Bessie, with Anders at my side. "Thank God, you showed up in time," I say, throwing my arms around her for a quick hug, then stepping back. "Where's Mala? Did she call you?"

"Yes, she said there were armed men at the hospital. Do you know what the hell's going on here?" Bessie's dark brow creases as she motions a deputy toward Anders. "Someone find a key and unshackle Detective Anders."

"Thanks," Anders says, but I can't tell if he means it. He rubs his wrists. "Are these the only men you've taken into custody? Alonso Estrada is responsible for kidnapping Dena's friend Gabriella. Ferdinand's men took him."

Bessie keeps an eye on the room as she speaks. "Gabriella's safe. Her injuries are being seen to in the ER. We also intercepted the men holding Dr. Estrada. He's en route to the police station. Unfortunately we haven't located the man Gabriella calls Victor."

"Victor escaped…" *No.* The terror I've been holding back rushes through me. "What about Mala? Tell me she's safe." I grab Bessie's arm. "Ferdinand said his men would get to her in time. He promised—"

Bessie's body tightens like a tightly wound spring. She shakes my hand off her arm, her own settling on the butt of her gun. "Ferdinand took Mala?"

"No, Victor. He shot her with a sedative, then he and two other men loaded her and another patient into an ambulance."

The tension inside Bessie snaps. She moves fast, broadcasting the information over the radio mike while dispatching officers still on scene to search the hospital. "What else can you tell me?"

"Dr. Estrada said he'd tell me where to find Victor if I protected him. This was his plan the whole time." I lean into Anders, speaking to him more than to Bessie since she won't understand. "It's why he gave Victor the tissue samples. Why he kidnapped Mala. She's his insurance policy."

Anders places his hand on the small of my back. His warmth spreads, banishing the chill in my body and bringing clarity to my tangled thoughts. Estrada and Ferdinand are the links to everything. And if the only way to get Mala back is by making a deal with the devil, then so be it. But I won't go forward alone.

Bessie pulls car keys out of her pocket and hands them to Anders. "Detective, you've been reinstated for duty. Get to the station and find out what Estrada knows." Her cold gaze shifts to the handcuffed man surrounded by deputies. "I'll meet up with you after I speak with Ferdinand Lafitte."

"Bessie," I swallow hard, "what if Mala's—"

"Best you know up-front, Dena. I don't deal in what ifs. We will find Mala. Whatever it takes. Now go. I've got a mess to clean up."

Anders leads me outside. Police cars fill the parking lot, blocking the front entrance. A large crowd stands behind them. We find Bessie's car parked off to the side of the building. It's a secluded corner, blocked off from view of the parking lot. For the first time in what feels like forever, we're alone. Safe. I can finally breathe.

Anders and I share a look, just one. But it says everything. He opens his arms, and I fall against him, hugging him tight. I don't want to ever let him go. "Tell me everything's going to be okay," I whisper against his chest. "Even if it's a lie, I'll believe it if it comes from you."

"Everything will be fine. We'll find her."

"I believe you. In you. *Always.* But you need to have faith in yourself…and in me. 'Cause if you don't and you let yourself be captured by Ferdinand or anyone else, ever again, without a fight, I'm gonna kick your perky ass."

Anders laughs. "So you meant it when you said we're a team? You're not afraid I'll hurt you?"

"I love you, Michael Anders. It would break my heart if I lost you, and I'm more afraid of that than I am of anything the shadow might do."

"I couldn't bear it if I hurt you in any way." He lifts my face and presses a kiss to my lips. "That includes breaking your heart. I may be the avatar of Death, but I live for you. You called me from the darkness. You brought light to my shattered soul and made me whole."

Aw, that's the cheesiest and sweetest thing anyone's ever said to me.

I brush a tear from my eye, then hug Anders again. We were pieces of a puzzle scattered into the wind, brought together and made stronger together. I'm not afraid to face whatever fate throws at us next. I will fight for my family, my friends, and myself. I'm living this second shot at life to the fullest, without wasting any of these precious moments hiding in shadows, wishing for Death. 'Cause I'm already held safely in his embrace.

Did you miss Mala and Landry's story? Please turn the page for an excerpt from *Dark Paradise.*

CHAPTER 1

Mala

Floater

Black mud oozes between my toes as I shift my weight and jerk on the rope, sending up a cloud of midges and the rotten-egg stench of stagnant swamp water. The edge of the damn crawfish trap lifts out of the water—like it's sticking its mesh tongue out at me—and refuses to tear loose from the twisted roots of the cypress tree. It's the same fight each and every time, only now the frayed rope will snap if I pull on it any harder. I have to decide whether to abandon what amounts to two days' worth of suppers crawling along the bottom of that trap or wade deeper into the bayou and stick my hand in the dark, underwater crevice to pry it free.

Gators eat fingers. A cold chill runs down my spine at the thought, and I shiver, rubbing my arms. I search the algae-coated surface for ripples. The stagnant water appears calm. I didn't have a problem wading into the bayou to set the trap. I've trapped and hunted in this bayou my entire life. Sure it's smart to pay attention to my instincts, doing so has saved my life more times than I can count, but this soul-sucking fear is ridiculous.

I take a deep breath and pat the sheathed fillet knife attached to my belt. My motto is: Eat or do the eating. I personally like the last part. A growling belly tends to make me take all kinds of stupid risks, but this isn't one. If I'm careful, a gator will find my bite cuts deeper than teeth if it tries to make me into a four-course meal. Grandmère Cora tried to teach her daughter that the way to a man's heart was through his stomach. Since Mama would rather fuck 'em than feed 'em, I inherited all the LaCroix family recipes, including a killer gator gumbo.

Sick of second-guessing myself, I slog deeper into the waist-high water. Halfway to the trap, warm mud wraps around my right ankle. My foot sticks deep, devoured. I can't catch my balance. *Crud, I'm sinking.*

Ripples undulate across the surface of the water, spreading in my direction. My breath catches, and I fumble for the knife. Those aren't natural waves. Something's beneath the surface. *Something big.* I jerk on my leg, panting. With each heave, I sink deeper, unable to break the suction holding me prisoner. Gator equals death…But I'm still alive. *So what is it? Why hasn't it attacked?*

A flash of white hits the corner of my eye—

Shit! I twist, waving the knife in front of me. My heart thuds. Sparkly lights fill my vision. Blinking rapidly, I shake my head. My mind shuts down. At first I can't process what I'm seeing. It's too awful. Too sickening. Then reality hits—hard. The scream explodes from my chest, and I fling myself backward. The mud releases my leg with a *slurp*. Brackish water smacks my face, pouring into my open mouth as I go under. Mud and decayed plants reduce visibility below the surface.

Wrinkled, outstretched fingers wave at me in the current. The tip of a ragged fingernail brushes across my cheek. It snags in my hair. I bat at the hand, but I can't free my hair from the girl's grip. She's holding me under. Trying to drown me. I can't lift my head above the surface. *She won't let me go!*

My legs flail, kicking the girl in the chest. She floats. I sit up, choking. I can't breathe and scream at the same time. I'm panting, but I concentrate. *Breathe in. Out. In.* The girl drifts within touching distance. Floating. Not swimming. Why doesn't she move? Is it stupid to pray for some sign of life—the rise of her chest, a kick from her leg—when I already know the truth?

Water laps at my chin. I wrap my arms around my legs. Shivers shake my body despite the warmth of the bayou, and my vision's fuzzy around the edges. I'm hyperventilating. If I try to stand I'll pass out. Or throw up. Probably both 'cause I'm queasy. I close my eyes, unable to look at the body any more. Which is so wrong. I've studied what to do in this sort of situation. Didn't I spend a month memorizing the crime scene book I borrowed from Sheriff Keyes? *Come on, Mala. Pull it together.* A cop—even a future one—doesn't get squeamish over seeing a corpse. If I can't do something as simple as reporting the crime scene, well, then why not drop out of college, get hitched, and push out a dozen babies before I hit twenty-five, like everyone else in this damn town?

I lift my hands to scrub my face. Strands of algae lace my fingers. I pick them off. My legs tremble as I rise, which keeps me from running away. I have to describe the crime scene when I call the Sheriff's Office, and I imagine myself peering through the lens of a giant magnifying glass like Sherlock Holmes—searching her body for clues. Each detail becomes crystal clear.

Her lips are slightly parted, and a beetle crawls across her teeth, which are straight and pearly white, not a tooth missing. She's definitely a townie. A swamp girl her age would have a couple of missing teeth, given she appears to be a few years older than me. Her expensive-looking sundress has ridden up round her waist. Poor thing got all gussied up before she killed herself.

The deep vertical cuts still pinking the water on both of the girl's wrists makes my stomach flip inside out. I double over, trying not to vomit. It takes several deep breaths to settle my gut before I can force myself to continue studying the body.

Long hair fans out like black licorice around her head, and her glazed blue eyes stare sightlessly at the heavens. Faint sunlight glistens on the flecks of water dotting her porcelain skin. I've never seen such a serene expression on anyone's face, let alone someone dead, like she's seen the face of God and has found peace.

After seeing her up close and personal, I can't stomach leaving her floating in the foul water. Flies crawl in her wounds, and midges land on her eyes. Slimy strands of algae twine through her hair. Soon the fish will be nibbling at her. Unable to bring myself to touch her clammy-looking skin, I take a firm grip on her dress and drag her onto the bank—high enough above the waterline that she'll be safe from predators while I get help.

I'm halfway across the stretch of land between the bayou and my house when a shiver of foreboding races through my body, and I slow my pace. *Shit! I took the wrong path.* Usually I avoid traveling through the Black Hole. It's treacherous with pockets of quicksand. Cottonmouths like to hide in the thick grass, beneath lichen-smothered fallen trees. Those natural obstacles are pretty easy to navigate if you're alert. What makes the hairs on the back of my neck prickle is the miasma that permeates every rock and rotten tree in the clearing I cross to get home. A filmy layer of ick coats my skin and seeps in through my pores until it infects my whole body with each step. I feel…*unclean.* I'm not big on believing in the whole concept of evil, but if there's any place I'd consider to be tainted ground, I'm walking across it.

Instinct screams that I'm not alone. I'd be a fool to ignore the warning signs twice. If I listened to my instincts earlier, I never would've found the body. I stretch out my senses like tentacles waving in the wind. Nothing moves…chirps, or croaks. A strange, pungent odor floats on the light breeze, but I can't identify it. My darting gaze trips and reverses to focus on the *Bad Place.* I swallow hard and yank my gaze from the dark stain on the rock in the middle of the circle. Mama said our slave ancestors used this area for their hoodoo rituals because the veil between the living and dead is thinner here.

It's always sounded like a whole lot of bullshit to me until I stumbled across the blood-stained altar and shards of burnt bone scattered across earth devoid of grass or weeds—salted earth, where nothing grows. Mother Mary, it creeps me out.

'Cause what if I'm really not alone? What if something stands on the other side of the veil, close enough to touch, but invisible? Watching me.

Whatever's out here can go to the devil 'cause I'm not waiting to greet it.

By the time I burst out of the woods that border our yard, the sun has started its downward slope in the sky behind me. I double over, hands on my knees, to catch my breath after my half-mad run. Our squat wooden house perches on cinder-block stilts like an old buzzard on top of the hill. The peeling paint turns the rotting boards an icky gray in the waning light, but it's sure a welcome sight for sore eyes.

With a final glance over my shoulder to be sure I wasn't followed, I dash beneath the Spanish moss–draped branches of the large oak that shades our house, dodging the darn rooster running for me with tail feathers spread. I brush it aside with my foot, avoiding the beak pecking at my ankle.

"Mama!" My voice trembles. I really wish my mother had come home early. But the dark windows and empty driveway tell me otherwise. I track muddy footprints across the cracked linoleum in the kitchen to get to the phone.

Ms. Dixie Fontaine answers on the first ring. "Sheriff's Office, what's your emergency?" The 9-1-1 dispatcher's lazy drawl barely speeds up after I tell her about the dead girl. "All right, honey. I'll get George on over. You be waiting for him and don't go touching the body, you hear?" She pops her gum in my ear.

A flash of resentment fills me, but I'm careful to keep my tone even. "Don't worry, I know better, Ms. Dixie. I only touched her dress—to drag her from the water."

"That's fine, Malaise, quick thinking on your part. Bye now."

"Bye," I mutter, slamming the phone in the cradle. I breathe out a puff of air, trying to calm down. I'm antsy enough without having to deal with Ms. Dixie's inability to see me as anything but a naive kid. I'm not an idiot. How can she think I'd make a rookie mistake like contaminating the crime scene? I've been working with her now for what? Nine…no, ten months. Hell! What does it take to prove myself to her? To the rest of the veterans at the sheriff's office who remember every mistake I've ever made and throw them in my face every chance they get?

Disaster. That should've been my name. Instead, I've been saddled with Malaise. Well, whatever. I stomp into the bathroom, slip off my muddy T-shirt and cut-off jean shorts, and take a scalding shower. I scrub hard to get the scummy, dead-girl film off my skin. It takes almost a whole bottle of orchid body soap to cleanse my battered soul and wash the tainted, dirty feeling down the drain with the muck.

The whole time, three words echo in my head. *Deputy George Dubois.* My heart hasn't stopped thudding since Ms. Dixie mentioned his name. The towel I wrap around my heaving chest constricts my rapid breaths like a tightened corset. Hopefully, I won't do an old-fashioned swoon like those heroines from historical novels when I see him.

It's a silly reaction, but George comes in third on my list of People I Want to Impress the Most. It's not that his six feet of muscled, uniformed hotness tempts me to turn to a life of crime just so he'll frisk me and throw me in the back of his patrol car. Nope, that pathetic one-sided schoolgirl crush passed after we graduated and started working together. I'd be as cold as the dead girl if I couldn't appreciate his yummy goodness, but the last thing either of us need is for a romantic entanglement to screw up our professional relationship.

George epitomizes everything I want to become when I "grow up." He graduated from Paradise High School my freshman year and went to the police academy at the junior college. Once he turned twenty, he got a job at the Bertrand Parish Sheriff's Office.

When news of a part-time clerical position floated around town, guess who stood first in line for the job assisting Ms. Dixie with the data entry of the old, hardcopy crime reports into the new computer system. It's not always what you know at BPSO, but *whose* ass you kiss to get hired as a deputy. The recession left few open positions, forcing rookies to compete against seasoned officers who were laid off at other agencies. I don't have family to pull strings for me, but I've made job connections with people in positions of authority while obtaining practical experience working for the Sheriff's Office. I refuse to leave my future to the fickle whims of fate.

My last year at Bertrand Junior College begins in two months. I'll graduate with an Associate of Arts degree in Criminal Justice. I haven't decided whether to transfer to a larger university for a BA, but if not, I will definitely enroll in the police academy next summer. One year. I just have to survive one more boring year, and I'll finally get to start living out my dream of becoming a detective.

Calm down, Mala. I fuss with my thick, russet curls for a few minutes in the bathroom mirror then give up and pull it back in a high ponytail. My hair's a lost cause with the darn humidity frizzing it up. I finish dressing in my best jeans and a lavender T-shirt. Rocks pop beneath tires traveling down the gravel driveway. Instead of remaining barefoot, I slip on my rain boots, not wanting to look like a complete heathen or worse, reminding the higher-ups at the crime scene of my true identity—the prostitute's bastard.

Rumors about Mama's choice of occupation have been whispered about since before my birth. You'd think being the daughter of the town whore would be humiliating enough to hang my head in shame. Then add in the fact that most folk also think she's a broom-riding witch. The kids in school were brutal, repeating as gospel the stupid rumors they overheard from their parents, who should've known better. It boggles the mind that people in this day and age can believe ignorant stuff like Mama can hex a man's privates into shriveling if he crosses her. The only good thing about being the witch's daughter is it keeps most boys from straying too close. I don't have to deal with a bunch of assholes who think I'll blow them for a couple of twenties and an open bar tab like Mama.

With one last rueful glance at my face in the mirror, I shrug. This is as good as it's gonna get. I run onto the front porch and freeze halfway down the steps. The patrol car I expect to see in the drive turns instead into a good view of Mama on hands and knees beside her truck with a flowerpot stuck under her chin as she pukes in the geraniums. *Crud! Georgie will be here any minute.* I've got to hide her in the house. She can spend the night heaving up what's left of her guts in the toilet without me babysitting her.

Mama senses me hovering. She rolls onto her backside and holds out her hands.

"Don't just stand there gawkin' like an idiot, help your mama up," she says.

With a heavy sigh, I trudge to her side. I grit my teeth and lift her to her feet while she flops like roadkill. Upright, she lists sideways. A strong wind would blow her over. The vomit-and-stale-beer stench of her breath makes my nose crinkle when she throws her skinny arm around my shoulders.

"What you been up to today?" She tries to trail her fingers through my ponytail, but they snag on a knot I missed. She jerks her hand free, uncaring that it causes me pain since she's purposely deadened her own feelings with booze. Mama can't cope with her life without a bottle of liquor in one hand. It's like the chicken-and-the-egg question. Which came first? Was her life shitty before she became an alcoholic, or had booze made it worse? I can't see how it could be better, but maybe I'm naive, or as stupid as she always calls me.

I rub at the sting on my scalp. "Why are you home so early?"

She sways. "Can't I miss my baby girl?"

"Missing me never slowed you down before. What makes tonight any different?"

"Why you so squirrelly? You act like you don't want me here." She pulls back far enough to look me over. "Expectin' someone or you all dressed up with nowhere to go?" She cackles, slapping her leg like she's told the funniest joke ever.

"Georgie Dubois's coming out."

"Why? I know the deputy's not comin' to see you."

I grit my teeth on the snappy comment that hovers on the tip of my tongue. "Found a dead girl floating in the bayou."

Mama pulls her arm back and strikes cottonmouth quick.

I end up flat on my back with stars dancing before my eyes. My cheek burns. I blink several times, trying to clear my head, then focus in on the shadow hovering over me with clenched fists. "God damn it! Are you crazy?" I roll over and stagger to my feet. She steps forward again, fist raised.

"Don't you dare, Mama!"

"Don't take the Lord's name in vain. Or threaten me."

"I haven't threatened, *yet*. But I swear, you hit me again, I'm out of this rat hole you call a house. I've earned enough scholarship money to move into an apartment."

"Why you sayin' such things, Malaise?" Tears fill her eyes.

Money. The only thing that still touches Mama's fickle heart.

"You just backhanded me, Mama! What? Do you expect me to keep turning the other cheek until you break it? Or accidentally kill me like that girl I found…"

Mama's mocha skin drops a shade, and she sucks in a breath. I don't think it has to do with any feelings of regret. No, it has to do with the girl. She hit me after she heard about George coming out for the body.

"Why do you look so scared?" Suspicion makes my voice sharp. "What did you do?"

Mama staggers toward the house.

"Don't walk away from me," I yell. "What's going on? Georgie will be here any minute. If I've got to cover for you, then I need to know why or I might let something slip on accident."

Mama makes it to the stairs and collapses onto the bottom step. She buries her face in her palms. Shudders wrack her body. "I need a drink, Mala. There's a bottle in my bottom drawer. Bring it out to me."

"That's not a good idea…"

She lifts her head. Her dark brown eyes droop at the corners, and I see the faint trace of fine lines. Strangest of all, her eyes have lost the glazed, shiny appearance they held a few minutes earlier. *The news shocked her sober.*

"I'm not askin' again, Malaise. Get in there if you want to hear the story."

CHAPTER 2

Mala

Trigger Happy

I scramble up the stairs. It doesn't take but a minute to find the bottle hidden under her nightgowns in the dresser drawer. The seal on the bottle of Johnnie Walker Red remains intact. She must've been saving it for a special occasion. That doesn't bode well for the direction of the conversation we'll be having in a moment. I don't bother with a glass. Mama always says, "Don't need one for beer. Don't want one for liquor." I ease down the staircase. She doesn't even look up, just holds out a shaking hand.

"Want a swig?" she asks, opening the bottle with a deft twist. A slight smile dances on her lips. "No? My, my, such a good girl I got. Funny thing is, girl, I was just like you at your age. Thought I was better than my mama. Thought she was trash."

Silence fills the space between us, but I twitch first. "That's not how I feel—"

"Don't lie. I see it in your eyes. You'll learn different when your time comes." Her chapped lips purse. She takes a long drink and sighs. "Come on over here. Sit by me, *cher*."

I shuffle forward then stop.

She stretches out the arm not holding the bottle. "Come on, I won't bite."

When I sit down beside her, she pulls me close, and I lay my head on her shoulder. For a long minute, we sit in silence, staring out toward the woods. The sun has almost reached the tips of the moss-draped trees, and the clouds have turned crimson and gold. Day and night. Love and hate. One can't exist in the world without the other. They come together at twilight—the perfect symbol for my chaotic feelings for Mama because, as much as I hate how she treats me when she's drunk, I still love her.

"Mama, I'm sorry I cursed you," I whisper, head tilting to stare into her pensive face.

She squeezes my shoulders. "Don't worry, *cher*. I won't be around to hurt you much longer."

"What does that mean?"

"Means I had my death vision and I'm gonna die. Soon. I'd hoped to keep the news from you for a while yet, but I need to set my affairs in order before I pass."

I snort and pull free of her embrace. "That's silly, a death vision." The wellspring of anger reserved just for her crazy shit has been tapped, and it bubbles up again. "The drink has you hallucinating."

"Wish that was the case, Malaise. The day's comin'. I'm not sure exactly how or when, but it's tied to that girl you found. I dreamed about her." She takes another drink then burps. "S'cuse me."

I shake my head. Mama, the epitome of a southern lady.

"I don't believe in dreams that foretell the future." My arms fold across my chest with a chill that caresses my spine like an accordion being played by a zydeco master. "You're just *crazy*—"

She rolls her eyes at me then shakes her head. "Sure, I'm crazy. I know I am, but it's those dreams that done drove me nuttier than Ida Jean's fruitcake, not the other way around. After I die, the visions will pass on to you like mine came from my mama and hers from her mama, and so on, all the way back to mother Africa. Then you'll sit on my grave and beg my spirit to teach you how to control the horrors you see." She takes another drink. "Maybe I'll have forgiven you by then and will help you out."

"I'm not sitting on your tomb. That's creepy. And I'm the one who should be forgiving you," I say, voice rising. "Why you always got to turn things around and make yourself the victim?"

"Talk to my bones and find a bottle of whisky. Both'll be your best friends. Helps ease the pain of dreaming of deaths you can't change."

I roll my eyes, careful not to let her see. No use arguing when she refuses to listen. "Tell me about the girl."

"Long black hair? Blue eyes to match her fancy sundress?" Mama sits the bottle between her legs. "A spoiled, rich brat from town."

"Yeah, I guess. You met her before?"

Red and blue flashing lights and a siren drift from the end of the long driveway leading to the house. The patrol car's wheels had rolled over rain-filled puddles that splattered the sides with mud during its close to thirty-minute journey through unpaved woodland.

Mama reaches for the railing and uses it to pull herself to her feet. "I'm going to bed. You tell little Georgie Porgie to tell his daddy hello for me. We go way back, me and Dubois senior. He'll remember me."

Does that mean Georgie's dad and Mama did the nasty back in the good ol' days? *Eww.* "Yeah, sure," I drawl. *Thanks, Mama. Scarred for life with that image.*

I squeeze my eyes shut and shove the thought of Mama dying into the farthest recesses of my mind. As much as she drives me crazy, I love her. The idea that she won't be around forever terrifies me.

George parks his patrol car and steps out with a scowl. My gaze travels over his body. I compare the change in his appearance. It's been a month since he went to the graveyard shift, and the beginning of a Dunkin' Donuts belly stretches his starched, tan uniform shirt, but he still looks mighty tasty.

He catches me staring. A smile lights up his face. "Hey, Mala Jean." He waves me over. "Dixie said you found a body?"

"Uh yeah, down in the bayou." My feet tangle together. I must look as drunk as Mama when I stumble over to him on wobbly legs. *Stupid feet.* "Just you coming for her?" I ask, glad my voice doesn't shake too. I wipe sweaty palms on my jeans. *I am a professional.*

George blushes, a light dusting of freckles standing out against his pale skin. The setting sun brings out the fire in his reddish-gold hair. "Sheriff Keyes, Andy, and Bessie are out on Route Seven. A bunch of buffalo broke free of McCaffrey's pasture and ran out into the road. It caused a major pile-up."

"Merciful heavens, anyone dead?"

"Four buffalo got killed. No human fatalities, but some pretty serious injuries. A little boy needed to be flown over to Lafayette. The sheriff's ETA is in an hour with the coroner." He remembers to take a breath before continuing, "So, where is my crime scene?"

"About half a mile away. Got a flashlight? It'll be dark by the time we get there."

George climbs back into his car and comes out with a long-handled flashlight and his shotgun. He pulls a mini-flashlight from his duty belt and hands it over.

"Okay, let's go," I say, leading him into the woods.

He walks with the shotgun pointed skyward, alert for trouble. His eyes scan the dense foliage completely oblivious to my desperate attempts to keep the conversation going so I don't have to think about our destination. How can silence be so deafening? *Say something. Anything.*

George clears his throat. "How's your ma? She been staying out of trouble? I haven't seen her at the station for a few days."

Heat floods my cheeks, and my steps quicken. I swallow hard around the lump in my throat. "Mama's doing just fine, Georgie." Somehow I manage to answer without my voice betraying the immense humiliation I feel. Why did he have to go and irritate me by bringing up Mama? "I'm sure she'll be real grateful for your concern over not seeing her in the drunk tank."

God love him, but it takes a few seconds for the sarcasm to sink in.

"Oh, Mala, you know I didn't mean anything bad by that. I hadn't seen her is all, and I usually see her every weekend…uh, this isn't going too good for me, is it? Might be better if I shut up, huh?"

My eyes roll at George's horrified tone. He has a good soul, not a mean bone in his body, and the faux pas leaves him flustered. Wanting to put him out of his misery, I look over my shoulder with a forced grin that I hope doesn't scare him. "Don't worry. You mess with me, I mess with you."

"Still, I'm sorry. I wasn't thinking. Truth be told, I'm a little nervous." He gives me a sideways glance. "I wouldn't say this to anyone but you 'cause…"

"'Cause you know I'll have your back?" I arch an eyebrow and echo his relieved smile. "Stop avoiding the subject by buttering me up with compliments. What's wrong?"

His hand tightens around the shotgun. "Fine, but don't laugh. Swear."

I cross my heart.

"I've never seen a corpse before, and Sheriff Keyes expects me to work the crime scene alone until he arrives with the coroner." He pauses, and I give him a blank face—the expression I hide behind whenever someone says something hurtful. Or in this case, to keep from laughing my head off over seeing big, bad, ex–football player, super-cop Georgie shaken. It makes him a little less superhero-like and more human.

He gives me a relieved smile. "I don't want to make a fool out of myself."

"Don't worry, I won't let you do anything stupid, like vomit on the body," I tease. A slight chill in the air makes me shiver, and I wrap my arms around myself for comfort. I smell the sulfur stench of the water before I see the girl's body lying on the muddy bank. "There she is."

George plays the flashlight across the corpse. "Oh Jesus, damn it," he whispers, voice choked up. "It's Lainey—Elaine Prince."

"*Lainey.*" I sigh the nickname. Knowing it makes her feel real. She didn't before, not totally. I turn to George, unable to face her glazed stare. "She's exactly how I left her."

"O-oh, well, that's good."

We stand side by side over her body, coming to grips with the harsh reality of her death in our own ways. Seeing her again stirs up volatile emotions I refuse to contemplate too closely. I can't afford to look weak, and breaking down in front of George is not an option. Finally, I can't take the silence and ask, "You gonna pass out?"

"Nah, I'll be fine. I knew Lainey." George clears his throat. "She's…she was a couple of years ahead of me in school. I had a huge crush on her in ninth grade."

He squats down beside Lainey and pulls her dress down over her legs. I almost remind him to put on gloves, but it doesn't matter. Any evidence probably washed away in the swamp.

"Lainey comes from a good family," he says. "Her father's a well-respected preacher. Her mama's always donating time. You know, doing good deeds like feeding and clothing the poor. They'll be crushed."

My rubber boots squelch in the muck as I hunker down next to him. "Prince, huh?"

The name sends tendrils of unease down my spine. The image of Landry Prince's gray eyes form in my mind. His heavy stare followed me whenever I walked past him at school. I memorized his schedule last semester to avoid going to the places where he hung out with his friends. I'd shaken him until a few weeks ago when he started coming into Munchies on the weekends when I work a second job—not sure why he finds my waiting tables so fascinating. The irritating thing is he never speaks to me. Hell, he doesn't even come in alone. He has a different bobble-headed girl clinging to his arm each time, but do his dates keep his attention from turning to me like a needle drawn to a lodestone? Nope!

George glances over at me. The shadows make it difficult to read his expression, which means he can't see how freaked out I am either. "Her younger brother, Landry, went to your school."

My chest tightens. I can't breathe. I close my eyes and focus on drawing in air.

Crap, she is *related to him. My juju's the worst today.*

"Mala, are you okay?"

I twitch, blinking in George's direction. I wipe my sweaty palms on my jeans. "Oh, yeah, Landry got accepted to play football at the JC. I've seen him on campus."

I try to picture Landry's face, but I've always avoided studying him too closely because he makes my stomach squiggly. The only image that forms clearly is of eyes like the sky before a hurricane. The rest of his features blur and morph into his sister's bloated face and dead-eyed stare. My stomach sours like I ate a tainted batch of crawfish, and I swallow hard. Desperate for a distraction from how queasy I feel, I walk over to a downed log and sit down. "He's never said two words to me, but he struts around campus like he's the king and we're subjects who must bow down before him. He's an arrogant jerk."

Landry watches me, Georgie, like I'm a deer he's tracking. I shiver, rubbing my arms. I've had boys interested in me before. Some hate me. Others are scared or curious because of the witchy rumors. But Landry…he creeps me out but also strangely fascinates me. I can't tell what he's thinking, and the touch of his eyes on my skin feels…electric, like when thunder rumbles overhead just before lightning strikes. I hate it.

George follows and sits beside me. His arm brushes mine. "Sounds about right from what I know of Landry, but Lainey was a good person." I can't see his eyes, but I feel his gaze fall on me. "You know, Mala, you've never gone out of your way to try to get to know folks. Not everyone has it out for you."

I tense up. Of all people, he knows better than anyone the sort of special hell my life has been. "Maybe if I hadn't been bullied all through high school, I'd be more social, Georgie. I can't help that I didn't always have clean clothes, let alone name brands…" I trail off, feeling hot and sticky. *Hellfire! Arguing over the body of a dead girl. How low could I get?* "Look, I have my reasons for not liking Landry, but this is his sister, and I don't mean to disrespect the dead."

George blows out a breath, running a shaky hand through his hair. "No, it's my fault. I shouldn't have said anything. It's not the time or place."

"But you *did* say it."

"Yeah, I did. 'Cause it's true. And life's kind of short to leave things unsaid, don't you think?"

No, I've never thought that. I draw in a deep breath. His fresh, clean scent washes away the scent of decay. George bumps his shoulder into mine, and I almost tumble off the log.

"Damn it, Georgie." I jab my elbow into his side. "How about if we agree to disagree on this issue and call it even?"

George's mouth opens. I can tell by the set look on his face that he has an argument prepared and ready to launch. Then his eyes follow mine. When his gaze lands on Lainey, he shudders. The radio connected to his belt crackles. He speaks quietly into the microphone attached to his lapel and then turns to me.

"We'll finish this discussion later. Sheriff Keyes, Detective Caine, and Coroner Rathbone are at your house with the crime scene techs. You okay to get them alone?"

"Sure, if you aren't too scared to stay here by yourself. I think you'll be fine. Just march around and make a lot of noise to scare off any critters. Don't get trigger happy when we return and shoot us on accident," I tease with a flashlight-enhanced grin, then shut off the light to fade ghostlike into the brush.

* * *

The moon lets in faint light through the treetops. I allow my eyes to adjust, then lead my group toward the crime scene. Sheriff Keyes, the parish coroner Dr. James Rathbone, Detective Bessie Caine, and two crime scene technicians with their large flashlights and bags of equipment follow like the pack of stampeding buffalo that caused the traffic accident.

Damn. I'm sick of this crawling, choking feeling of dread. It smothers me with each step. My breaths quicken. I desperately try to take my mind off of seeing Lainey again. I really, really don't want to go back. But I owe it to George to suck it up. Only a selfish loser would abandon him when he's waiting for me. Plus it's part of the job description.

Sheriff Keyes pats my shoulder, and I flinch. "Are you doing okay?" he asks.

My voice cracks, but I manage a shaky smile as I say, "Well, sir, stumbling across that girl's body tonight certainly put some gray hairs on my head. I'll look as stately as you soon enough, if I'm not careful."

He runs his fingers through his silver hair. "I've seen a lot of untimely deaths in my life, and it's never easy or kind on the living."

My head drops as I sigh. "No, it's not."

"All things considered, you handled a difficult situation like a professional."

Joy rushes through me. I squeeze my hands together and hold in my squeal. It won't do to act like a dippy-brained teenager after getting such a high compliment from my hero. The sheriff doesn't know it, but he's the closest thing I have to a father figure. I've idolized him ever since I was a little tot, hanging onto Mama's skirt and trying not to cry as she was carted off to jail. He teases me to make me feel normal. And I tease him back to feel strong. He'll never admit it to me, but he likes my spunk. I overheard him tell Bessie so.

Keep it cool, Mala. "I hope you'll remember you said that when I apply for deputy next year and not all the silly things I've done since you've known me, Sheriff."

He gives me a weary smile. "I don't think that will be a problem. Ah, Bessie's coming. I'll let the two of you take point."

"Yes, sir."

When the chief detective reaches me, I wrap my arm around her waist. "Hey, Bessie, *konmen to yé?*"

"*Çé bon, mèsi,*" Detective Bessie Caine says, squeezing me so tight that I almost trip. When she loosens her grip enough for me to step aside, I see her solemn expression, but I also detect a bit of a twinkle in her dark eyes. She's always been nice to me. Hell, to be honest, she raised me. At least once a week, when Mama got too drunk to drive home, Bessie dragged her out of the bar and dropped her off at the house. She even stayed a bit to make sure I had something to eat since Mama tended to forget that a growing girl needed food.

Bessie sighs. "So, tell me what happened."

I shrug and pull from the safety of her arms. "Pretty much what I told Ms. Dixie. I found the girl—Lainey Prince—floating in the bayou…"

Bessie places her hand on my shoulder and squeezes. "You didn't mention a name when you called, Malaise. How do you know her?"

"I don't. Georgie recognized her. Speaking of, maybe we can move a little faster 'cause he's all alone and kind of freaked about the gators."

Sheriff Keyes chuckles from behind. "Oh, is he?"

Instant regret stabs a hole in my chest. I didn't realize he'd be able to overhear our conversation. Why did I open my big mouth? Not wanting to make George look bad, I say, "George secured the crime scene, and he's protecting it from gators. I also saw tracks this morning for Mamalama. She's the biggest razorback we've got in these parts. It's lucky I found Lainey before that old boar came for water and smelled her, or the boar might've eaten her."

Sheriff Keyes points the flashlight directly at my face. "That's a gory thought."

Blinking, I shrug and pick up my pace. "I like to watch mob movies. Pigs eat anything. I've heard the best way to dispose of a body is to throw it in a pigpen. Not that I've been researching body disposal for a specific reason or anything." *Oh God, Mala shut up.*

Bessie's shoulders twitch, her version of a knee-slapping guffaw.

I blush and duck my head, wishing I could rewind the last few minutes. Great. I protected George's reputation by making myself look like a blithering idiot.

The report of a gunshot fills the air and, with it, a shout.

"Georgie!" I yell, and lurch forward. *I never should've left him alone.*

ACKNOWLEDGMENTS

To the readers of the *Dark Paradise* series, thank you. If these novels allowed you to escape for a single second from the troubles of your daily life, then I truly have attained my dream. To receive news about my upcoming releases, exclusive excerpts, and give-aways, sign up for my newsletter: http://eepurl.com/9xH8X

The *Dark Paradise* series was a labor of love, and I am grateful to the many people who have helped me along the way. Without your support, I would not be seeing a lifelong dream come true. My love and gratitude goes to my family, whose unwavering support inspired me. Nate, my soul mate, thank you for talking me off of the ledge whenever I wanted to quit and for keeping me supplied with chocolate and peach tea. Kierstan and Maxwell, Mama could not have done this without your patience and love. You inspire me every day. Dreams are attainable when your loved ones believe in you. Never give up. To my parents and, later, my in-laws, you cultivated a love of reading and writing in your children and grandchildren. Thank you for that gift. To my supportive siblings, I love you.

To my amazing agent, Kathleen Rushall, you are my champion, a friend, and the Ned Stark of my heart. You never gave up hope and found us the perfect home in Grand Central Publishing. To my amazing editor, Alex Logan, I appreciate the opportunity that you have given me. You amaze me with your questions, your insight, and your willingness to push me to be the best that I can be. My gratitude to Madeleine Colavita, Lynne Cannon Menges, Julie Paulauski, Jodi Rosoff, Siri Silleck, and the rest of the extraordinary Grand Central team who work so hard behind the scenes to make their authors feel special and wonderful.

A special shout-out goes to the amazing folks at AQC, especially the Speculative Fiction group. I found you when I needed you the most. Thank you to my amazing critique partners. Kate Evangelista, you were the first person other than family to read my work. Thank you for letting me know that I didn't completely suck at writing and for being a mentor, a friend, and a psychic twin. You taught me how to grow in my craft, supported me when I thought all was lost, and cheered me on when things went well. Carla Rehse, Sarah Gagnon, and Martha Mayberry, my writing sisters, you mean the world to me. Thanks for reading my rough first chapters and making them shine. Donald McFatridge, King of Echoes, thanks for getting my twisted sense of humor by being even more twisted. You're the funniest man I know. Michelle Hauck, Queen of Plotholes, thank you for catching my dangling threads. Without you nothing in this story would make a lick of sense.

Thank you Joyce Alton, Jennifer Troemner, Diana Robicheaux, Debra Kopfer, Jordan Adams, Jason Peridon, Kierstan Sandro, Bessie Slaton, Jonathan Allen, Christine Berman, Lyndsay McCreery, and Margaret Fortune. You all rock! I couldn't have done this without you.

To my wonderful friends and coworkers at BCP, thank you for listening to my crazy ideas. You supported me when I only thought of this as an unattainable dream. I appreciate each and every one of you.

ABOUT THE AUTHOR

Angie Sandro was born at Whiteman Air Force Base in Missouri. Within six weeks, she began the first of eleven relocations throughout the United States, Spain, and Guam before the age of eighteen.

Friends were left behind. The only constants in her life were her family and the books she shipped wherever she went. Traveling the world inspired her imagination and allowed her to create her own imaginary friends. Visits to her father's family in Louisiana inspired this story.

Angie now lives in Northern California with her husband, two children, and an overweight Labrador.

Sign up for Angie's newsletter to hear about her upcoming releases, exclusive excerpts and bonus scenes, and giveaways. http://eepurl.com/9xH8X

For more information about Angie, visit her here:
http://anjeasandro.blogspot.com/
Twitter @AngieSandro
http://facebook.com/pages/Angie-Sandro/
253044268078356